THE NEPHILIM SEED

a novel

THE NEPHILIM SEED

a novel

JAMES SCOTT BELL

BROADMAN
& HOLMAN
PUBLISHERS

NASHVILLE, TENNESSEE

0-8054-2438-5

Published by Broadman & Holman Publishers
Nashville, Tennessee

Dewey Decimal Classification: 813
Subject Heading: FICTION
Library of Congress Card Catalog Number: 2001025059

Library of Congress Cataloging-in-Publication Data
Bell, James Scott.
    The Nephilim seed : a novel / James Scott Bell.
      p. cm.
    ISBN 0-8054-2438-5 (pb.)
    Medical ethics—Fiction. 2. Human experimentation in medicine—
Fiction. 3. Mothers and daughters—Fiction. 4. Single mothers—
Fiction. 5. Women lawyers—Fiction. 6. Kidnapping—Fiction. I.
Title.

PS3552.E5158 N4 2001
813'.54—dc21

                                                    2001025059

1 2 3 4 5 05 04 03 02 01

For Glenn and Carolyn Kirby

PART ONE

There were giants in the earth in those days;
and also after that, when the sons of God came in unto
the daughters of men, and they bare children to them,
the same became mighty men which were of old, men of renown.

GENESIS 6:4, NKJV

1

Dr. Sterling Brown felt something on the back of his neck. He spun around.

Nothing.

Shaking his head, he forced a chuckle at his nervousness. No one was following him into the Universal Sheraton Hotel, least of all the devil himself.

Or was he?

Brown wondered. He had never considered himself on the charismatic side of Christianity. He was raised without religion, became an evangelical in college, and now, as a professor of philosophy at Butler Theological Seminary, he was that hybrid of academic and believer that modern society looked on with such skepticism.

At fifty-one, he was in love with the life of the mind, knowing this was God's call for him. A Ph.D. in philosophy from the University of Chicago preceded his doctorate in theology from Butler. He lived and moved in the realm of ideas. Machinations of spiritual warfare were not in his realm of expertise.

Yet he'd had the oddest sensation of that very thing in the last few weeks, as if legions of Satan's minions were gathering on some spiritual battlefield, determined to bring him down.

And he didn't wonder that it should be so pronounced tonight as he checked into the room that had been reserved for him. In approximately six hours he would be awakened by the desk. That would be 2 A.M. Brown would hop in the shower and try to freshen back to wakefulness. He would brew a cup of coffee in the small maker provided by the hotel, then await the limo driver, who would arrive by three.

Then Dr. Brown would be whisked to the small studio in Hollywood, where he would have makeup applied in preparation for his debate on *The Today Show.*

The show was broadcast live at 7 A.M., east coast time. That was four out here in Los Angeles. Brown knew he'd have to be on his toes. His mind didn't generally have to cogitate in the middle of the night.

He also knew his opponent would be fresher, being on the east coast. Dr. Bently Davis was professor of biological sciences at Harvard University and an outspoken critic of the Intelligent Design movement, which Brown would represent.

Brown was one of the leading exponents of ID, which had stunned evolutionists around the world in recent years. ID offered reason and evidence, scientific evidence, that life was designed by intelligence and could not be a random, purposeless accident.

Everyone in the field knew that Davis, who had tried to marginalize ID as just another "crazy, creationist plot," was livid that ID was not going away. Indeed, it seemed to be picking up steam.

This appearance on *Today* would be a major step forward for ID theory. A national show giving time to the topic! Brown knew Davis must be absolutely beside himself. In the past, when debating creationists, Davis always managed to put his opponents on the defensive, make them look silly. If Brown could hold his own with the great Davis, what a coup that would be. Millions of people would be hearing a viable alternative to evolution, instead of the evolutionist propaganda that had remained fairly well unchecked for a century.

And then they would hear something more.

Brown was not going to be the one on the defensive this time. He was going to challenge Davis with a question that could blow the Harvard professor right out of the water.

Sterling Brown had become an expert on the issue of bioethics. The rise in the ability of scientists to intervene in the genetic makeup of living creatures created a whole new arena of moral and theological conflict. Brown was sure that biotechnologies, in the hands of sinful man, would create rampant biological chaos, with long-term consequences scarcely conceived. Indeed, if unchecked, such technologies could result in the very end of mankind.

So Brown firmly believed. To many, even some of his colleagues, he was considered a crackpot. A man without evidence. A prophet without honor.

All that had changed two weeks ago. Knowing he was to debate Davis, Brown had E-mailed a friend on the east coast. Bob Thomas was a pastor who kept up on the latest news, and if there was anything interesting in the recent past regarding Davis and his views, Bob would know about it. Davis was always showing up on op-ed pages and in magazines. Perhaps Bob knew a nugget or two Brown could use.

What he got back was a cryptic message that amounted to a potential bombshell. Bob had uncovered a seemingly innocuous report about a small bio-tech startup in Cambridge called UniGen. The company was trying, like many others, to patent synthetic genes, what could potentially become the dominant currency of the twenty-first century. That alone was not earth-shattering news.

What was shattering, to Bob Thomas at least, was that one of Davis's former students had committed suicide. The student was the son of Bob's closest friend, and that friend had told Bob that his son had been acting strangely ever since taking on a job the previous summer. At UniGen.

In which Davis was a controlling partner.

Bob, in his E-mail, said his friend was sure there was a connection. But the police had dismissed him out of hand. There was absolutely no evidence, they said, linking the suicide to anything at UniGen, least of all Bently Davis, whose reputation was impeccable.

"So why don't you ask Davis this question?" Bob urged in his E-mail. "'Professor Davis, are you familiar with a company called UniGen?' He'll have to say yes. Then ask this follow-up: 'Professor, has UniGen in the past, or does it have a plan in the future, to experiment on human beings?' Ask him that, and let the whole country watch his reaction. I'll tape the show and then show it to the police. It may be a start."

For several days after the E-mail, Brown had prayed. He did not want to slander anyone but after much struggle decided this was not slander. It was a simple question and a relevant one to the debate. In fact, he came to believe it *should* be asked. Human experimentation was an affront to God. Let Davis deny that his company would ever do such a thing.

And so Brown was prepared to go forward. He had done the right thing, gathering information beforehand. It was fundamental for debaters to be prepared. The only thing that bothered him was his sense that Davis might somehow have done the same thing with him. And illegally.

Someone had tapped into Brown's computer system. He was sure of it. Was it just a computer hacker's prank, or was something more going on here? Whoever had done it would have had access to some intimate writings and thoughts. Someone working for Davis? Or was this just pure paranoia? Regardless, Brown would need greater security in his system, and soon.

But as he stepped into his hotel room, Brown reminded himself that his greatest security was God. Why did he keep forgetting that, or taking it for granted?

Turning off the lights, Sterling Brown dropped to his knees by the bed and prayed. He thanked God for the opportunity to present the case for design to a nationwide audience. He asked for wisdom and guidance in confronting Davis with the big question, and that whatever happened, God would use him to bring out the truth.

He ended his prayer as he always did, with thankfulness for his wife and two children, blessings that had enriched his life beyond all measure. And then for his brother, who was lost and searching for his own personal truth.

Then Brown stripped down to his shorts, slipped under the covers, and went to sleep.

A harsh ring awoke him. It was the front desk, as ordered, waking him at two. Brown followed his planned routine, and the limo arrived at three on the dot.

Brown joined the driver at the front desk. He was a pleasant young man, intelligent looking with striking eyes. Brown thought the ladies must go wild over him. He introduced himself as Anthony.

They entered the night, where the limo awaited near the front entrance. *Quite a treat,* Brown thought. *Just like a movie star.* He settled in and scanned the urban landscape as Anthony guided the limo onto the Hollywood Freeway. The night was curiously still at this hour. Brown looked up into the Hollywood hills, dark and brooding under a veil of fog. The lights permeating the shroud were like diffuse, feral eyes.

"What do you do when you're not driving a limo?" he asked Anthony.

"I like to read," the driver answered.

"That's great! Not many kids your age seem to do that."

"Don't know why."

"What sorts of things do you like to read?"

"Anything and everything," he said. "I like Stephen King and Dean Koontz, but I also like to read about science and philosophy."

What a wonderful development, thought Brown. *To have found in this transient relationship a wealth of common interests. And how delightful to find them in such a young person. If only more of my own students were so inclined.*

"What philosophers do you like?" Brown asked.

"I've been reading a lot of Nietzsche lately."

"Ugh." Brown couldn't help himself. "Can't stand him myself."

"Why not?"

"Well, for one thing, I find his concept of the master race appalling."

"But what if it's true?"

This was an interesting and ironic turn, Brown thought. Here he was on his way to debate one of the most important issues of the day with a leading intellectual scholar, and he was already into a discussion with a limousine driver over the meaning and worth of Friedrich Nietzsche—at three o'clock in the morning!

God must have a sense of humor.

"I don't happen to think it's true," Brown said. "I think his philosophy was influenced by a pathological childhood. Did you know Nietzsche may have been infected with syphilis passed through his father?"

Anthony was silent for a moment, then said, "His philosophy can stand or fall on its own."

"I wonder," Brown said. "His rage against Christianity may have been a neurosis, not clear thinking."

"But you can apply that to anything."

"How so?"

"Are you a Christian?"

"Yes, I am."

"Then no doubt you're aware that Paul was a latent homosexual. Does that mean Christianity is untrue?"

Though Anthony had said it in an odd monotone, Brown had the sense that there was intent behind the accusation, a focused hostility.

"Anthony, I don't know where you heard that," Brown said.

"From a Christian scholar."

"What?" The very idea was anathema to Brown.

"Sure, a bishop, Bishop Spong."

Oh, thought Brown, *that explains it.* Bishop John Shelby Spong was an Episcopal clergyman who had fallen off the deep end and now wrote harebrained books with bizarre views about Christianity.

"Anthony, I really think you have to explore this issue further than Bishop Spong."

"Maybe you're the one that needs to explore further," Anthony snapped.

This was not needed. Brown should have been gathering his thoughts for the upcoming show, not fighting with a limo driver on the way to the studio. It was almost as if Davis himself had planted a shill to get him upset before the appearance.

Brown decided to change the subject. "Are we almost there?"

"Soon enough," said Anthony, in a clipped, emotionless tone. Brown said a silent prayer for him. Maybe after the taping he could have a further chat with this intelligent young man and perhaps steer him back toward the Truth.

They rode in silence all the way to the off-ramp at Vermont Avenue. With eyes closed, Brown composed himself and returned again to his preparation to meet Davis.

Clever to a fault, Bently Davis was a strong adversary. He'd come to prominence in the '70s, a sort of scientific *wunderkind,* with the publication of his book *Watchmaker without Eyes.* This popularization of the neo-Darwinian theory had brought Davis wide acclaim and ensconced him as the "voice of reason" against a revival of religious sentiment and new interest in something he hated passionately, creation science.

Brown knew there were things about Davis, just as there were with Nietzsche, that went a long way to explain his vehemence in denying any possibility of God. There had been rumors about a troubled childhood, though Davis had worked for twenty years to shut off any access to his past. It was as if Davis had invented a new life for himself, starting with his position at Harvard and the publication of his book. There had been several since, all *New York Times* bestsellers.

Brown had read them all, and while he sharply disagreed with each, even to the point of anger, he sensed within the lines a man who was on the run from God. Perhaps this morning a seed would be planted inside Davis that would one day help him turn away from his view of a purposeless universe and his interest in messing with human beings. Brown issued a silent prayer that this would be so.

The limo turned left on Vermont and drove into deeper darkness. Strange how the march toward dawn had not brought any increase in light. Indeed, the streets were penumbral, almost supernaturally so.

"Is it much farther?" Brown asked.

"Not much," Anthony said.

"Look, I'm sorry we got into a little argument there. A limo ride isn't the best time to get into the major issues of life, is it?" Brown gave a little laugh.

Anthony did not laugh. "It doesn't matter anyway."

"You sound fatalistic."

"It's all a crock, Doc, and you should know it."

The driver was threatening to take him down another path of argumentation, so Brown let it go.

They were in a remote residential area now, and that seemed strange. Where would a television studio be? *We must be close,* Brown thought. And then the limo began an ascent up a hill.

"Where are we?" Brown asked.

"Almost there," said the driver.

Brown checked his watch. 3:15. Still plenty of time.

The limo pulled to a stop.

Looking out the window, Brown saw a blanket of fog stretched out below him, covering Hollywood. It was eerie, like they were in the sky somewhere, looking down on a lost world.

10

The door opened, and Anthony announced, "We're here."

Brown stepped out into the night, looking for a building of some sort. There was none. Grass and weeds met Brown's feet. This appeared to be a vacant lot of some sort.

"What's going—" Brown started to say. He stopped when he saw the gun pointed at him.

"Turn around," Anthony said.

Stunned beyond belief, Brown froze.

"Turn around."

"Anthony . . ."

"No more talk!" Anthony raised the gun to Brown's face and pulled the trigger.

Click.

No shot, no bullet between the eyes. Brown saw the exasperated expression on Anthony's face as he looked at the weapon that had misfired and started fiddling with an adjustment.

Sterling Brown ran.

How can this be? his head screamed. No answer came. He kept his legs moving.

He could not see through the soupy fog, but he was silently thankful for it. Escape was possible. He had kept in shape, running every other day, and now that would serve him . . .

He fell . . . down a hill on the other side of the lot. Brown felt no pain from a bullet. He hadn't been shot. He slid on his backside down the moist grass of the hillside.

At bottom, with skinned arms and ripped pants, Brown looked back up through the fog. He sensed, rather than saw, his executioner chasing him.

Brown got up and tried to run again.

But his knee betrayed him, twisted on the way down the hill. Hot jolts of pain shot through his body.

He would have to limp.

He struggled forward.

Behind him, the sound of loose dirt falling.

Which way to go? Brown pressed ahead into the blanket of mist and felt a sense of menace he hadn't experienced since Vietnam. For a split second he was back in the dense jungle east of Khe Sanh, in the latter days of the Tet offensive. Hell, he learned then, was not in the gunfire. Hell was in the not knowing when it would come.

That was the feeling now. Not knowing where this mad gunman was or why he was trying to kill him, when a bullet might rip the air and enter his body.

In the foggy thickness he found pavement. A street. If a car were to whiz up through the fog he wouldn't see it until the last second. But hearing nothing, he continued on, struggling to the other side.

If only he could find a house, a refuge, anything. A place to hide.

Looking behind him he saw nothing but the gray heaviness of the air. He listened, did not hear a sound.

Hope.

He came to a patch of grass. Mown grass. A residence. Farther still, the outlines of a house, a front door. He pushed his aching legs by sheer will.

Somewhere a dog barked in the night.

Up the walk, onto the porch now, Brown wondered if the occupants would be that rare exception in Los Angeles, people with an unlocked front door.

No way. The door was secure.

Brown rang the doorbell.

Nothing seemed to stir in the house. He pounded on the door.

No answer.

Brown looked back the way he had come, and the mist seemed to move, take shape, like some apparition in a horror movie coming to life.

A dark figure emerged through the haze, moving purposefully but without haste. Almost as if he knew exactly where Brown would be.

Dr. Sterling Brown could only turn and, back against the door, watch helplessly as Anthony approached him.

"Why?" Brown called out. "Why are you doing this?"

Anthony came to within three feet of him and stopped. Brown could see his face, and what he saw rocked him.

Anthony's eyes were luminescent, red. Animal-like, but more than that—demonic. Yet that was not the scary part. What was scary was the fact that the face that held them was impassive, as if this evil were the most natural thing in the world.

Brown looked down and saw that Anthony no longer held the gun. Instead, in his right hand, he gripped a knife with a huge, jagged blade.

And then in a voice that seemed to come from some abyss, Anthony said, "I teach you the Superman."

Brown recognized the words of Nietzsche.

"Man," Anthony continued, "is something that is to be surpassed."

He raised the knife.

Janice Ramsey blamed herself for what happened in the supermarket that day. And she was convinced the guilt and despair over it would be a punishment that would last forever.

The day had started with such promise. Literally. Her ten-year-old daughter, Lauren, had managed to squeeze from her mother a pledge that they would go out to dinner at a fancy restaurant that evening. "A real dress-up place," Lauren said. "Not Wendy's like usual." There was a Wendy's in Melrose Park that Lauren loved to an almost fanatical degree. So to have her suggest something different was special indeed. "Because *you're* special, Mom," Lauren had said.

Janice nearly cried at those words. She did cry when Lauren then told her she had saved up twelve whole dollars so she could help pay for the dinner, because she knew how hard Janice worked.

The gesture meant more to Janice than words could express. Since the awful divorce, which she had not wanted, Janice was fearful Lauren would be ripped apart inside, that she would somehow blame her mother for all that had transpired. It was irrational to believe that, Janice knew, but irrational was the only way to describe the events of the last two years.

Sam had started out as a supportive husband. There were the usual stresses and strains of a modern marriage between two professionals, though Janice put her career on hold to stay at home while Lauren was young. But they always seemed to work things out and agree on the most important issue—their daughter.

That was before Janice reclaimed her Christian faith and went back to church. Sam, for reasons unknown to her and which he would not discuss, grew increasingly hostile about it. But that was not the worst of it. The worst was that his hostility led to violence.

Twice Sam had hit her. Across the face. Hard.

He had never done anything like that before in their entire marriage. It was shocking, out of character, horrible.

After the second time she begged Sam to go to counseling with her. He refused and avoided the issue altogether. He dealt with it by staying away from home longer and longer. He made several business trips from their suburban Chicago home to the east coast. Sam was in pharmaceuticals and apparently had a big client in Massachusetts somewhere. He never told her; he just took the trips.

Janice refused to consider divorce. She was convinced the physical violence was an aberration, related to stress or perhaps some chemical imbalance in Sam. It was possible his brain was not in equilibrium, which happened sometimes with Type-A personalities. She was convinced that part of her duty as a Christian wife was to help Sam get through this troubled time. There was also an element of plain doggedness. Janice would tough this out, as she had done all her life. Growing up poor and an only child, she had learned early on how to take care of herself, especially after her dad walked out on her and her mother. Janice had never experienced the luxury of self-pity.

Now, with a daughter of her own, she was determined to make the marriage work, even with a husband who was roiling out of control.

Then one day Sam abruptly moved out and served her with divorce papers. He would not communicate with her except through his lawyer. Divorce was inevitable.

She decided to make the best of the situation. She would not fight about community property or deny visitations with Lauren. She would cooperate with Sam to make this as easy as possible on their daughter.

But when Sam went to court to try to get physical custody of Lauren, Janice fought back. What did it was the little item in Sam's motion papers, which said he objected to Lauren being raised "under religious duress."

Duress! He might as well have accused Janice of brainwashing their only child!

The one time she managed to get him on the phone he would not listen to reason. His animosity toward her beliefs was rabid. "You're not going to raise our daughter to be a religious nut!" he shouted.

Stunned, Janice snapped, "Like me?"

"Exactly like you!" And he slammed down the phone.

There was just no explaining it. This was not the Sam Ramsey she had fallen in love with. Something terrible had gone wrong with him. She didn't think it was an affair that caused all this . . . this *hatred*. And this hard, hurtful attack in court to wrest Lauren from her.

As an insurance defense lawyer, Janice had no experience in the tumultuous world of family law. She had to find and fund a private attorney who specialized. Fortunately, she found one who was both fair and reasonable. It would cost, but it had to be done. Contested custody proceedings were awful, but that was Sam's choice. He was vicious and cruel, and Janice was worried that he might, in fact, hurt Lauren.

A judge would make the determination.

One day before the hearing came the incident in the market. It happened just after she conducted a tough, stressful deposition with a man who was suing Starbucks for a product defect in their custom cups, the kind with a screw-on top. He had purchased coffee, and as he tipped the cup for his first sip, scalding brew ran out all over his hand. He'd suffered severe burns on most of the back of this hand and a small burn on his chest.

He wanted thirty million dollars.

Or his lawyer said he did. Janice knew Larry Carter only by reputation, but he was supposed to be one of the slickest PI attorneys in all of Chicago, a man who brought outrageous lawsuits hoping for a quick but hefty settlement.

For three hours Janice questioned Carter's client, Stanley Jackowski, about his life, his work, and his coffee-drinking habits. Carter was no help, interrupting with a lot of meaningless and improper objections. Playing hardball.

Emotionally spent, Janice took the rest of the day to research cases on Westlaw and go over a few other case files. The one thing that kept her going was knowing that the sooner she finished her work the sooner she could pick up her daughter from day care and get ready for their dinner.

She finished early, and that gave Janice and Lauren time for a little shopping before heading home. Lauren brought Janice such comfort that she almost forgot about the day she'd had.

"You know something?" Janice said as she wheeled a cart down the soup aisle of the market.

"What?" said Lauren.

"You make me very happy."

Lauren hugged Janice hard. "I'm not letting go," she said, laughing.

Janice laughed too. "I don't want you to."

"Not ever?"

"Well, maybe for dinner, huh?"

"I'll think about it."

They laughed again.

That's when Janice saw the man.

He was a flash of color at first. Appearing out of nowhere, he rushed by like a sprinter. Everything that followed seemed to happen in the same instant. He bumped hard into the shopping cart, which hit Janice in the hip. Janice was knocked backward into a row of soup cans. Lauren screamed in surprise.

Janice's immediate thought was the man was being chased by someone, for some reason, and in his haste had happened to run into her.

Then she realized he had her purse.

Instinctively, Janice gave chase, shouting at the top of her voice, "Stop him! Somebody stop him, please!"

Down at the end of the aisle, she saw the man, her purse under his arm, jump up and over a checkout counter. He landed on the other side, shoved a bug-eyed box boy out of the way, and dashed toward the door.

"He's got my purse!"

A somnolent security guard, well past his prime, stirred near the produce section. Janice saw him fumble for his walkie-talkie as the purse snatcher disappeared outside.

In her head she started to click off everything that she was about to lose. Driver's license. Credit cards. Pictures of Lauren. State bar ID. Keys to the apartment.

The apartment! Now this snatcher would know where she lived.

The thought chilled her.

The automatic doors strained open as Janice shot out to the parking lot. She saw cars moving in haphazard fashion through the aisles and people pushing carts.

No sign of the snatcher.

How could he have gotten away so quickly?

Then heavy breathing at her left hand. The so-called security guard. "Did you . . ." he huffed. "Did you get . . . a look at him?"

"No," Janice snapped, "he just came out of nowhere. I think I can tell you what he was wearing."

"The police . . . the police will be here . . . soon."

"Are there security cameras in the store?"

"Yes, ma'am."

"Well go mark them. I'll want to look. I can't believe this is happening!"

"I'm sorry."

"Me too."

She trudged back inside, a thousand thoughts and emotions whipping through her brain. She did not need this. Not with the custody hearing tomorrow and the Jackowski case and dealing with Carter and now her dinner date with Lauren spoiled.

No, she wouldn't let it be. She wouldn't. Her time with her daughter was sacred. She would shake this off and make the best of it. She would go to dinner and . . . pay for it *how?*

Maybe Lauren's twelve bucks would have to be it. Maybe it was a Wendy's night after all. At least they could get dressed up.

Janice felt the looks of the mass of shoppers, none of whom had made a move to help. Another indication of modern life, the terminally apathetic.

Now where had she left Lauren? Right. Near the soup.

Janice quickened her step, looking. What must her daughter be thinking? Is Mommy OK?

No, Mommy isn't OK, but she soon will be. A spicy chicken sandwich and fries is all that . . .

Lauren was not at the shopping cart.

She was probably up front at one of the counters, looking for her. Sure. There was a logical explanation. Even so, Janice felt the chill of panic arise inside her.

"Lauren!"

No answer. In a run-walk, Janice got to the counters and scanned the store up and down. "Lauren!"

A short man with a ruddy face and half-tied necktie on his short-sleeved white shirt skidded up to her. He had a pin that said *Manager* on his shirt pocket.

"Ma'am," he said with some panic, "we're terribly sorry about what—"

"My daughter!"

"—happened with your . . . daughter?"

"I can't find my daughter."

"Oh gee."

"Help me, will you?"

"But . . . yes . . . we're terribly sorry. We'd like to give you a coupon for—"

"Please!"

Red blotches appearing on his cheeks, the store manager said, "What does she look like?"

"A girl, ten years old, blonde hair in a ponytail. Please look!"

"Oh gee."

The store manager turned and conferred with the corpulent security guard, which only increased Janice's panic. Little help was going to come from that quarter.

Janice ran up and down aisles, out into the front, back into the store, covering every inch of the place with her feet and eyes.

No sign.

"This can't be happening," she whispered to herself. "Dear God, where is she?"

Slumping by the water fountain in the front of the store, Janice closed her eyes. She opened them when the voice of the store manager came at her. "The police are here, ma'am."

Janice looked through the double glass doors and saw the police vehicle rolling to a stop.

"They'll take care of everything," the manager said, his voice reeking with anxiety.

Janice said nothing.

"We won't need to consider . . . a lawsuit, now will we?"

Janice looked at him incredulously. "Don't worry."

He sighed. "Thank you."

Two young police officers, a male and a female, came through the doors.

"Over here," the store manager said, waving a hysterical arm. "This is the woman whose purse was taken."

"Ma'am," the male officer said. "My name's Hanson, and my partner's name is Denton. Can you tell us what happened?"

"My daughter is missing!" Janice said. "She was taken."

"I thought this was a purse snatching."

"I don't care about the purse. Someone has taken my daughter. Please help me."

"Better call Wright," Hanson said to Denton.

"Sure thing," the woman replied. She went back to the police car.

The scene began to take on the look and feel of a nightmare. And just as in a nightmare, Janice felt powerless to do anything about it. She wanted to, needed to, but was stuck here.

Her daughter was gone.

Dear God, she was gone.

If Jedediah Brown could have put his hands around the skinny detective's neck and gotten away with it, he would have. In a second. The guy was driving him nuts.

Stupid cops with their by-the-book and we'll-be-in-touch procedures. Maybe they were bound by rules and regs, but in life you have to know when to bend the rules. And Jed Brown knew. That's how he made his living.

Maybe the skinny cop—Mitchell was his name, about five-ten, mid-thirties—was upset about that. Cops didn't like bounty hunters. Professional jealousy. Bounties went where they pleased and knocked whatever heads needed knocking, without having to beg some judge for a warrant, or answering to some supervisor who might be having a bad day.

Bounties were independent, and that's just the way Jed Brown liked it.

He knew Mitchell was nervous. Brown had a sixth sense about such things, having worked the bounty trails for twenty of his forty-five years. When you're out locating skips and fugitives, you get to know people, and even the smallest of reactions. People try to fake you out, but a good bounty can smell fear.

This Mitchell was a study in nervousness and professional conflict as they sat at his desk in the Hollywood Police Department. Mitchell kept tapping his index finger on the steel desk, and stared at the patch over Jed's left eye.

"So your answer is what again?" Jed Brown said, resting his two huge arms on the desk so Mitchell could see the merc tattoo—a sword with a viper wrapped around it—on top of his muscular right forearm.

Looking down at the tattoo, then back up at the bounty hunter, Mitchell swallowed and said, "All we can."

"That's what I thought you said. I just couldn't believe I heard it." Brown leaned back. His copper-colored hair, streaked with soft gray lines, was pulled back in a ponytail. He spoke through a bushy mustache of the same color. "You think I'm one of them little old widows up in the hills coming down because her dog Fluffy is missing? Is that what you're thinking, Detective Mitchell?"

"Now wait a minute—"

"No, you wait a minute. I want details. And I'm going to keep on wanting details. I'm going to be on you like ugly on a frog, Detective Mitchell, because this is personal."

"I understand."

"And don't try to con me with psychobabble 101. Just give me the Jack Webb."

"The who?"

"Didn't you ever watch *Dragnet?*"

"No."

"And you're a cop?"

"What has this got to do with anything?"

"Jack Webb was Joe Friday, the greatest cop who ever lived, and all he wanted was the facts, ma'am. That's what I want."

Mitchell continued to tap his finger on the desk. "I think I've gone over the facts as we know them."

"Go over them again."

Clearing his throat, Mitchell began, "Your brother was killed in the early morning hours of September 3. Cause of death loss of blood from a sharp object wound across the throat."

"I've got all that. Now I want to know who did it."

"We're working on that."

"Mitchell, are you going to give me details or not?"

"I'm afraid I can't do that. This is an ongoing investigation, and the details are confined to personnel."

"That's a lie."

"Excuse me?"

Brown looked at the ceiling and then ran his hand over his furry upper lip. "You heard what I said. The only reason you're not telling me anything is because you're afraid I might beat you to the punch."

Mitchell's tapping got more rapid. "This is strictly procedural."

"Listen, Mitchell. My brother is dead, and he shouldn't be. I'm the one that should be dead, not him."

Jed hadn't intended to say that; it just popped out. But as soon as he said it, he knew it was the perfect summary of what he was feeling. Sterling was the good kid in the family, the nice one, the Christian. Jedediah was the black sheep, the disappointment.

"Mr. Brown," said Detective Mitchell, "I'm very sorry about your brother. Believe me, we'll do everything we can to track down the person who did this."

Jed Brown slapped his hands on the desk with a *thwap* that broke through the office din and caused a few other cops to look over. "That's just it, Mitchell."

"That's just what?"

"You don't know where you are. *Person* who did this? You think this was some random Tom, Dick, or Harry? This was a professional hit, Mitchell. And I want to know why."

"As I said, we'll do all we can, look at every angle."

"I wish I could believe you, Mitchell, but you and I know that this is one case, one number, one blue binder, and this is L.A., California, man. You'll do what you can, but you got a mountain of other unsolveds. I'm gonna do my part."

Mitchell cleared his throat. "You can't do that."

"What did you just say?" Jed put a glare into his good eye.

"Citizens who interfere with an investigation can be charged. You leave the police work to us."

Jed Brown stood up, to his full six-foot-four. He towered over Mitchell, who remained in his chair. Jed allowed the nervous cop a few moments of uncertainty, then said, "I only have one thing to say to you, Mitchell."

"Yes?"

"Which way's the bathroom?"

Detective Mitchell blinked with surprise, then indicated toward the front desk. Jed leaned over and put his beefy hands on the sides of the desk. "And Mitchell . . ."

Mitchell's half-full coffee cup crashed onto the floor, shattering and spilling brown liquid all over.

"Sorry," said Brown as Mitchell shot out of his chair and surveyed the mess.

"Oh man!" Mitchell said, leaning over and opening a desk drawer, reaching for a wad of napkins. He started throwing them on the floor to soak up the spill.

"No more coffee for you, Mitchell!" shouted another detective from across the room. A few others joined in laughter.

Jed threw his leather jacket over his arm and said, "Clumsy me."

"Just get out of here," Mitchell snapped, moving napkins around the floor with his foot.

"You'll keep in touch, won't you?" Brown turned and made his way toward the front desk. He walked past the suspicious desk sergeant and out to the main hallway, where the men's room was. He entered, found a stall, and latched himself in.

Then he took his jacket off his hand to look at the small police notebook he had lifted from Mitchell's desk after spilling the coffee.

He knew he would have only a few minutes at best, so he didn't waste time. There were about ten pages of notes. Using a micro digital camera, Jed Brown took a picture of each page.

He flipped the notebook closed and put his jacket over it.

The suspicious guard eyed him closely as he walked by again. "Forgot my keys," Jed explained.

Mitchell was still dealing with the spill and broken coffee cup. Jed threw his jacket on the desk and picked up the keys he'd purposely left behind. "I'm going to send you a new coffee cup."

"There's no need."

"I want to. I really do. People will tell you, I'm a man who pays his debts." He picked up his jacket, leaving the notebook on the desk.

"And they'll also tell you," Jed said before leaving, "I'm a man who makes sure other people pay theirs."

Ten minutes later, owing to the light traffic in Hollywood, Jed was back at his apartment on Ivar. As he opened the door to the one-bedroom on the second floor, he was hit with a wave of smells—a volatile mixture of beer, unwashed dishes, and dust.

Welcome home, he thought.

Living this way had its advantages, though. The low rent and overhead left Jed with enough money to run his business—finding people for a price. He had enough left over from his erratic income to purchase the technology that made tracking possible. And living alone made the money go further. No one to take care of. No one to worry about. No one to rip out your heart.

He set his digital camera by his laptop computer. He connected the camera to the laptop by a cable, then fired up the computer. Once everything was ready, it took just a few seconds to upload the images on the camera to the computer screen. He was now able to scroll through the notes of a police detective with an active case.

Before sitting down to read, Jed pulled a Coors out of the refrigerator and popped it open. *Beer for lunch is probably not a good idea,* he thought. *But what does it matter? It's taking away some of the pain. Of losing Sterling. Of more imbalance in the world.*

Sterling and he had been different ever since he could remember. Sterling had the good grades, the people talking about what a good boy he was. The adults all shook their heads when Jed's name was mentioned. He was well aware of that, the way children pick up on those signals.

But that didn't mean he hated his brother. It was the opposite. Sterling was always looking out for Jed. Six years older, Sterling was not a playmate. He was a real big brother. More than once Sterling had taken care of a bully on Jed's behalf. Jed was never reticent about getting in a scrape, even if his opponent was older and bigger. That reputation invited harassment. Sterling had to temper those confrontations on many occasions.

Once, after a ninth grader had bloodied Jed's nose, Sterling took Jed aside and told him he'd better "wise up."

"Meaning what?" Jed wanted to know.

"Meaning," Sterling said, "if all you do is fight all the time, you'll end up looking like Bozo the clown, with a big red nose. Jesus said, 'Blessed are the peacemakers.'"

Sterling was always quoting the Bible. Even as a kid. He went to Sunday School every week even though their parents didn't go to church. Jed knew Sterling was into this God stuff. It was all confusing to Jed.

Now the kid who had known his Bible, the one who had grown up and studied theology—who had even influenced Jed to give all that a try in the dark days after Vietnam—and the man who had been more generous and loving than anyone Jed had ever known, was gone from the world.

And Jed Brown was still here, sucking beer, wondering why.

He drained the beer and tossed the can in the sink. Then he got another one and sat down with it at the laptop.

And started to read.

4

Mommy said never be scared, Lauren thought. *Be like David. The Lord is my shepherd.*

Over and over, in her mind, she repeated the words. She was scared, more scared than ever in her whole life, but she wasn't going to let them know it.

Even within the restraints, even with the tape over her mouth, Lauren knew she had a choice. She could give in to the fear or believe God would help her.

The Lord is my shepherd . . .

The car was speeding. She sensed it, even though she was on the floor in the back, looking up at the interior lamp, hearing the hum of the engine, feeling the vibration of the tires on the road.

Mommy said never be scared . . .

Being tied up like this was, in a way, familiar to her. That dumb Tommy McIntire had tied her to a tree with nylon rope a few months ago. They were playing with some other kids in the little park near her house when Tommy, two years older, had suggested playing "hostage." Lauren thought it would be fun. She had no way of knowing Tommy was more interested in the hostage part than the rescue part.

He tied her up and convinced the other kids to ditch. They ran away, and Lauren was left secured to the tree. She was scared. She started to cry. A nice old man had untied her, but not until several minutes of fear had gone by.

The same kind of fear she felt right now.

Be like David.

She could hear them talking. What they said sounded funny.

The man with the deeper voice said, "She's a little young, don't you think?"

"That's the point," the other answered.

"I mean, it's really just a theory."

"Yeah, but in theory it should increase the effectiveness."

"Developmental potentiality?"

"Yeah."

"But what about negative potential?"

"Such as?"

"Accelerated mutation."

"Always possible. But that only puts selection to work. And gives us more information."

"Cool."

Lauren couldn't make sense of the words. But she had a feeling, one that wouldn't go away. She had the feeling they were talking about her. And what they were talking about was not nice.

Be like David.

The Lord is my shepherd.

After that awful time with Tommy McIntire, Lauren had cried in her room until her mother got home. When she told her how scared she was, how she could never go outside again because Tommy would get her, her mother had sat down on the bed and lifted her onto her lap. It was warm and soft there, like always.

"Do you remember what I told you about how God uses these bad things?" Mommy had said.

"Um, I think so."

"How?"

"For good."

"That's right. All things work for our good if we just trust in him."

But how was Tommy McIntire tying her up to a tree a good thing? Lauren didn't ask but squeezed closer to her mother, where safety was sure.

"Do you remember David and Goliath?" Janice asked.

"Yes, Mommy."

"David was just a boy. He wasn't a soldier. When he first saw the giant Goliath, he had every right to be scared."

"Was he?"

"No."

"How come?"

"Because he knew God, and he trusted God. The big old army of Israel was out there on the field, and they were scared. Because they weren't trusting God the way David did. So they were shaking in their sandals when that nine-foot giant stepped out and made fun of them."

"He made fun of them?"

"Yes. He was saying he was the best thing out there and he could beat anybody they sent to him, and he kept challenging them."

"Tommy McIntire is like that."

"But David was not afraid. And when he heard what Goliath was saying, he looked around at the soldiers just standing there, and he said, 'Hey! This is a disgrace! Who is this uncircumcised Philistine that he should defy the armies of the living God?'"

"What's circum . . . ?"

"I'll explain that later. But it meant that Goliath was an enemy of God, and David knew that God's people could never go down to defeat. God had a purpose for them, and God never goes back on his promises."

"Wow."

"So when David went out to meet this big warrior, all he had was a slingshot and some rocks. But he wasn't afraid. He knew God was with him. And he got Goliath with the first rock. Bam!"

Her mother had slapped the bed then. Lauren laughed.

"And it was David who wrote that beautiful psalm we always say. Remember? 'The Lord is my shepherd.'"

"I remember, Mommy."

"So the next time you feel afraid, be like David. Trust in God. Pray to God. Will you do that, Lauren?"

"Yes, Mommy."

Be like David . . .

The car drove relentlessly forward. The vibrations made Lauren drowsy. The two men in the front had stopped talking for the moment. Lauren tried to think of them as two giant Tommy McIntires. Bullies. Mean. But they didn't know what they were in for. Did they think they could act this way and God wouldn't see?

Be like David.

The Lord is my shepherd.

●

"If you'll just calm down, ma'am."

"I can't calm down!"

"We can only—"

"This is my daughter!"

Four hours had dragged by since the kidnapping. Four agonizing hours while horrific pictures of imagined harm weaved in and out of Janice's mind. The police officer, whose name was Wright, seemed frustrated with her.

Nor did it help to be sitting in the claustrophobic office of the store manager. It only aggravated the feeling of impotence she felt. They had brought her a sandwich and a Snapple lemonade. She had touched neither.

"Have you looked at the security cameras yet?" she asked.

Wright heaved a sigh and shook his head.

"Why not?"

"They were out."

"What?"

"Yeah."

"Why?"

"Don't know."

The store manager, who had been pacing near the wall, suddenly stepped forward. "They were on this morning, all systems checked out. We weren't negligent; we followed normal routine!"

With a wave of the hand, Wright silenced the manager. "Now tell me, in detail, just what happened."

Janice told the story, each word an agony. By the time she finished, her head was pounding. A throbbing numbness gripped her behind the eyes.

Officer Wright looked at his notes a moment, chewing the eraser of his pencil. "Now I'm thinking there might be a connection between your daughter's disappearance and the man who snatched your purse. A highly unlikely event which happens in close proximity to another highly unlikely event."

"Planned?"

"Maybe. Do you know anyone who would want to take your daughter?"

She knew, of course, but realized she hadn't wanted to say it. Now she was compelled. "My ex-husband."

"And why is that?"

"We're in a custody battle."

Wright nodded. "This happens more than you know. One parent takes it out of the courts and into his own hands. Grabs the child, goes underground somewhere."

"And it can be years," Janice uttered in spite of herself. "Maybe never."

"We can finish this later," Wright suggested.

"No," said Janice. "The sooner the better. What more do you need?"

"Can you think of any reason your husband might do this now?"

Janice wiped her eyes with a balled-up tissue. "Only that we have a custody hearing tomorrow. Maybe he thought he was going to lose. He hates to lose." She thought of all the arguments they'd had and how Sam had never backed down. Not once. She had tried to work through those times, submitting herself to him for the good of peace in the house. Lauren would cry at their arguments. Janice couldn't stand that.

Now it was clear to her that this was Sam's ultimate move. His big score. His attempt to destroy her.

"We'll have a man question your ex, Mrs. Ramsey."

Without thinking about it at all, Janice said, "Taylor."

"Excuse me?"

"Janice Taylor is my name now. It belonged to my mother." The moment she said it, she felt an exhilarating cleansing. It was a strong name. She'd always loved it. Because her mother bore that name and from her Janice had learned the value of hard work, of honesty, but most of all of honoring God.

It was that ethic that Janice carried with her, through school, through a scholarship to Illinois University, and all the way through to the University of Chicago, one of the finest law schools in the country. She owed it all to the name Taylor.

And that's who she would be again.

The fresh feeling of starting over was the one thing that kept her from collapsing in total exhaustion when she finally got back to her apartment and rousted the manager to let her in. But once inside, Janice was met with a melange of other emotions, especially loneliness and loss. *Lauren is not here! Where is she? Is she safe? Is she dead? Is she scared now, without me able to wrap my arms around her?*

The questions pounded her mind until she thought she might go crazy, might be unable to turn them off.

She grabbed the phone and called her mother. She kept in regular touch, at least once a week, but most often more. Tonight she needed the comforting voice of her mother more than ever.

"Hello, Jan," Mary Taylor said. She was now sixty-three but still strong and ever the optimist. "How's everything?"

Janice told her. It was hard. The words sometimes stuck in her throat. But finally the whole thing was out.

Mary Taylor paused before responding. "I will call the prayer chain at church tonight," she said. "We are going to hold you and Lauren up."

"Thanks."

"Are you all right?"

"No."

"Want to come down here for awhile?"

"No, Mom, I feel like I've got to stay available, for the police."

"I'll pray for the right person to come along and help."

"The police are doing all they can, I guess."

"I'll pray just the same."

"I know you will, Mom." Janice had always admired her mother's praying. Never a doubt. Never a waver. Only a warrior on her knees, in all sorts of circumstances. When Janice had gone to law school, she had come to rely more on her mind than on prayer. In fact, she had stopped attending church by her third year. Now it was time to return to what really worked.

Once she was off the phone, Janice knelt at a chair in the living room. It had been so long since she'd prayed on her knees. She prayed what her mother had suggested, that the person or persons who could most help would come her way, that she would be prepared for anything.

And then she crawled up on the sofa, kicked her shoes off, and, fully clothed, felt her body finally shut down.

Jed watched the man's eyes widen as he told him about the time he set a guy on fire.

He was a squat little man, bald, and wore a short-sleeved white shirt with a loosened, pale blue tie. He sat behind a nondescript desk in an office off the garage area. Outside the window, through the venetian blinds, Jed could see four limousines parked in their spaces. One of them was being washed by a Latino man in brown overalls.

"Yep, I didn't really mean it to happen," Jed said. "The first time, that is."

The man at the desk swallowed.

"See, the dude had jumped bail before, got nailed, escaped. Not from me. When I nail a dude, he stays nailed. So they call me up and say can I get him, and I say, you know who you're talking to?"

As if answering the question himself, the man at the desk nodded.

"He was a feisty dude, this one, name of Stevenson. I kick in the door of his girlfriend's place, and see him go for a weapon. So I take out this—" Jed removed a small spray bottle from his jacket pocket and held it out for the man to see—"a little

Mace, which is alcohol based. I give it to the guy right in the face. *Tssss!*"

The man jumped at Jed's sound effect.

"But the guy keeps going. Big guy, too. And so I figure I have to bring him down with this."

Jed removed his M-26 Taser gun from his other pocket. The bald man's eyes expanded to their full extent.

"So bam, I hit the guy with a zap, right in the chest, and guess what? The spark sets off the Mace! Yeah, man! All of a sudden, this guy's head is on fire. He looked just like a Roman candle. Can you dig it?"

The man sat frozen in his chair.

"I asked you a question," Jed said ominously. "Can you dig it?"

The man nodded.

"Say, *I can dig it.*"

"I can . . . dig it."

"Good, good. So I'll ask you for the last time. I want the name and address of the driver for the limo on September 3, paid for by CBS."

"But I can't—"

Jed held up the Mace.

"Please," the man begged. "If anything happens. . ."

"Nothing's going to happen," Jed said, "except a few questions. Oh, and the fact that your head won't melt."

Quickly, the man turned to his computer screen and started tapping the keyboard.

●

Working was pointless. The deposition Janice was supposed to summarize might just as well have been three hundred pages of blank paper. The words swam around like so many gnats—random, meaningless, and ultimately annoying.

It wasn't just fatigue. She had fought nausea all through the night, getting only snatches of sleep. Lauren kept flashing into her mind, and every time she did, Janice would utter a prayer. She pleaded with God to protect Lauren and asked for peace. Peace came and went, like waves crashing then receding from a rocky shore.

When morning came, she tried to carry on as if it were a normal day. She made coffee, forced herself to eat a bowl of oatmeal, tried to read Ebert's movie review in the *Sun-Times*. Her mind refused to focus.

Maybe work would do it.

It didn't. Janice found herself staring out the window of her tenth-story office over Michigan Avenue, wondering if her daughter was out there in the faceless mass of pedestrians. Was she scared? Crying? What?

At ten-thirty she finally called Mr. Bollington. Her immediate supervising partner, Bollington had taken Janice under his considerable wing— he was a six-foot-seven former Chicago Bulls basketball player who carried on his competitive inclinations in the courtroom. A master trial lawyer, he defended companies on behalf of their insurance carriers. He hated fraudulent claims as much as he hated the Utah Jazz.

"I'm sorry, Ray," Janice told him. "I can't get it together today."

"Hey there," Bollington said in his familiar West Virginia twang. "I told you this morning you ought to get on home."

"I thought work would help. There's really nothing I can do until I hear from the police. Plus, I have the hearing this afternoon."

"The custody thing?"

"Yeah."

"You got yourself a full plate. Why don't you just go home?"

"I'd sit there, too. Can I just stay here?"

"You do that little thing. Anything I can I do for you?"

"Pray." Ray Bollington was a Christian, one of the reasons Janice had hooked up with his firm a year ago.

"You got it. Call me if you need anything."

Janice spent the next few minutes looking out the window and talking silently to God. It helped. She remembered something she'd told Lauren a few months ago, when that awful boy had tied her to a tree. She had told her to be like David, to trust in God. They had sat on Lauren's bed and talked about it.

Smiling at the memory, Janice, for one instant, felt a solid sense of peace. It was shattered by the ringing of her phone.

Her assistant, Margo, said it was an Officer Wright.

Janice punched the line. "Yes."

"Mrs. Ramsey?"

"Taylor."

"Oh yes, sorry. This is Officer Wright. I wanted to get back with you. We questioned your husband last night."

"Ex-husband."

"Right, right."

"And?"

There was a long pause. Janice's skin began to tingle. "We don't think he's involved."

A surge of disbelief hit her. She had been so certain it was Sam. "Why don't you think so?"

"A couple of reasons. I have a lot of experience here, and I was able to look him in the eye as I questioned him. Plus, he can account for his whereabouts for the last four days, in detail."

"Yes, but that doesn't mean he didn't hire people to do this."

"Of course not. And we're not ruling anything out . . ."

The way Wright said *anything* made Janice tremble slightly. Surely he wouldn't be suggesting . . .

"What do you mean by that?" she asked.

"Just that we're keeping all possibilities open."

"Including what?"

Wright did not answer immediately.

"Officer, what are you talking about?"

"Ms. Taylor, can you account for your whereabouts the last week or so?"

Janice almost dropped the phone. "You can't be serious!"

"This is just—"

"Did Sam suggest this to you?"

"He indicated . . ."

"Indicated *what?*"

"That you had exhibited, well, unstable behavior in the past."

"Unstable!"

"Is that true?"

"Unstable!" Janice shouted. Then she realized how unstable that sounded. She tried to force herself to be calm. It didn't work. "He's a liar."

"Ma'am, I realize this is hard for you."

"How could you even think this? I love my daughter."

"Of course you do. And sometimes people do things out of love that they shouldn't."

"Like kidnap their own child?"

Silence on the other end.

"This is too absurd," Janice said.

"Maybe, but we have to follow this up. Can we meet sometime today?"

Twin jackhammers drilled Janice's temples. "Today . . . I . . . I have a court hearing."

"After that?"

"I don't know . . . maybe."

"We really need to hop on this."

"Can I call you?"

"Please do. Or I'll call you."

"Fine."

"Mrs. Rams . . . Taylor?"

"Yes."

"I'm sorry it has to be this way."

"Me, too."

She hung up.

The nightmare had intensified. Janice had no idea how she made it through the next three hours. But when she finally got to court, and sat down next to her attorney, Pamela Fordyce, nausea eddied inside her.

For a moment Janice thought she might simply pass out. She had been in many courtrooms but always as one of the lawyers. Now she was just another name in just another family law dispute, of which hundreds were heard here every month. At least Pamela was good. And a Christian. It had been difficult to find someone who shared her faith who was able to survive in the tumultuous world of family law. But Pamela was one.

Unfortunately, Sam's attorney, Grayson Yates, was reputed to be the best family law attorney in the city, and a man who would do anything to break down his opposition.

Hearing the courtroom doors open, Janice turned and saw Yates enter, with Sam close behind.

Yates was in his fifties, with a head full of white hair, and trim. He wore a crisp gray suit with a burgundy tie. A gold bracelet glistened on his left wrist. Yates nodded at Pamela as he took to the opposite counsel table. Sam didn't look at Janice. His eyes, cold and inert, stared forward.

Once more, Janice puzzled over Sam's unbelievable change of character. He was like another person. Was there some deep, dark secret about his past that he had never revealed to her, something virulent that had taken root inside him and was now fully grown in all its toxic profusion?

Janice's stomach turned over again as she remembered why they were here—to do battle over the future of their daughter. It seemed almost surreal now that Lauren was missing. But Pamela had counseled going through with this initial hearing anyway.

The judge, a fiftyish woman with deep lines in her face, called the case.

Both attorneys stated their appearances, then Yates took to the podium to argue.

"Good morning, your honor," he said graciously.

The judge said nothing.

"We are here to argue for a change in custody, based on the fact that the child's mother is unfit. We have several arguments to make in that regard, and—"

"I've read the papers, Mr. Yates," the judge snapped. "Is there anything new?"

"As a matter of fact, there is," Yates said.

Pamela stood up immediately. "Your honor, I object. We haven't been served with any notice of a new substantive issue."

"Is that true, Mr. Yates?" the judge asked.

"It's only because we have just become aware of it, your honor. I'm sure if I could be heard—"

"I want to hear it first," Pamela said. She had warned Janice that Yates would try to pull something like this.

"Sit down, Ms. Fordyce," the judge said. "We're all here, so let's hear about it. I'll give you adequate time to respond if you need it."

"Thank you, your honor," said Yates. "It seems the child was in the care of the respondent only yesterday, your honor, and that through a lack of care, or deliberate plan, was kidnapped."

"That's outrageous!" Pamela said.

"Hold it," said the judge. "Just hold it right there. Now, Mr. Yates, are you telling me that the child is missing?"

"Yes, your honor."

"Since yesterday?"

"That's right."

"And you're alleging that this was *what* now?"

"Either an egregious lack of care or, if your honor please, a scheme to have the child hidden from Mr. Ramsey."

Pamela said, "Your honor, we must be heard on this!"

"You will be, Ms. Fordyce," the judge said. "Mr. Yates, just give me your factual statement."

"Certainly. Respondent was in a market yesterday with the child and left her unattended for a period of time. During that time the child was taken. While this may have been negligence on the part of the respondent, the circumstances do give rise to some questions. The kidnapping could have been a purposeful act. Either way, the child is missing. The police are looking for her right now. This is obviously of grave concern to Mr. Ramsey and calls for an expedited decision. We would like your honor to declare full custody for Mr. Ramsey. The child is clearly at risk with the mother."

Janice sat frozen, with a mixture of incredulity and outrage. Though she knew Sam had told the police she might be behind Lauren's kidnapping, never had she thought he would go so far as to allege this in a court of law. There was no evidence. Yet there it was, from the mouth of Sam's lawyer, like a shotgun blast to the stomach.

The judge called on Pamela to respond.

"Your honor," she began, "I am almost speechless at this outrageous accusation. My client was indeed at the market with her daughter, when someone grabbed her purse. She simply gave chase, during which time her daughter was taken. It seems like this was a planned abduction, yes, but the real suspect is sitting right over there."

Pamela pointed at Sam. He shot her a look full of venom.

"Your honor," said Yates, his hands outstretched. "This is pure desperation."

"Is it?" said the judge. "Why shouldn't I consider the possibility of your client being culpable?"

Yates nodded. "Because my client will take a polygraph, your honor, with any examiner named by the court or opposing counsel. He is anxious to do that. The question is, will the respondent do the same?"

Of course, thought Janice. But Pamela said, "A polygraph is unreliable, your honor."

"But it is a factor to consider," the judge said. "And I have a feeling I'm going to need all the factors I can get on this one."

"Perhaps, your honor, you would like my client to testify," Yates said. "He is willing to put his credibility on the line right now."

The judge glanced at the clock, and Janice got the terrible feeling she wanted to dispose of this matter quickly. Not a good thing for a family law judge.

"All right, Mr. Yates," the judge said. "I will give each party the opportunity to testify. Agreed, Ms. Fordyce?"

Pamela whispered to Janice. "Are you game?"

"Let's do it," Janice said. Despite everything she'd seen in her years practicing law—the manipulations of the system, the bald-faced lies, the trickery of attorneys who put winning above all—she still believed in the power of truth. She would raise her right hand, swear to tell the truth and nothing but, and the judge would see there was no substance to the slander coming from Sam and his attorney.

"We're prepared to go forward, your honor," Pamela said.

"Very well then," said the judge. "Mr. Ramsey, you may take the stand."

●

Dewey Handleman flew over the polar ice cap, arms outstretched, weightless.

Eyes closed, he felt a cool rush of energy unlike any sensation he'd experienced in his seventeen years. It was . . . pure aliveness. No, something more: a transcending of life. A flight into another plane of being.

They said it would be like this, but no verbal description could do this justice.

He opened his eyes, hovering in the sky, even as the rational part of his brain reminded him he was sitting in the back of a Dunkin' Donuts in Cambridge, just a few blocks from Harvard Square. No matter, he was beyond space-time limitations, even if it was merely a product of a chemical high. This must have been a little like those "trips" they used to take in the '60s but better because the LSD they used left nothing of value to the brain.

This was different. This was biological history.

Dewey left the ice cap momentarily and considered the glazed donut in his hand. Every part of it was new to him, as if he were seeing the *essential* glazed donut for the first time. He was an explorer of donuts, and he laughed at the wonder of it.

Even donuts! Even on this level he had surpassed humanity! No one could see like he could.

His left hand, which held the donut, still looked small to him, though every line and pore was a universe of newness. His one regret in all this was that there would be no physical change. If only he could have become a size equal to his brain power. Even before the process he was a genius, but that genius was housed in the scrawny little body nature had saddled him with.

Now he was going beyond genius, and by all rights his body should go with him. They had called him "Wimp" in high school, an insult that quickly became a nickname. Fortunately he got into Harvard early and escaped Brooklyn as soon as he could.

Closing his eyes again, Dewey drifted through the sky above the earth, euphoric. He could stay like this forever, in a state of suspended and eternal delectation. Unemotional yet profoundly enjoyable, just like they had told him. . . .

A darkness overshadowed him. It was sudden, violent.

He shook, keeping his eyes shut, curious. What was this?

It lasted but a moment, yet in that instant he sensed something completely irrational—the presence of evil. *Personal* evil. Evil incarnate.

Like some scene out of an *Exorcist*-type movie!

How could that be? He didn't believe in that nonsense. Demons and devils? Of course not.

Was this just some weird mutation of imagination? Some blip in the treatment? Had to be. Why else would he have this type of vision at all?

The shadow passed as quickly as it had come, but it seemed to Dewey that it didn't completely disappear. It was as if it was, well, waiting somewhere. Ready to make a reappearance.

The door of the donut shop opened, and Dewey came out of his trance. A cool breeze shot into the store. Dewey felt it with every part of his being. He was more alive now than at any time before in his life. Fantastic!

Behind the breeze was a street person. Dewey recognized him. He hung out in the area, and Dewey had passed him many times before. He was bearded, brown, his clothes hanging on him like a fungus. His tennis shoes were unlaced, in the manner of former psychiatric patients. He shuffled rather than walked.

Dewey watched him with utter fascination, for he sensed again the heightened perception that had been promised, that would soon become a permanent faculty of his brain. As if looking at an amoeba through a microscope, Dewey examined the vagrant as he approached the counter. He wasn't one of the pit rats who hung out at the MBTA station. Those were mostly kids anyway—skinheads, gutter punks, homeboys, Goths. No, this vag was a ding, a crazy. What would he do? Dewey observed.

"Coffee," the dirty man said, in a soft, apologetic voice.

The woman behind the counter, an aggressive looking Asian, seemed to recognize him. "No coffee! You go!"

Ah, Dewey thought, *competition! The eternal struggle.*

"Coffee," the man repeated.

"You no money! You go!"

The man turned from the counter but made no move toward the door.

There were two other people in the shop—an older man reading the *Boston Globe,* and a female student-type sipping coffee and studying some papers.

Dewey, seated in the rear, analyzed the scene with clarity and fascination, anticipating all the moves.

First, the vag would shuffle toward the old man and hold out his hand. The old man would shake his head. Then the vag would try the woman, and she would not even look up to acknowledge his presence.

"You go now!" the woman at the counter would say once more, followed by, "I call police!"

But the bum would not listen. Finally, he would shuffle back to Dewey and ask for a dollar.

All this happened instantly in Dewey's mind and then happened in real time. This new clarity was a real trip. He could see the future!

So now the man was standing before him, hand out slightly as if trying not to give offense, but soliciting just the same.

"A dollar?" Dewey said. "In the old days it used to be a dime."

The man looked puzzled.

"You know," Dewey said, "as in, 'Brother can you spare a . . .' ? That was during the Great Depression, a time and place you would have fit into nicely."

The man just stood there.

Suddenly it occurred to Dewey that for this moment he owned this man. Actually *owned* him. And there were a number of ways he could use this ownership. This would be a situation that would come up over and over again, Dewey knew, as the process continued and the full effect finally took hold.

So what to do with it?

"Come on," Dewey said, standing and grabbing his backpack full of heavy textbooks. He walked to the counter as the vag followed, pulled out a dollar and laid it in front of the shocked woman. "A coffee for my friend," Dewey said.

"No coffee for him!"

"Look, here's the money. I'm buying him the coffee."

"He no stay!"

"That's fine. I'll take him with me. He's a friend of mine."

The counter woman looked back and forth between Dewey and the man several times, then turned and fetched a coffee. Dewey smiled at his new friend. The vag silently looked at the floor.

"You both go now," the woman said as she placed the coffee before Dewey.

Dewey picked up the Styrofoam cup and with a nod of his head motioned for the man to follow. They stepped out into the cool afternoon air.

"Thank you," the man said, arm outstretched.

Dewey held the coffee back. "Not so fast, friend. Let's walk a little. Where do you sleep?"

The man hesitated, looking at Dewey, suspicion etched across his dirty face.

"Come on," Dewey said, "I just bought you coffee."

"What do you want from me?"

"Just information. You're helping me."

"How?"

"Look, I'm a student at Harvard. You, obviously, are not, unless you're in the theater department." Dewey laughed, delighted with himself. He had never been witty in his former life. Apparently one of the side benefits of the process was a wry sense of humor. "I'm interested in how you got this way."

"Why?"

"Maybe I can help."

"I ain't got much help from nobody. Not since I got back."

"From where?"

"The Gulf, man."

"Gulf?"

"Desert Storm."

"Interesting."

"Can I have the coffee?"

"Show me where you sleep."

"I will, I promise."

Dewey handed the man the coffee, feeling a little like the guy who tosses fish to the performing seals.

After a sip, the man started walking down the sidewalk. He took Dewey half a block without words, then turned down an alley. Midway in the alley was a dumpster.

The man kept walking, Dewey following, until he stopped by the dumpster.

"In there?" Dewey said. "You live in there?"

"You think I'm a pig?" the man said.

Dewey held his tongue. The man pushed the dumpster forward, revealing a small, square, iron door embedded in the brick wall.

"Used to keep munitions in these things in the 1800s," the man said. "Now it's mine."

"Prime property, huh?"

"Yeah."

"Well, it's like they say. Location, location, location."

"Huh?"

"Never mind."

The man sipped his coffee. Dewey watched him as he would a bug pinned to a corkboard.

"Where you from?" Dewey asked.

The man's look of suspicion gave way to one of utter need. "Can you help me?"

"Maybe," Dewey said.

"They took away my meds," he said. "They won't take me back."

"You were in an institution?"

The man nodded.

"And now you're out, and you have no medication?"

"They're full up at Pine Street. Forget about it. I need meds, man. I . . ." He stopped suddenly and looked at the ground. A strange gurgling sound came out of his mouth. At first Dewey thought he might be choking on something, then realized the man was crying.

What to do now? Dewey felt himself stepping outside his own body, observing himself as he studied this weeping street person, watching to see just how he, Dewey, would react to this display of human misery.

He waited for an emotion to kick in, wondering what it would be. Disgust? Empathy? A heightened sense of identification? A total repulsion? What?

Nothing came. Dewey realized he was thoroughly dispassionate, and that pleased him.

But that's what they had promised. This new freedom from emotion. It was working, actually working!

Suddenly he felt himself lift his backpack by one strap, swing it around in a large arc and then land it with full force on the back of the vag's head.

He went down with a guttural moan, hitting the pavement with a thud, twitching once before becoming motionless.

Dewey looked at the squalid heap, now wondering how he would feel about what he had just done. And when he felt nothing, he said softly, "Interesting."

Looking up and down the alley, Dewey saw he was alone. He hit the man four more times with the backpack.

Then he walked out of the alley.

"Please state your name for the record," Grayson Yates said.

"Samuel P. Ramsey."

He was still handsome, Janice had to admit. But long ago that had ceased to be an attraction for her. Inside he had grown ugly. An interior repulsiveness had taken hold, like blight in the pith of a tree. She had agonized about the source of that decay for years but still could not explain it. It was as if he had been injected with a slow, spirit-withering contagion.

"Mr. Ramsey, you are the ex-husband of the respondent, Janice Ramsey?"

"Yes."

"And you have a daughter?"

"Lauren."

"How old is she?"

"Ten."

"Currently the respondent has physical custody?"

"I hope to change that."

Sam looked at Janice then, and she physically shook. His eyes were devoid of humanity, at least toward her. What had she done to deserve such hatred. Nothing! Yet his glare pierced her like a hot poker. In spite of everything, she had invested a significant portion of her life and emotions in Sam Ramsey. That wouldn't just melt away.

Grayson Yates said, "With regard to the unfortunate events of yesterday, the disappearance of your daughter, would you tell the court if you are in any way responsible for this."

Coolly, Sam turned to the judge and said, "Absolutely not. I was on a business trip back east, and my flight came in late last night. I had a message on my machine to call the police. When I did, I was given the news about the abduction. I was devastated, your honor, and I thought immediately that my ex-wife had something to do with it."

Pamela shot to her feet. "Objection, your honor. That's pure speculation."

"Overruled," said the judge. She turned to Sam. "On what do you base your opinion?"

Sam nodded earnestly at the judge. *He's playing her,* Janice thought immediately. He was selling her, like just another prospect. The problem was he was good at it. If nothing else, Sam was a master salesman.

"My ex-wife has become part of a religious sect," Sam said, "which teaches intolerance and bigotry. They have a record of interfering in family affairs, and she has told me directly that she will never allow me to have any influence over my own daughter."

That was a lie! But Sam had delivered it so convincingly Janice wondered if he somehow believed it. No way. There was something else at work here. A darkness. Janice sensed it. Sam embodied it.

"I have no further questions," Grayson Yates said. He turned to Pamela and, with a smug nod, retook his chair.

Pamela stood and addressed Sam. "Mr. Ramsey, you say you were on a business trip yesterday, is that correct?"

"Yes."

"That doesn't mean you couldn't have hired someone to kidnap your daughter, does it?"

"I didn't."

"Excuse me. I asked you if you *could* have."

"I did not hire anyone to kidnap my daughter."

"Your honor," Pamela said, "will you direct the witness to answer my question?"

Seeming exasperated, the judge snapped, "He's answered it. Move on."

The rebuke was like a slap to Janice. The judge was clearly biased now, for whatever reason.

"Very well then," said Pamela. "Mr. Ramsey, have you ever hit your wife?"

"Objection!" Grayson Yates shouted.

"Yes," said the judge. "I'm going to sustain the objection."

"But your honor—"

"No, Ms. Fordyce. This is a limited hearing on custody. We're not going to revisit the marriage."

"But surely this has relevance," Pamela said. Her neck was reddening.

"I rule that it does not," said the judge. "Do you have anything further?"

"Mr. Ramsey," Pamela shot at Sam. "If it was within your power, you wouldn't hesitate to take your daughter away from my client, would you?"

Leaning forward, Sam looked coolly at Pamela Fordyce. "I would not so long as the law allowed it. And that's why I'm here."

It was a perfect answer, perfectly delivered. It seemed almost rehearsed, as if Sam had anticipated that very question. Or been prepared for it by Yates.

Pamela said, "Then your answer is yes, you would."

This time, the judge did not wait for an objection. "He has answered the question, Ms. Fordyce."

"Nothing further," said Pamela, apparently reading the same writing on the wall as Janice.

Before stepping down, Sam said, "Thank you, your honor." The judge smiled and nodded at him.

"Call Janice Ramsey," Pamela said.

Janice took the stand and was sworn.

"Janice," said Pamela, "did you abduct your daughter?"

"Absolutely not," said Janice, her entire being squeezing every last drop of sincerity out of her answer. She wanted—*willed*—the judge to see her veracity.

"Did you engage anyone to abduct your daughter?"

"No, I did not."

"Do you have an opinion as to who might be behind this abduction?"

"Objection," said Yates.

"Your honor," Pamela said, "Mr. Ramsey was allowed to speculate. I'm simply asking my client the same thing."

"You don't need to explain the facts to me, Ms. Fordyce. I'm sitting right here. You may answer the question, Ms. Ramsey."

Janice opened her mouth slightly but stopped. Part of her wanted to shout it. *Yes! Sam! He had her taken! He would do it!*

But another part of her, the stronger part, knew that it *was* speculation. She had no way of knowing, let alone proving Sam's involvement. Not yet, at least. Sam had lied openly. People did that all the time in family court. She could not.

"I don't have a strong opinion," Janice said finally. "I'm not going to accuse Sam Ramsey without any basis. I just want my daughter back." Janice's eyes suddenly became wet. She fought hard to hold back the tears.

"That's all, your honor," said Pamela.

Janice was halfway out of the witness chair when she was knocked back by the voice of Grayson Yates. "Just a couple of questions, Ms. Ramsey."

Blinking her eyes to bring back focus, Janice watched him approach. The tiger image came back. Yates seemed ready to pounce.

"You love your daughter, don't you?" Yates said. His voice rolled out like sonorous musical tones.

"Of course I do."

"Very much."

"Yes, more than I can say."

"Would do anything for her?"

"Naturally."

"Whatever you thought to be in her best interest?"

Spinning a web. That's what he was doing with his seemingly innocuous questions. Janice had enough trial experience to know exactly what was happening. As a lawyer, she could step back and analyze. But as a witness under oath, having to answer questions, she was too close to see the entire pattern.

Just the truth, she told herself. Just keep telling the truth. "I always do what is in my daughter's best interest."

"You're a member of the Oak Park Bible Church, are you not?"

The sudden shift was a typical cross-examination tactic. What was Yates driving at? Sam's outburst about a "sect" had alerted her to a possible, extreme line of attack. But there was something more going on here. Yates had that look.

Truth. Truth.

"I am," said Janice.

"How long have you been a member?"

"About five years."

"You like it?"

"I love it. It's a wonderful church."

"You take your daughter there?"

"Yes, of course."

"She goes to Sunday School there?"

Before Janice could answer, Pamela objected on grounds of relevance. The judge overruled her.

Yates said, "That church has become a big part of your and your daughter's life, has it not?"

"That's what church is, a big part of one's life."

"You would consider the people there to be your spiritual family?"

"Yes."

"You have stated that to Mr. Ramsey before, haven't you?"

"I may have."

"In fact, that was one reason for the breakup of your marriage. You put your church family ahead of your own husband."

"Objection!" Pamela said.

"Sustained," said the judge softly.

"Well, let me ask you this," Yates said as he moved to the counsel table and picked up a file folder. Glancing at the contents he said, "Do you know the Reverend Greg Arsenault?"

"Yes."

"He is, in fact, the minister at Oak Park."

"Associate minister."

"Do you know him well?"

"Yes I do. He's a wonderful man."

"Wonderful?"

"Yes."

"And his views on what's good for children are wonderful, too?"

"Definitely. He oversees the children's ministry, and the kids love him."

"Including your daughter?"

"Yes."

Where was he going with this? Trying to tie Janice and Greg together in some kidnapping scheme?

"Are you aware that the good reverend was once arrested for child abduction?"

No, Janice had not been aware of that. What she did know was that Greg had done some things in the past that some might have called extreme. Like civil disobedience in front of abortion clinics. He was, no question, a man who put his faith and beliefs into action.

"No, sir," she said.

"And that he once wrote—" Yates looked at a page in the folder—"'A spouse with a hostile, unbelieving husband or wife is compelled to take every action possible to secure the salvation of his or her children.' Were you aware of that?"

"No."

"Do you agree with it?"

The question was a snare. "I would have to read it in context," she said.

"You can't answer directly?"

"It's not a simple yes or no, Mr. Yates."

"But in principle, do you agree with it?"

"I agree that I take my faith seriously."

Yates took a step back and smiled. "Of course you do," he said. "No further questions."

There was no need to continue, Janice knew. A good cross-examiner knew when to stop, and often the best time was when heavy implications hung in the air to be breathed in by judges and juries. Yates had polluted the courtroom well.

Janice's legs were wobbly reeds as she returned to her chair. Pamela patted her leg comfortingly, but Janice felt like she'd been dumped and rolled by a crashing wave. She looked at Sam, who returned her gaze.

How, she asked with her eyes, can you do this?

He smiled.

●

"She's in danger," Janice said, "I can feel it."

Pamela put her hand on Janice's shoulder. "I know what you're feeling."

"Do you?" Janice snapped. Pamela sat back, as if cold water had been splashed in her face. "I'm sorry," Janice said. "You didn't deserve that."

"Believe me, I've heard worse."

They were sitting together on a sofa in Pamela's law office. It was a modest suite in a building where Pamela shared a receptionist and library with other lawyers. But though unpretentious, it was comfortable. A place to set people at ease. Janice knew that as a family law attorney, Pamela needed to make people feel comfortable from the moment they walked in the door.

"One time I had a Christian man, quote unquote, come in for a consultation," Pamela said.

"How do you handle that?"

"I always ask if the party has gone to their pastor first. If they're Christian, it needs to go through the church."

"Sam never went to church with me, not once."

"Well, this guy got very upset with me when I suggested it. He said he hadn't come to me to get a lecture about his faith. He had come to give me a substantial amount of money to stick it to his wife."

"Wow."

"I told him I wouldn't take his case. At which point he called me the Whore of Babylon."

Janice winced, but Pamela laughed and said, "I have no idea of the theological significance of that. I've never been to Babylon."

Laughing in spite of herself, Janice felt more at ease. Pamela was not only an amazing lawyer in this swamp called family law; she was also a wonderful friend. "Do you ever regret going into law?" she asked.

Pamela thought a moment. "To be honest, sometimes. I get frustrated with the system. It's hard for one person to make a difference. But I guess no one ever promised it would be easy. How about you?"

"I feel the same way sometimes," Janice said. "Sometimes it's just like I'm a cog in a giant machine, going through the motions. Once, just once, I'd like to stand up before a court, maybe even the Supreme Court, with everything on the line, and make a winning argument. Use all the stuff up here"—she pointed to her head—"that I learned in Constitutional Law and just blow them away."

Nodding, Pamela said, "Yeah. I know. Someday you will."

The good feeling lingered for another moment, then Janice was thrown back to reality, and her daughter. "I can sense that Lauren's in trouble. And I know Sam is responsible."

"You can't be sure about that," said Pamela. "But if the proof is there, we'll find it. That's what we've got to bring before the judge. Not feelings."

"I know, I know." Janice's legal training told her Pamela was right, but her mother's instincts battled against that cold, objective conclusion. "I have to talk to him."

"Sam?"

"Yes."

"That's not a good idea."

"I have to. I have to do something."

"Janice . . ." Pamela stopped herself, looked deep into Janice's face. She seemed to be reading her eyes. Then, nodding slightly, she said, "I understand."

"You always do," Janice said.

"What if you find out Sam had something to do with it?"

"Oh boy."

"What would you do?"

"I think I would do something really bad."

"How bad?"

"Just don't let me have a baseball bat in my hand."

"Ouch."

"I know that's not right."

"I can't picture that, Janice. Not you."

"Me neither." Janice looked at the ceiling and sighed. "This is all so unreal. It's like a movie. These things don't happen in real life. I mean, nothing like this has ever happened to me."

"Can we have a prayer together?"

"Oh yes."

Pamela took Janice's hand as they bowed their heads. "Lord God," Pamela said, "I ask right now that you look after Lauren, wherever she is, and that you deliver her from evil. Protect her, Lord. Keep her safe. Bring her back to Janice quickly. And protect Janice, Lord. Give her an extra measure of faith. Give her wisdom, and bring her into contact with those who can truly help her. Show her what to do. I ask all this in the name of our Savior, Jesus Christ. Amen."

When she opened her eyes, Janice felt the warmth of peace. She suddenly thought, *Be like David.*

"I'm ready to see him now," she said.

"Sam?"

"Yes."

"Be careful. Be *very* careful."

"You just prayed for me, right?"

"Right."

"Then why should I be afraid?"

The Lord is my Shepherd. . . . The Lord is my Shepherd. . . .

Lauren repeated the phrase over and over, not just a prayer now but a lifeline. Her bladder was full, and the vibration of the car was making it hard to hold it in. She didn't want to wet in the car, because they probably wouldn't care, and then she'd be lying in it on the back floor.

The Lord is my Shepherd. . . . The Lord is my Shepherd. . . .

"Check on her," a voice said.

She didn't see but sensed the one in the passenger seat looking back at her. Lauren steeled herself, trying not to show them any fear. She had heard from her daddy that animals sense fear and will attack. She was sure these men who had her were animals.

But she could not control her squirming. Her condition required it. She had to hold it in.

"I think," the other voice said, "she might have to go potty."

"Oh, man!"

"Hey, when you gotta go."

And the two laughed.

"Ask her."

The observant one moved, and Lauren looked up. She saw his face. It was not what she expected. Her imagination had conjured up a twisted pug-face, a typical TV villain's face, or something from a comic book. But it wasn't like that. He was young, probably twenty or so, and looked not like a TV bad guy but a TV heartthrob. He would have fit in easily among that seemingly endless herd of faces that trundle through television's idea of what teen life is like. Lauren never watched those shows. Her mother wouldn't allow it. But at school all her friends had pictures of them from the magazines.

His hair was perfectly combed and his eyes . . . his eyes almost gleamed.

He reached his hand toward her face and grabbed one end of the tape across her mouth. With a quick *riiip* he pulled it from her, and it stung. Big time. But she did not cry out.

"Hey," Heartthrob said. "You have to go potty?"

The way he said it confused her. He wasn't mean about it, but he wasn't caring, either. It was as if he had no feelings at all.

"I want my mommy," Lauren said.

"I asked you a question."

"Yes," she said.

"All right, we'll pull over. You stay put." Heartthrob turned to the driver and said, "Find a spot."

"Got it," the driver replied.

Lauren held on with all her strength, sensing the car slowing. There were no other sounds except the beating of her own heart.

Finally the car was still. She heard a door open and Heartthrob got out. Then the back door opened and he said, "Come on."

He reached in and lifted her from the floor. Her hands were tied behind her, and she felt a shooting pain in her shoulders. Then she saw sunlight coming through a shroud of dark clouds. It was cold, wherever they were.

And where was that? The terrain was unfamiliar to her. They were near some kind of field, one that looked tended to. A farm perhaps. A few paces to the right was a grove of trees; she didn't know what kind. There were no buildings anywhere. She heard a car *whish* past on the highway.

"Hurry up," the driver said from inside the car. Lauren caught a short glimpse of him. He seemed fat.

"All right, come on," Heartthrob said, taking her right arm and leading her to the trees. "Get this over with."

Their steps made crunching noises on the weedy ground as they walked.

What if she screamed? Would someone hear her? Not likely, given where they were. And even if she did, maybe they'd kill her on the spot. People did things like that. Horrible things.

A fresh wave of fear welled up inside her. *Be like David.*

Now at the trees, Heartthrob let go of her arm. "Do it quick," he said.

"I need to take my pants off," she said, embarrassed.

"Oh, right." Heartthrob reached in his pocket and came out with a Swiss Army knife—just like the one her Daddy had. A flood of memories hit her then. *If only Daddy were here, he'd take care of me. Even though he's been mean to Mommy, he's not mean to me.*

She felt her arms go free. Heavy tape stuck to the tops of her wrists. Heartthrob reached down and tore the tape off. "Get going," he said, nodding toward a tree a few steps away.

Though she had to go badly, Lauren took her time walking to the tree. She was free, if only for a moment, and she wanted to enjoy it while it lasted. Just before stepping around the trunk, she looked back at her guard. His eyes seemed brighter somehow, as if reflecting the sunlight like tiny mirrors.

"Don't look," Lauren said.

"Don't worry." Heartthrob looked out toward the highway.

It took only a few seconds for Lauren to slip off her pants and underwear and feel sweet relief. For the moment, at least, she was happy.

And she started to think.

Maybe she could make a run for it. But how far would she get? Heartthrob looked like he was in good shape. He would easily run her down unless . . .

Lauren looked through the trees. It was an orchard of some kind, and the trees grew low and close together. If she could run in and out of them, under them . . .

No, too risky.

But what were they going to do to her? Would it be any worse if they caught her after an attempted escape?

She wished she knew what to do.

"He wants to talk to you," she heard Driver say to Heartthrob.

"Why didn't you bring the phone?" Heartthrob said.

"It's plugged in the lighter."

"Watch her."

She heard the driver say to her, "You finished yet?"

"Almost," she said. She took her time slipping back into her underwear and pants, and looked again at the tangle of small trees in front of her.

Slowly she came out from behind the tree. Driver was standing there. And he *was* fat. He didn't look like he could go up an escalator without losing his breath. Heartthrob was just getting into the car.

"Let's go," Driver said.

Lauren froze for one moment, and the decision popped into her head all at once. She turned her back.

"Come on," Driver said.

She ran.

"Hey!"

She didn't look back. She ran as fast as she could, ducking her head a little to get under the trees. And she started zigzagging in and out, like a slalom skier, only she didn't know where the finish line was. All she knew was that she had to keep running.

Behind her she heard the voice of Driver screaming something. It sounded like "Rance!" Maybe that was Heartthrob's name. The good thing was the voice was back where she had started. Driver wasn't following her, apparently wasn't even going to make the attempt.

She kept running. Wind whipped past her ears. *Dear God, help me find my way out!*

The dirt beneath her feet was soft, so she knew she wasn't running as fast as she could. But that meant her kidnappers would have the same problem, not to mention having to run practically doubled over to get under the trees.

Suddenly she was yanked back.

They had her by the shirt!

How could it be?

Flailing, she tried to break free, but she couldn't move.

It was over.

But they didn't say a word.

Lauren twisted in the grasp and saw what held her—a pruned tree branch, stuck firmly through her sleeve. Lauren almost squealed, but suppressed it, knowing even a little bit of noise could be a clue to her whereabouts.

Wasting no time, Lauren pulled at her blouse and let the sleeve rip.

Once more she ran. She went ten yards or so before a terrible thought hit her. She didn't know what direction she was going! For all she knew she could be running straight back to her captors!

Which way, God, which way?

She heard muffled voices in the distance but couldn't tell where they were coming from. Only that they were coming *nearer.*

Which way, God?

She heard a fluffing sound and spun around. A small bird was rustling in a tree a few steps away. For a short moment it stopped and seemed to regard Lauren, cocking its head, then flew off like an arrow away from her.

Lauren followed the bird.

She ran a good long stretch and, to her relief, didn't see the kidnappers. She paused for a rest, panting heavily, trying to listen.

Nothing but wind, and the desperate gulps of her own breath.

Then a voice. It said something very bad, and it was near.

What if they had split up? What if they were coming at her from two different directions?

Move!

Once more she took off, in and out of the trees, wondering if it would ever end. What if she was lost in a maze of trees, never to see the end? Trapped like a mouse, forever.

And then she saw it, what looked like a clearing up ahead. A field of some kind, green and lush.

A hot pain shot through her right foot. She went down. Dirt splashed up into her nostrils. She hacked.

But worse was the pain in her foot, like a knife had cut it. She pulled her foot up and looked at the bottom of her shoe. Blood was coming out of a little slit in the sole.

Lauren looked behind her. A spike stuck out of the ground at the base of one of the trees.

She tried to stand on her foot, but the pain was too intense. She could not run, only limp, and barely. It would only be a matter of time before the cut would take over and keep her from moving *at all*.

Get to the field, at least get to the field!

She half hopped, half ran to the edge of what turned out to be a cornfield. The stalks were low, coming up to her chin, but that might be enough for cover. With a quick look behind her Lauren pressed out into the field, a *shushing* sound enveloping her as she scraped the leaves.

Her foot was starting to throb, and her side was aching almost as bad. But she had to press on, had to.

For five minutes or so she ran-limped through the corn, until she could not physically go further. She fell down in between two rows of corn stalks, hiding herself in the cool green sea.

Now what?

Wait. Wait and hope they would give up. Hope her foot would feel better. And hope somewhere out here was a place of refuge.

She looked up through the stalks and saw a steel gray sky above her, with angry clouds massing like some evil army. She wondered how long it would be before the rain came.

And then, behind her, she heard a *shushing* sound. And voices.

Nice digs, Jed thought. Somebody was fronting this limo driver quite a wad.

So why was someone with a semipermanent hotel room in Beverly Hills driving a limo in the first place?

Jed walked the hotel lobby, all ferns and marble and gold and oak, catching hardly a look from the bell captain and concierge. With his pony tail and leathers, he could have been a rock star, after all. The only dubious glance came from a security guard in a dark blue coat. Jed could tell he was security from the way he scanned the lobby. None too subtle.

Ignoring him, Jed walked purposefully to the elevators.

A dapper, older couple gave him the twice-over as they awaited the elevator car. Jed turned his good eye to them and said, "Nice day."

The couple murmured some assent, but when they entered the elevator car, they stood in the back, huddled closely.

Jed got off on the tenth floor.

According to the information he'd squeezed at the limo place, a young man named Anthony ("Just

Anthony, that's all I know," the man had insisted) was staying in room 1006.

Now the only question was which approach? Direct or indirect?

Jed Brown had plenty of experience with both. Direct meant a knock, an opened door followed by a shoulder or boot, and came with a look of complete shock on the part of the inhabitant. The indirect method was safer but also more difficult. It meant gaining entry without anyone knowing it.

Problem was, Jed didn't fully know who he was dealing with, whether this Anthony was in or not, or how he would take an uninvited knock. But Jed's little man told him to be careful. Jed called his instincts—sculpted from innumerable contacts over the years with the broadest range of nefarious characters—his little man. He'd heard that from Edward G. Robinson in the movie *Double Indemnity.* Robinson, an insurance investigator, could always tell when something was wrong because his little man, right inside his stomach, would tell him so.

Now Jed's little man was saying Anthony would be one of the suspicious types, resistant, maybe even armed.

Jed walked back to the elevators, opposite which was an ornate glass table with two soft chairs beside it, a house phone, and a copy of *Business Week* on top. He took a seat, crossed his legs, picked up the phone, and punched 1006.

Three rings, then a clipped voice. "Yes?"

"I'm sorry, sir," Jed said in his finest, stuffy tone. "This is the front desk. How did you enjoy the champagne?"

"What?"

"The Veuve Clicquot you ordered, sir. Naturally, we wanted to be sure you were satisfied."

"I didn't order any champagne."

"But it . . . my, my."

"What is this?"

"It's just that, it has been billed to your room."

"Well take it off."

"I'm afraid I . . ."

"Afraid *what?*"

"I'm so sorry, sir. I can't do that."

"I didn't order any champagne!"

"But you signed the bill, sir. I have it here in front of me."

"You what? I'm coming down right now."

"Yes, sir, if you'll . . ."

Click.

Jed replaced the phone and picked up the copy of *Business Week*. One minute later a young man dressed in black pants and crisp white shirt appeared at the elevators. His black hair was slicked back and held down with some sort of industrial strength mousse.

Jed watched him jab the down button. *That's my boy.*

As soon as the elevator doors closed, Jed hotfooted to 1006. He gave himself four minutes.

From his jacket he pulled a key code card with two small wires attached. The wires went into a small, handheld computer. He stuck the key in the door's slot and hit the keypad on the computer. Small, red numbers swarmed across the LCD screen like bustling insects.

He could get a five-year stretch for even possessing this little device, and another ten for breaking and entering. But they would have to catch him, and they never would. Jed had been avoiding *they* for years.

Two minutes passed.

A door opened halfway down the hall, and a gray-haired gentleman in a pinstripe suit ambled toward him.

Jed waited until the man was about two yards away, then turned his head and smiled.

"Evening," Jed said.

"Good evening," the man replied, looking at Jed's hands.

"Can I ask you?"

The man stopped. "Yes?"

"You had any trouble with your key?"

"No, not at all."

"Well report it if you do. Hotel's had several complaints. Ask for security."

The man cleared his throat. "Uh, yes—"

"Have a good evening."

The man blinked once, then disappeared around the corner. From his look there was no way to know if the bluff had worked. Jed looked at the readout. The numbers had stopped. Jed pulled the key card from the door and heard the familiar *click*.

He opened the door and went in.

It was dark. The curtains were drawn, and no lights were on. Only a faint, bluish glow cast any illumination in the room. At once Jed knew this was the light of a computer screen.

Sure enough, a laptop sat on the desk by the phone. Jed gave the screen a quick scan. It looked like some sort of account information, perhaps a bank or mutual fund. He couldn't give it more time, however. Anthony would be back soon.

Quickly, Jed examined the room for weapons—all the drawers, the suitcase in the closet, under the bed. Nothing.

Satisfied, Jed waited in the bathroom. He took out his Taser, holding the Glock-sized weapon in his open palm.

And then, almost as if he'd been jolted by electric prods from the past, Jed's body filled with a sudden and ineffable sadness. He was not shocked, however. It happened periodically, like the flare-up of pain in a wounded limb. He'd had these spells for fifteen years.

Jed called these incidents "dark clouds." They rolled in quickly, like a storm in the Florida keys, poured out their vengeance, then cleared up as fast as they'd appeared.

He had learned just to grit it out.

Deep down Jed knew the clouds had to be connected to his soul—if he had one. Only now they seemed even more ominous, and he sensed the reason. His brother's death. It was not right. His brother had been the good one. If anyone had to die, it should have been Jed. Right now he wished it had been.

The last time he had seen his brother was Christmas, when they'd had that argument. How he wished he could take it back now! It echoed in his memory like a dead man's wail.

"Don't lecture me, Sterling. I hate it when you lecture me!"

"Why can't I share my concern with you, Jed?"

"Because it's Big Brother Syndrome. You think you have to save me."

"You've been running away from God long enough."

"If he's there, he can catch me."

"Not if you won't let him."

"Didn't God ordain this? All of it?"

"You can't blame God."

"Didn't God ordain my wife. . . ."

"The question is, what are you going to do about it?"

"I don't want to worship that kind of God! Can't you understand that?"

"You knew him once."

"You can have him, Sterling. Just leave me alone!"

"Will you pray with me?"

"No."

"Then let me pray for you."

"No!"

Sterling's wife had prepared a lovely turkey dinner. Jed tried to enjoy it, but it was no use. He didn't stay for dessert.

And now Sterling was dead, and Jed hadn't had the chance to apologize. And would never have that chance.

The room door opened, and Anthony charged in. He ran past the bathroom like a sprinter out of the blocks. Jed stuck his head out and saw that Anthony was frantically punching the computer keypad.

Jed stepped out of the bathroom. "Anxious, aren't we?"

Anthony, given a ghostly glow by the screen, spun around. For a moment Jed actually thought Anthony's eyes had a glow of their own.

"Steady, partner," Jed said.

"Who are you?"

"Let's talk."

"What do you want?"

"If you'll allow me, I'll ask the questions."

Anthony's body tensed. It was the coil of a cornered suspect. Jed could almost hear the gears grinding in Anthony's head, assessing the situation, wondering how to get out of it. How many skips had Jed seen suffer through the same, fruitless process?

"Don't even think about it," Jed said. He held up the Taser. "My little friend here can turn your Pat Riley hairdo into a waffle in two seconds. So why don't you just take a seat there on the bed?"

After a moment's hesitation, Anthony sat. He did not take his eyes off Jed. *A live one,* Jed told himself. *Be ready.*

"Turn on the light," Jed ordered.

Anthony reached for the switch for the bedside lamp and flicked it on. Now Jed took a fuller look. This was an intelligent-looking kid, trim and fit. Probably a go-getter, one of those twenty-somethings who was determined to grab all of the pie the world had to offer and not share any pieces.

Jed paced a semi-circle around the bed until he was on the same side as Anthony. Pulling a chair from near the window Jed slowly lowered himself into it, keeping the Taser visible on his lap.

"Now then," Jed began, "suppose we start with your whereabouts a week ago Thursday. Where were you?"

"I already talked to the cops. I don't have to answer questions from you."

Jed raised the Taser slightly. "I think you do."

"All right," Anthony said. "Big deal. I'll just tell you the same thing. I was driving a limo."

"For what party?"

"CBS."

"Occupant?"

"I forget his name. A doctor of some kind."

"Dr. Sterling Brown?"

"That might have been it."

He was lying. A name like Sterling would not have been an ambiguity. And if the cops had questioned him, surely it would have come up.

"OK. Where did you pick him up?"

"The Sheraton Universal."

"And what happened?"

"Nothing. Drove him to the studio in Hollywood."

"That can be checked."

"So check."

"When was the last time you saw him?"

Anthony's eyes looked up and to the right. That's when Jed knew for sure. That little nonverbal indicator was a sign of making up a story. When people's eyes go to the right, they are accessing the right-brain, the seat of creative imagination. That's how they make up stories. Jed had seen it many times before.

"Let's see," said Anthony, "I opened the door and let him out, and he was greeted by a guy from the studio, who started walking him toward a door. I got back in the limo and drove out of the gate."

"Did the gate have one of those up-and-down things?"

"Yeah."

"What color?"

At that, Anthony's expression froze.

For an instant time stood still.

Then everything seemed to happen at once. Anthony made a quick move behind him and suddenly had a knife in his hand. Jed aimed the Taser at Anthony's chest and triggered, but with perfect timing Anthony whipped a pillow in front of him, shielding himself from the prongs. They thudded into the padding, diluting the charge.

Anthony flashed out toward Jed, who barely had time to react. Jed twisted right as the knife blade thrust toward his heart. It caught his left sleeve, cutting through the leather, slicing skin.

Jed brought his right fist down on Anthony's arm with every intention of breaking it.

Anthony cried out, recoiled. The knife was still in his hand.

Jed was up in a split second, kicked at Anthony's wrist with his boot. Solid contact, like a punter in football.

The knife flew up and hit the ceiling, then fell straight down. Jed jumped for it, expecting company.

He had none. He stood up, holding the knife at the ready, waiting for something else—a chair, a table lamp—to be thrown at him.

Instead he saw Anthony, his back to the curtains, inexplicably holding the laptop computer. In all this he had chosen to grab the laptop. Why?

"It's all over, pard," Jed said. "Now you just take it real easy. All I want to know is why you offed my brother. I know you were in the hire of somebody. You tell me what you know, and I'll see to it the D.A. makes you a deal."

Anthony said nothing. With the laptop clutched to his chest with one hand, he reached behind him with the other, ruffling the curtains.

"Don't try anything, son," Jed said. "You took your best shot and lost. I don't want to mess you up, but I will if I have to. Now who are you working for?"

Anthony's lips slowly parted, showing teeth. It was not a smile, but a sneer. And once more, Jed was sure he saw a luminescence in Anthony's eyes. Like a cat staring into headlights at night.

Then Anthony spoke. "All truths are soaked in blood."

Before Jed could react, Anthony flung the curtains, slid open the glass door to the balcony, and dashed outside.

Jed ran for the curtains, knowing then the unthinkable was about to happen. All he saw the moment he got outside was the soles of Anthony's feet as they shot downward.

At the ledge, Jed saw the body falling like a missile toward the street below. It landed on the roof of a black, formerly pristine Lincoln which was parked in front of the hotel. A chorus of screams rose up to Jed Brown.

He raced back into the room, grabbed his Taser and the knife. For what he was about to do he gave himself five minutes.

He opened the door, careful not to leave prints on the handle and walked casually to the elevators. No one joined him on the ride down.

The lobby was already a flurry of activity. Looky Loos crammed themselves near the front doors, trying to get a peek at what happened.

Jed pushed his way past the small crowd and out to the sidewalk. He had three-and-a-half minutes left, according to his own timetable.

Three-and-a-half minutes to take advantage of the chaos. After that, security would be thinking too much. And cops would be starting to arrive.

Where Anthony's body had fallen, a ring of people was already formed. Jed could hear a voice telling people to get back, get back. That would be the security guard he had seen earlier in the lobby.

Indeed it was, trying everything he could to force order on a tense situation.

Three minutes.

Jed removed a leather fold from his pocket. Inside was a phony LAPD badge and a photo ID.

Jed shoved his way to the inside of the circle. As the security guard whirled around to stop him Jed flashed the badge. "Keep these people back, will you?" he said sternly, then flipped the fake credential closed.

"Yes, sir," the security guard said, immediately going back to crowd control mode.

One-and-a-half.

Anthony was sprawled out, face down, like a busted mannequin. Bloodstains and broken computer parts were scattered around the body.

Jed knelt by Anthony and made sure of the obvious. Dead. No question.

He focused on Anthony's right arm. It was tucked under his body, as if he were holding something close. Jed reached under the right shoulder.

"Shouldn't you wait?" It was Security. An amateur forensic expert!

"I'm doing the prelim," Jed said.

"Without gloves?"

Oh, great, Jed thought. Now he had less time than he thought. Ignoring the guard, Jed felt around under Anthony's body, lifting the shoulder slightly with his other hand.

"Hey, I don't think you should be doing that," Security said.

Jed closed his hand around a hard object.

"Who are you?"

Standing, Jed said, "Harry Callahan. LAPD."

"Let me see your badge again."

In the distance, Jed could hear a siren. It was approaching fast.

"You keep these people away from the body," Jed said, backing up.

"Hey—"

"Or it'll be your hide!"

"Hey!"

Jed turned and pushed through the knot of bystanders. Without looking back he began to run.

Cold.

Wind.

Sputtering of raindrops.

Alive.

Alone.

Lauren lay like a ball on the chilly, damp ground. Stalks of corn rose around her like sentries. Had she really spent the night here? Or was this a vivid nightmare from which she *really* had to awaken?

No, it was real.

And they hadn't found her.

She was *free!*

But *where?*

Her right foot ached. The wound. How bad was it? She sensed it would be bad indeed.

She coughed. Sniffed. A cold!

That's when she lost it. She had kept herself from crying before, but now the tears came in sheets. She wanted her mother. More than anything, she wanted to be in a warm bed with Mom sitting on the side, stroking her hair, giving her hot soup, taking care of her like always.

In her sense memory Lauren could smell the

Vick's VapoRub that Mom used to spread on her chest. She loved the smell, even though it was strong at the start. How she wanted it now.

Lauren put her face in her hands, and her hands on the dirt, and she wept.

Several minutes went by before Lauren managed to control it. She knew she had to. She couldn't stay here in the field. She would have to move.

Be like David.

Didn't God take care of David?

He would do no less for Lauren Ramsey! She believed it, firmly. And stood up.

A pervasive ache covered her foot, all the way to the ankle. Bad, very bad. She could not move.

Had to move!

Like a hopscotch champion, Lauren bounded on her good leg through the rows of corn stalks. The rain was starting to come down heavier now, soaking her hair and clothes, making her feel like a heap of rags thrown in a pool.

The ground, muddy, was no help. She slipped and fell twice trying to find her way out of the green maze.

And heard a noise.

It sounded like a machine.

She hopped toward the noise. It got louder. And then she was out of the corn. A flat field stretched out before her. She felt like she had just come up for air after being dunked under ocean waves.

And there, not far away, sat a man on a tractor. Coming her way.

He was wearing a blue raincoat and hat and seemed to be dragging something behind him. Looking backward, he couldn't see her.

Could she trust him? She now knew there were people out there who did bad things. But there was no way to avoid it. She stood there and waited for the man to look up.

When he did, she waved her arms.

A look of total shock covered the man's face.

●

Bently Davis was in his element.

Moving silkily around the front of the auditorium, packed with wide-eyed Harvard freshmen, Davis felt less like a professor than an artist. What was in front of him was not a classroom of students but a mass of clay blobs. Clay to be molded by the tools of thought, rhetoric, and charm. Of all the courses he had taught, from the graduate level on down, this was Davis's favorite. Introduction to Life Sciences, a freshman requirement. All those malleable young heads, the best and the brightest. He was shaping not only minds but history. It was the future sitting before him, and they were in his hands.

Especially girls. They always sat in the forward rows in Davis's classes. Each year there was a new crop, and they no doubt had heard the stories. For the last several years running, Davis had won the informal "sexiest prof on campus" poll run in the *Crimson*. He did nothing to dispel the reputation.

His shoulder-length steel-colored hair was curly, thinning on top but full on the sides. He wore a loose fitting sweater which revealed a gold chain around his neck, and casual slacks.

"After sleeping through a hundred million centuries," he told the student assemblage, "we have finally opened our eyes on a sumptuous planet, sparkling with color, bountiful with life. And yet even now there are countless millions who shuffle through this life without any wonder about it, devoid of curiosity or eagerness. And such were some of you!"

He paused then, to make eye contact with as many faces as he could. Part of it was dramatic intent, but Davis also liked to play a little game with himself. He wanted to see if he could find the face of a doubter, one who was going to be a problem child and would need a little extra work. It was his goal in Life Sciences to make sure *every* student left the class with an unwavering belief in raw naturalism—that the universe was an impersonal pool of matter, nothing more or less.

Of course, there were always stubborn ones, and usually one or two who stuck it out until just before the end. Almost always it was a Christian student from a podunk town and a podunk church, determined to cling to the fairy stories Mommy and Daddy had filled his head with.

In a few short moments Davis was sure he had found the one—a boy in the aisle seat, halfway back. Davis gave him an extended look.

"Well, there will be no sleeping in this class. We are casting off the soporific nostrums of this quaint culture and moving forward with our eyes wide open, not wide shut. Consider yourselves lucky to be here. You are at the top of the Darwinian-intellectual food chain. And we're going to gorge ourselves."

The laughter came, as it always did. Davis had honed this lecture into a successful stand-up routine.

"Yes, evolution will be one of our companions along the way, and I hope, dearly hope, there are not many of you who think that an intelligent Creator of some kind has knitted you together, as it says in some book or other."

Some more laughter, as Davis intended. He never said "the Bible." He always alluded to "some book or other," luxuriating in his created irony. He shot a quick glance at the boy he had pegged earlier, and sure enough his face was furrowed. Worried. The initial shock had set in.

"I know the reality is that there are a few of you in here. But by the time you finish this class, there will be a cleansing. I consider it a duty, part of my Harvard-inspired duty, to clear out that religious muck from your heads, because ladies and gentlemen, as surely as a Jeep sinks in quicksand, your brains will die if left in the bog of your childhood religionism."

A blond co-ed in the front row flashed a perfect smile at him. Davis thought she looked a little like Marilyn Monroe, or maybe Madonna. Either way, he sensed she would be the first of the new semester's crop to garner some "extra credit" with the professor within the next few weeks.

"Yes, we are in a new millennium, yet over half the people of these United States say that they don't believe in evolution! Imagine that! Something that is just as much an established fact as fingernails and freight trains is *not* believed! Why *not?*"

His voice rose, like a trained actor's.

"It's because of this defect in the psychological history of our species, religion. You find this aberration at work even today, with know-nothings still clambering for the equal treatment of creation and evolution in science classrooms. Equal indeed! More like evil. I mean that. Listen: it is absolutely safe to say that if you meet somebody who claims not to believe in evolution, that person is ignorant, stupid, or insane!"

Davis paused again, for effect. He had stolen that last line from Richard Dawkins, the Oxford atheist. But he didn't care, because conversion was more important than copyright, and he had a class to convert. Also, he considered Dawkins a prig and a coward, because he would not debate creationists. Davis reveled in it.

"Ladies and gentlemen, it is not farfetched in the least to say that we are a culture at war. It is a war against religious bigotry. The enemy is fundamentalism, of all kinds. This is your boot camp, your basic training. You will be the foot soldiers of a grand and brave new world. It starts here. Are you ready to join? Are you ready to take the future as your own?"

Some students stood and applauded. The Marilyn Monroe had positive desire in her eyes. Davis winked at her.

And the boy in the aisle seat? He was still seated, but his face belied a growing anxiety.

All well and good, thought Bently Davis. He was sure this boy would be coming to his office soon, perhaps that very afternoon.

Let him come. It would be a game. How fast a conversion?

Davis ended the lecture early, as he always did. It was a teaser, mostly, getting the students' appetites whetted. Better a little yeast at first, let it ferment naturally.

Which reminded Davis, as he strolled across the Harvard campus after class, it was time for a crisp glass of Chardonnay while he worked on his new book. The one he'd received the half-million-dollar advance on. The one that would be his masterpiece.

In his mind, as he walked, he went over the opening words again. He practically had it memorized. His agent, and then his editor, both warned him it was too much for the book, but Davis insisted. This was not going to be another run-of-the-mill *New York Times* bestseller. This was going to a bow shot over a two-thousand-year-old ship, the ship of Western religious tradition. It would begin this way:

God is dead!
That is the single truth upon which all of reality is based.
It is an exercise in freedom and joy.
What has God ever brought us but pain and suffering? Guilt and
*   imprisonment? Despair and agony?*
God is dead!
Science has proved it.
The brave ones have lived it.
I choose to be one of the brave.
I will live on the side of nature.

The words pleased him, quickened his step. He felt the same charge throughout his body that he had when he first wrote them. It was not, he noted with a smile, unlike what he felt when he laid eyes on a pretty young student.

His editor had pleaded with him to cut those opening words. Too much market resistance. Hang the resistance, Davis had told him. If it came, Davis would meet it.

And then he uttered to himself a little doggerel he'd composed just the day before:

God is dead,
O praise be!
The job is open.
God I'll be!

He laughed out loud, but only because he knew he was on the verge of something just like this. His efforts were going to bury religion in the ground with a stake of rationality through its heart. Then, from out of that fertile soil would rise the new giants in the earth. Led by Bently Davis.

And in the process he would reap the benefit of his industry with untold wealth. Bill Gates had done it with technology. Davis would do it with biotechnology—and something more, something so explosive and mind-bending it would change the course of humanity forever.

It was a good time to be alive, he reflected. A good time to be Davis.

**10**

His name was Turner, and he was a farmer. "Last of a breed," he told Lauren. "I take from the land what it gives me. But soon enough there'll be those telling the land what it can do for itself."

Lauren, warm at last, sitting wrapped in a blanket by the fireplace, liked the man. He was older, like grandfather Joe, and friendly. His big white mustache reminded Lauren of a walrus.

The rain continued to pour outside the small house where Mr. Turner lived. He had two dogs and a cat, but no one else. He hadn't explained, and Lauren didn't ask. All she knew was he had a phone and she would be able to call her mother. Right after she finished the hot chocolate he had made her to warm her up.

"They call it 'biotechnology,'" Mr. Turner said as he poured himself a cup of coffee. "You know what that means?"

Lauren shook her head.

"Means they can manipulate nature from the laboratory. Can stick genes they make into crops and animals, making 'em super crops and super animals. But nobody knows what that's gonna lead to. Don't know what's gonna happen to the birds and insects that eat all that new chemical stuff. What it's gonna do to God's world. I'm not gonna be a part of it, that much I can tell you."

Lauren liked listening to him. His voice was comforting. She knew she could trust him.

"Now let's take a look at that foot," Mr. Turner said.

Lauren obediently lifted her right foot to him. He took it gently in his hands and looked at it, rocking his head from side to side. "Now that don't look too bad," he said finally. "Nothing that a little iodine can't handle. Just the same, I think I better run you in to see the doc in a little while."

"May I call my mother first?"

"Course you can, darlin'. Let me go get the medicine, and we'll be in business."

As he passed her, he gave Lauren a gentle pat on the head. She smiled and sipped her chocolate, listening to the rain. If she weren't so anxious to see her mother, she might have liked to stay right here for awhile, listening to Mr. Turner tell more stories.

She found herself thinking about the whole confusing episode. Who were those men who had taken her? It had been the most frightening experience of her life. There she was, one moment looking at the back of a box of Cap'n Crunch in the store, and the next a hand had covered her mouth as her body was lifted off the floor.

Everything after that happened so fast. Being bound up, thrown in the back of a car, riding for who knew how long.

Why?

Didn't kids get taken sometimes for money? Her mother wasn't rich, but she *was* a lawyer. Maybe that was enough.

But then there was Daddy. Daddy had a lot of money, especially lately. He had told her he was doing very well as a salesman for a company that made drugs to help people. That could be it. Maybe they were going to ask her daddy for money.

She finished her hot chocolate with a last, full gulp, put the cup down on the hearth. The little living room was cozy, covered with pictures of Mr. Turner and various people. Maybe his kids.

She heard a messy noise, probably Mr. Turner rummaging through the medicine cabinet. Her mother used to do the same. It reminded her of home.

She looked into the small fire Mr. Turner had made. It was so nice and warm. They didn't have a fireplace in her mom's apartment. This was fun. She watched the flames dance around, getting lost in the bright yellow jig.

The fire reminded her of another Bible story her mom had told her. The one about those three men with the funny names. The first time Lauren had heard those names and tried to say them back, it came out, "Shadrach, My Shack, and A Billy Goat." How her mother had laughed at that one!

They had been thrown into a big fire by that king with the funny name—they all had funny names in the Bible, except David—but they weren't burned. There was somebody else in the fire with them. Mommy said it was Jesus, before he was ever even born on the earth.

Cool, Lauren thought then.

Cool, she thought now. And she felt like Jesus was there in the room with her, in Mr. Turner's house. He was with her, just like her mom said he would be.

She heard Mr. Turner coming back toward the room.

"I like your fire—"

Before she could finish, a hand was over her mouth. Another hand gripped her neck like a steel trap. She sensed a figure moving, rolled her eyes right and saw him.

Heartthrob.

Drops of rain stood out on his hair. And then, in a voice that was chilling because of its calmness, he said, "You, little girl, are a real pain."

11

Janice had a feeling she should turn and get away. Fast.

She thought for an instant it was a message from above, a warning. But she quickly decided it was her own fear. She loathed facing Sam and knew he would get angry. He would say terrible things. She didn't need that.

But this was her daughter's life, and she needed to look Sam in the face. Read him. She had to know.

She knocked on the door of Sam's house. He had paid three-quarters of a million for it. He had been sure to let her know the exact price. It was his way of rubbing her face in an asset she couldn't touch.

But could he have hired men to take their daughter and then lied about it?

The door opened.

Janice felt her entire body tense.

Sam stood there, cold. Wordless.

"We need to talk," Janice said.

Sam stepped aside, motioning her in.

The house was spacious, fully loaded with the best furnishings. All this after the divorce. Janice was sure Sam had hidden assets during the marriage, but she didn't have the spirit to fight about it. She wasn't interested in his money, just Lauren.

"Sit," Sam said, more as an order than an invitation.

"No thanks," said Janet. "I just came over to ask you one thing. Did you take her?"

One corner of Sam's mouth veered upward. "Ah, so the accused becomes the accuser."

"How can you spread those lies about me?"

"How do I know they're lies?"

"You can't be serious! To think I'd take Lauren away like that? And for you to go into court with your fancy lawyer and—"

"Careful. You're a pretty fancy lawyer yourself."

"Where is she, Sam?"

"You have such a high opinion of me."

"Did you take her?"

"If I did, sweetie, do you think I'd tell you?"

"Sam, please don't call me *sweetie*. It's beneath you."

"There is much that is beneath me. Come on." He walked away from her, and she followed. In the living room, wide open and white, Sam sat on a large sofa. "Let's at least be civilized about this."

The way he said it made Janice tense even more. It was as if the word *civilized* was a weapon and a rebuke, as if he was accusing her of *not* being civilized. But what could that possibly mean? He was the one who had caused all the trouble in the first place, and continued to do so. Was this just another one of his mind games?

Janice refused to sit. "All I want to know is where Lauren is."

"I don't know," Sam said evenly, without a hint of emotion.

"Aren't you concerned?"

"Should I be?"

"How can you be so calm about this?"

Sam shrugged his shoulders. "I have nothing to fear."

"Our daughter was *kidnapped.*"

"So you say."

"What do you mean by that?"

"I still don't know you didn't do it."

A bolt of anger shot through Janice. Her face flushed. She told herself to keep cool. Sam, for his unfathomable reasons, had made it his goal in life to upset her at every turn. She wasn't going to let him.

"You've done some pretty strange things in your time," Sam said.

"You're being hateful, Sam."

Sam stood up and walked to the bay window that looked out on his extensive back yard. The lights of the Chicago skyline were visible in the distance, sparkling urban diamonds. "*Hateful* is a pretty strong word, Janice. I don't hate anyone. I simply can't stand weakness."

"I don't know what you're talking about."

Sam faced her. Janice had the oddest sense that his eyes were shining. "I'm talking about you and your simple mind and your embrace of insanity. That's what Christianity is. A form of insanity."

That came out of left field. It sounded strange, even for Sam. He hadn't been happy when Janice decided to return to church. He'd even made a few condescending remarks. But this was different. There was a boiling hostility in his words, well beyond what the context, hostile enough as it was, called for.

Maybe it was because the stakes were raised. Lauren was the stake. He would say anything to upset her. In the past Janice might have simply walked away from a conversation like this. Not this time. "I'm here to discuss Lauren."

"I *am* discussing Lauren," Sam said. "I'm not going to have you passing on this insanity to my daughter. That's why I'm going to take her away from you by court order."

"You won't be able to," Janice said, "unless you've already done it by force."

For a moment Sam looked taken aback. Maybe he had expected Janice to fold, like she'd done before in the face of confrontation. Then his face became hard once more. "I'm telling you I did not have anything to do with Lauren being kidnapped. And even if you weren't behind it, I hold you personally responsible for it. She was in your care, and you lost her. That's why, when she's found, she's going to live with me. Maybe you'll be allowed to see her, but only with strict supervision."

Janice's head went light for a second. "You really have gone off the deep end."

"Don't you wish? But you know that's not true. You know that I've got the means and the will to make your life a living hell. That is just what I intend to do until Lauren is safely with me. Unless . . ."

"Yes?"

"Unless you simply agree to let Lauren come live with me. That would be best for everyone."

"Not a chance."

"Then I will see to it that Lauren hates you for what you're doing to her."

"What *I'm* doing?"

"I will make it my sole mission in life to do this."

"Why, Sam? Why are you this way?"

Voice rising, Sam said, "You can't possibly understand! You are a blight on nature, an aberration. I don't expect aberrations to be able to think rationally. I expect them to wither and die."

Now Janice was sure Sam's eyes were aglow. Was he reflecting light? But the only light in the room was behind him.

"I thought I could be reasonable," Janice said. "But it's obvious there's no talking to you."

Sam almost growled. Janice shuddered at the sound. But she refused to back down.

"But let's be clear on one thing," Janice said. "I will not give in. I will not go away. I will not give up Lauren. If you choose to fight, I will fight back. I will never give up. I don't care what happens to me. Lauren is my only concern. And it's evident to me that allowing you to have her would be the worst thing possible for her life. I will not let it happen. God will not let it happen."

Sam took one step toward Janice, saying, "There are other ways."

Janice had no idea what he meant by that, but it was clearly a threat. A physical threat? She wouldn't put it past him, not after the last five minutes.

"I'll see you in court," Janice said, turning toward the foyer.

"You'll see me now."

He took another step toward her.

Danger. She sensed it, could not dismiss it.

Janice started walking toward the front door.

Sam practically jumped to the door, his back to it, arms outstretched.

"Please move, Sam," Janice said, at the same time knowing he had no intention of moving. Instead, he reached behind him without looking and secured a bolt on the door. It clacked shut with a fearful finality.

"I'm not finished with you yet," he said.

"Sam, move."

"You know something? You're still a very lovely woman."

Janice felt a mass in her throat, as if it would block the air.

"Oh yes," he said. "Lovely."

●

This time Heartthrob sat in the backseat with her. They had tied her hands again with that heavy tape, and also her feet. At least, for some reason, they hadn't taped her mouth.

"Now look," Heartthrob said, once Driver had the car in motion, "trying to run away like that is not going to work."

"What did you do to Mr. Turner?" Lauren said.

"Don't you worry about him."

"I want to know!"

"I said not to worry. We wouldn't hurt a nice old man, would we Steve?" Driver said, "No."

But Lauren knew. Somehow she just knew that poor Mr. Turner was dead. A ball of emotion filled her throat.

"My name's Rance, by the way," Heartthrob said. "No need for you to be scared."

"Then how come I'm all tied up? Where are you taking me?"

"You've got to trust us."

"But why are you doing this?"

"Lauren, do you like mystery stories?"

"How do you know my name?"

Rance's face pinched a little, and he looked toward Steve. To Lauren it seemed like he'd made a mistake.

"Smooth move, eggnog," Steve said.

"Who cares?" said Rance. "We knew she was a smart girl."

How did they know?

"So," Rance said, "do you like mystery stories?"

"I guess," Lauren said.

"Nancy Drew?"

"Sure." Lauren did love the Nancy Drew stories. Also Sherlock Holmes.

"Well, think of this as sort of a mystery. A game we're playing. Soon enough, you'll get the answer, and when you do, you'll be happy."

"Why?"

"Ah, I can't tell you right now. That would give away the mystery. You see?"

Lauren sighed. Although only ten, she had a sense when she was being spoken down to. God, her mother told her, had given her a good brain. She was smart, and she picked things up.

What she was picking up now was the fact that two young men were in on some sort of scheme to kidnap her, probably for a ransom from her father.

She also knew from mystery stories that the detective always liked to get people to talk. If they did, they might reveal information that would be helpful. So, if her captors wanted to play a game, she'd play, too. The game would be, Get Them Talking.

"You guys are breaking the law, you know," she said.

"Law is a man-made construct," Rance said. Lauren didn't quite understand that, but she did note a certain arrogance in tone. She remembered her mother telling her no one is above the law. Maybe these two, for some reason, thought they were.

"What does that mean?" Lauren asked.

"You wouldn't understand," Rance said. "Not now. In a few days, though, I think you will."

"How come?"

"That's part of the game."

"What if the police catch you?"

"They won't," Rance said. "They can't."

"Why not?"

"Because they're dumb."

Steve snorted a laugh in the front seat. "They're mutants," he said.

"Yeah," said Rance, laughing in agreement.

"Mutants are from science fiction stories," Lauren said.

"Hey, right on," said Rance. "And what makes you think you're not in one?"

"Cool it," Steve said.

"What's the difference?" Rance said.

"The difference is it's not time. Not yet."

"You worry too much." Rance looked at Lauren. "Don't you think he worries too much?"

"I don't know him," Lauren said. "Why does he worry?"

"All right," said Steve, "enough talk. Just everybody shut up and let me drive."

"OK, Mr. Sensitive," Rance said. Again to Lauren: "Just one more thing, little girl. If you try to run away again, Steve and I will have to do something we don't want to do."

Lauren looked into Rance's eyes. They were cool, sparkling blue but without emotion. "What?" she said.

"Hurt you," Rance answered.

Fear rushed back into Lauren, enveloping her.

"And now that you know that," Rance said, "we can enjoy the ride, right?"

It was crazy.

Unbelievable.

Sam had an animal look in his eyes. No, more than that—nocturnal eyes, like an animal that could see in the dark. Janice knew then, as clearly as she knew anything else, that he was going to assault her. He planned to take all her dignity away with an unspeakable act of male violation.

How could this be happening?

She took a step backward.

Sam advanced a step, a crooked smile on his face, like he was enjoying her torment. Now there was no doubt he was completely over the edge. Something had happened to him. And now something was going to happen to her.

She backed up farther, back into the living room.

Sam followed, taking his time, one slow step after another, as if orchestrating the building up of tension. She was his plaything. He was seeing how far he could take this. Emotionally first. Physically next.

Could she grab something to hit him with? Janice looked quickly around the room, but nothing was within reach. In the middle of the room, on a glass table, was a small, marble sculpture. It would be just the thing if she had it, but the last few moments convinced her it would be fruitless to try. He would be all over her if she made a sudden move.

"Stop it, Sam."

"You just don't understand me."

"I understand you're crazy."

"You haven't got the capacity to understand me."

Capacity? "Don't do this," Janice said. "You'll regret it."

"Will I? The only thing I regret is not doing this sooner."

There would be no reasoning with him. That was obvious. It was a physical duel. She was sure to lose. Sam was always in good shape. He worked out regularly, lifted weights. It was almost an obsession with him, some quest for physical perfection.

Taking in the room as a whole with a quick glance, Janice suddenly ran into the adjoining dining room, putting the elegant table between her and Sam.

Sam bared his teeth. It was at once animalistic and something more than that. *Superhuman* was the word that came into her mind. Sam seemed like he was full of greater capacities for physical harm and evil intent than a normal human being.

Is this what a psychopath is like?

The closest Janice had ever been to a real psycho was in her law school days, when she'd worked on a student project helping prisoners with appeals. At the state prison in Joliet she was interviewing a young drug dealer when another prisoner suddenly attacked him on the other side of the visitor's screen. The attacker actually bit into her client's neck! It took three guards to pull him off.

And as Janice sat there, frozen in her chair, the psychotic prisoner looked her straight in the eye even as he was being taken away by the guards. He was about thirty years old, with a long scar on his cheek. His look chilled her. It was like he was memorizing her face.

Later she found out that he was a serial killer, and something more—a devil worshiper. Oddly, this was a connection prison officials and law enforcement failed to take seriously.

Now, staring at Sam, there was a hint of that same look. He was a man whose conscience was warped and who was capable of doing *absolutely anything*.

"Do you think you can stop me?" Sam said, crouching at the other end of the dining room table. "Think you can play ring-around-the-rosy all night?"

She did not reply. What was the point?

A quick look at the table. Janice saw a place setting there. The only possible weapon was a fork. She snatched it.

"Oh," Sam said derisively, "so now she's going to stick me. Is that it?"

She would if she could. But she was going to keep that table between them as long as possible.

With one hand Sam grabbed the table's edge and, with frightening ease, threw it on its side. The contents crashed on the hardwood floor.

In the shock of the moment Sam spoke, eerily calm. "Don't you realize religion is a sacrifice of all freedom? It's self-derision, self-mutilation. Do you think I'd ever let you do that to my daughter?"

He began walking toward her, the barrier gone.

All thought left her. Her body was ablaze with feeling and adrenaline.

Sam was five feet away, advancing slowly.

Janice reached behind her, felt her hand wrap around the back of a wooden chair.

For a long moment time stood still, like a freeze-frame shot in a horror movie. Janice saw the entire frame at once: Sam's otherworldly face, with its grim mocking; the mess on the floor of an otherwise immaculate house; her own image, gripped with fear yet alive with an innate drive for self-preservation, and not just self, her daughter; the soundless night outside.

And then he sprang.

His body shot forward so fast he became a blur. He grunted. Janice swung the wooden chair in front of her. She heard a hard *thwack* and knew, without seeing, that the chair's seat had undercut Sam at the knees. The force of his impact pushed her backward as Sam went toppling over the chair, landing to her left. He shot a hand out and for a moment had her by the ankle. But his grip gave way as he tumbled away.

Janice ran back through the living room toward the front door.

Behind her Sam's voice issued a shrill epithet, filled with rage. His resolve would be redoubled, Janice knew. She had to get out.

A few feet more and she would be at the door. Could she make it outside? And even if she did, would he pursue her, like an animal after its prey?

It was a chance she'd have to take.

She reached the door, grabbed the fancy gold handle and yanked down.

The door didn't budge.

The bolt.

Janice heard a scuffling sound from the living room and the bestial snarling of something not quite human.

Reaching up, she fumbled with the bolt. It was locked in place.

Sam had made sure she couldn't get out of the house.

Janice shot toward the stairs. Maybe at the top she would have an advantage, able to throw something at him.

She started up.

Sam's feral sounds were patient. Like an animal closing in for the kill.

Janice made it to the top of the stairs and around the corner, hoping there would be something she could get her hands on.

Nothing but an empty hall.

On the wall she saw a large mirror in a gold frame.

She heard the first of his steps on the staircase.

"Janice!" he shouted. "Don't make me come up there, dear."

Then a second step.

Janice lifted the mirror from the wall.

"Janice, sweetheart," Sam said, his voice sounding like another she'd heard. Where? Then, suddenly, she remembered. It was just like the much-parodied voice of Jack Nicholson in the movie *The Shining*. She'd seen it years ago but never forgot that Nicholson crazy-voice. She half-expected Sam to say, "Heeeerrrre's Johnny!"

Another heavy step. "Don't you realize," Sam said, "that in the beginning was nonsense, and the nonsense was with God, and the nonsense *was* God?"

Gripping the bottom of the frame with both hands, Janice waited. She would have to select the perfect moment, or the surprise would be gone.

"I'm trying to save our daughter, don't you see that?" Sam's voice was getting closer. Janice put her back against the wall, afraid the sound of her breathing would give her away. "What I am going to do to you now will be your cleansing."

One more step, Janice thought.

"Listen to me!" Sam shouted.

Now!

Janice swung the heavy mirror out and to the right. It cut through the air and crashed into the wall. Janice heard glass shattering as she followed the mirror's momentum around the corner. Immediately she saw Sam halfway down the staircase, smiling up at her.

"Predictable," he said.

Janice stood at the top of the stairs holding a heavy frame with a cracked mirror. It might as well have been a neon sign that said *idiot*.

"Now why don't you just accept it?" Sam said.

"Stop, Sam."

He took a step upward, his eyes, shining like red bulbs, locked on hers.

Janice raised the mirror and threw it at Sam.

She did not stay to see if it made contact. As she raced down the hall, she did hear a muffled grunt that gave her hope of a few more precious seconds.

She ran to what she thought was the master bedroom. When they were living together, Sam always kept a handgun in the bedside table. If she could lock the door and find a gun, maybe she could hold him at bay until she got out.

Janice took a quick look behind her. Sam, still taking his time, was just now at the top of the stairs.

Janice ran into the bedroom, slammed the doors shut, secured the lock. Sam would have the key, but maybe not on him. More precious seconds.

She was in darkness. Where was the light switch?

She heard Sam's heavy steps getting closer.

She swept her hand along the wall, looking for a switch.

"Sweetie?" Sam said.

Where is that switch?

The steps were just outside the door now. Janice heard Sam's heavy breathing.

Then she found it, turned on the light.

Janice saw the bed, covered with a black spread. The entire room was a portrait in dark colors, as if here was perpetual night.

"Open the door, sweetie."

There were no bed tables. The room was almost ascetic in design. No frills. A desk by one wall.

"If you don't open, I'll have to open it myself," Sam said.

Janice ran to the bed and started feeling under the pillows. Silk sheets, nothing more.

Sam knocked on the door, like a friendly salesman.

Dropping to one knee, Janice looked under the bed.

Another knock, harder this time. "Sweetie?"

She could check the desk or the closet, but knew she had time for only one. Where would Sam hide a weapon?

She chose the closet. She opened the double doors to a swarm of expensive suits. The upper shelf held various items but nothing resembling a gun.

"Come on, sweetheart."

Janice frantically felt behind the boxes on the shelf.

Sam pounded on the door.

Janice felt nothing but wood.

Whump . . . Whump . . .

Sam was putting a shoulder to the door.

Janice threw everything on the shelf to the floor. *Please, let there be something.*

There was. Just as the bedroom doors crashed open, Janice put her hand around the butt of a revolver.

She whirled to face Sam, who, except for a little heavy breathing, seemed calm.

"Hello, sweetie. In the beginning was nonsense, remember?"

"I don't want to shoot, Sam," Janice said. Her hand was shaking so much she wondered if she could. She remembered an FBI agent telling her once that they always aimed for the chest, because that was the largest mass, and easiest to hit when your nerves were on edge.

As hers were now.

Sam stopped, smiled. His eyes gleamed.

"It always helps," he said, "if the gun has bullets."

That's when she knew it was over. Just to be sure she aimed the gun at the floor and pulled the trigger.

Nothing but a harmless *click.*

"Did you really think you could get away from me?" Sam asked, taking a step toward her. "Knowing that I didn't want you to get away?"

Janice couldn't move.

"If I were the angry sort," Sam said, "this would make me angry. That you would think so low of me. But I'm not angry. Not at all. I'm content."

He put his hands on her shoulders. His fingers dug into her skin.

"No Sam!"

"Powerless."

"Please!"

"Powerless."

Sam swung her to the side.

Her head hit the doorjamb. Lights exploded behind her eyes.

The vicelike hands pushed her into the wall again. Again her head slammed against hard wood.

"Sam, please . . ." Her voice sounded distant to her.

"Powerless."

She slid into darkness.

13

It wasn't supposed to be this way. It was like a pain, in the head, where there should have been calm, peace, absence of emotion.

Dewey Handleman analyzed his condition and found it strange.

He had always been a deep thinker about himself and existence. Even at age five, his parents' friends *oohed* and *ahhed* at the cognitive proficiencies of little Dewey. At six, his vocabulary was like a normal high schooler's—better, in fact, considering the public school system in Brooklyn. He was close to master strength at chess when he was just seven. He spent Saturdays during the summers cleaning the clocks of the old *patzers* in Washington Square, garnering praise and comparisons to Bobby Fischer.

And he asked penetrating questions of the rabbis whenever his family went to synagogue. One, Rabbi Milder, Dewey almost drove nuts. "Why does God allow suffering?" Dewey kept asking. None of Rabbi Milder's answers made sense to him. Finally, the rabbi told Dewey he didn't know why God allowed suffering, but he, Rabbi Milder, must have done something terribly wrong to keep hearing the same question over and over from such an annoying boy.

Dewey didn't go to synagogue after that. His parents, marginal on religion anyway, didn't force him.

When Dewey got accepted to Harvard at age sixteen, he went gleefully. Anything to get out of Brooklyn and its acceptance of the mundane. Maybe he'd find some answers to his questions at the greatest university in the land.

The problem of suffering still haunted Dewey. He grabbed hold of the philosophy classes—and the professors—but still found no satisfactory answer.

The only prof who reached him was Bently Davis. Davis said it wasn't suffering that was the problem, but our response to suffering. Change the response, which is just a chemical reaction in the brain, and you change suffering to something else—*not* suffering. Just an event, no more, no less.

Here, at last, was an original idea. It was that prospect of changing his own emotional reaction that got Dewey to sign up for the project in the first place.

So why was he feeling so upset about the death of one street person, the one he'd killed?

He had seen the item in the *Boston Globe*. Here in his one-room apartment, at night, alone, Dewey always felt the most secure. But he was not secure as he read. The *Globe* had the story on page 6:

Homeless Victim Was "Gentle Soul"

They called him Mike Meds. That wasn't his real name.
But it describes the plight of the man found dead and alone
in an alley just off Massachusetts Avenue last night.
The denizens of the streets here describe the dead man as
a former mental patient who would not harm anyone.

"He kept asking for his medication," said a woman who refused to be identified by name. "He never wanted to hurt nobody. He was a gentle soul, you know?"

Police are still working on a positive identification of the deceased. But the street people knew him. And they are scared.

"Anybody can get knocked off anytime," said a man known as Hungry Sal. "And who's gonna care?"

And that's the way it should be, Dewey thought. *No one else should care about the elimination of a vag. It should be cause for rejoicing among civilized people. One more cancerous spot on the lungs of society cut out. Gone. Leaving us just that much healthier.*

So why did Dewey feel this pang? This was supposed to have been eliminated entirely.

For one, frightening moment, Dewey wondered what would happen if the elimination didn't work. What would happen if his new capacities had to battle the old responses? Had anyone thought of that? Wouldn't that lead to a sort of insoluble conflict, ending in a kind of insanity?

Quickly, he shook it off. He didn't want to think of that. He was already in process, so there was no turning back.

Suddenly, the darkness returned. The same personification of evil he had sensed yesterday in the donut shop. Now he didn't even have his eyes closed! What was happening?

He had the sense this darkness was watching him, though the room was filled with light.

"Stop it!" he said out loud, grabbing the sides of his head.

The darkness remained. And it spoke.

Not in words, but through some sensory perception deeper than words. Like when one awakes from a dream with emotions raw and realigned.

"Stop!" he repeated.

But it did not stop. It lingered. Hovered. Stated its presence again.

Then came the answer. Not from Dewey, but from some other source outside the rational realm. This answer was the opposite of the darkness. It was less pronounced but still present, quiet yet insistent. For a split second Dewey had the feeling this opposite was calling to him to *feel.*

Feel what?

Guilt.

He slammed the *Globe* on the floor.

I will not care about a worthless life! He told himself. *I will never care. Never.*

He didn't want to! They had promised!

He remembered when he was eight and his dog had been hit by an ice cream truck. Before that he had never encountered death—if you didn't include Mrs. Morelli across the hall, who always gave him candy but smoked five packs a day of the stinkiest cigarettes ever invented. Now his dog, a mutt his father brought home from the pound a year before, was a lifeless heap.

Dewey cried right there in the middle of the street. A mistake. Some of the tough kids saw him. They gathered around him in a lazy circle and started laughing at him.

Laughing!

His dog wasn't even cold, and they were laughing at him, calling him a baby. He ran at the biggest kid then, put his head down and tried to ram his stomach. But the kid jumped out of the way, and Dewey went sprawling.

They laughed even harder.

It haunted him, their laughter, long after the incident was forgotten, even by the tough kids themselves.

Dewey never forgot. He hated what he felt, hated being weak. Wimp, they called him. He cared what they called him and didn't want to care. Ever again. He was mushy inside. He wanted to be steel.

That's when he had lost himself in horror movies. The classic Universal pictures, like *Frankenstein, Dracula,* and *The Mummy.* But also the bloodier versions from the sixties. Dewey always sided with the monsters. They were hated just because they were different and because they were strong.

Dewey would be stronger than all of them. And that's what Davis had promised him. The process would make him what he had always wanted to be—the monster that would not die. That's why he'd jumped at the opportunity.

And it seemed to be working. Until now, with this residue of sympathy, these visions of light and darkness!

He couldn't take it. He *wouldn't* take it.

They had promised. And if need be, he would make them keep their promise!

●

"All right?"

It was a voice echoing through a distant canyon. Janice, still in darkness, heard herself groan. Her head felt like a tanker had run over it.

"Easy, take it real easy."

A man's voice.

Sam!

"Please," Janice said, then opened her eyes.

And yelped.

"Whoa, whoa!" the man said. It was not Sam. He was not anything like Sam. He was more like . . . an ex-con. A *crazy* ex-con. How else to describe the eye-patch and untamed hair?

Yet he wasn't making any sudden moves. He was kneeling beside her. Gentle.

"You all right?"

"No," Janice said, looking around. Still in Sam's bedroom. But where was Sam?

"Hurt?" the strange man asked.

Yes, all over the back of her head, spreading like a crown and down to the bridge of her nose. "What's happening?" Janice said.

"You tell me."

"Who are you?"

"Nobody. What's your name?"

She didn't answer.

"Sam Ramsey your boyfriend? Husband?"

Janice blinked into further awareness. "You know Sam?"

"I do now. Only he doesn't know me. And he doesn't know what hit him." The man took Janice by the arm and gently pulled her into a sitting position. She leaned back against the wall.

Then she saw Sam. He was lying on the floor, face down. "What . . ."

"Don't worry," the man with the patch said. "He'll be out for a little while. Maybe the sleep will do him some good. He'll just have one whale of a headache."

"I don't understand."

"I haven't got time to explain. Can you get up?"

Shards of pain shot through her head as she struggled to her feet, with the man's help. The room spun like a runaway carousel.

"I still don't . . ." she started to say, but stopped when this person began walking around the room, looking at every portion of it. He went to the desk and started opening drawers, rifling through them.

"What are you doing?" Janice said.

"Looking."

"Who are you?"

"Where does he keep his bills, papers, stuff like that?"

Janice looked quickly at the heap that was Sam. Even after what she had just been through, she felt a throb of compassion for him. Would he even wake up? Just what had this intruder done to him? Why should she even be here talking to him?

"We'd better call the police," Janice said.

The man turned to her, and she realized just how big he was. "That would not be a smart move."

Her concern expanded.

"Tell me what's going on," Janice demanded.

"I'm going downstairs now. If he moves, call me."

"Wait!"

He didn't. He was out the bedroom door.

Janice put her hand on the top of her head, trying to lessen the pressure. It didn't help.

She followed the man down the stairs.

She found him in the room Sam used as an office. He was already well into the desk drawers. She heard crumpling sounds.

"I have to know what you're doing," Janice said.

"Not now."

"I *will* call the police." She didn't pause to think that this man might hurt her worse than Sam. Yet there was something about his frenetic searching that told her he wasn't out to do her harm. He was here to find something relating to Sam and for what appeared to be a very important reason.

The man stopped. "Look, from what I can tell this is a domestic violence case gone nuts. You were here, let me guess, to hassle him about support payments or visitation, right?"

How did he know? "That's not any of your concern."

"Cops hate these cases. Chances are you'll get dragged into it further than you want. Now how well do you know your ex?"

"Why?"

"I have my reasons for asking."

"I thought I knew him, but he's changed."

"How?"

"I don't know. Colder, harsher."

The man's uncovered eye widened. "We need to get out of here. Now." He made a move toward the door.

"Wait. I don't know who you are or what you're doing here. Why should I go with you?"

The man steadied his one-eyed gaze at her. "Because if you don't, you could end up very, very dead."

14

The student's name was John Phillips, and Davis could read him like a book.

A bad book, Davis thought. "Sit down," he said.

Bently Davis's office was like a living organism. Every inch of space was taken up by books, plants, artwork, computers, papers, file cabinets, and eccentricities—framed baseball cards, a signed 8 x 10 of Jimi Hendrix, and even some African artifacts. It was not messy, however. In its own, unique way it seemed a fully functional mass, each part consistent with the whole.

John Phillips sat in a director's chair opposite Davis's desk. Davis noted the kid wore the same anxious expression he had in the lecture. As if he expected Davis to rip his whole world apart. Well, if need be . . .

"You wanted to see me," Davis said.

"Yes, Professor Davis." He was not a bad-looking kid, but his face belied a thorough innocence. He wore a brand new Harvard T-shirt. "I'm in Life Sciences."

"Ah yes. Big class."

"Really big."

"Where you from?" Davis already knew the answer, having accessed the kid's transcripts and Harvard application via computer.

"South Dakota," John Phillips answered.

"Big town or small town?"

"Small, I guess you could say."

"This is a little culture shock for you then."

"Totally."

Davis leaned back in his swivel chair and put his feet up on the corner of his desk. "Don't let it throw you. You'll get used to it."

The student nodded, without smiling.

"Now what can I help you with?" Davis asked.

"Well, it was about something you said in the lecture."

"At least I know you were paying attention." Davis laughed good-naturedly.

Phillips didn't laugh. "Something you said about your duty, your Harvard-inspired duty, to clear religion from our minds."

"I think I said religious muck."

"Yes, you did."

"And?"

"Well, I . . ."

"Go ahead. You can speak freely."

"All right. I found that offensive."

"That's the way I intended it."

The young man looked surprised.

"Part of my job here," Davis said patiently, "is to shake students out of their comfort zones. That's the only way real learning can take place, you see? We have to realize that so often religion offers the opposite of learning. It stagnates the mind, tells it to stay right where it is."

"But that's not really so."

"No?"

"And if someone has religious beliefs, you shouldn't interfere with that."

"Why not?"

"Because . . ."

Davis took his feet down and placed his elbows on the desk, a more confrontational position. "John, are you a Christian?" Davis already knew the answer.

"Yes."

"What denomination?"

"Assemblies of God."

"So you don't exactly see things the way, say, the Baptists do."

"Not on everything, no."

"What if you're wrong?"

"Excuse me?"

"What if you are wrong about something, and the Baptists turn out to be right?"

"Well, then I'd be wrong, I guess."

"And you don't see eye to eye with atheists, either."

"Of course not."

"But what if *they* turn out to be right?"

"I don't believe they are."

"I'm asking you *what if?*"

John Phillips squirmed in his seat, the pained expression returning to his face.

Davis said, "All I want you to do is open your mind up to the *possibility* that you may be wrong. If the evidence is not there, if the arguments and facts don't convince you, at least you'll have given them a chance. Isn't that fair?"

"But the way you say things, it's like you're trying to make us feel stupid or something."

"That's part of the painful process of growing up, John. Sometimes we look at what we're like as children and realize just how stupid—or at least naive—we were. At that point we have a choice. Do we remain in that innocent state, or do we move on, with courage?"

"But I strongly believe there is a God. I strongly believe in Jesus. I don't think that's stupid at all, and I don't think it's right to make me feel that way."

"Are you at least open to the possibility you might be wrong?"

"Not on that, no."

"Not even if there is evidence to the contrary?"

"I don't think there is."

"Would you be willing to look at it if there were?"

"I haven't seen any."

"What about the evidence for evolution?"

"I don't believe there is evidence for it."

Davis picked up a note of combativeness in the tone. That was not surprising. Evolution had long been a favorite whipping boy of fundamentalist Christians, and these creationist types always sounded defensive. Davis usually made short work of them.

"So you believe the earth was created in six days a few thousand years ago? And that all the life we see around us was set in place by God?" Davis would frame the issues first before cutting out the empirical legs from the kid.

"For me the issue is that life had to be designed by an intelligent agent."

Davis squinted. So this was another of the new breed. The so-called "intelligent design movement" was getting very annoying to Davis. As far as he was concerned, it was just old-style creationism gussied up in new and misleading verbiage. But it would not go away. It would not be marginalized. And, in fact, some of its exponents were actually gaining a foothold in certain sectors of academia. Like that Sterling Brown. At least he was no longer a problem.

"There is no evidence for that idea," Davis said sharply. "Can you give me any?"

"The way I see it," John Phillips explained, "design is an inference that comes from observing the evidence. If nature is not capable of producing what we see by chance, we can start to infer that intelligence is behind the design."

"Nonsense."

"Why?"

"Because that is not the way science is done. Science deals with reality, not fantasy."

"But, Professor, if reality includes an intelligent designer, science is missing reality by ruling that out from the start."

Suddenly Bently Davis felt a frustration he hadn't experienced in years. This student across from him, who he was sure would be an easy mark, was exhibiting a logical potency that wouldn't just fade after a few slick arguments.

What this student represented, Davis realized, was something like evolution in *ideas*. A virus that is subjected to antibiotics eventually develops a resistance. The resulting strain is stronger and can't be conquered by the old treatments. That's precisely what was happening here, Bently Davis mused. Creationism, so easy to knock out of innocent heads before, had become stronger after years of opposition. It was infecting minds and staying there.

And here before him was a prime example.

"Mr. Phillips," Davis said, "we have a long way to go in class. I have a feeling we'll have more conversations along these lines. And to tell you the truth, I look forward to them."

A glimmer of hope shone on the face of the student. "Really?"

"Oh yes," said Davis. "I look forward to them indeed."

Looking somewhat mollified, the young student excused himself and left the office.

For a long time Bently Davis sat there, looking at the empty chair.

Another elimination? Perhaps. Probably.

It could be done, of course, but he didn't like this fraying of the edges. Things weren't going as smoothly as he wanted.

He turned to his computer and punched in for E-mail. Several messages were waiting, but only one with the reference "NE."

Davis opened the message. Onscreen he saw this:

#skpo$)kjf;!lsik))¢7(*76hd,xh^wpkjhghie9/cv,.sp3e0∞8j•
ªHhlwk©^83wlsn^&69l^902H^$3(0–_976xKCM;'-
90&689º—8,.xk_094385-8wyqBujl=u88#¢8-∞§ghOl¨øl

A point and click later, the message was downloaded. Then Davis opened the encryption-decoding program. A split second later he read:

Anthony dead. Self-destruct. Someone found out about
him. No identity, partial description. Looking for man with
patch over one eye. Will follow up.

Dead? Anthony?

And who was this man with a patch?

Yes, there were going to have to be eliminations. Maybe even a lot of them.

Davis got up and locked his office door. He took out his keys and unlocked the bottom drawer of a steel filing cabinet. From this drawer he removed a small safe.

Placing the safe on his desk, he entered the combination and opened it. He removed the small vial and syringe from the safe. In one minute his injection was ready.

He took it under his tongue.

When he was finished, he replaced all the items, then sat back in his chair and closed his eyes.

Euphoria was immediate and all encompassing. All would be well again. The project would get back on track. The little girl would soon be here. All would indeed be well.

With a smile, he started whispering, over and over:

God is dead,
O praise be!
The job is open.
God I'll be!

15 Janice Taylor, formerly Ramsey, could not believe two things.

The first thing was that she had been able to drive four hours in the middle of the night.

The second thing was that she was on the road with a man she would have run away from in normal circumstances.

His name was Jed Brown, and he had an incredible theory. But it made a crazy sort of sense, and so here they were.

After leaving Sam's house this man actually convinced her to give him a ride to a small coffee shop—he apparently liked obscure eateries of all types—to explain himself.

"My brother was murdered," was the way he started the conversation, and that got her attention right away. It didn't let up from there. "The cops were treating this as some sort of street killing, the chuckleheads. It took me about two seconds to figure out they were out in the bleachers."

"How?" Janice asked, surprised at her own fascination with this strange man.

"Instinct. It's my business."

"What business is that?"

"I find people. For a price."

"You're a bounty hunter?"

"We prefer to be called disappearance consultants."

She looked at him for an extended moment, focusing on the eye patch. "If I may say, doesn't your appearance make you stand out?"

"The only time people I'm tracking see me face-to-face is when I'm ready to bag 'em."

"You must be licensed by the state."

"Of course."

"Let me see it."

Jed gave her a half smile. "Very good," he said.

"Very careful," she said.

He showed her his credentials. "I can make a call to verify," said Janice.

"I'll give you the number."

Janice thought a moment, then said, "Keep going."

"I lifted a lead from a cop and followed it up."

"What do you mean 'lifted'?"

"Stole."

"From a police officer?"

"Sure."

"And you didn't get caught?"

"Hey, I was born to steal from police officers."

Janice shook her head. What manner of man was this?

"And I found the guy who killed my brother," Jed said. "He was up in a fancy hotel in Beverly Hills. That means money. A lot of it. He was a young guy who drove a limousine."

"Why did he kill your brother?"

"That's what I'm not sure of. It was a professional hit, meaning he got paid to do it."

"Did your brother have enemies?"

"I can't figure that one. He was an academic, a theologian. He didn't go around making enemies, at least not ones that would kill him. He did have this thing about modern science."

"What kind of thing?"

"That it was going too far. You know, cloning people and all that."

"That hasn't happened. Yet."

"Sterling was sure it was on the way and made a lot of noise about it. But so do a lot of other people. I don't think there's a connection there. He was going to be on TV that morning."

"The morning he was murdered?"

"Right. My mom called me and said he was going to be on *The Today Show,* talking about the evolution thing. Maybe there's some connection to Sterling being on the show. But who would murder him for that? Katie Couric? No, that doesn't make any sense either. There's something out there that's very weird, because the guy I found, this Anthony?"

"Yes?"

"Get this. When I had him cornered in that hotel room, he turns around and takes the big dive."

"I'm sorry?"

"Jumps out a tenth-story window. Kills himself."

Janice's breath left her with a jolt.

"But even crazier was what he did right before that. He grabs his laptop computer and goes down with it. Is that a kick in the head or what?"

"Why did he do that?"

"To keep me from getting the information that was on it. He knew I was on to him. He didn't want me to get the answers. He didn't want me or anybody else to get it so bad he killed himself and smashed his machine. Now what do you suppose that means?"

Janice thought a moment, took a sip of coffee, then said, "He was part of some group?"

"Very good. He died for the cause, whatever that cause is."

"Where does Sam come into all of this? If this all happened in L.A., what does that have to do with Chicago?"

Jed grabbed the saltshaker and poured a little salt on the table. Janice found herself watching both this strange ritual and the sword-and-snake tattoo on his forearm. Suddenly, she wondered what would happen if someone she knew walked in and saw her with this man. What would she say? *Hi, this is Jed, and he's a bounty hunter. Join us?*

"I found a phone number in the jumper's coat pocket," Jed said. He tilted the saltshaker slightly and pushed the base into the small pile of salt on the table. He did this delicately, like a man placing a fuse in a bomb. Then he took his hand away. The salt shaker stayed tilted on the table.

Jed admired his handiwork for a moment, then looked at Janice. "I traced the number to your husband's house."

"You can do that?"

"Surely you don't believe anything is private anymore, do you?"

"Maybe I did."

"And then I hopped a plane, caught a cab."

"Just like that?"

"In my line you have to move fast. I want to know why my brother was killed."

"How did you get in the house? It was locked from the inside."

Jed snorted a laugh. "Please. A Rabson latch? I've seen tougher locks on child-proof aspirin bottles."

"At least you came along at the right time."

"He was going to kill you."

"How do you know?"

"Body language. I speak it fluently."

Janice shook her head.

"Now let me ask you one," Jed said. "You were there for a custody thing, right?"

"How do you know *that?*"

"Divorce, child, mother at house of ex who is looking to do her serious harm. Why else would a mother do that if it weren't for the protective instinct? I've seen it a thousand times before. Well, maybe a hundred."

"You're absolutely right. He's been after custody of my daughter."

"How old?"

"Ten. Her name's Lauren." At the sound of the name, Janice felt hot tears run to the bottom of her eyes, threatening to pour over. She held them back. But it must have been obvious.

"He took her, didn't he?" Jed said.

Amazed again, Janice said, "I think so. She was kidnapped, but Sam denies he had anything to do with it."

"He strikes me as a very ruthless guy."

"You think Sam is involved in your brother's death?"

"Yes."

The news stunned her, even though it didn't seem surprising. The way Sam had been acting, and his behavior this night, made it clear he was capable of just about anything. But murder?

"I haven't got all the pieces yet," Jed said, "but I'm hoping you'll help me find them."

"What can I do?"

"You can listen. And you can think." He reached into the leather shoulder bag he had brought with him and pulled out the papers he had taken from Sam's house. They looked like bills or statements. He shuffled through them and put them down, one by one, on the table, in some sort of order he had come up with himself.

He did this lightly. It was almost like he was placing feathers on a sleeping person, trying not to wake him up. At one point Janice leaned forward to ask a question, and Jed said sharply, "Don't bump the table."

She shook her head, and he pointed to the salt shaker. "Don't want it to tip over," he said.

The juxtaposition of these two images—a man intent on unpackaging a murder plot and a joker playing little parlor tricks—was almost surreal. She didn't know what to make of this fellow across from her. He *looked* like someone she would want a hundred-yard buffer zone around. Wild, ponytailed hair, eye patch, and tattoo were not usually associated with what her mother called *breeding*.

And yet, underneath all that, she sensed a torment. Like something, somewhere, had kicked him hard on the inside.

He was an interesting study all right but also someone to keep at arm's length.

"Here," he said, looking at a statement. "What is UniGen?" He turned it toward Janice.

"I'm not sure."

"There are a lot of them here. They look like income statements."

"Sam was a salesman for a pharmaceutical company, or so I thought."

"Did he travel?"

"To the east coast a lot."

"What cities?"

"New York. Boston."

"UniGen has an address in Cambridge."

"What does that mean?"

"It means I'm going to Cambridge. You want to come with?"

"Why?"

"Because I have a feeling your daughter might be there."

Janice stared at him. "How do you know?"

"Instinct. You in or out?"

"You just expect me to go? Like that?"

"Like that."

"With you?"

"With me."

"Alone?"

"I'm not picking up any hitchhikers."

At least he was direct. "But I don't know anything about you."

"Listen, lady, somebody offed my brother. And there may be a connection between that and your daughter. I'm going to try and find out, and I usually find something. If you want to be there when it happens, fine. If not, fine. Just tell me."

Janice could hardly believe she was thinking about it. But getting out and actually trying to do something would be a relief. Besides, the recent experience of having been thought an actual suspect was disconcerting. The police were not going to move on her behalf any faster than they were now doing.

Excusing herself, Janice called Pamela for counsel. After telling her of the attack by Sam and her rescue at the hands of a mysterious tracker, Janice informed Pamela that she was thinking of going with the man to look for Lauren. Pamela at first questioned Janice's sanity. Janice surprised herself at how determined she was to go. She *had* to take some sort of action. And somehow she sensed she could trust this man.

Pamela finally came around, and Janice asked her to keep praying. Then Janice called the office and left a message for Ray Bollington. She had two weeks vacation coming, and her immediate work was covered. Good old Ray would surely understand.

"I guess I'm going," Janice said when she rejoined Jed Brown.

"Good," said Jed. "We'll take your car."

And that's how, after stopping to pack a bag, Janice found herself driving drowsily toward the dawn, with a man she barely knew snoring softly in the passenger seat. All the while, she prayed. She prayed to keep awake and alert. She prayed that the stranger in her car might actually be able to do something to solve this nightmare.

But mostly she prayed for Lauren, and for the Lord to keep her surrounded by angels.

16

Lauren did not like being blindfolded again. This time, at least, Rance had been nice about it. Only it was a chilling niceness, the kind where you know a person is up to something. So what was it they were up to?

She was in the back seat again, sitting up. She had promised to behave, and they had made clear that she'd better.

Why?

Her mind had gone over and over the snatches of conversation she'd heard over the course of this wild ride.

There had been that talk about *mutants*.

And then, *It's not time.*

Before that, something like, *It's never been tried on one so young.*

Young like *her,* obviously.

They were going to *do* something to her, *because* she was young. That was the conclusion she reached. And it was something that could harm her in some way. Would it make her a mutant?

She thought of poopish Tommy McIntire then, because he was always such a bully, and her mom told her bullies were all cowards underneath. If Tommy were here, in her place, he would be real scared, she knew.

But she wasn't going to be. She knew God was with her; her mother had told her so and had taught her the Twenty-third Psalm when she was six years old. Whenever she was scared, even when Tommy tied her to that tree, she said to herself, *I will fear no evil for Thou art with me.*

The car took a turn onto a gravel road. Lauren could hear the crunch of the tires on rocks, and the ride got bumpier.

"Over there," she heard Rance say.

"Got it," said Steve.

Where were they? She had no idea. It just sounded out of the way, like when her dad took her on a hiking trip and got off the main road. She was being taken to a secret hiding place, of that she was sure. That's where they would do the thing to her that they had been talking about.

The car drove on for another ten minutes or so, bumpy all the way. Then it started to slow, and finally stopped.

Car doors opened. Someone grabbed her arm.

"Let's go," Rance said.

He pulled her out of the car. Her feet hit rocky ground. She slipped. Rance lifted her and started her walking. She sensed a coolness in the air, a bit of moisture, like fog. Her mind filled with images: gnarly, leafless trees under a dark sky, silhouetted by the light of a full moon. Bats.

Don't worry, she told herself. *The Lord is my shepherd. These guys don't know who they're up against.*

"Watch your step," said Rance, guiding her upward on some stairs that felt and sounded like old wood. They groaned and creaked under the weight. She counted five of them to the top, and then she was pulled forward again. She sensed herself going through an open door, then a feeling of being inside. There was a musty smell, like old carpet.

Behind her the door slammed shut, and some locks—three? four?—were engaged. And then her blindfold was removed.

At first her vision was blurry, but gradually she regained focus. It appeared to be a cabin, complete with log walls and hardwood floor. It had a strange feel to it, sort of like a failed experiment—as if someone had once planned to live here but had long since abandoned it to creeping decay.

"Sit down, sweetie," said Rance. "Make yourself at home."

Steve disappeared into what Lauren thought would be the kitchen. Rance leaned casually on a large mantel, watching her. Lauren watched him back. She did not sit.

"Listen," said Rance, "you need to get used to being here. We're going to hang here awhile."

"Why?" Lauren asked.

"I can't tell you that right now, sugar. But I promise you're going to like it."

"I don't like it now."

"But you will."

Keep them talking. Look for clues. Lauren Ramsey is the new Nancy Drew, solving the case!

"Why should I believe you?" she said.

Rance smiled an easy grin. "Because I know things you don't know. I know how things work. You ever heard of Harvard?"

"Of course. It's a college."

"The best. Steve and I go there. We're smart guys. Are you smart?"

Lauren shrugged. She got mostly As and Bs, but struggled with arithmetic.

"Well," Rance said, "wouldn't you like to be smarter than any kid in your class? Wouldn't you like to go to Harvard someday?"

"I want to be a teacher."

"Teacher! Whoof. How much does a teacher make?"

"I don't know."

"Don't waste your time, little girl." Rance tapped his head. "Be smart. Smarter than all of them. And you can rule the world."

Lauren frowned and stared.

"Are you scared?"

"A little."

"Why not a lot?"

Lauren wondered for a moment if she should answer, then decided to go ahead. "Because God is watching us."

Rance's casual smile left as quickly as a breeze. For a moment Lauren wondered if he might spring at her. He had the look of a coiled animal. But just as quickly he reclaimed composure and shook his head. "That's a shame," he said.

"What is?"

"A nice little girl like you, believing in God."

"Don't you believe in God?"

"Of course not."

The assurance of Rance's dissent entered her like a chill wind.

"You want to hear why?" Rance said.

"No, thank you."

"Well, you won't have to hear about it from me. Soon enough, you'll discover it for yourself."

She had no idea what he meant, but somehow knew it was all mixed up with that stuff about mutants and "one so young."

"What are you going to do to me?" she asked boldly.

"What makes you think we're going to do anything?"

"You brought me here to do something."

"Don't worry, little girl, everything is going to be fine. We have food; we have some books and games. This will be like a vacation for you."

"I don't want a vacation. I want to go home."

"Not yet," Rance said. "And just in case you have any thoughts about leaving, we're in the middle of a huge forest, miles from anybody. Even if you could get out, you wouldn't last a day. And if you did, we'd find you. We have dogs that love to eat human flesh, and we put lots of poisonous snakes around."

His eyes almost glowed when he said that. Lauren wondered if a shaft of light from outside had suddenly flashed across his face, causing the reflection. But the two small windows in the cabin were curtained. No light from the outside could make it in.

Then Rance said, "You hungry?"

●

"Tell me about your daughter."

Jed Brown was driving Janice's car. The bounty hunter was methodical in his questions, like a good investigator. Janice cooperated fully. If this would help get Lauren back, she'd do it. She'd do just about anything.

"She's beautiful, wonderful," Janice said. "Of course, I'm completely unbiased."

"Of course."

"But she's the light of my life. She's smart and funny. I love being with her."

"Sounds perfect."

"Close," Janice laughed. "But she has the normal kid foibles. She loves fast food, especially Wendy's hamburgers."

"That's normal."

"You're a big help."

"I live on fast food. And Wendy's makes a mean burger."

What kind of man is this? Janice suddenly wondered. *What has happened to him that brought him to this unique profession?* She wanted to ask *him* questions, but an odd shyness stopped her. *Why should I feel that way?* she wondered.

"Now tell me about Sam," he said.

Her shyness increased. Why? Was this suddenly too personal, too revealing? Or was it because she was revealing herself to another man? She reminded herself this was business, and he was a professional, just as she was. His profession was hunting people, of course, but it was a profession just the same.

"He changed over the last few years," Janice said. "He's not the man I married."

"People change."

"But it was such a drastic change, like he'd suffered through some terrible trauma or something. I felt such guilt over it, like I was the cause of it."

"Were you?"

She shot Jed a glance, feeling slightly insulted. But she quickly concluded that was just his way. He was not one of the smooth talkers.

"I honestly don't know. The direction I was moving was radically different from where Sam was going."

"Explain," said Jed.

"About five years ago I returned to my faith."

In a clipped, almost clinical voice, Jed asked, "You'd been away?"

"I was raised in the church, in a small town in southern Illinois. When I went to the University of Chicago, I left that part of my life behind."

Jed grunted slightly, the way people do when acknowledging something familiar.

"What?" Janice asked in response.

"Nothing," Jed said. "You fell away, as the saying goes."

"Yeah. A long way. It lasted all the way through law school and beyond. When I met Sam, I was clerking for a federal judge and wondering which high paying job I'd take. Sam was pulling down about a hundred and fifty thou a year. We were going to make a pretty good economic summit. That's the way he put it."

"You married him for money?"

"No. I married him because he looked like Al Pacino."

Jed Brown chortled.

"The fact that he was so successful was not a minus," Janice continued. "At that point in my life I was ready to grab for the brass ring. Having Sam along for the ride was a bonus. But Sam could also charm a donut off a Teamster. He had an easy sense of humor and a smile to die for."

"Sounds like Mr. Perfect."

"I thought so. And I thought we were the perfect couple." Janice was amazed at how easily this was pouring out of her. "For a couple of years, we were."

"And then?"

"Lauren was born."

"That should have been a good thing."

"It was unplanned. Sam did not want a child. He wanted to be a DINK."

"Double Income, No Kids?"

"Right. He liked his freedom, wanted to take off and travel whenever the spirit moved him."

"So how did he handle it?"

"Coolly. Lauren was the first strike in our marriage. When I quit my first law firm so I could be at home with Lauren, that was the second strike. Money wasn't a problem, but Sam objected anyway."

"What was the third strike?"

"When Lauren was four, I had to make a decision about whether she was going to grow up with Christianity, like I did. But I had to put my own house in order first. I wanted to go back to church. When I tried to discuss this with Sam, he clammed up. He said, 'She's fine with what she's got. Let's leave it at that.' But I couldn't leave it at that. I was feeling pulled back toward God."

For a long moment Jed was silent.

"So, like I told you, five years ago I came back to the Lord," Janice said.

"Great." He sounded oddly distant when he said that. Janice tried to pick up a visual clue from his face, but it was impassive. "What did Sam do?"

"Nothing overt. He just started to grow distant. He spent more and more time away from home. On the road, business all the time."

"Not uncommon."

"But then one night, about three years ago, he hit me. It was so totally unlike him. We'd had our arguments, sure, but Sam never once came close to violence. But it wasn't even the physical blow that scared me so much. It was the look in his eye when he did it."

"What sort of look?"

"Almost a deadness. No emotion at all. Like a machine, or an animal. It was scary."

"Why didn't you take Lauren and leave?"

"I thought I could help Sam through this. I loved him."

"And you wanted to save him."

"But I couldn't get through to him. He hit me again one night a few months later. I did almost leave then, but he left before I did. He wouldn't go to counseling. He ended up filing for divorce."

"Were you relieved?"

"Of course not. I didn't want to give up on Sam. But he gave up on me. There was no way I could stop him. When he decided to go after Lauren, I had to fight back."

Jed nodded slowly, reflectively. Then he said, "Life stinks."

"But I believe God somehow, some way, is in everything, that—"

"Yeah, yeah."

"You don't believe that?"

"In a word, no."

"Why not?"

Jed stiffened slightly. "Let's get back to Sam. We have to think this through. Describe exactly what he did last night from the moment you walked into his house."

Janice recounted the events, reconstructing them as exactly as she could. At one point she mentioned that Sam said some odd things.

"Explain," Jed said quickly.

"Well, he said something that sounded almost like a quote. Something like the Christian faith was a sacrifice of freedom and self-confidence."

"Be as clear as you can," said Jed, sounding as if this was crucial.

"That was it. And that Christianity is self-derision and self-mutilation. Isn't that bizarre?"

"Anything else?"

"Yes, he kept twisting John 1:1."

"In the beginning was the Word," Jed said.

"Only Sam said, 'In the beginning was nonsense, and the nonsense was with God, and the nonsense *was* God.'"

Jed said nothing, looking at the road ahead of him.

"What do you make of all that?" Janice said.

"Funny in a way."

"Why funny?"

"Because that's the way I feel."

Janice felt strangely hurt by his comment. They had begun to get somewhere in this enterprise, and he knew she was a Christian. She knew he wasn't, was in fact hostile about it. But why did he have to make such comments?

"But that's not the point," Jed said, almost as if he sensed Janice's feelings. "The point is that the guy who jumped out the window on me said something weird, too, just before he dove."

"What was that?"

"He said 'All truths are soaked in blood.'"

"What do you suppose that means?"

"All I know now is that we have two guys doing bad things, and spouting bizarre sayings as they do. To me, that adds up to something."

"Like what?"

"I don't know."

"Does any of this have anything to do with my daughter?"

"Not yet. But as Quasimodo used to say, I have a hunch."

"You're a strange one, Mr. Brown."

He did not move his eye from the road. "I was born to be strange."

"Tell me something about your background."

"I'm tired. Let's give it a rest."

"Wait a second," Janice said. "Here I am pouring my story out to you, and you won't give me the time of day. That's not fair."

"Hey," Jed Brown said. "Who ever told you life was fair?"

17

Dewey Handleman was still awestruck at the amount of raw brain power that could occupy such a small space. Usually, genetic research facilities occupied four times the floor space as UniGen. But then, smallness had its advantages—secrecy, flexibility, ability to move fast.

That was how Davis had designed it, of course. Dewey had received the entire history of the place when he signed on for the project. It began, like all entrepreneurial success stories, as an idea in the head of a visionary.

That idea was coupled with a technology, in the form of Davis's partner, Dr. Lyle Burack. Together, they had formed UniGen with one purpose in mind—to build it quickly into the dominant company of what some called the Biotech Century.

What Microsoft was to the information age, UniGen would be to the age of genetic engineering.

That vision, along with stock options, was what drew Dewey Handleman in the first place. Davis had spotted his enthusiasm right away. Dewey had been in the front row in Life Sciences, and it hadn't taken long for him to excite Dewey about "the Nephilim seed," Davis's shorthand name for the project.

If Dewey had been religious, he would have called his participation in the project a transformation of the spirit. As it was, Dewey was confident he would indeed be transformed into one of the brightest and richest citizens of the twenty-first century.

Now this hitch had come up. Why was he having visions and a bout of feeling for this hapless homeless person? The injections were supposed to eliminate those. But here they were, and he had to give them voice.

It was a strange and contradictory situation. That was why he was here early. Before he took the next injection, he wanted to clear some things up with Davis.

For some reason security had been beefed up at UniGen. Such precautions were not uncommon at bio-tech companies, where secrecy about research was a necessity. A leak of a new development to the wrong people could potentially cost billions of dollars. This was high stakes all the way.

But this seemed to be overkill. Three security doors, two walk-through scanners, and four security guards.

To Dewey, it was a wonderland of possibilities. Ever since he was a kid, Dewey Handleman loved puzzles and problems. The more complex the better. Reading true crime books fueled his interest in figuring out the human drama. From there, it was a short walk to speculation about the other side, the criminals. Dewey loved to sit and figure out plans—plans to rob the neighborhood bank, or hold up a Brinks truck, or take a trip to the racetrack and walk away with a ton of cash. In his mind he knew how he would do it all.

His mind got cracking every time he came through the security at UniGen. How would he frustrate it if he wanted to? Almost without effort he had formed a preliminary plan. If he really wanted to trot off with some secret technology or piece of equipment, he knew what he'd do. It would be bold, all right, but fun. The ultimate puzzle solved. After passing through the final security check, Dewey was let into the lab area. He paused there a moment to appreciate once again the scope of the project. It was unlike anything in history, well beyond the predictions of even five years ago. What Davis was doing with the human genome was similar to what Edison did with light—only on an exponentially larger scale. Edison had merely illuminated the world; Davis was going to rule it.

If Dewey ever walked out of there with even an iota of information, it would be devastating to their plans. But of course he wouldn't. He had been screened and was an eager participant. And once the process got to you, it was like an addiction. He did not want it to stop.

"Good morning, Mr. Handleman," said the young technician, Harris. Dewey didn't like him. He called Harris the "head lab geek" behind his back. Dewey could eschew false formalities, being one of the subjects. In the pecking order Dewey considered himself far ahead of Harris, who was merely a paid lackey. Harris didn't even know the essence of what he was injecting into the arms of Davis's specially selected subjects. That was part of the security, too. Harris had been told a new genetic-vitamin was being tested, nothing more.

"You ready?" Harris asked.

Everything inside Dewey screamed *yes!* His body was crying out for the next injection. They had said there would be a certain amount of what they called *yearning,* in order, Dewey knew, to avoid the word *need.* Dewey was smart enough to know he was addicted. Just like any mainliner on heroin.

But he had one advantage, a mind that could fight back. Even if it was only for a moment. So with a flexing of mental power, Dewey said, "Not yet. Is Professor Davis in?"

"I haven't seen him today."

"I called ahead. He was supposed to meet me here."

"I don't keep his schedule. You want to roll up your sleeve?"

Dewey made no move to do so. "How about Dr. Burack?"

"He's here, but he's with someone."

"That's OK. Hang tight, Harris." Dewey started down the hall.

"Wait, you can't just . . ."

But I can "just," Dewey thought without stopping. His body was trembling, a sign of his need for the virus. Fighting it, Dewey continued to Burack's door, around the corner. This deep in UniGen, there was not a need for further security, other than an occasional stroll-through by a hired guard. Dewey gave a quick knock on the door and opened it.

Dr. Lyle Burack was seated at his immaculate desk. At forty-five he was trim and tanned, with a full head of black hair and a resumé as long as the eastern seaboard. Across from him sat a man Dewey had never seen before. He wore a red-knit shirt that stretched tight over heavily muscled arms. His blond hair was trimmed military style.

"Excuse me a moment," Burack said to the man, then to Dewey, "What do you mean barging in here like—"

"I need to talk to you," Dewey said. "I came early to talk with Professor Davis, but he's not here."

"Can't this wait?"

"I'm supposed to get an injection. I want to ask a question first."

Burack frowned at Dewey, thought it over, then said to the blond man, "We'll take this up later."

The blond man nodded, stood. He turned to Dewey and glared. Dewey saw the man's jaw twitch like it was being spring-loaded. Then the man left the office, shutting the door behind him.

"All right," Burack said. "What is so important that it couldn't wait?"

Dewey sat in the same chair the blond man had occupied. "I'm just a little unclear on a couple of points. When I signed on, I was promised full disclosure."

"Of course. Nothing has been kept from you."

"I hope not."

Burack leaned back in his leather chair and pulled at his lower lip. It was a habit, Dewey had come to learn, indicating analysis.

"That's your privilege, Mr. Handleman. We want you to be fully confident in what we're doing. But you already made this decision."

"I did, yes, and I'm still down with that. But I can't help thinking certain things."

"Interesting," Burack said, looking at the ceiling as if gazing into the heavens. "Isn't that the big question?"

"What is?"

"Whether we can help what we think. That's a conundrum the project may answer." Burack looked back at Dewey. "Think of it. One of the puzzling questions of all existence, and we're on the verge of pulling back the veil!"

Dewey nodded, feeling a hint of the intoxication he always experienced when in a room with Davis or Burack.

Burack stood and came around his desk, sitting on the edge to face Dewey. "Hold out your arm," he said.

For a moment Dewey hesitated, then obeyed.

"Now," Burack said, "whenever you feel like it, I want you to flex your wrist."

"Just flex?"

"That's right. Up and down. Whenever you decide."

Dewey paused, then flexed his palm-up hand toward himself.

"Do that three more times, whenever you decide."

Three times Dewey flexed.

"Now," Burack asked, "what began the process that led to those actions?"

"I just did it."

"Who decided?"

"I did."

"Did you?" Burack stood again and whirled toward his office window, which looked out on a garden area. "A few years ago I led a neuroscience experiment just down the hall here. We had a group of volunteers do exactly what you did. A clock allowed the subjects to note exactly when they decided to act, and by fitting electrodes to their wrists, I could time the start of the action. More electrodes on their scalps recorded a particular brain wave pattern which occurred just before the action. Every time."

"What was it?"

"I dubbed it 'readiness potential.' And it has nothing to with what religions or psychologists call the self. There is no self. Only readiness potential."

"But doesn't my will do it?"

"You have no will. What people call will is nothing more than a creation of genes in a unique environment."

"But that's what I can't seem to get around. I did something to somebody the other day, and I got bothered about it. I thought that wasn't supposed to happen."

"You merely had collateral empathic sensation. Quite common."

"But what's the source of that? Why do we feel it?"

"Evolution," Burack said simply. "Our species developed some adaptive advantage in this feeling."

"What sort of advantage?"

"We can't go back and spot it, of course. But it's easy to come up with possibilities. That's the strength of Dr. Bently Davis."

Burack sat back in his chair. As he looked at Dewey, he tugged again on his lower lip. "Are you having doubts?" Burack said.

"I just want to be sure."

"Sure about what?"

"That I'm not giving up something."

"Like what?"

"Myself."

"There is no self."

"You said that."

"Look Dewey," said Burack, using the first name for strained familiarity. "The world is rapidly dividing, like a giant cell. There will soon be only two groups. There will be a cognitive elite and all the rest. The elite will control everything, be richer than everyone else, live longer, accomplish more. The only question you face, and I face, and everyone faces is this: Which group are we going to belong to?"

Dewey nodded. He had heard all this before and did not protest. He needed to be convinced again.

"Now what we are doing here has a double benefit, as you know," Burack said. "Not only will you take a quantum leap in cognitive ability, but you will also share the wealth in the patenting of the process. Think about it. What is it that every parent is going to want for his or her child?"

"Intellectual advantage."

"And will they buy it?"

"Of course."

"And we'll have the patent. They will buy it from us. Do you realize what this means?"

"Yes." It meant wealth beyond belief. Power. Control. "But at what cost?"

"There is no cost," Burack said sharply. "There is only gain. Imagine all useless emotional sensation being eliminated from your brain. Everything that holds us back from absolute adaptive superiority will be gone."

"Human evolution in overdrive."

"Exactly! How can you even think there's a cost except to those who are weak and should be eliminated?"

"I guess so."

"You sound less than convinced."

"Maybe I need some time." Even as he said this, Dewey's body shrieked for the luxuriance of his next injection.

Burack stood. "We don't *have* time. All of this has been worked out, and you have signed on. There is no going back."

Looking at the floor, Dewey said nothing. He wondered whether the faint chill he felt in his back was the product of evolution or his mind.

"Question," Dewey said.

Burack looked at his watch. "I don't really have—"

"One question."

"What then?"

"Why am I having visions?"

"What sort of visions?"

"Religious. Good and evil, that sort of thing. I don't believe in any of that. Why should the process do that to me?"

Burack shook his head. "That's not been a problem so far."

"Well it's a problem now."

"What you need is time to chill out."

"Answer me!" Dewey stood, his fists clenched at his side.

Burack stood also. "Who do you think you are to yell at me like that?"

Breathing hard, Dewey felt a lightness in his head. But he would not back down. They always thought the wimp would back down. Not this time. "You're not telling me something."

"You have everything you need to know!"

Dewey's body again cried out for the injection. Burack was right. Dewey was his slave, like any junkie to his dealer. He looked at the floor and tried to think of something to say.

"The gentleman that was just in here," Burack said.

Dewey raised his head.

"Karel Van Hoorn. Brilliant. Used to work undercover for the Dutch government. He has a special function here."

"What?"

"Enforcement."

The chill Dewey felt grew colder.

"He spent several years doing covert work. They taught him well."

"To do what?"

"Damage control."

It all became clear then. "You're telling me basically to shut up, get on with it, or I'll have my legs broken or something, is that it?"

"Pretty much correct. Only the last part, about your legs? That's incorrect. It will be your brain."

"What about my brain?"

"It will be removed for research." Burack looked at his watch. "Now isn't it time for you to get your shot?"

**18**

"I registered us as Mr. and Mrs."

"You didn't!"

"I did."

"You don't think I . . ." Janice couldn't finish the thought. So this was how it was to be. He'd brought her to a motel outside Cambridge and now was making his intentions quite clear. "I don't believe you—"

"Relax," Jed said, a lilt in his voice. "I registered us as Mr. and Mrs. Bosco Minuski."

"I don't care if you registered us as Ken and Barbie!"

"You don't think I look like Ken? I mean, after a meltdown?"

"I don't consider this a joke."

"This is perfect."

"What is?"

"You see, Mrs. Minuski, we are having a huge fight. That's why I got us separate rooms." He held up two key cards like a pair of aces. His uncovered eye twinkled like a mischievous kid. "The guy at the desk said he understood."

In spite of herself, Janice smiled. "You must be the life of the party when you finally catch somebody."

"At least *I* think so. Shall we?"

Janice took a key and got settled into her primarily orange room, unpacking her small suitcase. She reminded herself this was for Lauren. She ignored the jolts of nervousness that shot through her like static snaps of electricity.

Fifteen minutes later Jed knocked on her door.

"Quaint, but livable," he said.

"What's our next move?" Janice said.

"I suggest you take a nap."

"Do I look that bad?"

"You don't look bad at all," he said, with a hint of warmth that she hadn't heard in his voice before. But he looked immediately disturbed at his utterance and quickly added, "But get some shut-eye just the same. I have a lead to follow up, and we can talk tonight."

"What's the lead?"

"A guy Sterling knew, Bob Thomas. He lives in Waltham. I found his name in Sterling's book."

"What's the connection?"

"Only that he lives in Waltham. It may be nothing, but there was a note on Sterling's desk calendar, dated two days before he died. It was to call this guy Thomas."

"Why don't you just call him on the phone?"

"I tried a bunch of times. Busy each time. Bob Thomas, or somebody who lives with him, loves to talk."

Janice looked at the bed, which appeared to be extremely soft. "The nap idea's a good one. I'll wait to hear from you."

"Pleasant dreams," Jed said. Then he walked out the door.

Janice secured the door with the chain lock, then slipped out of her clothes. She had packed only a few things in a modest bag, expecting this to be a short trip. At least she had remembered a nightgown.

She prayed before getting into bed. When she did, sleep came swiftly.

•

You fly, and are above it all. Lights, cars, city, buildings, people, state, world, earth.

You soar, because you see. See connections no one else can see.

Timeless, wondrous, connectiveness.

What the ignorant call God, you see has connection. You feel that bliss the mystics call God, but it is not God; you know that. You are not at one with the universe; you have made the universe one because you know the beginning, middle, and end. You have seen it and made it comprehensible, touched now with that part of your brain never tapped, the neural miracle of it all, in the sense that miracle is man.

Soaring, you are at peace.

Dewey Handleman lay on his bed, trancelike, smiling, soaring. As if above the clouds. Then suddenly falling. Down through the clouds. Why? What was this? No!

"Help!"

Why hadn't they told him?

"Help!"

•

Jed listened to classic rock on the drive to Waltham. Stones. Beach Boys. Beatles. A musical tapestry of his adolescence. When things were simple. Better.

Back when Sterling was alive. When there was still hope and belief.

But that was the past. Buried. *Keep it that way,* Jed reminded himself.

Only now something wanted to perform a resurrection of remembrance. That something was this Janice Taylor.

Why was she getting to him? It wasn't attraction, was it? That wouldn't have been surprising, because she was a good-looking woman. But he hadn't felt attraction to a woman in a long time, indeed resisted it. His companionships had been void of the personal. They were physical only. Jed was content to keep it that way. That way you didn't get close enough to get hammered again.

So what could it be? Was it her innocence? What else do you call it when someone holds on to a childlike faith in something you know is a lie?

But she was intelligent, not naive. Her Christianity was not some flabby thing stuck to a weak mind. Was that the problem? Was he intimidated by her in a way? Or merely fascinated?

Crosby, Stills, and Nash harmonized from the radio about the Marrakesh Express. Jed turned up the volume. Enough reflection. Let's rock.

Three songs later Jed pulled into a gas station in Waltham, got directions to the address he'd copied from Sterling's book. It was a nice, tree-lined street with well-appointed homes. On any other day a slice of suburban normalcy.

But not today, with questions to be answered.

The home was two-story, white with blue trim. Plush, green lawn. Jed brought the car to a stop right in front of the walkway.

As he got out his little man shouted a quick warning.

But the street was quiet. No one in sight. Only some cars parked.

One of the cars seemed to have a personality. It was dark blue, parked across the street and down a way, facing Jed's direction. Had there been some movement in the car? Jed wasn't sure, only that his little man told him to look that way.

Jed made a mental note to check out the car later. Then he walked up to the front door and knocked.

A moment later it opened, a chain lock allowing only a crack. A man peered out.

"Bob Thomas?" Jed said.

"Yes?"

"I wonder if I might have a word with you?"

"Who are you?" The voice sounded suspicious, tired, sad. The part of the face Jed could see looked lined, the eyes vacant. Why?

"My name's Jed Brown. I'm Sterling's brother."

The silence that followed seemed laden with apprehension.

"You need to get out of here," Thomas said.

"I've come a long way."

"Please leave."

"What is going on, Bob? I have to know!" Jed put his hand on the door just in case Thomas decided to close it.

"Please, I'm afraid. It's all been too much."

"Afraid of what?"

"Afraid. I don't know . . ."

Heaving a sigh of frustration, knowing there was information here he had to get, Jed said, "Look, Bob, I think you were one of the last people to speak to Sterling before he was murdered."

"Murdered?"

"You didn't know?"

"Your brother you said?"

"Yes. Did you speak to him?"

"No. You don't understand."

"What don't I understand?"

"You're talking about my son."

"Your son?"

"Bob is my son."

"May I speak to him?"

"He disappeared three weeks ago."

The words hung heavy in the air.

"You haven't heard from him?" Jed said.

"Please go. There have been phone calls. I'm afraid. If they see you here . . ."

"If *who* sees me here? Mr. Thomas, can I come in?"

"I can't help you."

"Wait—"

Thomas pushed the door closed, in spite of Jed's hand. He stood there for a moment, wondering if he should knock again. But he decided to leave it alone. The old guy inside was dealing with enough.

But it remained that Bob Thomas—Junior—was gone. But where? The little man was grumbling.

A squeal of tires. The blue car from down the street made a quick U-turn and raced off in the opposite direction.

Go! the little man shouted.

Jed went. He jumped in Janice's car and turned the key.

And sat there. It wouldn't start.

Pounding the dashboard with his fist, Jed unleashed a string of expletives. Ten minutes later, with some prodding, the car started. There was no way he'd be able to find the blue car now.

He headed back toward Cambridge. Clouds had started to roll in from the east. It would be a dark night.

**19**

The dream came just before wakefulness. Janice was on the edge of a cliff over a deep crevasse, molten lava flowing everywhere. It made an angry sound as it splurged, almost a growl. It was red death. Blistering steam rose up, enveloping her. Then she heard a voice.

On the other side of the crevasse, clinging to a branch, was Lauren! And she was crying hysterically. "Help me, Mommy! I'm falling!"

In the dream Janice's feet would not move. "Hold on, baby!" Janice screamed. "God will help you. Hold on!"

That's when she awoke. And immediately wept.

She was perspiring. What time was it? All she knew was that the light of day which had managed to eke through the window curtains was no longer there.

She stumbled to the shower, let the warm water bring her back to relative calm.

As she toweled off, still disturbed by the dream, she heard a pounding on the door.

She wrapped the towel around her and went to the door, looking out the peephole.

It was Jed.

"I just got up," she said.

"Meet me at the coffee shop on the corner in fifteen minutes."

"All right."

Jed was waiting for her when she got there. He was sitting in a booth near the rear, his leather shoulder bag on the seat next to him.

"You always have that bag with you," Janice said as she sat opposite him. "What's in it?"

"The secrets of the universe," Jed said.

"All in that one bag?"

"Great bag."

"No, really."

"Tools of the trade. And a change of underwear."

Janice shook her head and picked up a menu.

"Have anything you want under ten bucks," Jed said. "We're on a budget."

"You're so kind," said Janice. "Don't worry. I'll buy."

"You?"

"I'm essentially hiring you to find my daughter, right? I'll spring for the meal."

"Now ain't that a kick in the head?"

A waitress took their order—bowl of chili for Jed, chef's salad for Janice.

"Did you find anything in Waltham?" Janice asked.

"Only that my brother's friend is dead."

"Dead?"

"Car accident. Only the father doesn't think it was an accident."

"What's that mean?"

"I don't know. It causes me concern."

"So what do we do next?"

"We eat."

"I mean about finding my daughter."

"Tomorrow we pay a visit to UniGen. We go together. I will tell you exactly what to say and do."

"Where did you learn all this cloak-and-dagger stuff?"

"You just do it. You pick it up."

"Are you good at what you do?"

"The best."

"Humble, too." Janice studied his face for a moment. The two sides of it seemed to be signals for her feelings. The eye patch was on the forbidding and dangerous side. His good eye had a vulnerability to it she couldn't quite figure out. She felt both guarded and drawn to him.

"Now will you tell me something about yourself?" Janice said.

"There are some things you need to know and some things you don't."

"Then I'll ask you questions."

"Why?"

"Because I'm a lawyer. That's what I do."

"I plead the Fifth."

"This is not a criminal inquiry."

"I plead it anyway."

"How did you become a bounty hunter?"

Jed paused, his good eye narrowing. A half smile that said, "I'll play for now," appeared on his face. "Needed a job," he said. "I knew a guy who was doing it. He said I could make some money. And off I went."

"You took to it?"

"Like a cowboy takes to snuff."

"How long has it been?"

"About twenty years."

"That's longer than most corporate employees these days."

"No benefits, though."

"Family?"

Jed shook his head.

"What about your parents?"

"Mom in Pasadena. Father dead."

"Any brothers or sisters?"

"Just Sterling."

"Ever been married?"

"Next question."

"I'm sorry. I didn't mean to pry."

"Of course you did. That's what you do."

They didn't speak for several minutes. The waitress appeared and set down their food without a smile, then slid away.

"Do you mind if I say a prayer?" Janice asked.

"Just don't do it out loud."

She bowed her head, prayed for Lauren and thanked God for the food. Then she looked at Jed. He was pouring diced onions into his chili. "Why did you reject Christianity?"

He looked at her with a sharp scowl. "Who said I rejected it?"

"I don't know," Janice said, puzzled at why she had phrased the question that way. "I just got the feeling you were a believer once, since you knew John 1:1."

"Let's move to another topic."

"Why won't you talk about it?"

"Why should I?"

Something like an invisible wall of ice went up between them. Janice felt the chill. It was a thick wall, too. And it had a sign on it that said *No Trespassing*. Janice could have dropped the subject right there, left him alone. And if this had been any other circumstance, she would have. But nothing was normal about this man or her involvement with him. She wanted to know more.

"Because nothing is more important than what you believe about God."

Jed said, "You sounded just like Sterling then."

"I would like to have known him."

"There wasn't a greater guy in the world."

"Yet you disagreed with him on Christianity. Why?"

"That's my business."

"Why?"

"You want to believe in God, fine. If that helps you make it through the night, OK. But it's what we do on our own that makes the difference. I don't believe there's a God up there pulling strings. We pull our own strings. I believe man has to do it for himself."

"Sort of a self-help existentialism?"

"Where'd you learn those fancy words?"

"I read a book once."

"Me, too. And we're all we got. Man is man. Existence exists. A equals A."

"I couldn't go on if I really believed that."

"Why not?"

"Because man has done a pretty lousy job with the world."

"Oh right. Because of sin."

"Yes."

"Well, man does some pretty righteous things, too."

"Such as?"

"Technology. Man is killer on technology. You want to tell me that we're not a whole lot better off than we were a hundred years ago?"

"We have more technology, yes. But how do we use it?"

"Some good, some bad."

"And what do we do about the bad?"

"We let the market decide. Let people sort it out for themselves. If something is meant to be, it will survive. Things will get better."

"According to whom?"

Jed shrugged. "The market."

"That scares me."

"The world is a scary place."

"But God does make a difference, in many different ways."

"He watches out for his little sheep?"

"Yes."

"So where was he when your daughter got nabbed?"

Janice sat back with a jerk.

"And where was he when Sam was about to mess you up? Was it God who saved your neck, or was it Jed Brown, disappearance consultant?"

"We don't always know how God works."

"Easy for you to say. But not very helpful when it comes to real life. Now why don't you eat your salad before it wilts?"

The aggression in his voice unnerved her. "I'm sorry if I went too far."

Jed did not answer. He sat stock still and appeared to be looking over her shoulder.

"Don't turn around," Jed said.

"What's going—"

"Do exactly what I tell you."

Janice's heart pumped harder. She waited for him to give her directions, but he said nothing. He kept his eye on something behind her.

"When I tell you," Jed said, "I want you to get up and very slowly walk past me. There's a ladies room at the end of the counter. Go in. Don't come out until I get you. Understand?"

Janice swallowed.

"Remember," Jed said. "Slowly. And don't look behind you."

He waited . . . waited. "Now," he said softly.

Janice stood up and began walking toward the ladies room. The others in the half-full restaurant went on as if life were normal. Janice felt an urge to glance behind her but suddenly, of all things, thought of Lot's wife. Better to do what Jed said.

She pushed into the ladies room, which smelled like artificial lemons. She was alone.

How do you kill time in a bathroom, she wondered. She took a look at herself in the mirror. Her lids were heavy and under her eyes were dusky half-moons. She winced and turned on the faucet.

She splashed a little cold water on her face. A triggered memory surged into her head—Lake Michigan. Nine years ago. Lauren's first experience with water outside a toddler tub.

As Sam sat on the beach reading a book—why wasn't he interested in his daughter's adventure?—Janice carried the bare-skinned Lauren to the water, stepping in until she was waist deep. Then she gently lowered one-year-old Lauren so her tiny feet just cut under the surface.

In her arms Janice felt Lauren's initial jump at the new sensation, saw a look of confusion on her face. Then Lauren began to kick and splash. And laugh! Lauren seemingly wanted to soak up every bit of this fresh experience.

Soon Janice was hopping up and down, lowering her daughter into the water up to the neck, Lauren laughing at everything.

"Look, Sam!" Janice shouted to the shore, but Sam had either not heard or ignored her.

As she gazed into the sink in the diner bathroom, Janice wondered if she would ever again hold her daughter and hear her laugh.

Where was Jed?

Janice looked at her watch, estimating five minutes had passed since she'd left the table.

She paced for a minute, leaned against the wall, and prayed.

The bathroom door swung open. Janice straightened.

It was the waitress. Unsmiling and silent, she barely gave Janice a look as she entered a stall and latched it shut.

How much longer? Should she just walk out? Jed had told her to stay, but for how long?

The toilet flushed, and the waitress emerged from the stall. She went to the sink and washed her hands. She acted as if Janice was not there. She grabbed a paper towel and started drying her hands.

"Excuse me," Janice said.

The waitress turned and looked at her.

"The gentleman I was with . . . You served us?"

A barely perceptible nod from the waitress.

"Can you tell me if he's still out there?"

"He left."

"Excuse me?"

"A few minutes ago."

"Is he coming back?"

"How should I know? He paid and left a tip, walked out. You two have a fight or something?"

Janice rushed out of the bathroom, charged through the restaurant and out the door. The night had somehow grown darker, even with the diner sign's yellow luminosity. She walked quickly back toward the motel, her head a whirlpool of confusion.

She was almost jogging when she got to the edge of the parking lot near her room and then stopped as if she'd run into an invisible wall. As creeping vines of fear brushed inside her chest, she looked up and down the small lot. There was no mistake about it.

Her car was gone.

**20**

Be like Daniel.

Lauren sat by the fire Rance had built, swinging her legs up and down, thinking about escape.

She would be like Daniel in the lion's den, another story her mother told her. God had kept the beasts from eating him. Surely he would keep the snakes and dogs from hurting her.

Of this she was absolutely sure. The only problem was getting out.

But she already had that planned. "I'm hungry," she said.

"What?" Rance said from the corner table where he and Steve were playing chess.

"May I have something to eat, please?" Lauren answered.

"You want some Ritz crackers?"

"Yes, please."

"In the kitchen."

"You get them," Steve said to Rance.

"No," Rance said. "I'm working on a gambit here."

Lauren slipped off the chair and headed for the kitchen. Steve got up from the chess game. "Then I'll watch her, you lazy geek," he said.

"You're the geek," Rance snapped.

Lauren thought they both sounded like Tommy McIntire. Two ten-year-old bullies facing off on the playground. And they were supposed to be college students? She could hardly believe it.

The small kitchen had dull, green wallpaper with pictures of yellow pears on it. There was a small refrigerator with an aluminum sink nearby.

"All right, you can have some crackers and a glass of water," Steve said sharply. He opened a cupboard and pulled down a box of Ritz crackers. "But that's it."

"Thank you," Lauren said.

Steve filled a glass from the tap, handed it to her. "Now go back out and sit and read," he said. "And be quiet." He waited until she returned to her chair before resuming his place at the chessboard.

Lauren watched the two staring at the pieces. The looks on their faces were intense, concentrated. She knew a few things about chess. She knew, for instance, that it took a long time to play a game and that the players usually tuned out everything else around them.

A good thing. It would fit in with the plan.

She munched a few Ritz crackers and sipped the water, which had a rusty taste. Then she was ready for the next move.

"May I have a glass of milk, please?" she said as sweetly as she could.

Steve grumbled. "No. Drink the water."

"But this water's yucky."

"Let her get a glass of milk," Rance said.

"You go with her," Steve said.

"Why? You afraid she's going to come back with a knife and kill us?"

"We're supposed to, geek."

"You're the geek."

"I can get it," Lauren said.

Steve sighed outlandishly. "I'll go with her, but next time it's *your* turn!"

In the kitchen Steve poured a glass of milk and set it on the counter, not handing it to Lauren. "That's all you get," he snapped. "Now go sit down and shut up."

Lauren padded obediently back to her chair. Steve plopped into his own chair with an expulsion of frustrated air.

OK now, sip the milk. Let some time go by. Don't get nervous.

Two gulps of milk later, along with one more Ritz, Lauren said, "May I go to the bathroom?"

Steve groaned. "Oh man!"

"Go on," Rance said.

"No way, it's your turn!"

"Oh, just let her go."

"No way! You go with her."

"You want to make me?"

Lauren kicked her legs vigorously. "Pleeeeze."

"Just go!" Steve shouted. "You got three minutes."

"Thank you," she said, all sweetness and light. She scurried to the bathroom as if nature were calling loudly. Once in she locked the door. She had three minutes to get out the window and as far into the forest as she could.

She had to stand on the tank lid to reach the window. It was a small window that looked to be a hundred years old. And it was stuck.

She pushed with both hands and grunted. The thing didn't budge.

What if she broke the glass? No, they'd hear it, and besides she'd probably cut herself trying to get out. *Little Girl Bleeds to Death in Forest. Film at Eleven.*

God, make it move!

Lauren put the pads of her hands just under the frame and thrust upward again. Her hands thudded against the wood, hurting her.

But the frame moved. Only half an inch, but it did move.

She tried the maneuver again, this time getting an inch more. Dust flew up from the sill, swirled by a cold wind from outside.

A minute or so had gone by. They'd be coming soon.

Straining against the window Lauren managed to get it almost all the way open.

Thank you, God!

"Hurry up," Steve shouted from the other room.

"Coming!" she answered. Then she pulled herself up and over the sill. For a moment she hung there like a sack of laundry on a fence. The moonless night opened its maw like a hungry monster.

She hesitated, looked out into the blackness. Maybe staying and taking whatever they were going to do would be better than this.

Be like Daniel, she reminded herself.

"Here I go, God," she said to the sky. Then she jumped from the window.

And ran.

●

"Something's wrong," Lyle Burack said.

He paced back and forth across Davis's office, fingers scrambling his hair.

"Calm down," said Davis with a clenched jaw.

"Something unanticipated. Dangerous, potentially." Burack stopped for a moment and shook his head. At the age of sixteen, Lyle Burack had envisioned himself graduating from MIT with a degree in biochemistry. He was in love with the life of the cell. Ever since he had found out about it in a book his mother had given him, he was compelled toward exploration of life's building blocks. If he could understand them, he reasoned even then, he could alter them. And that would mean the ability to change humanity.

His favorite movie then had been *The Island of Lost Souls,* the classic starring Charles Laughton as Dr. Moreau. Here was a man who was portrayed as a villain. Lyle Burack thought him to be misunderstood. Moreau, through his experiments, was changing animals into humans. He was manipulating evolution, and what was wrong with that? You either left evolution to chance, or you took hold of it.

But Burack would learn just how backward society could be when it came to pushing the scientific envelope. Especially those who claimed some sort of religion. Like the Christians who kept mouthing off about such necessities as fetal tissue research. Where did they think the great breakthroughs were going to come from, anyway?

So Lyle added to his visualizations his own breakthrough in biotechnology, but something he would keep secret until he could unleash it on the world. That way there would be too much momentum already established. The religious zealots wouldn't be able to stop him.

His nascent images coalesced into hard reality. Not only had Burack received his doctorate; he landed a prime associate professorship at no less than Harvard University. Even he had not dreamed of the opportunity that came to him next.

Like just about everyone else in the science department, Burack fell under the spell of Bently Davis. Here was a true visionary, besting even Burack himself. True, much of what Davis proffered was decades, perhaps even a century, away. But one had to be awed by the passion of the vision. What could man himself do with the tools of nature? What wonders could he accomplish if he took the random-variation element out of the evolutionary scenario, replacing it with purposeful design? Then he would truly realize the power that religions gave to some god or other— the power to create, mold, shape, and propel the human animal toward ever greater heights.

Burack and Davis had clicked immediately. In Burack, Davis had found the key piece he had been looking for, someone with the technical expertise to give body and bone to his conceptions. And in Davis, Burack had found someone with the wealth and entrepreneurial power to put together not just a research project, but a cutting-edge business—one that would make them both so wealthy, so dominant in their field, they'd be very much like the deities so many claimed. "Patents and positioning," Davis had told him constantly, "will make gods in the new millennium."

Thus UniGen was born. And thus was Burack able to step down from an associate professor's salary into a major stockholder in a company that would blow its competitors off the map.

Which would happen when the Nephilim gene was finally perfected for use in children. That was the key. They would have hundreds of thousands, then millions of people clamoring for the treatment for their offspring. Man was by nature competitive. Once it became known that you could buy a mental competitive edge, there would be no stopping the demand. It would perpetuate itself, like a beneficial mutation spreading through a genetic pool.

But Davis had insisted on one thing more—nanotechnological capacity. The delivery of computers the size of a blood cell. It was that aspect that had him worried.

"It's Handleman," Burack said. "He came to see me today."

"And?"

"He's reporting visions. Religious kinds of visions. Good and evil, the devil and God, I guess."

Davis stared at the wall, chewing silently on his thumbnail.

"The Nephilim gene we gave Handleman is supposed to incapacitate the God part."

Burack and Davis firmly believed the religious impulse in man was merely another product of evolution. Somewhere in man's ancient past a part of the brain had developed a God impulse which, at the time, conferred an adaptive advantage. Perhaps those without this impulse were too afraid of the world to move, physically or mentally. But the God part of the brain now gave ancient hominids a collective courage, and another step in the progress of the species was made.

But now the God part of the brain had outlived its usefulness. It was vestigial, like the appendix. No longer useful. Which is why the Nephilim gene, in addition to its neural networking capacity, was designed to incapacitate the God part.

"Maybe," Burack continued, "Handleman's brain is resisting incapacitation."

Once more Davis was silent.

"So is this a problem?"

"What do you think?" Davis said.

"I'm asking *you.*"

"Why should it be a problem, Lyle?"

Burack put his hands on Davis's desk. "Because I don't want anything to muck up the project. We have one shot to make money off this. The God part is peripheral to that. I don't want it messing things up."

"It won't be removed," Davis said firmly.

"We could lose it all!"

"You still don't get it, do you, Lyle?" Davis stood, his eyes taking on that lethal look he got when challenged. "It's just about the money for you. It's always been about the money. I'm interested in doing a work that will last forever. You've never seen that, have you?"

There was no talking to Davis when he got this way, Burack knew. Long experience had taught him that.

"I just want you to remember," Burack said, "who the other half of this project is."

"I haven't forgotten, Lyle. And I don't intend to."

Burack nodded but couldn't help feeling like that last statement had been a warning. He'd never felt that from Davis before. Was it anxiety? Davis did seem wound tighter than normal.

Without another word Burack left the office. But he made a mental note to keep alert. Very alert.

21

Something told Janice to stay right where she was. There had to be a reason for Jed's disappearance.

Had to be, or she was the world's biggest idiot. Had she fallen for a scam? Had a smooth-talking con artist, with an eye patch no less, talked her into trusting him all the way to Massachusetts and then left her high and dry as he took off in her car?

Could be. Her life had been weird for several days.

Yet she hesitated returning to her motel room. She stood at a far corner of the building, watching the nearly deserted lot, hoping Jed would drive back and explain himself.

And wondering if he had really seen something that spelled disaster for both of them.

She heard a car coming, saw the beams of the headlights flash across the row of motel doors. Jed? No. It was a police car.

It crept slowly into the lot, like a bloodhound sniffing for clues. It took its time cruising, shining its spot every now and then. Looking for what?

Her.

Somehow, she knew it was her.

Why? How did the police get involved in this? Was Jed a fugitive of some kind? That made sense. He was open about his methods. Maybe he'd killed a man. Or woman. Or several. Maybe he was on the run, and the police spotted him, and she happened to have a car he could take.

What a fool she'd been to trust him.

The police car suddenly burned rubber and tore out of the lot.

Decision time. Should she try to get in her room? Or was somebody watching? She felt like some cut-rate secret agent in a bad spy movie. But she clearly had to do something, take one step at least.

She paused a moment, then charged across the lot and quickly unlocked the door to her room.

The room was still orange, but there was one major change. All her belongings were gone.

Cleaned out! He had even stolen her pitiful few changes of clothes. What was he hoping for? Money? Humiliation? A little joke at the end of the day?

She heard a squeal of tires in the parking lot. The cops were back. She hadn't done anything wrong but felt like a trapped criminal anyway. Bonnie Parker in a cheap motel. The cops wanted her for something. Maybe Jed had put them onto her as a diversion.

Quickly she shut off the light and connected the chain lock. She didn't pause to consider what good it would do. If the police wanted to question her, she wouldn't resist.

Or would she? She realized for a crazy moment that she wasn't sure what she would do. Her nervous engines were in overdrive.

All she wanted was Lauren.

Footsteps running to the door. Someone tried to open it. Then a pounding. "Janice?"

It was Jed's voice. Janice stood still and silent.

"Janice, open the door!"

His tone was not desperate, but it was adamant.

"They're coming! I've got your stuff. Come on!"

Janice hesitated. Should she trust him again? He had come back, so her theory of abandonment was false. And he did have her things.

She unlatched the chain and opened the door.

"You sure take your sweet time," Jed said.

"Where were you?"

"Get in."

He grabbed her arm and pulled her toward the car. Only it wasn't her car. This one was black and sporty.

"What car is this?" Janice said.

"Rental."

Jed's pace was rapid. Janice got in and hoped for the best.

Wasting no time, Jed Brown floored the gas pedal and raced toward the back of the lot. He paused only a moment, looking up and down the street, before heading out.

"Where are we going?" Janice said.

"Away from here."

"Can you explain as you drive?"

With a smile, Jed said, "I was born to explain and drive."

Janice looked over the interior of the car. It was the finest of everything. "This isn't a rental," she said.

"In a way it is. I'll give the guy a few bucks."

"Who?"

"The guy I stole it from."

"Are you telling me we're riding in a stolen car?"

"Briefly." Jed took a hard turn and scorched onto the expressway.

After recovering her equilibrium, Janice said, "And where's my car?"

"It'll be safe. I left it in a no parking zone."

"What!"

"Relax. They'll impound it. It'll be safe for a few weeks, plenty of time to clear this all up."

"Clear what up? Why are we doing this?"

"You didn't stay in the bathroom like I told you."

"Hey, I'm sorry, OK? What was I supposed to think?"

"You weren't. That's why I put you there."

"I don't believe I'm hearing this!"

"Calm down and listen. I saw the cops drive by the coffee shop back there, slowly. Somebody put the cops onto us. It had to be Sam."

"But we didn't do anything."

"We only beat up your husband."

"In self-defense!"

"You remember *The Fugitive* with Harrison Ford?"

Janice blinked. "What has that got to do with anything?"

"Remember when he has Tommy Lee Jones at gunpoint in that drain passage? And he says, 'I didn't murder my wife.' And Tommy Lee Jones says, 'I don't care!' Remember that?"

"Yes, I remember."

"Well that was the right answer. It's like what I do. I hear all the excuses, all the stories, but I don't care. My job is to bring 'em in and let the courts sort it out. So the cops don't care what our story is. They just want to bring us in, and we can't afford to be brung. Not now."

Janice noticed she was clamping her palms together in a death grip. She separated her hands and shook them like dusty rags.

"Tense?" Jed said.

"Who, me? I'm in a stolen car! I'm accessory to grand theft auto! My own car's in a police lot somewhere, and they're after me for assault and battery. Why should I be tense?"

"You know," Jed said, "you're kind of excitable."

"And you're not?"

"Want to feel my pulse?"

"No."

"If it's any comfort, I've been in spots a hundred times worse than this. You got nothing to worry about. Trust me."

A short burst of laughter erupted from Janice. In that moment all the absurdity of the situation was too apparent to ignore. "Why not?" she said. "What more do I have to lose?"

"Well it's a good thing," Jed said, looking up at the rearview mirror.

"Why is that?"

"Because I think we've been spotted."

**22**

Lauren couldn't remember ever being in such darkness. Outdoors, at least. This darkness was a lot like her closet when she hid there with her stuffed animals. Light would sneak in under the door but die before it reached full illumination. Here in the woods the tiny rays of light from the stars fell lifeless, too.

The trees were shadowy sentinels. At least she couldn't hear anything that sounded like a snake or a lion, only the soft crunching of leaves under feet.

So far, so good, God. Now where?

She had no idea what direction she was going, but she was sure God would lead her. How? She didn't know. Maybe stick an idea in her brain. She didn't know much about the Holy Spirit, but her Sunday School teacher had told her it would guide her through life.

Well, now was the time.

Especially now, as Lauren's nose was hit with an odd smell. It was something like . . . old socks. For an instant she wondered if it was the odor of death. Dead snakes, maybe.

Be like Daniel!

She forced herself forward, unable to completely

calm her mind. Her mom had always told her she was "impulsive." When she asked what that meant, her mom said, "You like to act before you think."

The memory of it only added another tier of uneasiness to her thoughts. Should she have done this? Was this the dumbest thing ever, even worse than the time when she was six and decided she was going to Australia? (She made it two blocks before she saw an old and strange man standing on the corner, dressed in dirty clothes, who looked at her with cold eyes. She ran back home.) Was she just wandering farther into a wasteland that would mean starvation and death?

Stupid Girl Found Dead, the headlines would say, *Should Have Stayed Put.*

Maybe she should go back. They were outside now, no doubt, madder than wasps in an overturned glass. Looking for her.

She would keep on. Even if she had to stay out the whole night, she would find a way.

She had heard somewhere that a stream would always lead to civilization. She would find a stream and then a log on which she would float to freedom. Then the headlines would be different. *Brave Girl Escapes Kidnappers on Homemade Raft! Whole World Amazed!*

She was walking faster now, able to see only a few feet ahead in the gray-black forest. Then she stopped to listen. Was there a stream somewhere?

The only sound was some sort of buzzing. Mosquitoes maybe. Out to suck her blood and leave welts all over her. She hadn't figured on that. She did not get along with mosquitoes. One summer night she had been bitten so bad her arms looked like cobblestone streets. She was a meal-in-waiting for the flying blood suckers.

Then she thought, *What if Daniel had been thrown into a mosquito den? Wouldn't God have saved him even then? Of course! If God can close the mouths of lions, he can sure plug up the snouts of mosquitoes.*

"OK, God," she said aloud, "protect my skin!"

She looked behind her for signs of light, flashlights maybe, indications that Rance and Steve were on her trail. She saw nothing but more night and started off again, waving her hands around her head for good measure, just to help God with his current task.

She hadn't gone ten steps when her right shoe sank into a yucky, wet mess. Yelping, she stopped and pulled her foot out. It made a sucking sound, like a kid slurping up the dregs of a milk shake through a straw. She was wearing white Keds and knew this was the end of *that* color.

Her foot was soaked and heavy. Was this mud? Or a swamp? Or what? What if it was something dead?

Sick!

She knew it probably wasn't, but the night was doing something to her imaginings. *Why was it that the mind always goes to the grossest things and stays there?* She'd ask God someday.

Turning left, she made her way over soggy leaves and twigs, slowly, forming a map in her mind around the dank impediment. If it was a swamp, there was no way to be sure how big it was or where it ended, but she had to trust her instincts. They were all she had.

"God," she said as she walked trepidatiously forward, "keep me from quicksand too, OK? Show me where to go!"

Maybe because she had been so intent on getting away she hadn't realized, until now, how cold it was. Nothing like the wind in Chicago, of course, but cold enough to prickle her with icy needles.

Keep moving, she told herself, *keep that blood flowing.*

Something brushed the back of her legs. Something moving!

Spinning around, she heard herself shout, "No!" as if, like an obedient dog, the thing would slink away.

Looking down, she saw the shape. It moved like an animal with a quick jerk. Lauren jumped back, and the shape stopped moving. Not an animal. A bush of some kind. She could see in shadow some branches sticking out like knots of discarded wire.

It was that realization that set her off. If it had at least been a *living* thing, maybe that would have given her a feeling that life was around, somewhere, surviving, like she would. But this was a bush. A cold, uncaring, silent plant-thing, and she was all alone with it in the silence and the darkness.

She couldn't hold back the tears. They erupted all at once, and she cried them out, as if the more they came the more chance she would find her way back to her mother. And home. And life.

●

"Unbelievable!" Janice said. She had both hands firmly on the dashboard in front of her, as if she could steady the car this way. Or slow it down. But the opposite was happening. Jed was putting the pedal to the metal.

"Don't worry," Jed said, driving with one hand.

"Don't worry? We're being followed by the police! In a stolen car!"

"They haven't put on the lights yet. If I can keep a distance, they can't run a check."

"So you're speeding up? How does that look?"

"Like I'm in a hurry?"

"This isn't funny!"

"Then what do you suggest I do?"

Janice couldn't think of any reasonable alternative. She started feeling like the narrator of *A Simple Plan,* a book she'd read in law school at the suggestion of her Criminal Law professor. In the novel an otherwise normal guy descends further and further into a black hole of crime and murder through a series of small steps and bad choices.

Now several of those steps had been taken by Jed Brown, and she was right there with him.

Janice barely had time to notice but now realized they were heading across what had to be the Charles River. Ahead lay the night lights of Boston.

"And your plan is?" Janice said.

"A night tour," Jed said, checking his rearview mirror. "Ever been to Boston?"

"Once."

"Nice town. I busted a few people here."

"I'm filled with confidence."

They rode on in tense silence, until Jed pulled off, faster than he should have, into the flow of traffic on the city side. "I think we lost them . . . oops, no."

"Where are we going?"

"Ever been to Boston Common?"

"I don't want to go to Boston Common! I want to get out of this thing and return this car and call the police to find my daughter."

Jed screeched off onto a steep street that looked properly Bostonian— upscale dwellings melding into boutiques and antique shops. "Listen to me," he said, coolly. "The police are not going to help us."

"Well if we just explain—"

"My guess is a lot of phony information has already been provided to them. We are suspects, not victims."

"But we haven't done anything!"

"Except steal a car."

"You're no help!"

"We haven't got time to debate this. An APB is probably out, and we don't have long to tour."

Janice closed her eyes and prayed. In her head it came out something like, *Lord, give me wisdom.*

The tires squealed as Jed took a turn onto a side street. With lightning swiftness he pulled the car over to the curb between two other vehicles.

"What are we doing?" Janice said.

"Parking."

"Why?"

"You don't just pass up a parking space in this town."

Before she could say another word Jed was out the door and on his way to her side of the car. For whatever reason—fear? exhaustion?—she didn't make a move. Her door swung open.

"Come on," Jed said.

"Come on *where?*"

"I'll show you."

"I say we stop this right now."

"Can you trust me just a little further?" Jed said. "I want answers just as much as you want your daughter back. I can help you find her. I promise you."

He seemed suddenly vulnerable, as if he was pleading with her to believe him. He was like a man who wanted—needed—to be trusted. But he was also a dangerous man. He had proved that through his methods. They were beyond anything in her experience. She thought for a moment of simply telling him to go on by himself, while she took her chances with the police.

Then a picture of Lauren, all alone in some dark place, shot into her mind, and Janice found herself saying, "Well, we've come this far." She got out of the car.

Jed reached in the back and pulled her suitcase and his leather bag from the back seat.

"Now where?" Janice said.

"Under the ground," Jed answered.

With one sopping wet foot and a stomach growling like an animal, Lauren trudged onward. She was half convinced now that she had been a total stupidzoid to run out into the woods. She was lost, and though she was still confident God would not let her be eaten by snakes, she wondered if he would do anything about her stomach. Sometimes children died, even Christian kids, even when they prayed. She knew they went to heaven, but . . .

Not just yet, God. Please, not just yet.

Her thighs were starting to hurt and tighten. Once she nearly got a cramp and walked several hundred yards holding her hand on her leg.

What time was it? Late. But not late enough. It would be hours before daylight came.

The world around her seemed a shapeless mass of forbidding substances, like she had fallen into a vat of cold, dark Jell-O. She remembered a vivid dream she'd had when she was very young. In the dream a black, vibrating coagulation had sprung up under her and caught hold of her legs. It held her like tar, but this tar was alive! And it was pulling at her, sucking her in deeper and deeper as she kicked and struggled.

But the more she resisted, the stronger it became until it had her up to the neck. Just before her head disappeared from the world of light into the blackness of death, she tried to scream. But in the dream her voice was soundless.

That had been her first nightmare. Her mother had sensed something wrong and came into Lauren's room to hold her.

Now Lauren was starting to relive that dream, and she wondered if her mother could feel it now. Did she sense her daughter's distress? And would she come to her? Would she?

O please God, yes. Please get my mom!

She heard something and stopped. What was it? It sounded distant, and it sounded like a growl.

Her throat tightened as she strained to hear. What if it was a bear or something and it had her scent? She'd seen a show about that once on the Discovery Channel. Once they got the scent, it was all over. There was the hunter and the hunted. She knew which one she was.

There it was again. A low, snarling sound, loud and not too far away. It echoed, like she had heard a lion's roar echo at the Brookfield Zoo. It was enough to set her whole body vibrating with imagined fear. Exactly how she felt right now.

Again it came, only this time it sounded strangely mechanical. Not a bear at all. A car! Yes, a car of some kind straining up a mountain road!

And a road meant she was not lost! Someone would be along to help a little girl wandering in the middle of the night and . . .

A frightening thought intruded. She'd heard enough stories about abductions and horrors visited upon children to know that this was a dangerous option. Her mother's warnings about strangers came back to her.

But what other choice did she have? She was not going to stay out here anymore. And if God had protected her, like Daniel, from the snakes and bears, certainly he would save her from a bad man.

She uttered a prayer and started toward where she had heard the noise.

Only there was no more noise, the growling car having found its way and left. Lauren walked slowly but steadily in the direction she thought it had come from, listening for another sound to guide her.

She heard nothing.

After ten minutes of walking she hesitated, afraid that she might actually be heading in the wrong direction. What if she had? Maybe she would hear no more cars and be completely lost again. Out in the night, alone.

And it was getting colder. Her teeth were starting to do Morse code in her mouth as she wrapped her arms around herself.

What now, God? What now?

She heard a whooshing sound very close. Definitely a car! She wasn't far away after all!

She headed for the noise, faster now, determined not to let her new sense of direction fade. She had gone maybe seven or eight steps when the ground disappeared from under her.

A sense of falling, falling, then hitting a hillside with a thump and feeling her head snap back.

But she had landed on a carpet of leaves, and at least that softened the impact. After the initial hit she rolled, a wild rag doll, downward until stopped by the shoulder of the road.

Dazed, Lauren had no idea how far she had fallen. It seemed like a mile. For a quick moment she thought she had tumbled off a cliff into some secret place where no one would find her.

Then she heard it—a car, coming her way. Yes, there was a road here, a hard dirt road! And then light. Headlights. Heading for her.

She did not hesitate. Enough was enough. She was cold and tired and didn't care who it was. She'd just have to trust.

Waving her arms as the headlights came nearer, Lauren felt a fresh spurt of tears run down her cheeks.

The car slowed.

O please let it be someone nice. Please!

The car stopped. With the lights directly in her eyes, Lauren couldn't see. But whoever it was could see her.

A door opened, and for one brief, scary moment she thought, *What if it's Rance and Steve?*

Footsteps came toward her, and she could see a figure silhouetted by the back lighting. She put her hand to her eyes to shield the light but remained blind.

And then a familiar voice said, "Lauren!"

"Daddy!"

PART TWO

Can one be a saint if God does not exist?

—ALBERT CAMUS

**24** Down in the musty warmth of the MBTA station, Janice had the feeling she was in a netherworld. Like Hades, the realm of the dead. Slowly, inexorably, her sense of normalcy was melting away. She was being carried along in a flow she could scarcely understand, let alone control. All because of this man.

Janice became aware that Jed was looking at her. "What is it?" she said.

"Nothing."

"No, tell me."

He shook his head. "Weird."

"What is?"

"This. Your being here."

"I was just thinking that."

"I mean your being here with me. I work alone. I don't know why I even asked you to come along."

"You were offering to help me."

"I don't do that. People can help themselves."

She tried to infer his meaning, looking for clues under the surface. "That's a pretty bleak view, isn't it?"

"It's reality."

Janice shook her head. She suddenly felt like reaching out and putting a hand on his arm. Though she didn't, she said softly, "I don't accept that."

"Here comes our train," Jed said.

Jed was silent during the trip. When they finally stepped off the train and into the night, she was half-convinced he was making this whole plan up as he went along.

A few blocks of brisk walking brought them to an apartment building that looked to Janice like it came out of a Tennessee Williams play. If it had been a person, it would be a brooding Southern hulk like Stanley Kowalski—vulgar and dangerous.

"What are we doing *here?*" Janice asked as Jed approached the door.

"Almost home."

At least the place had a security buzzer. Jed pressed a button and waited, then a high, nasally voice crackled, "This better be somebody who owes me money."

"Data!" Jed said.

"Who is this?"

"Your worst nightmare."

"Oh, no."

"I have need of you, my alien friend."

"Forget it!"

"Data . . . ," Jed's voice had a warning tone.

"It's ten o-freaking clock at night, and I'm right in the middle of a game!"

"Game'll have to wait."

"What if I tell you to shove it?"

"Data, my compadre, you tried that six years ago, remember? And what did it get you?"

A short silence ensued, as if the voice on the other end was engaged in thought. Then the door buzzed, and Jed pushed it open.

The inside of the building was dank and smelled of old trash. A lone, bare lightbulb was all the illumination provided in front of the stairway.

At the top of the creaking stairs, Jed turned right and headed down a corridor to a door at the end. He rapped once on the door, its green paint slightly faded. Janice heard the jumble of a lock; then the door opened slightly, a chain across the crack. And behind the chain, a pair of small, ferretlike eyes.

"My man," Jed said.

"Don't man me, man," the nasally voice returned.

"Let us in."

"Who's us?"

"Got a friend with me."

"Oh man!"

"You'll like her."

"Her?"

"She won't bite."

"Do I have to?"

"Would I be here if you didn't?"

"Man!"

The door slammed, followed by the sound of the chain unlatching. Slowly the door swung open. The young man with the ferret eyes glared at Janice, then at Jed, saying nothing. He looked to be in his late twenties, had thinning hair wisping back off a huge forehead, and a large, hooked nose. He wore a drab red tank top—exactly the wrong choice for a thin body with spindly arms. The rest of his ensemble consisted of a pair of striped boxer shorts and sagging white socks.

"Janice, meet Data," Jed said as he led her inside.

"Hello," Janice said.

The reluctant host slammed the door.

"He named himself after that guy on *Star Trek*," Jed said.

"Next Generation!" Data corrected. "That's the show that nailed it! And I am Data, from the Omicron Theta star system."

"He won't reveal his real name," Jed whispered loudly, "which is only known to a few close companions, such as myself."

"You better not!"

"Don't worry, your secret is safe with me. For the time being."

Turning abruptly Data stormed back into the bowels of his apartment. And what an apartment. The first thing that struck Janice was the other-worldliness of it. It seemed like some science fiction fanatic's idea of a livable space, only without any thought of cleanliness or order. The walls were covered with posters of characters from *Star Trek: The Next Generation*—Captain Picard, Giordi, Wesley Crusher, Riker, but mostly Data.

The walls themselves were painted black but with stick-on stars of the glow-in-the-dark variety. The floor was a mess of discarded clothes, fast-food wrappers, and computer technical manuals of some type.

Jed followed Data. "We're going to need a place to crash for awhile."

"Why me?" Data said, kicking at a T-shirt on the floor.

"Because you're here, we're here, and something's come up."

Data threw himself heavily on a soft chair with stuffing coming out of one of the arms. He folded his own arms across his chest like a petulant child.

Matter-of-factly, Jed said to Janice, "Data here is a master of lying low. He was one of the best of the neo-hackers a few years ago."

"*The* best," Data corrected.

"Did a lot of low-level entries into systems, just for fun."

"It was art, man."

"People started to close in on him."

"In their *dreams*."

"But he always slipped away. In fact, he liked to try to make life nervous for his pursuers."

"*Did* make 'em nervous."

"What he'd do, moving around as he did, is find out who some of these people were, and then he'd find their cars."

"It was so easy."

"And he'd install a little tracking device under their cars."

"Made them myself."

"Then he'd track them by computer, find out where they went. And he'd send E-mails to them saying things like, 'I know where you were last night. You were at . . .'"

"That was so fun."

"But when he hacked into the Secret Service's secure system, they got seriously miffed. Especially when a few Clintonian tidbits ended up on the *Drudge Report*."

"Freedom of the press, man."

"So the Service got the top cyber sleuth in the country—"

"Don't mention his name!"

"—Seth Sellers—"

"Ahhhhh!"

"—who tracked our boy down."

Data jumped to his feet, his face red, and looked directly at Janice. It was like he was pleading his case to a jury, and she was the jury. "It took him *eight months* to figure it out, and even then it was only 'cause of one bonehead move I made. He *never* would have caught me! He's a fake, a sham, showing up on *Larry King* like he's some rock star!"

"But catch him they did," Jed said, "leading to a major federal complaint. They were gonna throw the proverbial book at him. So Data decided to skip bail."

Data plopped back into his chair, looking disgusted.

"Which is where I came in," Jed said. "It only took me two weeks to find him. It was just a mile or two from here, wasn't it?"

"I wasn't even trying," Data said.

"But as I was bringing him in, something very strange happened. I find out I kind of like the kid. He knows more about computers than anyone I know."

"You got that right."

"And so I tell him when he gets out to come look me up. I'll use him as sort of a consultant. He ends up entering a plea and does two years at Terminal Island. He gets out by helping the feds catch a couple other hackers."

"Easy marks. Amateurs."

"And now he does some work for me, whenever I have a skip on the east coast."

"He pays lousy," Data said to Janice. "He still owes me money."

"But Data is willing to offer me good terms, because I know something that he would rather I didn't know."

"Here it comes."

"I know his real name, where he lives, and what he does. And I know how he violates the terms of his parole."

"It's blackmail! It's un-American!"

"It's very American," Jed said. "Tit for tat. Quid pro quo. Anyway Data won't mind if we hole up here for a few days."

The prospect made Janice's stomach do a quick turn. But what choice did she have now? It was late at night, and they were here. She needed the time. Tomorrow they could concentrate on locating Lauren. That's what Jed did. She would give him the next couple of days to do it.

"This bites," Data said.

Janice didn't argue the point.

**25**

Now the kid seemed livid. Before, John Phillips was merely offended, somewhat confused. All of a sudden he was on a crusade.

"I'm going to lodge a formal complaint," he said.

Davis leaned back in his chair, closed his eyes, and sighed. Sometimes he wished the teaching role did not involve personal interaction with students. It could get to be so bothersome, especially with the naive ones, like this Phillips kid.

Yes, Davis had to admit, he'd come down a little hard in class that day. He had made the argument that Mother Teresa was, like every other creature, acting out of selfishness. She wasn't concerned with the poor; she was concerned about making it to heaven. The poor were just her vehicle. She stayed with them to prove herself to God so she could make it. And so we all act that way, with our selfish genes, for what is in our best interest.

Well, that must have done it for the kid, because here he was on some holy mission.

"You haven't given the class a chance, John," Davis said.

"This really stinks," Phillips said, his cheeks a

blotchy red. "My parents are coughing up practically all the money they have to send me here. I guess there are a lot of students in the same boat. If their parents, and the alumni, really knew what was being taught in some of the classes, there would be a real stink. I'm going to press this to the next level."

"Making it a cause?"

"If you want to call it that. I just want the truth to get out there. I want people to know."

Those words triggered a far-off memory in Davis's mind. *I want the world to know* were the exact words that echoed from the deep fog of his childhood. His mother had said those very words to him. They were on some street in his Texas hometown. She held his hand, walking him quickly.

"Why do we have to go?" the six-year-old said.

"That the world may know," said his mother, a plain but formidably built woman.

"Huh?"

She stopped, took the little boy by the shoulders. "I want the world to know, honey lamb, all about Jesus."

Even then there was something about that name that scared him. Was it the look in his mother's eyes? A look that told him this Jesus was not someone to mess with? Was it because of the awful thing that his mother was under this spell? The awful thing—his father leaving, just like that, no words, no nothing—had hit them both hard. Bently had cried for a week solid, but his mother had gone into a scary, quiet place.

When she came out of it, she was not quiet anymore. And she talked a lot about fire.

Bently didn't like fire. He didn't like the fire in his mother's eyes or the fire they talked about at the meetings—the fire where people burned and screamed forever and ever!

Bently heard all about that fire for the next three years, his mother telling him almost every night that he would go there if he didn't mind her, if he did certain bad things to people, especially girls.

One time, he remembered vividly, she told him about a race of giants on the earth, the offspring of demons and women. She called them by a strange name, the Nephilim. That's what happened when women gave themselves over to their base impulses. But Bently, strangely, had thought then it would be nice to be a giant. You could squash people that way— people who tried to hurt you, or scare you.

Then came the happenings with Mr. Johnson. Looking back through the haze of time, Davis knew that was the start of it, the beginning of the events that would spin him toward his destiny.

Harry Johnson was Bently's sixth-grade schoolteacher. Bently liked him. He seemed to have so much to say, so many fascinating things to show the class—especially when it came to science. What a universe was open there! Presented to him by a teacher, so it had to be real. Here is where his imagination could run free at last!

So Bently was pleased when Mr. Johnson actually came over to the house one evening, though he was embarrassed by the looks of the place. They lived in a run-down house near the railroad tracks, and mother didn't keep house much. Bently was the one who opened the door, and when he saw Mr. Johnson standing on the porch, he smiled.

"Howdy, Bently, old kid!" Mr. Johnson said. Mr. Johnson was in a tan suit. There was moisture on his forehead, and a few strands of his brown hair were stuck to his skin. In his right hand he held a small bouquet of flowers, like the kind you could pick up cheap at the A & P. (Bently had once got some for his mother, but she yelled at him for not being a good steward, whatever a steward was.)

"Your mother at home?" Mr. Johnson said, leaning forward to muss Bently's hair. When he did that, Bently smelled something funny on Mr. Johnson's breath. It was like he had something rusty in his mouth. Maybe that's why he was acting a little more, well, enthusiastic than usual.

That's when his mother came to the door. "What are you doing here?" she demanded. Bently thought that was rude, and the last thing he wanted was to make Mr. Johnson feel bad.

"It's my teacher," Bently said.

"I know who it is," his mother said, her eyes with that crazy look in them. Only this time she was looking at Mr. Johnson, like he was some sort of bad person.

"Myrna," Mr. Johnson said sweetly as he stepped through the door, holding out the flowers. "I thought we could talk about it."

"There's nothing to talk about, Harry Johnson. I want you to leave. Now."

Since his mother didn't take the flowers, Mr. Johnson handed them to Bently to hold.

"Now, Myrna, there's no need for that kind of attitude." Mr. Johnson looked at Bently. "Your mother really likes me, you see."

"Leave now!" Myrna demanded.

As Bently stood there, listening, he was fascinated by two things. First, that his teacher and mother even knew each other. And then that they seemed to have some sort of past. They were arguing about something that had happened, and his mother was upset about it. But his mother was always upset about something, so that was the part that didn't surprise him in the least.

Then Mr. Johnson did an odd thing. He put his hands on Bently's mother's shoulders! Bently had never seen, as long as he could remember, anyone touch his mother. She didn't even like him to touch her, even when he handed her things.

His mother just stood there, not making an attempt to get away but going as stiff as stone. Mr. Johnson was still flashing his lazy smile at her. "Myrna, don't you think I deserve a hearing?"

"You've been drinking," his mother said.

"Just a little hair of the dog," Mr. Johnson said. "It don't bite."

"I won't have this in my house!"

To Bently it seemed like nothing his mother said had any effect on Mr. Johnson. What a wonderful thing, he thought. How does he do it?

Harry Johnson reached into his trousers pocket and pulled out a dollar bill and handed it to Bently. "You run down to the drugstore and get yourself an ice cream," he said. "And then buy a comic book. You like Archie?"

"I guess," Bently said, not knowing who Archie was since his mother had forbidden him ever to look at a comic book.

"Well you go on now and don't come back until you see the clock say nine. You got that, Bently?"

"Yes, sir."

"Wait just one minute!" his mother said.

"Hold on, Myrna. We need to talk this through. You don't want Bently to hear all about it, do you?"

About what? Bently thought. He watched his mother's face quiver and twitch. Surely something beyond his understanding was going on in her head. But that's how he felt about most of what went on behind his mother's eyes. It didn't really surprise him when she looked at him and nodded assent.

Bently dashed out of the house, his heart dancing. Ice cream! All alone, so he could pick any kind! And a comic book! Mother hadn't said no, so he took it as tacit approval. He would get to find out about this Archie now. Oh wonderful new world!

At the drugstore Bently gobbled up a double scoop of tutti-frutti and still had enough left over for *two* Archie comics! Mr. Wilson let him sit at the counter and read about these funny kids with names like Jughead, Betty, Veronica, and Moose. He was in another world, a colorful world of actual fun, and he didn't want to leave it.

But Mr. Wilson shooed him out around nine-thirty, reminding him it was a school night. Reluctantly, Bently returned home.

He was greeted by a dark, still house. No one seemed to be inside. At first he was afraid to call out for his mother, fearing that she would answer in the darkness and scare him out of his pants. He felt for the light switch, flicked it on, and whispered, "Mother?"

He saw her sitting on the old sofa in the living room, her back to the door, hunched over. Bently thought she might be praying. But as he approached her, he became convinced something was wrong. Very wrong.

Bently took slow steps toward her, careful not to walk too heavily, fearing he might set her off. In the dim light he noticed her hair, normally pinned back severely, was loose and messy. And he saw that one shoulder of her dress was torn.

Who had done that? Mr. Johnson? No way. Mr. Johnson would never do anything like that. He was a teacher, respected in the community.

No, if anything, his mother had probably gone nuts over something, and Mr. Johnson had tried to restrain her. Anger welled up inside Bently. If his mother had made Mr. Johnson mad, Bently didn't know what he might do. Run away, maybe.

Bently accidentally bumped an end table. It scraped on the floor. His mother whirled around and glared at him.

"You wicked boy!" she screamed. "You wicked, evil boy!"

"Mother, what's wrong?" Bently said, trembling.

"Don't talk to me! You left me! You're wicked! You're all wicked! Evil!"

Bently shook his head. What had happened in this house while he was gone? His mother stood up, and the only thing Bently could think of was that movie he had sneaked into at the drive-in, *Attack of the Fifty-Foot Woman.* His mother suddenly seemed that large, that scary.

She raced to the kitchen, faster than he had ever seen her move, almost supernaturally fast, and came out wielding the wooden rolling pin—the weapon she used to mete out his punishments.

But he had done nothing wrong! Stunned by her vehemence, he was unable to move. "What did I do?" he said, tears forming.

She did not answer but whipped the rolling pin across his legs. Bently shrieked. "Mother, no!" he said, falling backward to the floor, coiling into a ball. He waited for the next blow.

It didn't come. He peeked upward, saw his mother hovering over him. Then she was beside him, on her knees, crying. "Oh my boy, my boy," she burbled. "My poor boy." She said nothing for several minutes, just rocked back and forth.

The next day at school Mr. Johnson asked Bently to stay in the classroom at lunchtime. He seemed his usual, jovial self.

"Your mother talk to you about last night?" he asked with a smile.

"No, sir."

Mr. Johnson came over and sat next to Bently. He put his hand on the boy's shoulder. "Bently, I think it's time you did some growing up. Your mother, she's not quite right. She's, well, sort of sick."

"Sick how?"

"Sort of in the head. Now people get like that sometimes. And it's up to us to help them. You want to help your mother, don't you?"

Bently nodded.

"We can do it. Together. I can help you *and* her. You just do what I say, and we'll see to it that your mother gets that help. It might be rough for you at first, but I think you can take it. Can you take it, Bently?"

"Yes, sir." He trusted Mr. Johnson. He would do the right thing.

"Fine, fine. I'll tell you exactly what to do. Just remember one very important thing. Your mother might invent a story to protect herself. She might say some terrible things about me. She might even say I did something very bad to her, but you can't believe it, Bently. She's not right in the head."

Bently knew that was true. He had known it for years. But his mother never did say anything, not even during the proceedings that followed. Not when the authorities came and took Bently away. Not during the court hearings when Bently testified like Mr. Johnson told him to. Not even when she was led out after the judgment that sent her to the asylum. It was like she had retreated to a dark, silent place and refused to come out.

As far as Bently was concerned, it was the silence of death. He never saw his mother again.

It was as if a giant boulder had been lifted from the boy's shoulders. He had one pang of guilt as they took his mother away from the courtroom for the last time, but it was a quick one. Mostly, he felt relief. He was *free*.

Mr. Johnson became a surrogate father to him. Even though Bently went to a series of foster homes, his beloved teacher kept in touch, kept opening up the wonderful world of science to him.

And protected him from religion. He taught Bently that religion was a system opposed to the mind and that it did terrible things to people, like it had to his mother. He gave Bently challenging books, which Bently devoured. His favorite was *Atlas Shrugged* by Ayn Rand. Mr. Johnson spent hours talking about that book—"The greatest novel ever written in history, without a doubt"—and said someday he'd take Bently to New York to meet the great novelist.

That trip was not to be. Just before Bently's senior year in high school, Harry Johnson died in a car crash. There were rumors that he had been drunk, but Bently didn't believe them. The town was in the grip of fundamentalism and always slandered those who didn't share the faith. Bently had even heard once, from an old biddy in the drugstore, that Mr. Johnson had actually assaulted some church women!

All the product of sick minds, Bently knew. Sick people. He couldn't get out of town fast enough. His grades got him into Harvard with a full ride, and he was ready to go.

At Harvard he met the next great influence in his life. Anton Puglia was a Harvard professor who, along with Timothy Leary, had championed the use of LSD for mind expansion. He got into trouble while

Bently was there, for his secret experiments with student acolytes. Bently was one of them, and the experience changed his life forever.

It was a peak experience, like some religious sages reported, but based entirely on chemical reaction. During one "trip" Bently saw the entire history and future of biological exploration in bold colors, with himself in the center, leading the world toward a period of greater freedom and potential than it had ever known—the potential of mind to evolve itself, ultimate power in the hands of man, finally free from the shackles of religious superstition and myth.

He, Bently Davis, would change the very course of mankind. The Beatles had recently said they were more popular than Jesus. Bently Davis would truly be more popular than Jesus, more influential. He would finally purge the stain that his mother had left on him.

From his graduation day in 1969, Bently Davis had shot like a rocket through graduate school and associate professorships, landing at Harvard in the fall of 1975. His first book, *The Brain of Being,* became a *New York Times* bestseller the next year, and his celebrity status was assured.

Now the foundation had been established, the base from which he would put into place the actual plan he had first envisioned during that wondrous LSD experience years before. The project he had dubbed, in his own mind, Nephilim.

●

And now a blip had appeared in the form of this student, John Phillips, who had decided to make a cause out of opposing him. Christians were becoming very troublesome of late, especially in the courts. The worst were the creationists, who wanted science classes in public schools to give equal time to Genesis.

What claptrap! The problem was there had been some successes, and these were picked up by the press. There had even been some embarrassing tabloid fodder, such as when the dean of the Harvard Divinity School had been removed because his Harvard-owned computer was filled with pornography downloaded from the Internet.

Davis did not need any of that, especially now, when the Nephilim seed was about to be taken to the next level. This John Phillips had to be taken care of.

"You want the world to know about my many sins, is that it, John?"

"In a way."

"Will you do me one favor then, before you take on this challenge?"

"What favor?"

"Will you let me show you, just once, what I'm doing for the good of man as I see it? I'm not an evil person, John. I'd like you to see that. Didn't Jesus say to go the extra mile? Would you do that for me? Would you let me show you my UniGen office and lab?"

Some of the fight had gone out of Phillips' expression. He thought it over, then nodded. "OK."

"Good," said Bently Davis. "That's very good of you, John."

**26**

Janice awoke gasping for air.

She'd had the same dream where she was on the edge of a cliff over lava flowing below. Lauren clinging to a branch on the other side, screaming, "Help me, Mommy! I'm falling!"

"Hold on, baby!" Janice screamed again in the dream. "God will help you. Hold on!"

This time the dream continued. The branch Lauren clung to was ripping out of the side of the cliff. Lauren shrieked louder and louder, desperate for help. Janice could only stand by, watching in horror, powerless, looking to the heavens for a miracle.

Surely God would come! He would send an angel!

"Hold on, baby!"

Then the branch gave way.

She awoke into another level of terror—she didn't know where she was. Dim, early morning light seeped through a small window covered by a yellow shade. She was on a lumpy bed folded out from a sofa. And for a few seconds she could not remember how she got there.

Then she saw a large poster of a space ship on the wall, and it all came back. But her realization was only slightly better than the nightmare. Her daughter was still missing.

She closed her eyes and prayed.

She threw on a T-shirt and jeans and headed for the kitchen. Data was seated at the kitchen table, in front of a laptop, fingers flying over the keyboard.

"There's coffee," he said.

"Thanks," she said, not at all surprised at how shaken her voice sounded. She found a cup in an open cupboard and poured herself coffee from what looked like an original Mr. Coffee machine.

"Where's Jed?" she asked.

"Am I supposed to know?"

Janice took a chair opposite Data. "I should thank you."

"For what?"

"Letting us stay here."

"Like I had anything to say about it."

"Thanks just the same."

"Oh man!" He leaned back in his chair, exasperated. "I was at level nine, and I didn't use the wizard key! Idiot!"

"Something wrong?"

Data slammed the laptop closed. "Forget it. Just forget it!" Without the screen in front of him, he looked at her. "What exactly are you two doing here?"

"Didn't Jed tell you about it?"

"I wasn't in any mood to listen to him last night."

"I'm sorry for the inconvenience. I'm looking for my daughter."

"She lost?"

"Kidnapped."

A bit of hostility fell away from his expression. "Didn't know that. How you handling it?"

"I just have to keep faith that God will help me find her."

"You believe in God?"

"Oh yes."

Data sniffed loudly, took a sip of his coffee. His hawklike nose disappeared into the cup for a moment. "That's old news," he said.

"God?"

"Yeah. See, we are evolving creatures. We each have a separate identity, and it's our job to take that to the limit." He leaned forward importantly, as if about to deliver top secret news. "But there are institutions that stand in our way. Government, church, anything collective. That's why I don't have a driver's license. I won't give my Social Security number to any entity. The Social Security Administration already has it, but *I* won't give it away."

"Why not?"

Data hit the table with his fist. "Because! The use of a single common identifier in multiple relationships represents the creation of an external analog of the individual!"

Janice blinked.

"Don't you see? That creates a surrogate shadow identity, which is narrowed and limited by the perceptions and purposes of those using the analog! If I give my Social Security number to any entity, it makes a caricature of my identity and is the same as committing identity suicide!"

OK, Janice thought. *Stay calm.*

"In the seventh season of *Star Trek: The Next Generation,* Data's cat, Spot, not only changed sex but also changed breed! People thought that was a mistake by the show. That was not a mistake! It was a message to us all. We can be transformed! We can transform ourselves! I don't expect you to understand."

"Well, I—"

"Ah, it's always like this. I think on multiple planes, and nobody seems to get all the connections. Do you know how frustrating that is?"

"I have a clue, I think," Janice said. She suddenly found herself liking this guy. Maybe he was nuts, but he was at least thinking about the deeper things of life, caring about them, which was more than she could say about most of her contemporaries. She said, "Try to explain Christianity to people these days. It's frustrating, too."

"That's because it's irrational."

"Any more irrational than a surrogate shadow identity?"

Data stiffened. "That's a verifiable fact!"

"I think Christianity is too."

"Not."

"I think our society has placed too much faith in material things and not enough on spiritual things. And yet people feel empty; they're searching for meaning, but they're not looking in the right places."

"Oh yeah? Where are the right places?"

"Where God has revealed himself."

"Or *herself.*"

Janice smiled. "Not."

"Or *itself.* But how do you know that's God and not a self-referential reflection based on a need for a superior analog of the self, when the self views itself and reflects that the analog is necessary for a fullness that is missed simply because of the reflection itself? Huh? How do you know?"

Janice blinked, unable to put any of that into workable English. "Because I do," she said.

Data threw up his hands and slapped his legs. At that moment Jed barreled through the front door, carrying a large brown bag.

"Bagels," he said, "and sweet rolls. Can't face the day without a good breakfast."

"Terminal!" Data said, in a way that made Janice think he was happy. When Data hungrily went after a bear claw, she was sure.

Janice selected a raisin bagel with cream cheese. Jed took a cinnamon roll. As they all munched, Jed said, "OK, boys and girls, let's get to work."

"Work?" Data said. "What work?"

"Finding a killer," Jed said. "And you, my friend, are going to help."

"Oh man!"

 Lauren had the most awful feeling she'd had in her whole life. Worse than the first time she had a bad dream and woke up and thought she was lost to the world forever. Worse even than the last few days when her life had been thrown into a giant blender.

Those feelings were bad, but this was worse because she shouldn't have been feeling this way at all.

She couldn't help it. Even though it was morning now, and her daddy was in the next room, the feeling would not go away.

The feeling that her daddy was not her daddy.

It didn't make sense, but there it was—the gnawing sense that he was a different person entirely. That something had taken over his body, like in that movie she had once seen on TV about the body snatchers who came in giant pods. She had been scared by that one, all right.

But how could that be? He *was* her daddy! He had found her when she was lost. He had told her not to be afraid of anything, that he would take care of her.

His voice was the same. His face was the same. He even smelled the same—slight scent of aftershave mixed with his own, unique, daddy smell.

But it just didn't feel *right*.

In the little bed she'd been given—just a mattress on the floor in the corner, with a pillow and a blanket, in a room with no windows—Lauren silently prayed that her daddy would be all right. That whatever was wrong with him wouldn't hurt him. And that he wouldn't hurt her.

Her head filled with memories. They were a mixture of good and bad. Well, maybe not bad. Sad was more like it. Sad because she loved her daddy so much but didn't get to see him nearly enough.

In fact, the happiest day and the saddest day she could remember were the very same one. She must have been five at the time, and Mommy said Daddy was going to take her out to a big dinner and the movies—*The Lion King*. Somehow Lauren sensed this was a major move by her daddy to make up with Mommy. Her parents hadn't been getting along well lately.

But that didn't matter! *The Lion King!* And she'd get to be with her daddy, who was gone so much of the time!

She spent the whole day just thinking about how wonderful it would be—all of them together, just having fun. It was the happiest she had ever been.

Then it all exploded. Daddy had come home in one of his moods. The dark kind, the kind that always scared her. She stayed up in her room but could hear the shouting going on downstairs. She knew all her dreams that day were gone now, shattered.

But before he left the house, her daddy came up to her room. He sat on her bed and put Lauren in his lap. She laid her head on his shoulder. He explained to her that he had to go away for awhile, maybe a long time, but that he would never stop thinking about her. She had cried then, and he stayed with her for a long while.

It was the last time he ever held her.

The man who was with her now in this cabin in the lost woods was different. He wasn't the same one who had held her. She didn't know how she knew, but she did.

Lauren stayed in bed, saying the Twenty-third Psalm to herself, until her daddy opened the door.

"Time to eat," he said.

"Daddy?"

"Yes?"

"Why are we here?"

Sam took a step into the room. "Don't worry," he said. "You're with me."

"I'm scared. I want Mommy. Where's Mommy?"

She saw his eyes grow hard and somehow—how?—glowing a little bit. It was so strange!

"It would be best for you to forget about your mother for now," he said.

"But Daddy—"

"I said forget about her. You're with me. You're safe now. Safe from *her.*"

But what did that mean? Why safe from Mommy?

"Now don't you worry about a thing. This will all be over soon, and we'll go back home. Together. You and me."

"I'm going to go home with you?"

"Yes. Wouldn't you like that?"

Not my Daddy. Not my Daddy.

"Yes, Daddy. I'd like that very much."

He smiled at her, but it wasn't a smile with warmth in it. It was the smile of someone who has just conquered an enemy. "Now come on out and have some cereal," Sam said. "Get dressed." He left the room, closing the door behind him.

This will all be over soon, he'd said. What would all be over? How soon is soon?

This time the trip had been to hell.

In his mind Dewey felt that way, that what he had experienced was some real manifestation of a place of eternal torment. Why hadn't they told him the visions would be like that? Why was he having visions at all?

Did anyone else in the project get them this way? Did Davis or Burack?

It had come an hour after his last injection. He was back in his room, lying on his bed, the familiar rush of warmth roiling through his head like a small brushfire.

Then, without warning, the visions.

Disembodied heads floating all around him. Bloated and ugly, horrific looks on their faces, as if they were being tortured. But no sounds came out of their screaming mouths. The heads just swirled around him like a demonic mobile. They seemed to be trying to tell him something but could not give voice to their torments.

Suddenly, a white-hot blaze erupted and consumed the heads. Just like that they were gone. But the conflagration remained, filling the room. If he hadn't been incapacitated with fear, Dewey would have jumped off his bed and run out of the building. But he was afraid that if he moved the fire would take him too.

All he could do was watch, wide-eyed. And in the midst of the fire, he saw two eyes, glaring, glowing—two monstrous eyes, as real as anything he had ever seen, yet a part of some other world. The eyes did not blink. They continued to stare at him, as if in warning.

The episode lasted fifteen minutes, but it seemed like hours. When he finally came out of it, Dewey swallowed two sleeping pills and managed to sleep, fitfully, through the night.

Then this morning he'd had a flashback. The same scene he'd experienced in his apartment erupted before him again on his way to class. This terrified him even more than the original vision. If it repeated, how many times would it happen? Was he going to be like a Jekyll, never knowing when he might be hit with the internal eruption of Hyde?

Why was he getting flashbacks at all? The Nephilim gene was supposed to work without these side effects. They told him that. They *promised* him that! Were they lying to him? Were they lying to everybody?

Davis and Burack. They had some things to answer for.

As soon as he had that thought, something more horrible than the visions seared into his brain like a hot poker. It was unbelievable, and it tore at him like nothing he'd ever felt in his entire life.

Dewey Handleman had the sudden urge to kill himself.

The urge was strong, almost irresistible. Dewey had flashes of how he might do it—jump in front of an MBTA train, get a gun, hang himself. The pictures kept coming, wouldn't stop. Dewey was watching a morbid mental movie about his own demise.

And even as he did, Dewey sensed the eyes, the ones he had seen glaring at him in his bedroom, were out there, watching.

Grabbing the sides of his head, Dewey bent over, put his head between his knees, and screamed.

"Hey," a voice said. "You all right, man?"

Dewey looked up without seeing. He jumped to his feet and started running.

"Hey!" the voice called out. "Your backpack!"

Hearing, but not caring, Dewey ran as fast as he could toward Cambridge Common, wondering if this was his last day—maybe his last few minutes—of life.

As he approached the highway, with the traffic racing by, he thought *Maybe a big truck would do it, end the visions for good.*

29

"You're about to see at work the fingers that poked the eye of our nation's top secret security system," said Jed.

"And got me twenty-four months for the trouble," Data added bitterly, his laptop booting up.

Janice said, "All from this one little computer on a kitchen table?"

Data huffed. "You just don't get it, do you? It's not about environment; it's about ability, connectedness, the fifth wave. We are moving into another dimension."

"A dimension not only of sight and sound, but of mind," Jed said in his best Rod Serling voice.

Data did not laugh. "It's all here for anyone with half a brain to see it! For you two I'm not so sure."

"Feeling testy, are we?" Jed said.

"Just give me something to work with here."

"Let's get warmed up first. You got a good online source for quotations?"

"Why don't you just use *Bartlett's Familiar?*" said Data. "That's baby stuff."

"Let's make it a game then. You show me how fast you can identify the author of the following quote. You ready?"

"What do I get if I win?"

"Another week of freedom."

Janice shook her head. This was a little like watching Abbott and Costello.

"Just give me the quote," Data said, "and keep an eye on your watch."

"All right. The quote is 'All truths are soaked in blood.' Go!"

Data's fingers became a flurry, like angry bees. The tapping of the keyboard was a plastic symphony. Janice watched with awe. If she was computer literate, this guy was Mozart. Every now and then Data would mutter something like "search engine" or "enter," his eyes never leaving the screen.

Suddenly he threw up his hands and yelled, "Time!"

Jed looked at his watch. "A minute forty-three," he said. "Not bad. Assuming you got the right answer."

"Of *course* I got it. It's right here." Jed and Janice craned their necks to get a look at the laptop screen. Janice read it aloud. "'All truths are soaked in blood.' Friedrich Nietzsche."

Jed and Janice looked at each other but said nothing.

"Hello!" Data said. "Somebody want to tell me what's going on?"

"Steady, Eddie," said Jed. "Check one more thing." He read from his notepad. "See if our man Nietzsche said something about 'in the beginning was nonsense.' Use *nonsense* as the key—"

"Don't tell me my job!" Data said, his fingers flying. In less than thirty seconds he pointed to the screen. "There it is. The full quote is, 'In the beginning was nonsense, and the nonsense was with God, and the nonsense *was* God.' Now you want to tell me about it?"

"Both of them," Janice said, "Anthony and Sam, they were quoting Nietzsche? What is that all about?"

"Connection," Data said. "It's all about connection!"

"For once he's right," Jed said.

"For once?"

"Now things get harder, the connection between UniGen and Sam Ramsey. There's something there I'm not clear about. Think you can get into UniGen's records?"

Already Data was tapping away. "That is so easy. I mean, if you know what you're doing, you can run an espionage operation from anywhere in the world. You can get the name of some dork at a nuclear lab, then get his credit ratings, bank statements, school records, his mortgage, his insurance, his hospital records even."

"That's scary," Janice said.

"Welcome to the brave new world," Data said, continuing his work on the keyboard. As he tapped, he hummed something to himself. It sounded like the *Star Trek* theme.

"What's up?" Jed said, removing a small notepad from his pocket, along with a pen.

"Patience. All good things take time. I'm routing this through San Juan, Puerto Rico. Don't want them tracing us, do we?"

"Data knows all about being traced," Jed said.

"Yeah, but it took them eight months! I was such a bonehead."

"Was?"

"Shut up. Look. UniGen. Hmmm. They've got this firewall. Well, let's just see about that." *Tappity tappity tap.* "More like a gas flame." *Tappity tappity tap.* "But that's not a problem for the Data man. No, not a problem. Wait . . . Here we go. Take a look."

Janice looked, breathed out a shocked burst of air. Sam's picture was on-screen.

"That the guy?" Data said.

"Yes," Janice said. "How?"

"They got something going where they want very specific ID requirements. You'll see this at many of your major corps now, especially when they're dealing with volatile stuff. Like bio-tech. They don't want anybody walking out with their secret to curing cancer."

On the screen Sam's face seemed hard and empty. "What does it tell us?" Janice asked.

Data tapped the keyboard. Numbers appeared. "Looks like he was employed beginning in 1992."

"What?" Janice said. "Sam didn't start in pharmaceuticals until 1994."

"Unless some yo-yo made a wrong entry, that's a lie."

Yes, Janice thought. *That's it. A lie. Sam had been living a lie for a long, long time.*

Jed said, "Any record of payments?"

After a brief finger dance on the keys, Data said, "Yep. We got payments going back to late 1993. That confirms it. Thank you."

"Can you cross-check with a name?" Jed asked.

"Come on, Klingon dog, give me a hard one."

"Fine, fine. Anthony."

"Anthony who?"

"Just Anthony. See if anything comes up."

With a shrug, Data went to work. As he did, Jed looked at Janice. "Anthony was the guy's name who jumped out of the hotel room, if it wasn't a pseudo."

Janice sat back for a moment and looked at the whole scene. It was amazing. These two improbable allies, Jed and Data, were doing some extraordinary things. Data seemed to have the ability to be anywhere in the electronic world at an eye-blink's notice. And Jed had a sense, an instinct, about finding anyone in the *real* world.

She was starting to be drawn to Jed in a way that made her nervous. She didn't want to be attracted to him. He was not a believer and was about as far from her idea of a man she could love as the ACLU was from The Family Research Council. But there it was, creeping up on her like a thief in the night.

"Nothing," Data said. "I come up with nothing."

"I *know* there's a connection," Jed said. "Anthony had Sam's phone number."

"Maybe they were dating."

"You sure there isn't anything?"

"Nothing that connects them."

"How about Anthony alone?"

"Let's see." A moment later Data said, "Ah, yes. Anthony Pellegro."

"There a picture?"

"No," Data said.

"Cross Anthony with the name *Brown,* see if anything comes up."

"OK."

Tappity-tap tap-tap.

"Now I get this guy."

Janice looked at the screen. A picture of a severe, square-looking man stared out at her.

"Karel Van Hoorn," Data muttered. "What kind of an alien name is that?"

"Dutch," said Jed, writing the name down in his notepad.

"What does that mean?" Janice said.

"It means," said Jed, "he's got a Dutch name." Janice's exasperation was apparently visible, because Jed immediately put up his hand. "It doesn't mean anything right now."

Data said, "Come on, people! How much longer are we . . ." His voice trailed off as he stared at the screen.

"What's up?" Jed said.

"I'm going," Data said, tapping away quickly. He shut down the computer and closed the top.

"What's wrong," said Jed. "What happened?"

"They found me."

"You got nailed?"

"Yeah! So?"

"What's this mean?" said Janice.

"It means," Jed said, "our computer genius here was caught."

Data's face was growing redder by the second. "I wouldn't have been if you two didn't distract me!"

"Does that mean they can trace it here?" Janice said.

Jed looked to Data for the answer. "I don't know," he said. "I went through Puerto Rico!"

"Great work."

"You're the one who got me into this!"

"Gentlemen, please," Janice said.

Ignoring her, Jed said, "OK, cement fingers, let's see what you can do with this." Jed reached into his bag and pulled out a square, metallic object the size of a pad of paper.

"What is it?" Janice said.

"A hard drive," Data said. "From a laptop computer. Am I right?"

"Right," said Jed.

"And a pretty gnarly one, too. What happened?"

"It hit the ground. From a great height."

Janice said, "That couldn't be the drive from Anthony's computer, the guy who jumped, could it?"

"Why not?" said Jed, smiling.

"How did you get it?"

"I took it."

"From the crime scene?"

"Where else?"

"That's—"

"Tampering with evidence at a crime scene, yes. Now are you ready to go?"

"Where?"

"To do a little sleuthing. Or you could stay here with Data while he works. He might even let you make him some macaroni and cheese."

"Let's go," Janice said.

"Oh, and one more thing, Data. Where are the keys to your car?"

30

Dewey Handleman lay on the sidewalk, motionless. All he was aware of were his breathing and the disjointed passing of cars and pedestrians. He must have looked like one of the homeless derelicts he would earlier have so easily eliminated.

He had barely kept himself from suicide. It had been close. Only the marshaling of all his mental power kept him from hurling himself in front of a truck. He had even picked the truck, an eighteen-wheeler just a hundred yards away.

It was rage that kept him from doing it. Rage that had been inside him for as long as he could remember. Rage that came out when he was picked on by the other kids. Like the time a big kid in second grade pushed him to the ground and sat on him. Called him names. Laughed. And Dewey had reached out and grabbed a rock and thrust it at the kid's face. When the kid cried out and the blood came, Dewey was happy. Rage worked.

And when he was in junior high school and they had pantsed him in gym class. Held him down and took his gym shorts, leaving him in the middle of the gym in his jock strap. That time the rage stayed with him for days, fueling his revenge. Each of the ones who held him down got a cherry bomb in his locker one night. No one was ever able to pin that on him.

Then in high school it was a festival of rage. No friends. Just enemies. The rage bubbled and would wait. Wait for the day when he would rise to such power no one would be able to laugh at him again.

He thought the project would be the fast way to do that. But now this. They hadn't told him about this. Only his rage had overcome the almost irresistible urge to self-destruct. Now Dewey vowed to keep that rage alive.

In the several minutes he lay there on the side of the highway he decided what he would do. It came to him clearly and completely, as if his brain had formulated the plan without effort and now presented it to him as a gift.

He slowly got to his feet and began walking north.

**31**

The Ford Escort smelled of old hamburgers. That didn't surprise Janice, since several McDonald's wrappers lay crumpled on the backseat. Sitting in the passenger seat, Janice got the uneasy feeling she was going to stick to the upholstery if she tried to move.

Jed, behind the wheel, said, "Sorry about the car. He's kind of a slob."

"Maybe he's just an absentminded genius."

"No, he's a slob. But under the circumstances these wheels are the best we can do."

"He was nice to let you use it."

"Not really," Jed said. "I told him I'd break one of his fingers if he didn't let me."

"That's horrible!"

"It's a guy thing."

They were heading toward Cambridge and the UniGen office. All Jed had said was he had a little plan. The day was overcast, befitting Janice's mood. Each moment that ticked by made her feel Lauren was farther and farther away.

"We'll do a little standard surveillance," Jed explained. "Maybe Sam, or this Karel Van Hoorn, will come out or go in."

"And if not?"

"Then we just get to enjoy a lot of time in this fine machine."

Janice sighed.

"How you holding up?" Jed asked.

"I'm holding."

"I know it's tough. I had a little girl myself once."

The announcement shook Janice. She'd had no idea, in fact couldn't help thinking of Jed as the quintessential single man—a lone wolf, a rebel. But a daughter? And it seemed he had not even expected the news to pop out of his mouth.

"You're a father?" Janice said.

"Forget it."

"No, really."

"It slipped out."

"Please tell me. I'd like to know."

"No."

Janice sensed the ice wall going up. *Leave it alone,* she thought instantly, but then realized she didn't want to leave it alone. Not this time. For years in her marriage she couldn't get through to Sam, could never get him to talk to her on a deep level. He stayed hidden from her. And it had cost her family big time. If she was going to continue on this quest, she was going to know who was with her on it.

"Look," she said, "I don't know who you think I am or what I might do or say, but you asked me to trust you, and I'm asking you to do the same. I want to know about your daughter. Please."

"You don't want to know."

"But I do. I really do."

"Look, her name is Melody."

"That's a nice name. How old is she?"

"Last time I saw her, she was three."

"When was the last time?"

"That's enough."

"Come on."

"Forget it."

"No," Janice said.

"Why not?" Jed said angrily. "What makes you so interested in my personal life?"

"Because you're a human being, that's all! Is that so difficult to understand? That I might want just a little human contact here?" Janice was surprised at the vehemence of her words.

For a minute Jed drove in silence. Finally, he said, "Human contact isn't all it's cracked up to be."

There was a deep sadness in his voice, a descent into quietness that signaled no further trespassing. Janice wanted to reach into that sadness for no other reason than to relieve suffering.

"Maybe," she said, "you'll feel differently in time."

"You mean God's timing, don't you?" A coolness had returned to his voice.

"Is that so hard to believe?"

"Yes."

"Why?"

"If there really is a God up there like you believe, like I used to believe, you know what I'd say to him?"

"What?"

"I'd say, 'What have you done for me lately, pal?'"

Then, through the ice wall, he said. "We're here."

●

Praying. Alone. Scared.

I bet Daniel was scared just a little bit. I bet Paul was scared. You gave them courage, right, God?

Lauren knew God would help her. She felt it almost immediately, a flood of courage entering her body, a new surge of strength. There was something strange going on here. Her father wasn't really her father. Something had happened to him, and she sensed it was about to happen to her.

Oh God, bring Daddy back!

That would be her prayer. Bring Daddy back to his senses. Maybe he was just upset over the fighting with Mommy about custody. He was stressed out; that was it. He'd get it together soon, wouldn't he?

She prayed that he would.

A quick knock, and the door opened. Her father said quickly, "What are you doing?"

"Just praying, Daddy."

"Come with me."

Lauren stood and walked to Sam. When she reached him, he took her by the hand and led her outside the cabin. She didn't see Rance or Steven anywhere.

The day was bright and sunny, and the light in the trees gave everything a garden effect. God's secret garden. It was almost like a message from him that everything was still beautiful, and she shouldn't worry.

But her father held her hand hard. He pulled her silently down the long road until he made a quick turn into the woods.

"Where are we going?" Lauren asked.

"Just a little farther."

Her hand was starting to hurt because of his grip. Was it going to be now? Was this terrible thing they were going to do to her about to happen?

Don't worry. Be like Daniel.

A small clearing opened up before them. It looked as if someone had purposefully cleared the trees to create a space. Lauren could see something in the middle of this clearing, slightly covered with leaves. It became clear that her father was taking her to this thing, whatever it was.

When they got to it, she saw clearly that it was a dead thing. An animal. She didn't want to see it. But when she resisted, Sam pulled her harder.

"Please, Daddy."

"Look at it."

"I don't want to."

"Look!"

He was going to make her, no matter what she did. With eyes half-closed she turned slowly toward the awful, dead thing. And when she saw it was a dog, she started to cry.

"Why, Daddy?"

Sam, his grip still a vice on her little hand, pulled her to him as he knelt down.

"I killed that dog," he said. His eyes were cold.

"Why did you do that . . . ?" This time she could not say the word *Daddy*.

"Because I want you to understand. I want you to see. I want you to know."

"Know . . . what?"

"We're all animals. You, me, your mother, that dog. Animals. And we are either going to be killed by other animals or survive. Do you want to end up like that dog?"

"No."

"Then you must become stronger than the other animals. The other human animals. That's why you were brought here. You are a very lucky little girl. You are going to be given a great gift."

As she looked into the darkness of her father's eyes, Lauren could not imagine what such a gift would be.

"A very smart man has given us a way to jump ahead of all other human animals. He has invented a way to increase the strength of your brain. To make it more powerful than you could ever imagine. Think of that, Lauren. You can have the greatest brain in the world!"

Suddenly his eyes took on new life, almost glowing with enthusiasm. Or craziness. "How can I?" Lauren asked.

"You can't understand it now," Sam explained. "You won't be able to appreciate it fully until after. But basically it is a way to speed up human evolution, by putting a special gene right into your brain. What this does is allow the brain to use more of its power than ever before. And because you're so young, you'll have a chance to develop it even further. You'll be the smartest person who ever lived!"

"But that's not right."

"What's not right?"

"God makes us who we are."

She felt her father—or what used to be her father—stiffen. The dead coldness came back to his eyes. "You have to forget all that. That's a lie."

"It's *not* a lie!" She tried to pull away from him, but he held her shoulders fast.

"Listen to me! You're just a little girl. You've been told lies all your life by your mother, by your teachers, by everybody except me. And I'm telling you now that you are going to get a greater gift than you could have ever imagined. But I need you to accept it, Lauren. If you fight it, something may go wrong."

Wrong?

"You have to trust me, Lauren. I'm your father—"

You're not my Daddy!

"—and I'm telling you not to fight this."

I will!

"Because if you do, you're just going to end up . . ."

Like that dog, right? That's what he's saying. Dead like that dog.

Oh God, make him stop now! Bring my real daddy back!

●

"Soda?" Bently Davis asked.

Of course John Phillips would say yes. Davis's research had revealed a ton of relevant information about Phillips, including the seemingly obscure fact that he loved Coca-Cola. But nothing was obscure if you knew how to use it. Even a Coke could be a weapon.

"Thank you," John Phillips said. "A Coke?"

Davis smiled. "Of course." They were in Davis's UniGen office, a large cube of pure white. Davis pressed a button on a console and said, "Karel, please bring Mr. Phillips a Coke, will you? Herbal tea for me."

Davis looked back at Phillips. "I want you to know, John, that I appreciate your giving me a chance to show you what I'm doing off campus. Sometimes people think Harvard professors are off in their own little worlds, with no connection to reality."

Phillips smiled. "Like Professor Dershowitz?"

"Ah, Alan," Davis said. "He's over in the law school, you know. Different breed over there."

Phillips laughed good-naturedly, and that's when Davis knew the rest would be easy.

"I feel we needed this chance to get to know each other," Davis said. "Mutual understanding and all that."

Nodding, Phillips said, "Yes, but I want you to try to understand where I'm coming from too."

"Naturally."

"God is the most important thing in my life."

Davis nodded, trying hard not to say something sharp edged.

"I feel like modern science doesn't appreciate at all the possibility that God is an actual reality," Phillips said.

"Well, that's not what Steve Gould thinks, is it?" Davis secretly loathed

Stephen Jay Gould but was always ready to trot out his name if it served his purposes. "Have you read his latest book?"

"Gould will give religion a bone but won't let it come to the table," John Phillips said. Davis had to admire that. This kid could turn a phrase. Harvard was full of rough talent, waiting to be mined. If Davis could polish this one up according to his own specs, he could be a real asset.

"But God is forever beyond the discipline of science, John. We have to acknowledge that."

"I don't think so. If we see evidence of a designer, why should science say that a designer can't possibly exist?"

"Because science works on the observable, John. Nothing more."

"I think science is arrogant," Phillips said.

Squinting slightly, Davis said, "What is arrogant about pursuit of truth, John?"

"Because naturalistic science, as it is widely practiced, operates as a kind of religion. Yet the scientists refuse to acknowledge that. It's like they have a set of blinders on."

"You think I wear blinders?"

Swallowing, John Phillips said, "Sometimes, maybe."

Karel entered the office carrying a tray with the beverages. Davis watched as Phillips took his Coke and gave Karel a perplexed stare.

"This is Karel Van Hoorn," Davis said. "One of my assistants. I'd be lost without him."

Karel nodded at the student. "Pleased to meet you," he said in a thick accent, pronouncing each word slowly.

"Thank you very much," Phillips said.

"That'll do, Karel," Davis said. Karel bowed slightly and left. Davis waited for Phillips to take a drink and then said, "You were telling me I wear blinders."

"I didn't mean to insult you, sir. It's more of a worldview idea, I think."

"Explain."

"The way one chooses to see things. Naturalism is a worldview. It takes as its starting point the assumption that everything in the universe is natural and impersonal, that there is no supernatural."

"Because it cannot be observed, John."

"But that just doesn't make sense," Phillips said, taking a big swig of Coke. "Just because something is unseen doesn't mean it doesn't exist."

"But how can science say anything about that?"

"There are clues. Design in nature is one of those clues."

"Design *by* nature, John."

"But nature doesn't design on the order of complexity we see. Look at the cell. There is no Darwinian explanation for what we see on the cellular level."

"There is, John. We just haven't found it yet."

Shaking his head, Phillips said, "Isn't that a cop-out?"

"No, John, it's the scientific method. Are you feeling all right?"

The young man had his hand on his forehead. "I don't know," he said. "My head . . ."

"Feeling sick?"

Phillips didn't answer. He dropped his glass on the carpet and put both hands on the sides of his head, rubbing at his temples.

"Let me call a doctor," Davis said.

John Phillips fell off his chair in a heap, thudding onto the floor, unconscious.

"Oh doctor," Davis said quietly. And then he smiled.

He buzzed for Van Hoorn.

When the big man entered, Davis said, "Take him to the cabin lab. We'll try the new gene on him."

Van Hoorn nodded, then said, "There was a security breach."

Davis felt a shot of nervous alarm. He didn't like it. "What are you talking about?"

"Somebody tapped into our system."

"Who?"

"We're working on it."

"Well you do that! I want to know where it came from! This is absurd!"

Van Hoorn said nothing. Davis did not like the fact that his emotions were running high. He thought he would have had more control than this.

It was the fraying around the edges that did it. Janice Ramsey had been traced to Cambridge, then lost. And someone was helping her. Was that the connection with this security breach?

If it was, there were some unanswered questions out there, things about the project's viability he didn't know. And if there was anything Davis hated, it was not knowing.

He would have to step up the plans.

The girl. She was the important one. It was time to do the girl.

 **32** For an hour Jed said nothing. He just stared across the street at the building he'd identified as housing UniGen. Janice didn't know what to say and so said nothing. She knew he wanted to be left alone.

Jed's revelation about having a daughter was explosive to her. She sensed in him a loss, a deep spiritual pain, yet he had rejected the spiritual.

He seemed beyond caring.

In a way Jed was like Sam, though to a lesser extent. Where Sam had fallen into a darkness of violence and evil, Jed had merely stepped into it. And he didn't seem to care if he went further.

All she could do was silently pray that whatever had happened to him in the past God would use to lead him back to the light.

"You hungry?" Jed asked without turning his head.

"No, I'm fine."

"There's a sandwich place."

"No, thank you."

"I guess I'm not very good company."

"It's all right."

"But this is what tracking is like. You spend a lot of time in cars, sitting."

"It must be very lonely."

Jed said nothing.

"What exactly are we looking for?" Janice asked.

"Any one of these guys," Jed said, pointing to the paper on the car seat that contained the images of the UniGen principals that Data had managed to save.

"What then?"

"We improvise."

"That's *it?*"

"You never know what'll happen. Depends on the people, the mix, the circumstances. You have to improvise. That's part of life."

Janice shook her head. "I guess as a lawyer I always want to know what the plan is."

"Not as exciting that way, though."

There was a hint of jocularity in his voice again. Janice smiled. "I guess not. I just wish we had more to go on."

"We've got some links."

"What links?"

"Nietzsche, first of all."

"What do you see there?"

"You know anything about him?"

"A little, from college courses. He influenced the Nazis, right?"

"Hitler took his concept of the superman and twisted it into the concept of a master race, sure. But Nietzsche was into a lot more than that. The death of God, the will to power. He rejected all religious understanding."

"An atheist."

"The atheist of atheists. For him all knowledge was invention, and inventions were lies. Religion was the biggest lie. So his only answer was to learn to lie creatively. Sort of like presidential politics."

He turned to look at her briefly. "Along with Darwin and Freud, Nietzsche is the big influence of our age."

"They all fell short, in my opinion."

"I don't know. Nietzsche may have been right."

"What?"

"Yeah. Which is a pretty terrifying thought, isn't it?"

"I don't buy any of it."

"Sure, but what if God really is dead?"

"Nietzsche is the one who's dead."

"But what *if?*" Jed looked at her. His face was now devoid of any jocularity.

"If that were so, life wouldn't be worth living."

"And now you know where I'm at."

Janice sensed the ice wall going up and said nothing. She closed her eyes and leaned her head back. In a few moments she found she was praying silently for Jed Brown.

When she opened her eyes, Jed was leaning forward. He had a small tube up to his eye. A telescope.

Janice looked out the window and saw a dark blue car pulling out of an underground garage.

"What is it?" Janice asked.

"I recognize the car. It was watching Bob Thomas's house."

Jed pulled the car into traffic. "And I think the guy driving is Van Hoorn."

"Who?"

"One of the guys Data brought up on the screen. I'm going to stay with him."

"Why am I not surprised?"

Jed kept a couple of car lengths' distance from the blue car. Janice had to admire his technique. Even in the midst of the city rush, Jed stayed with the blue car, timing stoplights perfectly, weaving when necessary. Obviously good at his job.

"I think there's someone in the car with him," he said at one point.

Janice's pulse accelerated. "Lauren?"

"Can't tell. But he keeps looking in the back. Don't get your hopes up."

But they were up. Janice kept a prayer looping through her head that Lauren would be there.

The blue car caught the 99 heading north. Jed let a little more distance form between the two cars. "Looks like a long haul," he said.

"Why?"

"Don't know. But I see this guy as a messenger boy. Only question is what is he delivering?"

The blue car kept on, as if taking a long, leisurely drive in the country. At least this part of the country was beautiful. Janice had always liked New England. She had been here once during the changing of the seasons, when the leaves were various shades of amber and gold. God's canvas. Janice allowed herself a small respite of enjoyment.

"He's going rustic," Jed said presently. "This is going to be tough."

"Why?"

"Because he'll spot me. Two cars on lonely roads. He'll know."

"What are we going to do?"

"Improvise."

●

Sam Ramsey sucked in a long breath of clean air, sensing every atom of it. The forest air was crisp, pure. Like his brain—pure thought power, pure potential—and devoid of the stale pollution of emotion.

That is what Davis had promised, and that is what he delivered.

Sure, there was a cost. Sam was dependent—an addict; he would admit it, but it was power he was addicted to, and Davis gave that to him. The power to overcome anything.

He would overcome Janice, too, when the time came. Wherever she was, whoever she was with (the guy who had knocked him out, and oh, how he would pay), Sam would make sure she was eliminated.

Then it would be just Lauren to worry about. Not that she would cause any worry. Once the injections started, she would belong to Davis, and Sam's debt would be paid. Davis would have his grand experiment, a child who would grow with increased capacities and eventually bear Davis his own child. Either voluntarily or involuntarily. In the womb or out.

And Sam would have injections forever.

That was the deal. The only thing Sam wondered was how early on Davis had decided Sam would go for it.

Sam first met Davis on a sales trip to Boston. Sam had been spending more and more time on the road—purposely. Janice was driving him crazy. Getting sucked back into going to church, talking about it all the time. It was a slap in the face, that's what it was. She had no respect for him at all.

When he'd made that final call one day downtown, he didn't really want to go back. He wanted to find something else to do. So when he saw the little notice about a lecture at Harvard, featuring Bently Davis, that was the ticket. The title of the lecture was "Who Needs Religion?" Perfect.

While Sam had heard of Davis—never read any of his books yet, though—he wasn't prepared for what he heard that evening. In the packed lecture hall this guy Davis absolutely mesmerized the place. Speaking without notes, moving around the stage like a leopard on the prowl, Davis threw out one dazzling idea after another. Each idea, it seemed, was a bombshell directed at firmly held religious ideas.

Sam got caught up in Davis's talk in a way that was almost adolescent. If he had been religious, he would have called it a religious experience. But it was merely the meeting of two minds—Sam's, poised and ready to hear the message; Davis, delivering it with the zest and eloquence of the greatest speakers of the age.

One part of the speech was so audacious, so clear and sharp, that the words still rang in Sam's head.

"Mother Teresa!" Davis had shouted, referring to the nun who worked with the poorest of the poor in Calcutta and who had been much in the news of late. "She is a selfish old woman! Just like all of us, possessed of the naturally selfish instincts evolution has given us. Why does she give her life away caring for those miserable examples of humanity? Out of some altruistic urge? Out of some perverse concept of love? No! What she is doing is buying her way into heaven! It is just another form of Catholic indulgence!"

Finally, Sam thought, *someone who tells it like it really is!* Someone who gave voice to the deep troublings of his own heart, inner currents that had been there since his Catholic school days.

That's why Catholics, Protestants, and any other religious sect were just as screwed up as everybody else, Sam now knew, because religion didn't recognize the evolutionary forces that shaped it!

A yearning of huge proportion welled up in Sam. He could not recall ever feeling this way. It was almost hypnotic. He had to meet Davis.

He waited over an hour after the lecture. Davis was surrounded by well-wishers, most of them young, most of them women. He held court as Sam, fascinated, watched. And overheard more dazzling ideas tossed out as easily as a farmer would scatter seed.

When Davis made for the stage door, the crowd having thinned out considerably, Sam stepped forward. His greeting was standard, but there must have been something in his eyes, Sam thought later. Davis must have seen it. Which is why he consented to have coffee with him.

Sam had poured out his enthusiasm. He wanted to know everything about Davis's beliefs and background. When Davis began with his own story, Sam was spellbound. He knew from the start that the man sitting across from him was a genius.

Davis spoke to him of Darwin that night, of the possibilities of human evolution. He tied it in somehow with the philosophy of Nietzsche, though Sam had no knowledge of the German philosopher. Even so, the way Davis explained it made so much sense. Some people were better than others. Some could become supermen. All it took was the technology. And the technology was almost here!

Sam knew about biotechnology. He knew many companies were going into the development of synthetic DNA for various purposes. What he was not aware of, and what Davis slowly revealed, were the astounding possibilities of computer chips to work directly on the human brain.

It was almost too much to believe—science fiction stuff—but Davis assured him it was almost here. It was called nanotechnology.

A nanometer, Davis explained, is one-billionth of a meter. A typical atom is .2 nanometers. The period at the end of a printed sentence is about 700,000 nanometers.

Using X-ray lithography, synthetic nanospheres containing millions of circuits could be produced, all on genetic material that would not be rejected by the human body. Then, once injected into the bloodstream, these nanospheres—programmed according to human design—could go directly to any portion of the human body they were directed to go.

We could, Davis said, become our own God! Christians believed that God programmed all of humanity with his Spirit. But it would soon be possible to do the very same thing, and more. We could program people with the right *philosophy.* We could do away with the weak-minded beliefs of the past and take away obstacles—like human emotion—that muck up the works.

How did he like that? Davis asked.

More than he could say, Sam knew. But it must have been evident in his expression, because that's when Davis asked if Sam wanted to be part of the greatest research project in the history of the world.

Sam agreed immediately and took his first injection that night.

With it came a clarity unlike anything he had ever known before and a euphoria that took over every fiber of his being. He wanted more.

And he got it.

As the weeks and months went on, Sam became more and more addicted to the Nephilim gene that was changing his brain and body.

Then, about a year ago, Davis asked him if he wanted to continue.

Of course! How could it be any other way? How could he possibly stop now?

Davis said the program was costly, and not all subjects could continue the treatments. But if Sam were willing to do one thing, it could be arranged to have him stay on the program forever.

Anything, Sam said.

Davis asked him about Lauren. Would Sam be willing to offer his daughter to the project? They needed to know how it would affect children and whether the new capacities would be replicated in offspring. Lauren would reap all the benefits of the program and then, when she was of age, have a child with Bently Davis.

It would be the ultimate experiment.

Sam quickly agreed; by that time his emotions were gone, and he could be completely rational about it. Nothing was wrong with the plan. His daughter was just another biological creature who could be used for the greater good.

The good, in this case, being the beginning of a new race of perfect people.

Now it was all about to happen. Lauren was in the cabin, awaiting her chance at immortality. Sam almost wished he could feel happiness now, just to enjoy the moment all the more.

Life was good indeed.

**33**

Jed chose to improvise just outside a little town Janice didn't catch the name of. It was quaint, though, with a definite New England twist. Tourist shops mixed with real local businesses. Lots of available parking spaces.

The blue car cruised through Main Street, Jed allowing more space.

Now they were on a road with two lanes and no traffic. Just the two cars.

Jed sped up.

"What are you doing?" Janice said.

"Passing."

He closed in on the rear bumper of the blue car just as it went into a curve. When they came out of it Jed gunned the Escort into the opposite lane in an attempt to pass the blue car.

Janice closed her eyes and kept them closed until she felt the car slow. When she opened her eyes again, she saw that the blue car was still in front of them.

"Lousy Escort!" Jed blurted. "It couldn't pass a butterfly."

The blue car was starting to pull away.

"Does he know?" Janice said.

"That we're following him? I don't think so. I think he just didn't want to be passed by an Escort."

"So now what?"

"We go for the road rage."

"Excuse me?"

"I'm going to chase after him like I'm mad."

"What good will that do?"

"I'm hoping it will slow him down." Jed had the Escort going seventy now. Janice thought for a moment it might be too much. She imagined the car breaking into a thousand pieces at seventy-five.

"He doesn't want some slob following him," Jed explained. "He's on a mission for UniGen. He'll stop and try to beat some sense into me."

"A fight?"

"Ever seen one?"

"What if he has Lauren in that car?"

"This is a chance to get her out."

A pounding started in the middle of Janice's forehead. She put her finger there and rubbed.

"Don't worry," said Jed. "I was born for this."

●

The man who used to be Lauren's daddy was trying hard to seem normal. He held Lauren's hand tenderly, but it was cold to the touch. Lauren didn't fight it. This wasn't the time.

He was walking with her a short way from the cabin, keeping his voice calm. That must be part of this thing they were going to do to her. Keep her quiet. Gain her trust.

"You have to know I'd never hurt you," Sam said.

"Yes, Daddy," Lauren said. She would play along for now.

"I want you to understand just what is going on here."

"All right."

The afternoon sun gave the forest a soft, nonthreatening hue. Lauren felt for a moment like God was showing himself to her.

"You know, there are people who have done wonderful things with science," Sam explained. "Did you know that?"

"Of course, Daddy."

"Sure you do. Science has given us medicine and drugs and things to keep us healthy."

"Band-Aids?"

"Yeah, sure. Band-Aids too. That's what's so great about science, you see? It helps people."

Lauren nodded.

"Now, I know a man who has invented a wonderful scientific thing," Sam continued. "It will help people be very smart and healthy."

"What is it?"

"Well, it's sort of like vitamins."

"I take Flintstones vitamins."

"Exactly. Just like that. Only this kind of vitamin goes right into our blood."

"How?"

"With a shot."

"I don't like shots!"

"Oh, this shot doesn't hurt at all. It's over very quickly."

Lauren didn't believe him. Shots always hurt a little. "Do I have to, Daddy?"

"Yes."

So that was it. A shot of some kind. That's the thing they were going to do to her. "What does this vitamin do, Daddy?"

"Well, it goes right up to the brain." Sam stopped, squatted down and held Lauren's shoulders. "There's actually a way to deliver what's called a synthetic DNA molecule."

"What's that?"

"A very amazing thing. It is actually delivered on a virus."

"Those are bad."

"Not this kind. It's what we call benign. That means friendly."

"A friendly virus?"

"Yes."

"I'm scared."

"You don't have to be."

He looked at her with those cold eyes. Lauren found no solace there.

"There's this thing called the blood-brain barrier," Sam said. "I don't expect you to understand, but it's wonderful. That barrier used to prevent molecules from being delivered to the brain. But the man I'm talking about has found a way to overcome the barrier. He attaches a certain kind of protein to the outside of the virus which overcomes the barrier. The protein is called a ciliary neurotrophic factor."

"I don't understand this, Daddy."

"You don't have to. All you have to know is that it works wonderfully. What happens is this. The DNA molecule activates certain parts of the brain that have not been accessed before. It stimulates a cascade of new cognitive ability!"

"Cog . . . ?"

"It's like this. Think of what happens when you tell two friends a secret, and then they tell two friends, and on and on. Or think of a waterfall that splurges along a series of rocky steps. The final result, the pool at the bottom, is many steps removed from that first waterfall, right?"

"Uh-huh."

"That's a cascade. What we are able to do is give people's brains that ability, something that's never happened before in human evolution. Isn't that wonderful?"

"I guess so," said Lauren.

"Look at me," Sam said. "I'm a thousand times smarter than I used to be."

"You got a shot?"

"Several of them. And it's a great feeling! Now you're going to get to experience it too. You're going to be the first child to get it. Doesn't that make you excited?"

Lauren said nothing. She was not excited. But she didn't want to say anything to make Sam upset.

"And guess what else?" Sam said.

"What, Daddy?"

"They will also put some tiny, tiny computer chips into you. Think about that! These will help you even more! This is called science, honey."

"Won't it hurt, Daddy?"

"No, I promise. You're going to be the smartest little girl in the whole wide world."

"When?"

"In just a few hours. Isn't that wonderful?"

No.

Lauren looked into his eyes, looking for the Daddy she used to know. Was he in there somewhere? The one who had once been kind to her? She kept looking, until Sam suddenly turned his head away.

"What's the matter, Daddy?"

"Nothing."

"Are you sick?"

"No."

"You're hurting my shoulder."

Sam snatched his hand away. He stood and looked up, as if searching for something. Then suddenly put his hands on his head.

"Daddy, what's wrong?"

"Nothing I said."

"I can pray for you."

"Quiet!"

"Please—"

"Quiet, quiet!" He turned his back on her.

Something was terribly wrong with her father. She didn't know why, but just then she had a thought. Maybe it was her daddy trying to get out again. He was lost inside that body and wanted out! She would pray for that. Oh, she would pray hard.

●

A slow-moving truck with "Wide Ride" across the back gave Jed the opportunity to catch up to the blue car. There was a house on the truck, taking up most of the two lanes. The blue car couldn't pass.

"Perfect," Jed muttered. He started honking at the blue car.

Janice saw the driver—Van Hoorn, Jed had called him—glare back at them.

"This is called forcing his hand," Jed said.

The blue car pulled to the shoulder of the road, near a field of dry grass. The wide ride lumbered on. Jed stopped the Escort about twenty feet away and said, "Stay on your toes."

Janice, at that moment, could not feel her toes.

Jed got out of the car. "Hey!" he yelled.

Van Hoorn emerged. He was dressed in a tight black shirt over a muscular physique. He looked dangerous. And angry.

"You crazy?" Van Hoorn screamed at Jed. "What you want?"

"Where'd you learn to drive, pal?" Jed said, approaching.

"You stop there," Van Hoorn said. His hands were empty, but Janice got the distinct impression they could be filled with a weapon at any time.

Jed stopped his approach. "Who you got in the car?" he said.

"Eh?"

"I said who is in the car with you?"

Van Hoorn's look grew harder. "I tell you nothing."

"You'd better start," Jed said. With a lightning move he pulled out his Taser. Van Hoorn's eyes widened. He said nothing.

Holding the Taser at Van Hoorn's chest, Jed called back to the Escort. "Come out here."

Janice didn't move. Van Hoorn looked at her. Their eyes met for a moment. A cold moment.

"I said get out," Jed ordered.

Slowly, Janice emerged.

"Go over and see who's in the car."

She didn't need another prompt. With Van Hoorn's eyes on her all the way, she ran to the blue car, hoping to find her daughter there.

But she wasn't there. Sprawled across the back seat was a young man.

"Well?" Jed said.

"I don't know who it is," Janice answered. "But he looks hurt."

"Is he alive?"

Janice looked closer. "He's breathing."

"Any blood?"

"No."

Back to Van Hoorn, Jed said, "So who is it, Karel?"

The sound of his name jolted Karel Van Hoorn. Clearly on the defensive now, maybe he'd give them the information they needed to find Lauren. Janice walked slowly toward Jed.

Van Hoorn maintained his icy silence.

"What about it, Karel?" Jed repeated. "You going to talk to me, or do we have to go back and see the town sheriff?"

Gears turned in Van Hoorn's head. His blue eyes darted back and forth between Jed and Janice.

"Put your hands in the air, Karel," Jed said.

Slowly, Van Hoorn raised his hands.

"Karel, make it easy on yourself," Jed said. "We only want to find out about the girl."

Janice watched for a sign in Van Hoorn's face. But he stayed impassive.

"You know about the girl, right?"

Van Hoorn just stared.

"Last chance," said Jed, putting his other hand on the Taser, aiming.

"You're not going to shoot me with that thing," Van Hoorn said.

"No?"

"You are crazy, but not that kind of crazy. Right, lady?"

"He's very crazy," Janice said. "I don't know what he's capable of."

"Thanks," said Jed.

"Don't mention it," said Janice.

"You both crazy," said Van Hoorn.

"Which is double the worse for you, pal," Jed said. He took three steps and put the Taser a foot from Van Hoorn's neck. "Now flap."

"Flap?" Van Hoorn said.

"Your lips."

Janice heard a car come whizzing down the highway. Maybe it was the combination of the two things, but in that instant Jed looked at her, and that was all Van Hoorn needed. He thrust his right hand out at the same time he whirled to the side. His hand grabbed Jed's wrist and pushed it downward. With his left fist he unfurled a wicked punch into Jed's face.

The car, a black Lexus, sped right by.

Jed stumbled backward. His foot hit a rock, and he went down. Van Hoorn was on top of him immediately. The two became a snarl of body parts.

Janice could see the Taser in Jed's hand and Van Hoorn's grip on Jed's wrist.

She took two steps toward them, a swirl of thoughts in her head.

The two men rolled over three times. Van Hoorn was on top. He was strong. Jed could not gain an advantage.

And Van Hoorn was slowly gaining control of the weapon. He was turning Jed's hand and arm toward Jed's body.

Janice waited no longer. She ran at the big man and threw her arms around his neck at the same time she wrapped her legs around his body. She felt the tendons in Van Hoorn's neck. They were like steel cables. She knew instantly he would be able to flick her off him in moments.

But moments were all she needed. She hoped.

Surprise worked for her. Van Hoorn's body jerked, his rage apparent, as he listed to the right.

Janice hit the ground, Van Hoorn's body pounding her down. Still Janice held tight. Her head crunched against some small rocks in the weeds.

She sensed Jed's body flailing.

And then Van Hoorn sent his elbow into her ribs. Pain exploded up her side. The air whooshed out of her lungs.

That's when she let go.

Van Hoorn's body slipped away. With her head on the ground, Janice could only see a swirl of legs and arms. And weeds. A thatch of brown grass ground into her eyes.

She closed her eyes and fought for breath. Her wheezing was audible as her lungs cried out for air.

She could hear the men crunching weeds, and then suddenly the noise stopped.

Janice opened her eyes again.

And saw Van Hoorn's back. He was on the ground.

"Janice!"

Jed's voice. Janice rolled onto her back, her face feeling raw, her side throbbing. She had no voice to answer.

"Just take it easy," Jed said. "Don't worry."

From the corner of her eye she saw Jed standing, holding the Tazer on Van Hoorn. Van Hoorn was not moving.

Breath came back to her slowly. She relaxed, breathed easy, waited.

The sound of another car came from the highway. Only this time it did not pass. Janice could hear it slowing, pulling to a stop on the shoulder of the road.

Help. Maybe it was someone who could call for help.

She could not see the car, but she could see Jed. His expression was taut.

Then a voice from the new arrival. "Put down your weapon!"

The unmistakable order of a man in uniform.

"Officer," Jed said. "Let me explain—"

"Put down your weapon now!"

Jed lowered the Taser to the ground.

When she was little, Janice often had dreams about being in a locked room. The room was always dark, and there were things that went bump. But the door was locked, and she couldn't get out.

Usually, she woke up screaming, and her mother would come in and stay with her, stroking her hair, until she went back to sleep. When Janice was around twelve, the dreams stopped. She hadn't had a similar nightmare since.

Until now.

Only this was real.

The bars of the holding cell were more secure than any door. The dim lighting, from a single bulb in the middle of the ceiling, was barely enough to qualify as illumination.

At least she had company.

Jed sat in the adjacent cell, one of four. Across from her was some kid, maybe nineteen, and in the fourth a man sleeping. From the sound of the snores, he was a drunk.

She wondered where Karel Van Hoorn was, and the young man who had been in his car.

For his part Jed looked uncommonly comfortable

in his cell. He was sitting with his legs up on his cot, hands folded in his lap. As if he'd been in this position before.

That set Janice off. "So *now* what?"

"We wait," Jed said.

"Wait! For what? For whom?"

"They'll be back in a while to tell us what's up."

"How long?"

"Don't know. These little towns have their own clock."

Janice couldn't remember the name of the place. She'd only gotten a quick glimpse of the sign from the back of the sheriff's Bronco. Oddly enough, it reminded her of a town she'd once seen in a Norman Rockwell print. Obviously, Rockwell had never been thrown in the slammer.

"But we haven't even had a chance to explain," Janice said.

"We will."

"Hey, what're you in for?" the kid across the way said. He had bleached-blond hair, spiked with gel, and wore a black tank top over jeans and boots. Both arms had tattoos up and down.

Janice didn't answer.

"You rob a bank, steal a car? What?"

"Ignore him," Jed said to Janice.

"That's right," the kid said. He was sitting on his cot facing outward, his knees up. "Kiss me off." Then he started to laugh. It was more of a cackle, a sort of crazed stream of noise.

Janice rubbed her temples. Her head was starting to beat a drum.

"Yessir," the kid continued. "That just about sums it up, don't it? Love thy neighbor as thyself. We're all living like Jee-zus."

The way he said it, exaggerating the name, set her off.

"Don't use his name that way," she snapped, surprising herself.

"What are you talkin' about, lady?"

"Jesus, that's who. Do you know Jesus?"

Jed said, "Don't go there."

Janice ignored him and looked at the kid. He stared at her with a mixture of bemusement and hate. But it was not focused hate, directed at her. She was just a representative. He hated everybody.

Why should she care? Why not just ignore him? Her nerves were frayed, she knew. That made her less than the model of civility at the moment. And being in a jail cell like a common criminal didn't help. She'd had enough of being pushed around for the moment. And maybe, just maybe, she wasn't just talking to one lost kid. She had not been able to crack through to Jed Brown directly. In a way this was a flank attack.

"Jesus?" the kid said. "Oh my *Jeezus?* Do I know *Jeezus?*"

"That's right." She remembered her sessions at Joliet. She'd looked into a lot worse eyes there. This kid wasn't going to get to her.

"What are you on, lady?"

"Just wanted to know."

"Give it up," Jed said.

Janice looked at him and said, "No." She was surprised at the sharpness in her voice.

"That's right, Popeye," the kid said. "You listen to the lady."

Janice could feel Jed smoldering, but he said nothing.

"So what about it?" Janice said.

"What's your game, lady?" the kid snapped.

"I asked you a question."

"So?"

"So it passes the time, doesn't it?"

"That's what we all got in here, baby. Lots of time."

"Time runs out. Then what?"

With a laugh the kid said, "Well, that's the question, ain't it?"

"What's your answer?"

"What is a nice, pretty lady like you doing in here, anyway?"

Jed snorted. "He's not going to answer you. He's afraid."

Suddenly the kid jumped up from his cot and grabbed the bars of his cell. His eyes were wide and wild. "I ain't afraid of nothin'!" he screamed, a spray of spit shooting out with the words. "You get put in here with me, and I'll show you afraid!"

Jed yawned and remained in his comfortable repose.

"You hear that, lady? I'll remember him!"

"I don't think you're afraid," she said.

"No way!"

"You'd answer the question, wouldn't you?"

The kid looked trapped now, like a caged tiger. He wanted to get at them, chew them up, but it wasn't going to happen. Not yet.

"You're starting to get on my nerves, lady."

"Good."

"Huh?"

"There's one way out for you."

"I'm not listening."

"You can dis the name of Jesus all you want, but that won't change the fact that he died on a cross for you."

"Turn it off!"

"You better get that straight before it's too late."

"Shut up."

"You better get your nose in a Bible and check it out."

"I said shut up."

"I won't shut up." Janice felt her face flush and her pulse rate jump.

The kid put both hands over his ears and screamed.

A moment later the jail door flew open, and a young deputy charged in. "What is all this?" he demanded.

The kid turned his back on him.

"Who was screaming?"

"The young man across the way," Janice said.

"Why?"

"Get her out of here!" the kid yelled. "She's crazy!"

"Now look here—"

Jed said, "Sir."

"What is it?"

"Any chance of getting out of here in the near future?"

The deputy shook his head. "Sheriff's out now. Probably won't be back for another hour."

Jed frowned, his eye patch dipping downward. "Where is he?"

"Taking those guys to their car, I guess."

"What guys?"

"The guys you came in with."

Grabbing the bars of his cell Jed pulled his face as close as he could get to the young deputy. "You mean he's letting them go?"

"That's right."

"Why?"

"You'll have to ask him. But my guess is you two are looking at an assault charge."

"Assault!" Janice blurted.

"That's my guess," the deputy said. "Now if you don't mind too much, will you keep it down in here."

"You're blowing it!" Jed said. But the deputy was already leaving. "Get back here! You don't know what you're doing!"

The deputy slammed the door behind him. Janice looked at Jed. All the cool was gone from him. He looked, for the first time since she'd known him, completely lost.

Then a wicked laugh came from the kid's cell. He was back on his cot, looking directly at Janice, cackling away. He laughed like that for a full minute, before finally catching his breath.

When he did, he said, "What's your Jesus gonna do for you now, huh?" Then he fell back on his cot.

For a moment Janice did indeed wonder what was going to happen next. Then she realized Jed had moved across his cell so he was right next to hers.

"Hey," he said quietly.

Janice came to him.

"I'm sorry," he said.

Feeling the first hint of genuine warmth from him, Janice was momentarily speechless.

"I'm sorry I got you into this mess. I mean, you're in jail. You shouldn't be here."

"You know what?" Janice said.

"What?"

"Peter and Paul did some of their best praying in jail."

When Jed smiled, it was like a thin ray of sunlight had penetrated a darkened room. "I just want you to know something," he said.

Janice waited, not wanting to blunder in with any wrong words.

"Back when I wouldn't tell you some things, it wasn't because I didn't trust you."

"No?"

"No. It was just that . . . I didn't want you to think less of me."

If Janice could have reached through the bars then, to touch him somehow, she would have. Jed turned his back and returned to the other side of his cell, where he lay down on his cot. His back was to her. Janice didn't mind. What had just happened was enough.

●

Go.

Don't go.

Do it.

Don't do it.

Stop!

Now!

They weren't voices, exactly, and yet they were—impulses with content inside his head. Dewey pushed his index fingers into his temples, hard, almost as if he would push right through to his brain to stop the argument going on in his brain.

And the voices had personality somehow. It was crazy, he knew, but discernible nonetheless. One voice—the one calling him forth to act—seemed tied to the demons he thought he saw. The other was gentler, benign, yet strong in its own way. How could any of this be? Was it just a malfunction in the circuits? Brain damage? Or something he currently did not understand?

"You all right, dude?" the man said.

Dewey brought his focus back to the man with one arm. He was scraggly—facial hair shooting out at odd angles—with a black bandanna covering his head. An outlaw all right. About as far removed from the tea-and-crumpets crowd as you could get in Boston without falling into the ocean.

The abandoned warehouse where they stood had shattered windows all around it. Target practice, the scraggly man had said. He liked to guarantee his goods. A few rusty chains hung from black joists in the steel-beamed ceiling. The only ambient light was a weak ray of sun that had to fight through dark clouds on the way to the ground.

Dewey kept rubbing the side of his head and said, "Fine."

"You better be," Scraggly said, "if you're gonna use one of these things."

Nodding, Dewey said, "I'm OK."

"You ever fired a semiautomatic before?"

"Sure."

"Liar."

"What does it matter to you?"

"Hey, no matter at all, dude. You want to blow your foot off, that's no hair off my back. I just like to think of myself as a teacher as well as a dealer. You buy from me, you get a lesson for free."

Do it.

Don't do it.

Dewey closed his eyes and breathed in hard. "Just give me the gun."

"Just give me the money."

Reaching into his pocket, Dewey pulled out the wad of hundred dollar bills—the entirety of his savings account. That this transaction was taking place at all told Dewey he still had the brainpower to force his will upon the world. It had taken him only two degrees of separation to find the scraggly gun dealer. The first was one of the denizens of his apartment building, a guy named Naylor, who had once sold Dewey an ounce of marijuana. That led to a bartender at a dive downtown who had grilled Dewey for half an hour before setting up the meeting and the specs by phone.

So now, as Scraggly counted the bills, Dewey was about to have his redemption at hand.

"She's all yours," Scraggly said, laying the nine millimeter handgun in Dewey's palm. "Tell your friends."

Scraggly turned and, boot heels clicking in the cavernous ruin, walked toward the shadows and then disappeared.

Do it.

Don't do it.

Now!

Stop!

From his pocket Dewey fished for the box of ammo he had purchased and proceeded to load seventeen rounds in the gun's magazine. Just as Scraggly, beloved teacher, had shown him.

Now! Stop! Now! Stop!

Suddenly the voices intensified, as if the moment of truth had arrived and the voices knew it even before Dewey knew it. And now he realized he would have to do something to still them or they would go on tormenting him forever.

His original plan began to change now, in a flash, as the volume grew louder in his brain. Without thinking about it, wondering even who was controlling his hand, he raised the weapon to his own head, his finger twitching on the trigger, his head swirling, his mind tumultuous.

Now! Now! Now!

●

The sheriff who ambled into the jail looked fat and happy—the sort with permanent job security no matter how incompetent he managed to be. Janice wondered who he was related to in the local government. Probably a cousin in a long line of country kin.

"How you folks doing?" he said in a weak attempt at casual courtesy. He was in his early forties, Janice guessed, with a substantial record of heavy meals behind him. The holstered revolver on his hip looked absurd.

"You sure took your sweet time getting here, sheriff," Jed said.

"Had to run me a couple of errands for the missus," he said.

"And where are those two jokers you let go?"

"Mr. Anderson you mean, and his son?"

"Anderson?"

"You folks are in a lot of trouble."

The kid across the way cackled like a mad rooster. "Didn't I tell you!" he screamed.

"Shut up, Lazlo," the Sheriff said. Then to Jed and Janice: "Local punk."

"Sticks and stones may break my bones," Lazlo said, "but Sheriff Egger will never hurt me."

"Shut up," Sheriff Egger repeated.

"I can't believe you let those guys go!" Jed said. "That's no father-son team, you yokel!"

"Now listen here, calling names isn't gonna—"

"Forget about that! That guy's name isn't Anderson, either."

"Sure it is," said Egger. "Saw the ID myself."

Jed shook his head. "Why don't you ask your local punk there how hard it is to fake an ID."

Lazlo laughed. "Piece of cake!"

"Shut up," the sheriff said.

"Look, Egger, there's stuff going down you have no idea about. You need to let us out of here."

"Well I can't do that. There's been a complaint."

"From a lying thug who is on his way to do permanent damage to who knows who?"

"All I know is—"

"You know squat!"

Egger started to turn. "If that's the way you're gonna be . . ."

"Wait a minute," Janice said.

The sheriff faced her.

"Watch out for that one," Lazlo said. "She's a religious nut."

"You a Jehovah's Witness?" Egger said, frowning.

"No," Janice said. "I'm a lawyer."

"Worse."

"For whom? Do you want me to start keeping count of the constitutional violations going on here?"

"That sounds a little like a threat."

"It is. This is shaping up to be a nice little exposé on *20-20*."

Sheriff Egger scowled.

"We could start with a little background material on this innocent-looking town and then proceed to the sheriff who doesn't care about the basic constitutional rights of American citizens. Like holding them incommunicado. Like keeping them from seeing a magistrate. Like being bought off by false witnesses."

The portly sheriff suddenly stiffened. Janice could see, from the faint light, small beads of perspiration popping up on his forehead. A thick silence enveloped the chamber.

Lazlo broke it. "She got you, Egger! She got you!"

With a sudden fury Egger pulled his revolver and pointed it at Lazlo. The kid scampered backward, terror spread all over his face.

"I warned you, punk!" Egger said, his voice cracking.

"Heelllppp!" the kid wailed.

"Sheriff!" Janice shouted.

Egger held the gun in position another moment, then slowly brought it down. "I'll deal with you later," he said. Then, turning, he said, "I'll deal with you two right now. And don't you think I won't. Both of you get to my office. Now!" He fished a wad of keys from his pocket, fiddled with them, then unlocked their cells.

"Get me out of here!" the kid yelled as Janice stepped from her cell.

"Don't worry," Janice said. "The Constitution is for you too."

"I don't need no Constitution! I need a bullet-proof vest!"

"Shut up," Egger said.

Janice and Jed followed him through the heavy door to the outer office. The last thing Janice heard before the door slammed shut was Lazlo screaming, "Don't leave me here!"

"I meant what I said," Janice told Egger. "You see that boy gets a lawyer."

"Whatever."

The deputy was seated at the front desk reading the *Enquirer*. Something about Michael Jackson and a "disappearing nose" was on the front page.

"Carl," Egger said to him, "why don't you go get me some cheese babka and pick up a little something for yourself."

"I'm not hungry," the deputy said.

"Then get hungry. Just get out of here."

The deputy understood. He put the paper down, gave Janice and Jed a quick glance, then left the office through the front door.

Egger sat in the chair behind the desk. He took the *Enquirer*, crumpled it up, and threw it in a wastebasket.

"Now look," he said. "I don't want any trouble from you two. I just want to follow procedure."

"The procedure," Janice said, "is we need to see a magistrate before the close of business. You know it, and I know it. I don't really care about your position here. You can be sheriff or dog catcher or Rex the Wonder Horse. But I do care about the law. You play fair, and the system will do its work. But you try to mess it up, and people are going to get hurt."

"You go, girl," Jed said.

Ignoring him, Janice said to Egger, "Now none of this has to go beyond this office. My friend and I will be happy to sign a notice to appear, and nothing more need be said about any of this. Except you must agree that if we come back here with proof that you've been had by another criminal, you agree to drop all charges. Fair enough?"

Egger slowly rocked back and forth in his chair. It squeaked rhythmically. "You won't go talking to *20-20?*" he said.

"They will not find out you exist," Janice said.

Heaving a sigh, Egger opened up a drawer and pulled out a couple of forms.

"And my Taser?" Jed said.

Egger swallowed. "Um . . ."

"What?"

"My other deputy . . . borrowed it."

"Borrowed! That's my property!"

"I'll see you get it back."

"When?"

Small beads of sweat popped out on Egger's forehead. "Soon?"

Jed looked about to explode. Janice put her hand on his arm and said, "Let's get out of here."

Egger looked like he would melt under Jed's stare. Then Jed turned for the door.

"Just one more thing," Janice said.

Egger raised his eyebrows.

"I meant what I said about that kid in there. I would hate to find out he'd had an accident of some kind. And I would appreciate it if you'd slip him a Bible."

"A Bible?"

"That's right. A little favor. Something else Barbara Walters never has to know about."

The sun was almost gone when she and Jed got outside. A hard orange burned in the sky. As they half jogged toward the impound lot, two blocks away, Jed said, "I can't believe those guys! But you, that was incredible. What a performance!"

"It wasn't a performance. I meant what I said."

"You're very good."

Janice smiled.

"Something else. How did you know he'd been paid off by Van Hoorn?"

"I didn't."

"Brilliant. Something I would have done."

"That's your test for brilliant?"

"One of them. You're a woman after my own heart."

"We'll look for your heart some other time. Right now we've got to find Lauren. Do you have any idea where to go next?"

Jed shook his head. "No. When we lost Van Hoorn, we lost the link."

"So what do we do?"

"Pray?"

Janice looked at him with total shock.

Jed shrugged. "At this point what else have we got?"

Half a block from the lot, just as they were about to cross the street, Janice felt Jed stiffen and turn. She heard what sounded like the shriek of tires. Following Jed's gaze, she saw a car down the street, headlights aimed at them.

"They've got us," Jed said quickly. "Come on!"

He pulled her arm and started them running down the side street.

35

Sweat was starting to sting the eyes of Bently Davis. Driving fast now, he had to make it to the cabin as soon as possible. Things were starting to get a little out of control.

Who had compromised UniGen's security? Was it some sort of inside job? But all of the insiders were accounted for.

Except Burack. Why would he be messing with anything? Professional jealousy? Ever since they started UniGen together, Davis had sensed a small but persistent envy in Lyle Burack. Maybe it was because Davis got all the ink, the accolades, while Burack felt he was stuck with the mundane, everyday running of the operation.

But would he sabotage the enterprise for that reason alone?

No, Davis decided. There was too much money involved. It had to be someone from the outside.

One of the subjects? Someone whose mind was operating at mega-level but who had somehow resisted the self-destruct fail-safe mechanism he and Burack had designed so effectively? Which one?

And that was not the only crack in the dyke.

Someone had hacked into the computer system. Someone who was very, very good at it. They'd almost identified the source, but whoever it was managed to get out before they could. How much information did he get and for what purpose?

And who was this one-eyed man with the Ramsey woman who had tangled with Karel Van Hoorn? That was another complication. Van Hoorn had been identified by this one-eyed man, and Burack had to go and spread a substantial amount of money in this little hamlet in order to get things straightened out.

Or was Burack behind all this after all?

Now he was back to Burack. The whole thing was a circle that didn't add up, didn't make sense.

He had to get to the cabin, get the girl injected, and take charge of the situation. Sam Ramsey, his first subject, would be all right. He had responded to the injections perfectly. Davis still remembered the excitement of those days. Of course, Ramsey had been well paid with stock options in the company. But he deserved them for being the first.

Now, in offering up his daughter, he was taking the next step.

Yes, Sam would be all right. Maybe he could have Sam take care of Van Hoorn and Burack.

Wiping the sweat from his forehead, Davis realized he was losing his grip. On the enterprise. On himself.

Things were beginning to crumble at the edges. Problems arising. People problems, the worst.

There would have to be some eliminations.

Reaching under his seat, Davis felt for his Smith & Wesson nine millimeter. Still there.

Jed pulled her into a small passageway between two small, commercial buildings. Behind them Janice heard the screech of tires.

"Who is it?" she said.

"Van Hoorn," Jed said. "Got to be."

"But why?"

"Come on."

Pulling her by the hand, Jed ran for a small path through a gardened area. Janice, in spite of everything, couldn't help thinking what a pretty town this was. They certainly kept things up in this place, anyway.

"Hey!"

The voice had come from the street. Whoever it was, was closer than Janice expected.

Then they hit the wall.

"No exit!" Jed yelled with obvious frustration. "Now I'm gonna have to take him."

He pushed Janice to the wall and then stepped in front of her, like a human shield. They were at the back of a concrete "U," the only way out being the way they came in. She could see past Jed's shoulder. It was darker in here than on the street, almost like dead night. Jed would have trouble seeing anyone. And he had no weapon. His bag was still at the impound lot.

"Steady," he whispered to her.

She heard footsteps coming their way. And then a figure, barely a shadow in the darkness. She felt Jed tense in front of her.

"Brown?" a voice said. A familiar voice.

"Oh no," Jed said.

"Oh yes, you idiot."

It was Data. His skinny form came closer.

"What are you doing here?" Jed said.

"Chasing you all over this stupid town! I come here to help, and you run away."

"But how did you find us?"

"You stole my car, remember?"

"Stole? You gave it to us."

"*They* don't know that."

"Who?"

"These local yokels. I got a call from a guy this afternoon, says they got a car with my registration in it. Asks me if I know anything about it. I could have said you took it without my OK. But being the nice guy I am, which I don't know why I am considering the way you have disturbed my peace, I tell him you do have it with my OK. He tells me you're in the lockup, and I tell him to give you a message to wait for me."

"I didn't get any message."

"Cops! What are you gonna do?"

"So you got a car—"

"Borrowed—"

"—and came up here—"

"—to find your sorry—"

"—because?"

Data folded his arms. Even in the dark, Janice could sense a smugness.

"Wouldn't you like to know?" he said.

"Come on, Data!" Jed exploded. He grabbed him by the shoulders. To Janice it looked like he could have snapped Data like a dry twig.

Shaking free, Data said, "Hands off! What I got is gonna cost you."

"*Cost me?*"

"That's what I said. You're gonna want what I got, I guarantee it."

"How much?"

"A steak and baked potato, with everything on it," Data said. "And a pitcher of beer. You in or out?"

"In! Now give."

"I'll give in the car."

"Car? Why?"

"Because if I'm right," Data said, "we don't have any time to spare."

36 Lauren prayed harder than she ever had in her life. She felt it, too. There had never been a need like this before. She sensed things were coming to some kind of head. It was in the way her father and the other two were acting. Nervous, somehow. Their cold control was starting to fray.

It was like the feeling she'd had once at school, when Bobby Altman and Jay Serico were acting up in Mrs. Gardner's class. She had given them lots of warnings, but they ignored them. They kept on giggling and talking. Mrs. Gardner had seemed tense that day, and finally she exploded. She screamed and yelled and even had tears in her eyes. She sent the boys to the principal's office, then sent everybody out of the room early for recess.

Only later did Lauren find out that a close friend of Mrs. Gardner's had died earlier in the week. That explained a lot.

There was that same feeling in the cabin now, only it wasn't because somebody had died. No, it was more like something was not going right. Lauren had no idea what that was all about, but she knew she had to pray.

Dear God, please bring me back to my mom soon. Please don't let anything happen to me because I know it would make Mom sad. And if you can do something to bring my daddy back, please do it, God. I don't want him to be mean anymore, and he's acting so different. I don't know why, God, but you do. Please help him. And please be with that nice Mr. Turner. Don't let him be dead, God. Let him be OK. OK, God? Thank you very much.

On her knees at her cot, she heard a door open, and voices. Someone new had come along. Something was about to change, she just knew it.

She listened closely to the voices. It was a greeting of some kind, then serious talk. She couldn't make out the words, only the tone. She recognized her father's voice. It had a strange quality to it, almost like he was afraid of something. Then an unfamiliar voice rose in what sounded like anger.

The talking went on for about ten minutes, then her door opened.

It was Rance. "Come on," he said.

Lauren got up slowly, not wanting to go with him, but knowing she had no choice. She felt a little like Daniel then. That's what she told herself. She was being led into what would be her lion's den.

Out in the living room of the cabin, she saw her father—the man who had once been her father—seated on one side of the room, looking away from her. Steve stood with his arms folded.

There were two other men in the room she had never seen before. One of them stood next to her father. He looked mean and strong. She had the feeling he was keeping an eye on her father, like a guard or something.

In the middle of the room was a man with long, curly gray hair and intense eyes, staring right at her. When he smiled, she felt prickles of ice all up and down her back.

"So this is Lauren," he said. He had that adult voice she couldn't stand, the one where you knew you were expected to stand there and be cute no matter what the adult said.

Lauren looked toward her father. He was still looking at the wall. His body seemed twisted, as though he were in some sort of pain. The mean man looked at him, then back at her.

"I'll bet you have lots of questions," the man with the curly hair said. "Like, who am I?"

She waited.

"My name is Bently Davis. I'm a teacher. I teach college. Have you ever heard of Harvard?"

Lauren nodded. She had heard her father talk about it once. It was supposed to be a big deal.

"Someday," Davis said, "you may go there. Would you like that?"

She shrugged her shoulders.

"Sure you would." He squatted then, looked at her at eye level. "But you have to be very smart to go to Harvard. Are you smart?"

Again, Lauren shrugged. *What was she supposed to say? Who was this man?*

"You look smart to me," Davis said. "You really do. That means you're able to understand things. Right?"

Now Lauren spoke. "I don't like being here."

"Sure, sure," Davis said. "But your daddy is here."

Lauren looked at her father. He was tensed up, still not looking her way.

"Doesn't that make you feel better?" Davis said.

"What are you going to do?" Lauren said.

Rance said, "She's a quick one."

"Hasn't your daddy explained this to you?" Davis said, his tone sharper.

Looking at him, Lauren thought she saw a nervousness there. Like he wasn't in full control, the way he wanted her to think he was.

Be like Daniel.

Suddenly, Lauren saw her father spin around in his chair and face Davis. "Maybe she's not ready," he said.

Davis stood up slowly. "What is that supposed to mean? What have you been doing up here this whole time?"

"Look, all I'm saying is, we want to have the conditions right. Right?"

"That was your job. Are you saying you failed in that?"

"All I'm saying is . . ."

"Just what are you saying, Ramsey?"

Lauren noted how Davis used her daddy's last name. It sounded harsher that way.

Her daddy looked at his feet and barely above a whisper said, "Nothing."

"All right then," said Davis. "When we're done up here, we'll show Lauren the whole place. She'll like that."

What did he mean?

Her daddy stood up then and said, "I'm going outside."

"You don't want to watch?" Davis said.

"No."

Davis seemed upset about that. In the exchange of looks, Lauren thought she saw a tension between them. But it also seemed like Davis was the parent and her daddy the child.

"Don't go, Daddy," Lauren said quickly.

Her daddy paused, a strange look on his face. Almost like some emotion was trying to break through, and it pained him.

"Maybe it would be best," Davis said. "Go on."

For a moment her daddy stood there, almost frozen, looking unsure what to do. And then he quickly ran out the door, letting it slap closed behind him.

"Daddy!" Lauren cried.

"He'll be back," Davis said. "And now are you ready for a great adventure?"

●

"I am such a genius," Data said.

"Will you tell us where we're going?" said Jed. He was driving Data's car now, according to the directions the hacker had given him. Data sat in the passenger seat. In the back Janice strained forward, wondering where they were headed.

"Tell me I'm a genius first," Data said.

"All right," said Jed, "you're a genius. An idiot, but a genius."

"Be nice!"

"Will you just talk?"

Janice said, "Will you two please knock it off?"

The two men fell silent.

"Just tell us what's going on," Janice said to Data. Then she added, "So we can truly appreciate your genius."

Data smiled. "That's the ticket. Because genius is apparently what this whole thing is about."

He took his laptop out of his backpack and set it on his knees. In a minute he was ready to put on a show.

"Now," Data began, "first thing I was able to do was access the information on that hard drive you gave me. That wasn't such a problem. What I found was a bunch of stuff that didn't make much sense, but I did find a very interesting file."

"What kind of file?" Jed said.

"I'm getting to that! It looked like a central document with several links. As I started to read it, I thought it was some sort of crazy treatise. It goes on and on. You remember Ted Kaczynski?"

Janice said, "The Unabomber?"

"Right. Remember, right before they caught him, he said he'd stop blowing people up if they'd publish his manifesto on how terrible technology is. Jerk. Anyway, it was this long-winded, rambling thing. Boring, really, but a window into the guy's mind. Well, this file is the same thing. Listen."

With a few clicks on the keyboard, Data scrolled some text across the screen and read aloud. "I say unto you there is no pure being. No gods, no forms, no substances, no things in themselves. All is only chaos, flux, and to that we must impose our will. You who say we must submit our will to that which is above us, when there is no above, are the cowards and dotards of our world."

"What's a dotard?" Jed said.

"A wimp," Janice said.

"Listen," Data insisted, reading on: "'I say unto you, all knowing is inventing, and all inventing is lying. All denial of this is a flight from reality and from existence itself. This denial is self-doubt, and self-doubt is weakness.'"

"Is there much more of this?" Jed said.

"Only about a hundred thousand words more," Data said. "But don't worry, I'm not going to read it all."

Janice said, "Sounds like the ravings of a lunatic."

"Sounds like more of that Nietzsche stuff," said Jed.

"Bing bing bing! Give the man a cigar," Data said. "Found a lot of cross-references. So we already knew that."

"You said you thought it was a treatise," said Janice. "What do you think it is now?"

"As I read this stuff, it became obvious that what the guy was writing was a novel."

"A pretty boring one," said Jed.

"Shows how much you know," said Data. "It reminded me of *Atlas Shrugged*."

Janice said, "The Ayn Rand novel? I read it in high school. Pretty bad."

"Yeah?" Data said. "It only changed the course of history!"

Janice shook her head. "Let's get back on point, shall we? You think this guy was writing a novel like *Atlas Shrugged*. So what?"

Data scowled at Janice.

"Don't offend our boy," said Jed.

"Because Ayn Rand wanted to install a whole new system of philosophy in the world," Data said. "She did it with a long speech made by her character John Galt. This book has the same feel to it. Right in the middle of this big speech is . . . here it is. Listen: 'God is dead. That is the single truth upon which all of reality is based. Just as nothing in biology makes sense except in the light of evolution, nothing in life makes sense except in light of knowing, believing, facing up to the death of God, once and for all. It is an exercise in freedom and joy.'"

Data looked up. Janice just shook her head. Jed kept his eye on the road.

"There's more," Data said. "'What has God ever brought us but pain and suffering? Guilt and imprisonment? Despair and agony? God is dead. Science has proved it. The brave ones have lived it. Those who deny this fundamental truth are the lost ones. They who seek to be saved are lost. Irony is the watchword of history! But their time is past. The forces of time and nature and the free mind of man shall take its course. They who cling to superstition will die out. I will help them in that process. I will live on the side of nature. And if I shall be resisted, what then? The fittest shall survive. I shall be the fittest. Survive. And thrive. And they shall call me, Nephilim.'"

The silence in the car lasted several moments. Then Data said, "I think this novel was going to be science fiction."

"Why is that?" Jed said.

"Because everything in this file is subsumed or linked to that name, Nephilim. It has to be made up."

Janice and Jed exchanged looks. "What?" Data said. "You've heard it before?"

"It's from the Bible," Jed said.

"It is?"

Janice said, "The Nephilim were a race of giants in the early part of Genesis."

"You mean like Goliath?" Data said.

"Way before Goliath," said Janice. "Before the Flood."

"If you believe in that stuff," said Data derisively.

"Shut up," said Jed. Janice was surprised at the snappishness in Jed's voice. Like he was jumping to her defense. He nodded at Janice and said, "Go on."

"The reference to the Nephilim is obscure," Janice said. "Some people say they were the offspring of demons, who came to earth and impregnated women."

"Now that would make a cool movie!" said Data.

"Not everyone agrees with that," said Janice, ignoring him. "But it's one theory. Others say that the Nephilim were the offspring of the line of Seth, the godly line, and the wicked descendants of Cain."

Data seemed suddenly pensive. "That's in the Bible?"

"Yes. Genesis chapter 6."

"Wow. That really *is* cool."

"And true."

Data looked at her sharply but did not respond. In fact, he seemed to be thinking about it. A small victory, Janice concluded. Then she said, "Anything else about this document?"

"Yeah," said Data. "I think the lead character here is based on a real person."

"Who?" Jed said.

"I'm not telling yet."

Jed slapped his hand on the seat.

"OK, OK," Data said. "I just had to set it up. I think what this is all about is Bently Davis at Harvard."

"The writer?" Janice said. "I know he's had a couple best-sellers."

"On science and evolution," Data said. "Very good. Well, if we keep reading in this thing—"

"Please," Jed said, "just the summary."

"Fine. We read on, and this character is proposing to speed up human evolution, using a form of injected virus to deliver synthetic DNA to the brain."

"Sounds like science fiction," Janice said.

"It's science *fact,*" Data said. "Or it soon will be. They can do incredible stuff with biotech, or haven't you been reading the papers?"

"Sure," Janice said. "I've heard about the wonders from Jed Brown."

Jed shrugged sheepishly.

"I'm not sold," Janice added.

Data said, "Well it's inevitable. You take that genie out of the bottle, and it's going to go the limit. That's what this character in this novel is saying. What he's claiming is that we can tap into our latent brainpower through biotechnology, making geniuses of us all. I, of course, don't need any help."

"That's debatable," Jed said.

"There's more."

"Give it," Jed demanded.

"Patience. Now listen how life imitates art. The third season kickoff show on *The Next Generation* was titled 'Evolution.' Dr. Paul Stubbs comes on board the *Enterprise* to conduct a time-critical experiment. But suddenly the computer systems on the *Enterprise* start to break down."

"Is there a point to this?" Jed said.

"If you'll listen! So they finally find out what happened. Wesley allowed two Nanites to escape."

"Nanites?" Janice said.

"Exactly. Tiny machines with billions of bytes of memory. They were designed to enter damaged but living tissue and make repairs. They were supposed to work alone, but Wesley taught them to work together and reproduce. So the two escaped Nanites have reproduced, and thousands of them are eating the memory chips in the ship's core computer!"

"This is just wonderful," Jed said, "but—"

"There's more! Data, LaForge, and Wesley get into the main computer to clear out the Nanites. But Dr. Stubbs jumps in and fires radiation into the memory banks, destroying the Nanites in the upper core! So the Nanites retaliate by pumping nitrous oxide into the main bridge! Data thinks these things are actually intelligent and contacts them through the Universal Translator! Data allows the Nanites to enter his neural networks so they can meet face-to-face with Captain Picard!"

Breathless, Data paused momentarily. Then he said, "Dr. Stubbs apologizes to the Nanites, and they agree to a truce. They help repair the main computer. Is that a killer story or what?"

Jed, seeming the slightest bit exasperated, nodded. "Wonderful. It's that nanotechnology stuff. Science fiction."

"Well," said Data, raising his eyebrows, "according to this document they think it's real. Whoever wrote this thing thinks it's happening now. I think so too. Now we get to the next part."

"There's a next part?" Jed said.

"Of course there is! All this is patty-cake so far! I next found a group of E-mail messages. This guy had been communicating back and forth from Hollywood to Cambridge. Where Harvard is located. Where Bently Davis is located."

"He was in touch with Davis?" Jed said.

"Pretty sure. Or someone close to Davis. Anyway, that's not the fun part."

"Fun?" Janice said.

"Look at this." Data scrolled some text onto the screen. Janice leaned closer. Onscreen she saw:

i¶ᵃᵒʰ∫¯MY∧T¢∧∧&;ᵒ≠)(&()•-=-I{IIU$#72LJ‡·°,·°% ®
¢£¶ᵃᵒʰ∫¯©UYi
I87)(*UUYGΔ˙ΔkNj#∞∧•ᵃᵃᵃ)^!I{i*ᵒj¨**H•(&*)(π¬˙°Δ
∂ç√¥®I•°°Ó"
∂˙´ÎØÒÔ₁°°¥KL˙©f≥µ∫−ᵃⱼœ˙Σ®

"Encryption," said Jed.

"An easy one," Data said. "Took me two hours of programming to crack it. Watch."

Data tapped a couple of keys and then read the screen:

> *brown may be on to us. somebody fed him information. don't know who right now. no matter. must be taken care of. proceed as discussed previously. await payment. usual transfer.*

Jed stiffened. "Brown! They mean Sterling!"

"Bing," said Data.

"So the other guy," Jed said, "the other end of these messages. It's Davis? From Harvard?"

"My guess," said Data.

"Then we have to talk to him."

"Precisely what we're going to do," Data said calmly. "We're on our way now."

Jed looked at Data quickly. "How?"

"It's a hunch, but a good one. We're only about thirty miles away."

"From what?"

"A cabin. There was a message connecting a certain event to a location near here. Directions and everything."

"What was the event?" Janice said.

Data hesitated before answering. "I found a message that was a list of what looks like key events in some kind of project. These are cryptic, but one item mentions a child."

"Child?" Janice said, feeling her nerves zap.

"Yeah. The only thing I can put together is that some sort of process is going to be applied to a child on a specific date."

"Lauren," Janice whispered.

"What date?" said Jed.

Data paused. "Today."

The car started spinning around Janice. She had to grab the seat back to keep from falling over.

Jed accelerated the car.

●

"I want my daddy!" Lauren cried.

"Then you'll be quiet," Davis commanded.

She stopped then, her chest heaving.

"If you want your daddy," Davis said, "then you'll do exactly as I say."

He had her, she knew. The way adults always find a way. What would Nancy Drew do? Keep him talking. Find something, anything.

"I want him now," she said.

Davis shook his head. "Not possible. I promise you, though, when we're all done here, you can see your daddy. He's just outside."

"I want my daddy in here."

"No."

"Then I won't be calm! I'll scream!"

Rance, who was standing by a wall, said, "I told you about her."

"Yes," said Davis. "A very smart little girl." He stood up. "All right, Lauren. We'll make a deal. You just do one little thing for me."

She eyed him suspiciously. "What?"

"You let me give you some vitamins, and I'll take you right outside to see Daddy. How does that sound?"

"I want to see him before."

"Now you're not being fair."

"Am too," she said.

"There are three of us here. We're all bigger and stronger than you. You wouldn't want us to get rough, would you?"

"I want my daddy."

"Because we can do that. And if we do, then you know what's going to happen?"

Lauren waited.

"We are going to give you the vitamins, and we are going to hurt your father too. That's what we'll do. And then you'll know that your actions here today made us hurt your daddy. Do want to feel that way?"

Hot tears stung her eyes. How could God be letting this happen? The mean people were winning. Her daddy had been mean, too, but he was just lost, and she prayed for him to come. If they hurt him, maybe he would never get back. And it would be her fault!

"I can see you're really thinking," Davis said. "And that's good. That's really good. You'll be able to think even better once I help you."

No way out. She finally nodded her head.

"That's the ticket," Davis said. "It's all going to be over before you know it."

He opened a small, black bag on the table and removed something. She wasn't sure what it was at first, but then he held it up to the light. It was a needle. He was going to give her a shot. She hated shots.

"Please, no," she said.

"It won't hurt, I promise."

"No, please!" Lauren backed up until she hit a wall. Then she felt a hand on her shoulder. It was Rance.

"Don't worry," he said. "You'll be like us. It's the best."

Davis stuck the needle into a small bottle and started to fill the syringe. Now they held her, firmly. Rance on one side, Steve on the other.

Holding her arms and legs down. And she was helpless. Just like when Tommy McIntire tied her to that tree.

Only Tommy was just a kid with a mean streak. These were adults, and they didn't care if they were mean. That was always the scariest thing to her. The way Rance and Steve looked when they found her at Mr. Turner's. She was sure they had hurt him, but they didn't show any signs they cared. Why were people like that?

"Now," Davis said, "don't you worry about a thing, honey."

He had finished with the syringe and was facing her. What made sense now was that she was going to be given something that would change her, the way it changed Rance and Steve. And her daddy. It wasn't just vitamins or being smart. It was something worse, much worse.

She opened her mouth to scream for her daddy, but a hand slapped across it before a sound came out. She tried to wiggle, but they were too strong.

Davis came into her sight, hovering over her like a bird circling a dead thing. He held the needle in his right hand and a swab in his left.

"I wouldn't hurt you for the world," Davis said. "You're my hope. You're what this is all about, Lauren."

Lauren felt him rubbing her arm with the wet swab, right where her elbow bent.

Closing her eyes, Lauren felt a short jab in the crook of her arm. It didn't hurt much at all. For that she was relieved. Then she felt a warmth running up her arm, like someone had shot chicken soup into it. Not an unpleasant feeling, either.

It was about a minute later, when her head started to feel dizzy, that she got scared.

They were still holding her, but she didn't fight them. That was the first effect she sensed in her mind. She no longer had the desire to fight. Something was happening inside her head, and she was just going to lie there and let it happen.

It was like that time she'd played statue-maker at school. One kid would take you by the arm and whirl you around like a sack on a rope. When you were good and wound up, the kid would let you go, and you'd spin away until you landed—sometimes on your feet, sometimes on the ground—in some strange position. Then you'd freeze, and the spinner would have to guess what kind of statue you were.

The time Lauren remembered she had ended up on the ground, flat on her back, looking up as the sky and clouds spun around over her head. It was like she was flying and spinning, up in the air and not on the ground, tumbling through air. She had no idea where she'd land.

That's what this was like now, the room spinning, the faces of Rance and Steve and Davis looking at her, as if waiting to see what kind of statue she'd become.

And then something else in her mind. A brightness. Suddenly everything seemed brighter, clearer. Not just what she was seeing, but what she was thinking as well. Like when she'd helped Mom clean the windows with Windex and just that little act would make the outside world sparkle more.

It felt so good! So this was what they were doing for her. Daddy had been right the first time. It was a wonderful thing. Why hadn't she trusted Daddy? Why had he been so upset just now? If he would only come in, she would tell him not to worry anymore.

Luxuriating in her new consciousness, Lauren was only vaguely aware of the voices. Something about having to "shoot him." Deep inside she knew that they were talking about her father. And then her mind went into a deep spin. All of that wonderful brightness and clarity swirled away, and a black hole opened up. She fell into it.

37

Janice was certain they were lost. Jed pulled over to the soft shoulder of the mountain road. Surrounded by the black forest, they seemed less like trackers than confused tourists. The headlights were a feeble antidote to the darkness.

"I know it's here," Data said, looking at the map on his laptop. "I put the coordinates together myself."

"That's comforting," Jed said.

"Look, you wouldn't even be here if it weren't for me!"

"My point."

"Can we just make a decision?" Janice said.

"I'm thinking," said Data. "I'd say just a few more miles ahead. A road."

Jed said, "And I say this is a bad idea. Let's get back to civilization. We could be out here forever and not know what to do."

Janice sat back and closed her eyes. Picturing Lauren, she silently prayed. She could hear her daughter's voice in her mind, calling to her. It was like that horrible dream she'd had, with Lauren slipping off a cliff into flowing lava. The dream came back to her. Lauren, slipping, about to fall.

Janice opened her eyes and looked out the car window. For some reason, she didn't know why, she strained to see something she just knew was there. A sign. A road sign, barely visible in the headlights several yards ahead. Suddenly she said, "Go!"

"What?" Jed said.

"Go on! Ahead!"

"Why?"

"Just do it."

With a shake of his head, Jed started the car forward again. "You're both nuts," he said.

But Janice knew he was wrong. As they passed the road sign, she could finally make out the letters. It said, "The Cliffs. 2 Mi."

The car could only go twenty miles an hour on the small, winding road. Janice tried to will it faster. When she realized she was stepping on an imaginary gas pedal, she sighed and sat back.

"If either of you have any other ideas . . ." Jed said.

"This has to be right," Data said. "I didn't see any other roads."

"What you don't see could fill a book."

"Hey, man, I'm the only lead you got!"

A fact that did not fill Janice with confidence. Only a few moments before, she had been relying on dreams to give her guidance. Sure, God used dreams in the past, but nightmares?

She felt a sudden wave of fatigue, physical and mental. The last couple of days had been pure torment. Closing her eyes, she put her head back on the seat and made a pitiful attempt to relax. But her mind kept whirring.

When the car started to slow, she sat up again. "What is it?" she said.

"This," Jed said, looking straight ahead.

Through the front windshield Janice saw a steel gate across the road. The headlights illuminated a "No Trespassing" sign on the front. A chain and padlock were secured to one side of it.

"We got some choices," Jed said. "We could get out and walk up the road on foot. But there's no telling how far it is or even if we got the right road."

"Has to be," Data said.

"Then you go," said Jed.

"What's the next choice?" Janice asked.

"Next choice is we double back and try to find another road, but there may not be one. And even if there is, it may not be the right one."

"Got to be around here somewhere," said Data.

"Third is we turn this around and get back to civilization, where we have a real chance to turn something up. Where we can actually see people."

"I swear, it's got to be around here," Data said.

"What do you say?" Jed asked Janice.

She didn't know. At that point all of the options—and none of them—seemed preferable. All she knew was she had to do something. Action was the only curative for her despair. Well, she'd come this far on a hunch. Why stop now?

"Let's walk up the road," she said.

"Right on," said Data.

"You're both nuts," Jed said. Then he opened the door and got out.

Flicking on a flashlight, the beam barely enough to rip a thin line in the blackness, Jed waited. Janice was getting the idea this was a fool's errand. But what did she have as an alternative?

The fact that Jed Brown was holding a gun did not add to her comfort level. Nor did it help that in her imagination some local hillbilly was sitting on a front porch with a loaded shotgun, just waiting for intruders, a hunting dog at his feet.

She got out of the car.

"Stay close," Jed said. "I don't want anybody falling and breaking an ankle."

"Don't worry about me," Data said. "I'm not going."

"What?" Jed said.

"I'll watch the car."

"You're a big help."

"Hey, I didn't want this gig in the first place!"

"Thanks, Data," Janice said, anxious to get on with it. "We'll be back soon. I hope." She took Jed by the arm and started up the road.

Wind whipped through the trees as the night air chilled. *Somewhere out here,* Janice thought, *might be Lauren.* She remembered the nights during storms when Lauren would want to come sleep with her. The little girl would crawl under the covers and snuggle up close, afraid of the noise.

Was she afraid now, with no one to comfort her?

The road was long and twisting. And uphill. Janice felt her thighs starting to cramp. But the prospect of finding Lauren kept her going. She'd fight broken ankles if she had to.

But what were they going to find when they got there? How could they get to Lauren, let alone take her from whoever was up there?

All she had was God on her side and Jed with a gun.

Pretty good odds, she thought. And what she realized now, to her surprise, was a warm feeling of trust for Jed Brown. That was new. And she liked it. She liked the feeling of being able to trust again.

"You doing OK?" Jed said.

"Sure."

"You sound out of breath."

"That's because I am. But I don't want to stop."

"When we get up there, I want you to stay back. It could get dangerous."

"I don't care."

"I don't want you getting shot."

"What about you?"

"I was born to get shot."

Janice put her hand on his arm, surprising herself and him. She turned him toward her. "I don't want you to get shot," she said.

He looked at her in the darkness, and she could barely see the broad lines of his face.

"Thanks," he said.

Janice squeezed his arm.

"You hear something?" Jed said.

Listening, Janice could only hear the wind in the trees.

"There," Jed said.

A crackling noise. One that was up ahead, but distant.

"What is it?" said Janice.

"I don't know. Could be movement. We're close."

They started forward again, picking up the pace. Janice felt her thighs balling up again but ignored it.

Using the flashlight, Jed guided them farther upward and around a bend. It was then that Janice realized what the sound was.

Fire.

Ahead of them, in the middle of the trees, was an orange blaze. The crackling sound was constant now. The wind shifted, and Janice was hit with the smell of smoke.

"Lauren!"

"Come on," Jed said, running.

She did, following him, ignoring the burning in her own lungs. It couldn't be, but it could. Lauren could be inside.

Oh God, no, don't let it be!

The last hundred yards seemed like a mile, but finally they made it to the gravel driveway that led to what used to be a cabin in the mountains.

It was entirely engulfed. The heat shot outward, Janice feeling it up and down her body. Jed, his arm up to shield his face, edged onward.

"Jed!" she called, thinking for a moment he was going to go inside.

He stopped, backed away. "It's too late," he said.

Janice started to run forward. "Lauren!"

Jed grabbed her with one hand, pulled her back. "We need to go back," he said. "We need to call this in."

"But my daughter!"

"There's no way to get in."

"Please!"

She felt powerless, lost. Then suddenly Jed put his arms completely around her, pulling her into him. She let it happen, putting her head into his chest. It was soft there.

Jed put one hand on the back of her head. "It's not over," he said.

Janice wondered.

She pulled her head back and looked once more toward the cabin. Flames shot into the air like fiery rockets, up into the air and to the sides.

A tree caught fire and began to burn.

"It's spreading," Jed said. "We need to get back."

Only force of will got her out of there. With a walk-jog, she and Jed made their way back down the road. In her heart she refused to believe Lauren was dead. But people who were mad could do anything, and Davis was a madman.

Running through the night, Janice felt herself break through a barrier. Maybe she'd had it there all the time, like the ice wall Jed had erected. Only hers was a refusal to face down evil. She had run from it, since the day she saw that prisoner in Joliet. She realized that's why she had chosen insurance defense work. It was not something that required a face-off against long odds.

Now that had changed. What Davis was doing was pure evil, and she was not going to run away from it.

Her body was fighting itself.

More than anything Janice wanted to stay awake, for news of her daughter. But almost as much she wanted sleep. She wanted respite from the pain of not knowing and from the sadness that was darkening inside her like some toxic spill in a defenseless ocean.

But the hard, wooden bench in the ranger station was not going to be any help in the sleep department. All she could do was lean her head back against the cold wall and close her eyes.

They had been here close to an hour now, and the fire trucks had long since been dispatched. Now it was just a matter of waiting. Data was, apparently, still in the car, having refused to come in for some reason.

Jed had been dealing with the ranger in charge, giving out information for his report. There would be a lot of explaining to do.

When Jed sat down on the bench, Janice opened her eyes.

"Well," he said, "we should know something pretty soon. They know what we're looking for now."

Janice nodded.

"How're you doing?" he said. His voice was softer than she'd ever heard it.

"I don't know," she said. "Hanging."

"You're hanging better than most," he said reassuringly. "I guess that's your faith, huh?"

She raised her head from the wall. She hadn't been thinking about it in those terms, but it was true. She was falling back on reserves of faith, even in the face of the hard questions she'd been asking God lately. It was part of the fabric of her thinking, and there was some relief in that.

"I'd like to have faith like that again," Jed said suddenly, quietly.

Janice felt herself reaching out to him, touching his arm, the smooth leather of his jacket cool under her hand. "You can," she said. "Of course you can."

"I'm not ready yet."

"Like that kid back in jail?"

Jed was still and silent for a moment, then nodded. "Maybe so."

"Pray."

"Not now."

"I'll do it then."

"You do it."

She closed her eyes.

A moment later she heard a buzzing sound from the console near the front desk. Then a voice crackling through the radio. Somehow she knew it was related to the fire.

She opened her eyes, though even that was a struggle. Her body wanted to shut down. As if he sensed this, Jed got up and took her arm, lifting her gently. Without another word they walked to the desk.

The ranger, a pleasant-looking fellow in his late thirties, was writing on a pad.

"News?" Jed said.

The ranger looked at them. "Yeah," he said, then stopped abruptly.

"Well, what?"

The ranger hesitated, then stood slowly with the pad. He kept his eyes on the paper.

"What is it?" Janice said.

"Just a preliminary," the ranger said. "They contained the fire."

"Is that all?" Jed said.

"No."

"What then?"

"I'm sorry, folks. They found bodies inside."

For a moment Janice hovered between wakefulness and unconsciousness, floating in a gray area, her mind flying away. And then she fell into Jed's arms.

PART THREE

Many men through their wickedness have burdens outside, but the greatest burden is the wickedness of their own hearts.

—JEREMIAH BURROUGHS

38

Janice had the sense that distant voices were calling to her, as if from across a wide valley. There were smells, too, acrid and smoky. Fire? Was she being called out of fire?

Lauren!

She shot bolt upright. Light flashed in her eyes. The air was cold. The room close. People around.

"Easy."

Jed's voice. And he was holding her gently at the shoulders. She was on a cot. A man in a ranger uniform—not the same one who had been at the desk—had his hands on his knees. "You all right, ma'am?"

"What happened?" she said, her voice seeming to come from a mile away.

"You passed out," Jed said. "A real good one."

She put a hand to her head. "How long?"

"Ten minutes, tops. You want to sleep? Gentle Ben here says you can have the room all to yourself."

Janice squinted at the ranger. He wore a name pin over his left shirt pocket. It said "Ben."

"I think I'm OK," Janice said, wondering if she was. Then the thoughts came streaming in. "The bodies! Lauren!"

As she tensed upward, Jed held her softly but firmly. "It's all right."

"Is she . . . ?"

"No. Report just came in. Two male adults."

Oh thank God. Thank you, God!

"But that means . . ."

"She's still out there. Somewhere."

The wisp of thankfulness she'd felt just a moment ago disappeared in a dark wind of despair. *What was the use? Why had God brought them all the way out here, so close, and yet let Lauren stay beyond her reach?*

She felt tears in her eyes and put her head down, fighting them. Then she felt Jed's hands squeezing her shoulders as he faced her.

"Hang on, Janice, hang on," he said. "Will you do that for me?"

"Sure."

"We're going to find her."

Janice wished she could believe him.

"We're going to find her," he repeated, "because I've got the scent."

"Is she out there, in the woods?"

"I don't think so."

Ben said, "We'll have a search party going out immediately, ma'am."

"I want to go with you."

"I don't think that would be—"

"The lady would like to go," Jed said, quietly but firmly. "And so would I."

"Of course," the ranger said. "But we'll have to wait until morning."

"But what if she's out there now?"

"We can't do much in the dark, ma'am."

Janice was about to speak when she felt Jed squeeze her arm.

"It's OK," Jed said. "We'll be back in the morning."

Somehow Jed's grip told her it was all right to leave. She didn't fight it. When they got out into the parking lot, they found Data tapping nervously on the hood of the car.

"About time!" he snapped. "We going home now?"

"Not just yet," Jed said. "Everybody in. Give me the keys."

Data blinked, then handed the car keys to Jed. He started up and took the car out of the ranger station lot, turning right on the main highway.

"Wrong way," Data said.

"Right way," said Jed. A minute later it was clear where he was going.

"What do you think you're doing?" said Data.

"Back to the scene," Jed answered.

"What for? They got cops for that."

"I like to see things for myself."

"I want to go home!"

"Soon enough."

"You'll get us all thrown in the can!"

"Relax, will you? We have a lawyer here."

Data shot a look at Janice, who was in the backseat. She smiled at him. "My fee is reasonable too."

At which point Data threw up his hands.

Five minutes later Jed pulled the car up to the gate that guarded the private road. A line of yellow tape was stretched across it. Data folded his arms and refused to budge. Before leaving the car Jed reminded him he had the keys.

The walk back up the road seemed endless to Janice. With each step she listened to the dead night, scanned the dark trees and wondered if Lauren was out there somewhere. At one point she called her daughter's name, receiving only the whispering wind in return. Jed put his arm through hers, silently comforting her.

When they reached the fire scene, Janice saw the flickering lights of some official vehicle out in front and a dark, uniformed man illuminated by them. He turned abruptly at the pair's approach.

"Hey, you folks can't be here," he said.

"It's all right," Jed said, pulling his credential from his pocket. "I'm a private investigator, and this woman is looking for her daughter. We have reason to believe she might have been here."

The man examined Jed's ID, then said, "I'm the investigator in charge, Sergeant Mullin. I'll want to ask you some questions."

"Of course," said Jed. "And I have some questions of my own."

"You want to go first?" Mullin said. He looked to Janice to be around forty-five or so, though it was hard to tell in the light. And there was a solidity about him that gave her reason to hope.

Jed said, "You figure arson?"

Mullin glanced at the remains of the cabin. Two of the four walls jutted up to points where the ceiling, completely caved in, once joined them. "Won't know completely until I get a closer look in the daylight. But my first look with the beam gives me a low point of burn on the northwest side, with heavy charring. That's a strong indicator."

"What about the bodies?"

"Won't know until the ME gets a look at them."

"But it's not usual to find bodies at an arson scene unless . . ."

"Right."

"Unless what?" Janice asked.

"Unless it was murder or mayhem," Jed said.

Shaking her head, Janice tried to imagine what might have gone on here. What was the connection to UniGen? Her daughter? Any of this? Did this nightmare have no end?

A crunching sound behind them. Janice turned and saw a monster. It's face was black and contorted, its eyes glowing. If it hadn't been holding a gun in its hands, she might not have thought it human. But she knew it was—human, crazy, and deadly.

"Don't move!" a screechy voice, a voice of desperation, cried out. "Or I'll kill you all!"

•

Bently Davis let the full fire of his rage burn. "How did they find us?" he screamed at Van Hoorn, who was driving Davis's car.

"I don't know," Van Hoorn said timidly.

"They followed you! You idiot!"

"No way they did. They were in jail."

"Not any more they aren't, are they?"

Van Hoorn was silent, his eyes fixed on the road ahead. Davis turned to the back where Sam sat with his daughter.

"How is she?" Davis snapped.

"Still out," said Sam. Lauren lay across the backseat, her head in her father's lap.

"Good. At least that part of it's OK."

"How long will she be out?"

"Can't say. The dosage was smaller than average but enough to effect a complete transition. At least according to Burack."

"I mean, she'll be all right, won't she?"

Davis let a stream of air out his nose in silent remonstrance. "What do you mean by that?"

"Nothing," Sam said, but to Davis it looked like *something*.

"What do we do now?" Sam said, then added, "With people looking for us?"

"We get back," said Davis. "We have plans to make. There's going to be a whole lot of unpleasant questions. But I'll take care of it."

"How?"

"I'll let you know on an as-needed basis." Davis didn't want to give out any more information than absolutely necessary. The project was threatening to crash around him, but he had a fallback plan no one knew about. It was a plan he didn't intend to implement unless all else had failed. Well, it was pretty close to that now. And in that instant he made the decision.

The plan would be put into action. That would leave only a few minor witnesses to handle, and Van Hoorn, chastened, would be more moti- vated than ever.

All will be well, Davis said to himself.

In fact, he willed it to be so.

**39**

Janice was sure of several things.

First, this crazy with a gun was the one who was responsible for the fire and the two dead bodies. He might have been an intended victim, maybe in league with the victims, and had escaped. But somehow that seemed unlikely to her, a negative hunch. He had a malevolent look, not the expression of someone who had escaped flaming death.

There was a second thing Janice felt assured of, and that was that this person, whoever he was, knew something that would lead them to her daughter. Like a connect-the-dots puzzle that begins to come into focus even before all the lines are drawn, this picture pointed to his complicity in matters relating to Lauren's whereabouts.

But the information he held might never be of use to anyone, for the last thing Janice was sure of—and, horribly, even more than the other two—was that one or all of them were going to die.

"Don't move one bit!" the crazy screamed. "I'm serious!" He alternated his aim between the three of them, finally fixing it on the uniformed Mullin who, Janice noted, was completely unarmed. He would be the first to go, she thought.

And the gunman was very close to firing. It was those eyes again, eyes that almost glowed. That was where the connection came, she realized. Sam's eyes had glowed in a similar fashion when he had attacked her. These eyes were in a face that was, Janice guessed, around twenty years old. The body was skinny and trembling, which made the danger of the situation all the greater.

"Now hold on there," Mullin said.

"Shut up!" Crazy screamed. "I'm the one talking! You're all part of this!"

Jed spoke. "Part of what?"

"Shut up!"

"What do you want from us?"

"You ignorant idiots! Don't you know what's happening? Don't you know he's coming?"

"Who's coming?" Jed said, his voice soft. Janice knew this was the voice of the seasoned tracker, the coaxing voice that probably had gone through many a door.

"Shut up!" Crazy shouted. "I'll tell you, you idiotic idiots! You think this is all there is, don't you? They said that's all there is; they told me that, but they *lied!* You hear what I'm saying: they lied! He's real, you dumb idiots! Real as anything. Real as you or me or this gun. And he lives in fire!"

Janice suddenly knew what he was talking about. Crazy or not, he was referring to the devil. And the devil was real; Janice knew that too. People had visions of Satan when in the grip of some hallucinatory stupor brought on by drugs or mental illness. She guessed drugs for this one.

"He'll come for you, like he came for me!" Crazy said. "But I'll send you to the pit first!"

"Hold on there," Jed said.

"I said shut up!"

"Maybe we can help you out of this thing."

"There's no help left! Can't you see that?" He raised the gun higher, pointed it at Jed.

Suddenly a voice from down the road shouted, "Hey!"

Data. Janice recognized the voice immediately.

Crazy spun around, the gun whipping along with his arm, and fired three shots—*batt batt batt*—in rapid succession.

"Data!" Janice shouted.

Now Crazy was jerking back toward them, and in that millisecond Janice prepared herself to die.

Then a blur from the right. Jed had sprung like some jungle animal who had been coiled, waiting for an opportunity. Crazy's shots had been that opportunity, and now Jed was on him, catching Crazy's right wrist in his hand and shoving the body to the ground. An eerie scream came from deep inside the gunman—like a madman's wail as he's thrown, straitjacketed, into a padded and windowless room.

Mullin jumped in to help, grabbing the gun out of Crazy's now immobilized hand.

Janice immediately ran down the road toward what she was almost sure would be a wounded, if not dead, Data. When she saw the dark, prostrate body face down and motionless in the moonlight, her worst fears were confirmed.

"Data!" she shouted as she ran up to him and sank to her knees. The moment she placed a hand on his shoulder he moved, rolling over onto his back.

"Will somebody please explain to me what is going on?" he said, his voice pregnant with animosity. Janice had never been so happy to hear an expression of displeasure in her life.

"You're all right!" she said.

"No thanks to whoever's shooting!"

"Come on," Janice said, helping him to his feet. "It's all right now."

Grunting, Data stood, brushing himself blindly. "I just got one thing to say."

"Yes?"

"This is the last time I go anywhere with you two."

Janice threw her arms around him, a gesture that mixed relief and reassurance.

Data cleared his throat. "Don't get all gushy," he said but made no move to break from the hug.

"Come on," Janice said, leaving an arm around him and leading him back up the road.

Crazy was being held face down by Jed as Mullin used rope to tie Crazy's hands behind his back.

"Who's this guy?" Data said.

"We're not sure," said Jed.

"This the guy who tried to kill me?"

"He's nuts."

That brought a deep, mordant laugh from Crazy. "Nuts you think? You are so clueless you don't even know. You don't even know what's in there. You don't even know where all the bodies are! You don't know about alternate reality!"

"What's he talking about?" Data said, suddenly seeming fascinated.

"Nuts," Jed repeated.

But Janice wasn't so sure. What other bodies? Where? Was one of them Lauren's? "Let me talk to him," she said.

"I don't think that's advisable," said Mullin.

"Let me try," she said. Then to Jed: "Would you sit him up, please?"

With a shrug, Jed pulled Crazy up by the shoulders and to a sitting position. "Watch him," Jed said. "He may bite."

Janice squatted in front of him. His face changed colors with the flickering lights of Mullin's vehicle. His eyes were seething with some feral rage.

"I'm an attorney," Janice said.

"So?" Crazy hissed.

"You may need my help."

"I don't need anyone's help."

"You could be in a lot of trouble."

"It's all of you who are in trouble." He smiled then, a sardonic reminder of his mental state. To Janice it only confirmed that something deeply spiritual was going on. The look reminded her of that prisoner at Joliet, the serial killer who had turned his worship of Satan into murder. Back then, as a naive student, she didn't know what to do in response. Now she did. If this was to be a spiritual battle, she would call on God and wade in.

She prayed quickly, silently, for God's help.

"You're talking about the devil, aren't you?" she said.

A sudden look of connection, almost respect, flashed into Crazy's eyes. "You know?"

"Yes," she said.

"He's real, isn't he?"

"Yes, but so is God."

Crazy looked suddenly confused.

"Tell me," Janice said. "Tell me about the other bodies."

His look returned to malevolence. "Why should I?"

"Because it's not too late."

"For what?"

"For you. To be helped."

Suddenly Crazy's eyes rolled back in his head. "AHHHHEEEEE!" he screamed, as if a horrific, convulsive pain had gripped his head.

"Careful!" Mullin shouted, grabbing Crazy's arms.

"Wait!" Janice said quickly. She reached for Crazy's shoulders and shook him. "God is here! He'll protect you! Do you believe that?"

"Help me!" he screamed, and then his head dropped forward onto his chest.

"Let us help you," Janice said softly. "What's your name?"

Slowly, the head came up. The fierce malignity that had been in his eyes was now faded. For the first time he looked remotely human. "Dewey," he said.

Janice glanced at Jed, who seemed astonished at this turn of events.

"Dewey," Janice said, "what can you tell us about the bodies?"

"Dead. I came for them."

"Who?"

"Davis."

"I knew it!" Data said.

Janice said, "Who else?"

"Them."

"Who?"

"All of them."

"Who were they?"

"Davis. Steve. Rance. And anyone below."

"Below?"

"Under."

"Under what?"

"The cabin. The underground. Where they made the chips."

Jed said, "What are you talking about?"

"Under the cabin!" Dewey said. "That's where they kept them."

"Kept what?" Jed said.

"Nanos."

"The what?"

"Nanotech?" Data blurted excitedly.

Dewey smiled, as if suddenly someone understood him. "Yeah!"

"No way!" Data said.

"Way," said Dewey.

●

Light. Far away. Dark light. Hurt. Head hurts. Who am I? Eyes. Open eyes. Fuzzy. Why fuzzy? Who? Face. Know.

"I'm here," the familiar face said.

Who am I? Lauren's mind repeated.

"Lauren?"

No, not Lauren. Lauren was just human. I am more.

She recognized the face of her father.

Now she understood.

40

"What's down there's amazing," Mullin said. "A concrete bunker. Like Hitler or something."

It was three o'clock in the morning, and Janice was operating on pure adrenaline. So many bizarre things had happened. And now, even more bizarre, they were back in the small sheriff's station where she and Jed had so recently been jailed.

Only this time it was Dewey—Handleman, his last name was—who was in the lockup while she, Data, Jed, and Sheriff Egger listened to what Mullin had to say. The office was cramped and cold, but Janice hung on every word.

"All sorts of instruments," Mullin explained, "computers, wires, I don't know what all. I'm not some computer geek."

"Hey," Data said.

"No offense. It's just that I'm a meat-and-potatoes kind of guy."

"Don't you realize what was going on down there?" Data said rapidly. "If what that guy said is true, they were making chips that could become part of human biology! I want to go back there and see."

"It's a crime scene," Mullin said.

"Oh, man!"

"They have two bodies down there, just like the kid said. I got their wallets. One of them was a Harvard student. John Phillips."

"How did he die?" Janice said.

"Won't know how they died until the medical examiner takes over. And we won't know what happened down there unless that kid tells us."

"He's insane," Jed said.

"Maybe."

"Who was the other one?" Janice asked.

"Guy named Bob Thomas."

Jed stiffened. "Bob Thomas?"

"That's what it said. Know him?"

"In a way. He had disappeared. His father told me."

"I've got to talk to him," Janice said suddenly. "Sam and Davis are still out there with Lauren, and he's got some information—"

"Now hold on one minute!" Sheriff Egger said, slapping his hand on the table. "This is *my* office and *my* deal, and I got a killer in *my* jail."

"Alleged killer," Janice said.

"Oh yeah, you're the lawyer. Well, nobody's going to talk to nobody until—"

"Excuse me," Janice said, "I want to talk to him."

"And I say you can't."

"I'm his lawyer."

"You're *what?*" The sheriff's face flushed, and his chin almost hit the desk. Janice caught Jed looking with a smile of what looked to be respect. She couldn't help smiling back.

"So if you'll allow me?" Janice said.

"Well I . . ." the sheriff stammered.

"Not much you can do there, Egger," Jed said.

With a growl the sheriff got up from his metal chair and started jangling his keys. "Well, the rest of you stay here."

"I'd like him to come," Janice said, nodding at Jed. "He's my assistant."

The sheriff rolled his eyes but didn't argue. Jed, still smiling, followed them.

Three of the four lockups were empty. Dewey was sitting in the cage that Lazlo had formerly occupied. "What happened to the kid?" Janice asked the sheriff.

"He's gone."

"Did he ever get that Bible?"

"You know, he asked for one right after you left. It kept him quiet."

"The Word is living and active," Janice said.

"Whatever," Egger said. "You've got ten minutes." He clambered out of the room.

Dewey was sitting on the metal cot bolted to the wall. His hair was wet and stringy, and he looked spent.

"Can you talk?" Janice said.

He looked at her without resistance but said nothing.

"*Will* you talk?"

Silence.

"Please," she said. "I only want to help you."

"You believe in God?" Dewey said, his voice low and weak.

"Yes, I do."

"That's what this was all about, you know. You all think things are so simple. You don't know anything."

"Will you explain it to us?"

"What do I get in return?"

Jed grunted. "He's sane enough to ask for tit for tat."

"Shhh," Janice said. She didn't want Jed tipping the precarious apple cart that was Dewey Handleman, to whom she said, "I will represent you, free of charge, in any criminal proceeding brought against you. That's my end. For which I want to know how I can find my daughter. Are we agreed?"

Dewey rose from the cot and ambled to the green bars of the cell. He put his hands around them like he was in some prison movie. "Deal," he said.

"All right then," said Janice. "Please. How does all this relate to God? And my daughter?"

"Way back there in evolution, when we were getting separated from the animals, something strange happened to our brains."

Janice didn't say anything. This was not a debate over evolution. She wanted to hear what he had to say, in full.

"We see evidence of this change in the Neanderthal site at the Shanidar Cave in the mountains of Iraq. You know about this?"

Janice shook her head. She only knew anthropologists liked to speculate endlessly about Neanderthals, without consensus.

"It's around sixty thousand years old, this site," Dewey continued, "and they found nine Neanderthal bodies, see. And one of these had wounds to its head that left him with a withered arm and blindness in one eye, during his lifetime."

"So?" Jed said, stepping forward as if genuinely interested.

"So that means this community of Neanderthals had to take care of this guy. He couldn't have survived without help. And that shows a little thing called compassion. It's a religious impulse. And then they found a grave of a young Neanderthal that had traces of pollen all around. That showed he was buried on a bed of flowers. Including hyacinth and hollyhocks, which were thought to contain healing powers. This is another indication of spirituality. Whatever it was that happened, it's the thing that separates humans from animals."

"Man becoming aware of God," Jed said.

"Or what he thinks is God. The brain may have developed this impulse, see, to give it an adaptive advantage. It helped our species develop courage in the face of a dangerous world, so we could continue our progress. It didn't mean God really exists."

"Go on," Janice said.

"It means, though, that our brains have a God part. It may be in the prefrontal cortex, which is responsible for the most sophisticated aspects of our minds. It's also the part of the brain that has grown the largest over evolutionary history. Ours is about 200 percent larger than what we would expect for a primate our size. Whatever it is, it is what makes people religious. It's also what holds us back."

"In what sense?"

"In a moral sense. That's what Nietzsche was talking about, see? Religion, especially Christianity, is pathology. We've outgrown our use for it, and now we need to allow our brains to use the prefrontal cortex for other purposes. Like expanding our intelligence."

All this sounded like something Data might have picked up from a *Star Trek* episode. But Dewey clearly believed it.

"That's what Davis's project is all about, see? He wanted to develop a technology that would retard the God part of the brain and use it for other, connective purposes. That's what this thing is all about!"

Dewey's voice had suddenly risen.

"Then why did you go after him?" Jed said.

"Because they lied to me! See, what they did was encode a destruct program in the nanochips. I figured this out; that's what it had to be. If something happened that threatened the project, and it was connected to you, the program told you to self-destruct."

Jed snapped. "That's why Anthony jumped out the window."

"And why I almost offed *myself*. But the only thing I did was think about it, see? I started seeing things, visions, and I started thinking about them, and that triggered the self-destruct! They took away my power to think!"

"Tell me about the visions," Janice said.

"Yeah, that's when it started to hit me. I started thinking about this God part and said to myself, what if it wasn't the product of evolution after all? What if it was put there by God, a real God, as the way to communicate with the brain? Isn't that what religion believes? You think we have souls, right?"

"Right."

"So maybe this is where the soul lives. Why not? And that's when the self-destruct really kicked in. But I fought it. I was too strong for them!"

"Why isn't it working now?" Jed asked. "The self-destruct, I mean."

"It ran its course, I guess. I don't know. But I fought it, and I won. And I went up there to settle accounts. But they saw me coming."

"Who?"

"Davis and that other guy, Sam something."

"Who else?" Janice said. "Was there a girl?"

"A girl? I didn't see one."

"What happened after they spotted you?" Jed said.

"They sent the goon after me, but I beat it into the forest. I waited, but he must have given up. When I went back to the cabin, I saw only Rance and Steve there."

"And you shot them?" Jed said.

"Me? Nah. Didn't have to."

"Why not?"

"Because somebody beat me to it."

Janice shivered, not knowing whether to believe him. He was unstable and perhaps just covering for himself. But he said it simply, and there was a patina of believability about him.

And that raised more troubling questions. If not Dewey, then who? Who had killed these people? Would it stop here? And where was Lauren?

"We've *got* to get back," Janice said to Jed. "We've got to find Lauren *now.*"

Jed said, "I think you're right."

"Can we do it?"

He smiled. "I've told you before; I was born for this. Let's go."

"What about me?" Dewey said.

"Don't say anything to anyone," Janice said. "I'm your lawyer. You speak only through me." Janice took a step away from the cell.

"Where are you going?" Dewey said.

"I'll be back," she promised.

**41**

The Boston Field Office of the Federal Bureau of Investigation at One Center Plaza is in the heart of downtown. It looks out, on one side, over Beacon Hill, toward the courthouse and Suffolk University. Behind it is City Hall and the John F. Kennedy Federal Building. It would be hard to find a better location for a local arm of federal justice. It is virtually equidistant from every area of the city.

The office opens precisely at eight-fifteen weekday mornings. On this morning Jed and Janice were outside the doors at eight. Two hours of sleep, caught in snatches, had been enough to recharge Janice's natural batteries. It would not be enough, she knew, to carry her through a week. She'd need a real long sleep soon. But now that was a luxury she could not afford.

When the office opened, Jed and Janice were the first at the reception desk, and their look must have signaled to the young woman at the window that real trouble was afoot. She did not hesitate in buzzing for an agent.

A few minutes later a blond man of about forty-five, somewhat short, with wide shoulders, stepped out to the reception area. "I'm Assistant Special Agent in Charge Eric Loveland," he said. "What can I do for you?"

"My daughter has been kidnapped, and we have reason to believe she's here," Janice said.

Loveland's eyes showed immediate attention. "You are?"

"Janice Taylor. I'm a lawyer from Chicago."

Loveland glanced at Jed. "And you?"

"Jed Brown, and I'm a skip tracer from Los Angeles."

"And your interest in this case is?"

"I'm helping Ms. Taylor."

"She's paying you?"

"No. Maybe we'd better give you the whole picture, from the beginning."

"I think," Loveland said, "that would be nice."

●

Dr. Lyle Burack could not stop shaking.

Dreams die hard, but dreams of multibillions of dollars die hardest. Something was very wrong, and the project was in danger.

He knew it, sensed it, even though the details were not yet forthcoming.

All he knew was he did not dare venture out of his house this morning. His imagination conjured up all sorts of dire consequences and surreptitious miseries, from surveillance by the Feds to a camera crew from *20-20* waiting outside his door.

Davis! Why hadn't he called? Where was he? *What was going on?*

Trying to calm himself, Burack, still in his robe and pajamas, padded to the kitchen for another cup of coffee. Yes, it jangled the nerves. He knew that. But the warmth was also some comfort. He'd take anything.

When he stepped into the kitchen, he screamed.

It was a short, staccato yelp of shock.

Standing there was the last man he expected to see here in his house.

"Karel!" Burack said. "What are you doing here?"

Van Hoorn, calmly leaning against the refrigerator, said, "I have news."

"Well what's all this sneaking around? You almost gave me a heart attack!"

"No one must know I am here."

Van Hoorn's low, modulated voice evidenced something sinister. Just as Burack had suspected. "What is it?" he said.

"We have trouble."

"What trouble?" Burack's body now shook with abandon.

"Sit."

"What?"

"Sit," Van Hoorn repeated, motioning to a kitchen chair. Burack complied. It was better that way. He thought for a moment he might faint. The chair would prop him up.

"Tell me," Burack said.

"Not much to tell. Breach in security. People know."

"What's being done about it?"

"All taken care of. Almost."

"What do you mean *almost?*"

"Still one more thing," Van Hoorn said. He moved toward the other side of the kitchen, temporarily out of Burack's sight line.

"What thing is that?" said Burack, growing slightly impatient with the enforcer's slow speech.

"Suicide," Van Hoorn said.

"Suicide? Did somebody commit suicide? Who?"

"You," said Van Hoorn.

It was the last thing Burack ever heard.

In his office at Harvard, Bently Davis breathed deeply and composed himself. Then he buzzed his secretary and told her to show his guests in.

Presently, through the door, came the FBI agent who had called—what was his name?—and the woman, Janice, the one Sam had warned him about. Following her was the bounty hunter with the eye patch, Brown.

Only three of them. This would be easy.

"Ah," Davis said, rising from his chair.

"Professor Davis, thank you for seeing us," the agent said, showing his credential. *Loveland.* That was the name.

"Of course," said Davis as he made eye contact with Janice and Brown. They had a wildness in their eyes as if moving in for the kill. This was just like evolution, Davis mused. Soon they would know who was fit to survive.

Agent Loveland said, "This is Janice Taylor and Jed Brown. They've come to me with a story and think you might have some information that would be helpful."

"I'll be glad to help in any way I can."

"Thank you. May we sit?"

"Certainly." There were two chairs in front of Davis's desk and one by the wall. Jed Brown took the latter. Davis settled himself back into his own swivel chair.

Loveland took out a small notebook, opened it, and said, "Do you know a Sam Ramsey?"

"Yes, I do," Davis said.

"How do you know him?"

"He's a sales representative. My company has done business with him."

"UniGen?"

"That's right."

"Do you know where he is right now?"

"No."

"When was the last time you saw him?"

"Four or five months ago, I think. I can check my records, if you want."

Loveland looked at Janice, and Davis caught the look. It confirmed for him that this was a fishing expedition on the part of the agent. Doing his job, following a lead, but only having the word of two civilians to go on. No sweat.

"Have you ever seen this little girl?" Loveland asked, holding out a wallet photo. Davis took the picture and recognized Lauren instantly.

"No," Davis said. "Who is she?"

"She's my daughter," Janice said, her voice like a knife.

"Cute," Davis said.

"Where is she?" said Janice.

"Am I supposed to know?" Davis said, opening his hands to Loveland. "What's going on here?"

"Ms. Taylor says her girl was kidnapped," Loveland explained. "She thinks the father brought her here and that you have knowledge in that regard."

Calmly, Davis said, "No, I don't. I'm very sorry to hear that, Ms. Taylor. I wish I could help."

"That's a crock," Jed Brown said.

Loveland raised his hand, signaling that he should do the talking. "Professor Davis, can you account for your whereabouts for the last forty-eight hours?"

"Certainly."

"And where were you?"

"Here. In Cambridge."

"Anybody see you?"

"A few people. I was working on my book."

"I'd like those names later."

"Of course. One of them was my partner, Dr. Lyle Burack. You'll want to talk to him."

Loveland wrote in his notebook. "Does the name Dewey Handleman mean anything to you?"

"Oh yes. He was a student of mine. Also a volunteer at UniGen."

"What did he do at UniGen?"

"Research assistant."

"I see. Professor Davis, I am about to ask you some questions that have to do with four deaths. That is, official investigatory questions. You are not under arrest, but you don't have to answer if you so choose."

"No, please, ask away. I'd like to help this woman find her child." He shot a quick glance at Janice, who looked mentally exhausted. Tense. And convinced that he knew something.

"OK then," Loveland said, "according to Mr. Handleman, UniGen has been engaged in research regarding human biology."

"That's right," Davis said. "We are a genetic research firm. It's what we do."

"Also, the use of tiny computer chips to alter people's minds."

Smiling, Davis said, "That's something that is years away from seeing the light of day."

"So you're not doing anything of that kind now?"

"No."

"In any research facility?"

"No."

"Does UniGen have a research facility anywhere besides Cambridge?"

"No."

"No secret facility out in a woodsy area perhaps?"

"No. We're a very small firm."

"And if Mr. Handleman were to say that such things actually took place, would he be lying?"

Davis nodded, prepared. "Agent Loveland, you may not be aware of this on the limited information you have, but Mr. Handleman had to be dismissed from UniGen a few weeks ago."

Loveland seemed surprised. This was the wedge Davis would place between Loveland and the woman. He would drive it further as the interview continued. "On what grounds?" Loveland asked.

"Drug abuse, I'm afraid," Davis said. "Mr. Handleman had a history of drug abuse and erratic behavior. He became a danger to himself and the firm."

Loveland looked at Janice then, and Davis knew the wedge was well placed.

"I see," said Loveland, writing something in his notebook. He did not follow up with a question.

"Wait a second," Janice said. "He's lying."

"Please," Davis said calmly.

"Does the term *Nephilim* mean anything to you?"

"Nephi-what?"

"Nephilim."

"I'm afraid I don't know what you're talking about."

Loveland said, "Ms. Taylor, let me—"

"No," Janice interrupted. "I want him to answer *my* questions. He's lying. He has my daughter!"

Good, Davis thought. *Let her vent her emotions. The wedge goes deeper.*

"Agent Loveland," Davis said, "I am happy to cooperate with you, but I can't put up with baseless accusations. I have classes to teach and business to attend to. Wild fabrications that come from a manifestly unstable person like Mr. Handleman shouldn't be allowed, should they? I'm a target because of position. If these people—" he waved his arm at Jed and Janice—"are setting me up for a lawsuit, I don't think the FBI should be a party to that."

"Lawsuit?" Janice said.

"Ms. Taylor, please," said Loveland. "I came here on your information only. I want to get to the bottom of this as quickly as you do. Your daughter's been kidnapped, but we don't know that Professor Davis had anything to do with it or knows anything. A charge like kidnapping can't be made lightly."

"But we have corroboration," Jed said. Davis glanced at the big man, whose good eye was glaring at him. "We have a computer file which shows Davis has a connection with something called Nephilim."

"And where is that file?" Loveland asked.

"With an associate of mine," Jed said.

"Can you get me that information immediately?"

"Sure."

Loveland stood. "Then I suggest we postpone any further questions until I get a look at that. Professor Davis, I repeat, you are not the target of any investigation. I'm just doing my job."

"I understand that," Davis said, rising and offering his hand to the agent. "And I understand the stress these people are under. Believe me, if I can help in any way, I will."

"Oh, you'll help all right," Janice said.

"Ms. Taylor," Loveland said, "it's time to go."

With that the agent raised his arm and guided Janice Taylor and Jed Brown from Davis's office, but not before one final look of contempt from the woman.

No matter, Davis thought. *The wedge is firmly in place. And it will stay.*

●

"He's lying!" Janice said.

"I don't know that," Loveland said firmly.

"But . . ." *But what?* The agent was right. If this were a trial, the judge would say all she had was hearsay upon hearsay, from Dewey Handleman through her. He had his job to do and was doing it. But the calm answers from Davis—and her emotional outburst, she realized—did not help one bit.

She felt Jed's hand on her arm. It was a comfort. "We'll contact you, Agent Loveland," Jed said. "Soon."

"I'll be waiting," he said.

Jed took Janice, via MBTA, to the impound lot in Boston (he knew where all the right places were, he explained), and Janice paid the fine to claim her car. All the while Jed calmed her, telling her he trusted Agent Loveland and once he had the information from the hard drive, he would follow up with Davis. In the meantime Jed would try to find Sam.

Jed drove her car this time, back to Data's apartment building. When they pulled up, Janice tried to quiet an increased feeling of desperation. There were so many connections that were tenuous. Why wasn't God dealing with the clear evil here? Why wasn't he leading her to Lauren?

She didn't even realize she had her head in her hands until Jed stopped the car and put his own hand on her shoulder.

"Hey," he said. "Hang in there."

"I'm trying," she said.

"You're holding up like a champ."

She smiled.

He said, "Sterling used to tell me about blessings through pain. I never got that. Where is the blessing in Sterling's death? And where is it with you, your daughter ripped away from you? I still don't get it. But I see strength in you."

Janice put her hand on top of his. In the silence she sensed that the wall of ice, for the moment at least, had dissipated.

"Come on," he said. "Let's finish this thing."

A cloud cover seemed to overcome Data's apartment building as they approached the front door. Jed buzzed the number. No response. He buzzed again, good and long.

Nothing.

"Not home?" Janice said.

"Maybe." But his look belied a sense of urgency. He proceeded to press every button on the console. "Shotgun approach," he explained.

A moment later the security door buzzed. Jed grabbed it and led them inside. Janice followed him up the first flight of stairs and down the corridor to Data's door. Jed's knocking got no response.

"I don't like it," Jed said. He removed a small, leather wallet from his jacket and opened it. Inside was a collection of thin metal tools. He selected one and began to pick the lock.

A few turns later and the door opened, tethered however by the chain lock inside.

"Data?" Jed said through the crack.

"Can you see anything?"

"No. But he's got to be in there. He attached the chain. Data!"

"Could he be hurt?"

"That's what I'm going to find out." It only took one shoulder thrust to rip the chain from its mooring. The door flew open, and Janice could see immediately that something was very wrong.

The apartment was completely torn up. Stuffing torn from the old sofa was strewn across the floor, furniture lay all over in broken bits, drawers had been pulled out and dumped. Even the *Star Trek* posters were ripped from the walls. Someone had done a thorough job.

"Data!" Jed shouted, running through the apartment. Janice looked in the kitchen, praying she wouldn't find a body.

"He's not here," Jed said, joining Janice in the kitchen.

"But somebody sure was." She looked around the mess and said, "And the computers are gone."

"Van Hoorn. They must have traced us when Data hacked into their system."

"So our hard evidence . . . ?"

"Is gone."

Janice felt a boulder drop inside her, a heavy reckoning from hard reality. Davis! He truly had this entire scheme under control. He had been cool for a reason. The only corroborating document that existed, so far as she knew, was gone now. All they could give the FBI is what Dewey had told them. But he was under suspicion for murder and had evidenced enough mental instability that his testimony would be worthless.

But what about the cabin and the secret lab underneath? Davis hadn't appeared concerned about it. Why not?

As Janice pondered all this, she noticed the kitchen window was wide open, the curtain flapping gently with the breeze.

"Jed, do you think he might have gone out this way?"

"Maybe," Jed said. "Let's look." He stepped up onto the sink, then, barely fitting, pushed himself outside. "There's a ledge here and . . ."

"What is it?" Janice said.

Then she heard Jed say, "Data."

Janice hopped up on the sink, feeling awkward squatting in the basin, to look outside. She saw Data, his back to the building, sitting on the ledge.

"Get away from me," he said quietly.

"What happened?" Jed asked.

"Get away, I said."

"Come inside before you kill yourself."

"Who cares?"

"What happened, Data?"

"You happened. You came in and ruined everything."

"Come inside and talk to us, will you?"

"They cleaned me out. Everything. All my computer stuff."

"Who did? Did you see anybody?"

"Somebody knocked me out."

"Can you describe him?"

"No."

"Come on in."

"Leave me alone."

"You want me to drag you in?"

"Get away!"

Janice reached out the window and touched Jed's leg. He looked at her, and she pointed to herself, indicating she wanted to try talking.

"Hey, Data," she said.

"You here too?"

"Yeah, it's me. I'm sorry for all this. I'm sorry you got sucked in."

"You didn't do it. It was *him.*"

"But it was my daughter that brought me here. And I want to thank you."

"For what?"

"For helping me. For putting yourself on the line. For getting shot at, and for letting yourself in for all this. It made a difference. And I'm grateful. I want you to know that."

Data paused, then said, "Fine. Now will you both go away?"

"We don't want to," Janice said. "We want you to come inside."

"Leave me alone, can't you?"

"That's not very Trekkian of you," Janice said. Jed flashed her an odd look, but it got Data's attention.

"What's that crack supposed to mean?" Data said.

Janice didn't have the faintest idea, except that she felt Data was, at that moment, a child pouting and like a child needed some parental counseling. Her instinct had told her to hit him where he was most vulnerable, and the only thing she could think of was his passion for all things *Trek.*

A passion Janice did not share. She had only seen a few episodes of the original TV show and a couple of the movies. So she said, "I just never saw anybody aboard the ship, the . . . the . . ."

"Enterprise," Data said.

"Right. Never saw anybody turn and run away from a fight."

"So?"

"Well, Davis thinks he has you beat. He thinks he can intimidate you. You want to let him get away with that?"

She saw Jed smiling at her and nodding. *Good plan,* he seemed to be saying.

"So what am I supposed to do? They took all my stuff!"

"Help us think, Data."

Now, for the first time, he turned to look at her. "Think?"

"Yes. You've got the best computer around in your head. We need your help. Please."

43

Agent Eric Loveland looked out from his office toward Beacon Hill. The gold-domed State House reflected the thin rays of sun that battled through the clouds. Just beyond it were the old brownstone and brick houses looking almost exactly as they did when Louisa May Alcott, Edwin Booth, and Julia Ward Howe, among others, had lived there.

Loveland liked the sights of the old city but now found himself wondering if the old was going to be forever lost to the terrible technologies he knew were coming. This story from Janice Taylor had enough bizarre detail to be the truth, yet his agent's gut couldn't help but be skeptical. Many a wild story had been dreamed up by people involved in domestic cases. He remembered one woman who had accused her ex-husband of being the mastermind behind the blowing up of the Murrah Federal Building in Oklahoma City in 1995. She'd supplied enough detail to make him spend a day tracking the guy's records. Turned out the guy was a plumber from Portland who was about as dangerous as Mickey Mouse.

Though Janice Taylor didn't strike him as the type, he also knew looks could be deceiving. He'd reached the point in his career where it was hard evidence that talked; the rest could walk, as far as he was concerned.

So where was the hard evidence in this case? Bently Davis, he knew, was one of the most highly respected academicians in the country. A best-selling author. A rich man, and therefore a target. And he seemed perfectly innocent when questioned.

But something, Loveland couldn't say what exactly, kept him thinking about this case. The whole thing about a secret lab in the woods (he was in the process of confirming that) and experiments with tiny computers in the brain. It was all so bizarre yet plausible. A new age was coming. If he was going to continue doing his job, he'd have to be ready for it.

It would all depend on whether that hard, corroborative evidence which the man, Jed Brown, had mentioned would be forthcoming. Loveland didn't like Brown. He had a thing against bounty hunters anyway. But in a pinch they could turn up some interesting stuff.

Loveland decided to do a quick scan of the news before taking lunch. He clicked his mouse, and his computer screen zapped to the Bureau's special LNA site, where instant local news access was provided twenty-four hours a day.

He scanned the provisional titles list, which were essentially summaries of the stories to be filed with various media in Boston and as far away as New York. Nothing much of interest.

Then he saw it. "UniGen Partner Dead. Suicide Suspected." He quickly clicked on it.

This was a story from the *Globe* set to go out to the wire:

> Dr. Lyle Burack, 42, a partner in the Cambridge-based genetic research firm UniGen, was found dead this morning in his home in Somerville. Cause of death has not been determined, but authorities are investigating the possibility of suicide. Sources close to the investigation say a note was

found at the scene. Burack was a partner in UniGen with Dr. Bently Davis, the Harvard professor and writer.

A dead partner and a note. A link to Davis? Lunch would have to be on the fly now. Loveland had some work to do.

●

"Daddy?"

"Yes."

"My head hurts."

"That will pass."

"It hurts very much. I'm afraid."

"That will pass too."

"I'm very afraid."

"No need."

"What's happening to me?"

"You're becoming new."

"New how?"

"Smarter. Better."

"But it hurts. Make it stop hurting."

"I can't."

"Please, Daddy."

"He'll make it stop."

"Who will?"

"Davis."

"I don't like him. Ohhhh! It hurts!"

"He'll make it stop!"

●

Data seemed to calm down a little once inside. Even as they found places to sit in the mess of his apartment, Data was returning to normal—what was normal for him, Janice mused, which meant relating everything to his favorite television show.

"This is so like the 'Conspiracy' episode."

Jed started to say something, but Janice, sitting next to him on what was left of Data's couch, touched his arm to stop him. She wanted Data to be free to talk as a way of relief. She could put up with it for a few minutes at least. Then they could return to the joint venture of finding her daughter.

Data continued, "See, an old friend of Picard's dies, but before he does, he warns Picard of a conspiracy to overthrow the Starfleet. So Picard puts Data to work——he always puts Data to work, you notice that?—and Data analyzes recent Starfleet command decisions. He detects a pattern, and Picard decides to check this out on Earth. As soon as they enter Earth's orbit, several admirals at Starfleet headquarters invite Picard to dinner."

"Nice of them," Jed said.

"Quiet," Janice said.

Data seemed to ignore them both. He seemed to be telling this to a theater audience in his mind. "Admiral Quinn says he can't come to dinner but asks to visit the *Enterprise*. But after he beams up, Picard has a feeling something's wrong and tells Riker to watch Quinn as Picard beams down to the dinner. Quinn starts beating people up, until Dr. Crusher zaps him with a phaser and examines him. She discovers a beetle has attached itself to Quinn's brain and is controlling his mental and physical activity."

Janice thought, *Life imitating art, or the other way around?*

"Riker beams down to the dinner, where everyone is controlled by the beetles on the brain. Riker pretends to be one of them but is faking it and pulls a phaser out on them. He and Picard find out that the leader is Commander Remmick, controlled by the mother creature. So they fry him."

Data paused, caught his breath. "So there you go. We got a brain-controlled conspiracy around us, but we got no idea where they're eating dinner. So we can't zap or—"

"Wait a second," Jed interrupted. "Dinner."

"Yeah, yeah?" Data said. "What about dinner? You hungry or something?"

"No, but Lauren is." He looked at Janice.

"What are you thinking?" she asked.

"My little man is talking," he said. "Where are we going to find Lauren? We have no clue. She's no doubt with Sam now. So when might they surface? For food."

"Maybe," said Data.

"They have to eat. My guess is that Sam wouldn't leave her alone, so she'd go with him when they went for food, to a store or . . ."

"Fast food," Janice said.

"What I was thinking."

Data slapped his thighs. "You know how many fast-food places we got around here?"

Jed turned to Janice. "Didn't you say Lauren liked a certain place?"

Janice thought a moment. "You mean Wendy's?"

"That's it." He spun back to Data. "They got Wendy's around here?"

"What do a I look like?" Data snapped. "The Yellow Pages?"

"You got a Yellow Pages then?"

"I used to."

"Find it."

"Oh man!" Data stood and stepped over some debris, making his way to the far wall where a small cabinet was overturned. He lifted the cabinet with one hand and reached under with the other. "You're in luck," he said, holding up a Yellow Pages. He threw it across the room to Jed.

Opening it up, Jed picked his way through until he came to the restaurant section. Janice leaned over to look. "Anything?" she said.

Jed scanned another moment, then said, "One. They got one! Can you believe it?"

"Where?"

"Looks like Chelsea."

Filled with a sudden surge of hope, Janice said, "Do you suppose?"

Jed turned and took her hand. It was a small gesture, but tender. "My little man is really talking," he said. "Could be nothing, but I'm thinking it's worth a try. And it's better than sitting around. What do you say?"

She felt, for some reason, that she should go with him. She didn't have a little man, but a still, small voice seemed to utter the word *go*.

"Oh man," Data said, "this is just like the episode where Picard hears voices, and Data figures out that a voice translator has been implanted in his—"

"Thank you, Data," Jed said.

"Let's go," Janice said.

The homicide detective, Murphy, was a throwback to **44** the Boston policeman of the early 1900s—florid faced and Irish, even the hint of a brogue in his voice. For Loveland—Ivy League educated but brought up in the sunny climes of Florida—it was like he had suddenly morphed into a scene from a 1930s Pat O'Brien movie.

"So how many suicides you investigated?" Murphy asked, leaning back in a squeaking chair at his desk in the squad room. The tone was a bit condescending.

"None," Loveland said.

"You Feds are above all that, huh? I get ten, twenty a month. If there's a suspicion about it, it goes through homicide. Most of the time it's a half-day thing."

"What's the main method?"

"You ever get any training at that fancy Quantico?"

"I had a one-day session on it."

"Uh-huh."

Refusing to take Murphy's bait, Loveland quietly asked, again, about the main methods of suicide.

"Gun or overdose," Murphy said. "We don't get many hangings anymore. Back in the old days it was more common."

"Why was that?"

"Because hanging was a form of execution. Now we're a lethal-injection society, a Dr. Kevorkian society, so people like the drug route. It seems a peaceful way to go."

"What did Burack use?"

"Twenty-two caliber bullet to the right temple."

Loveland nodded and took a sip of the battery-acid coffee he'd been given in a Styrofoam cup. "The reason I'm here, as you know, is that this may be connected in some way to some information that's come my way regarding Dr. Burack's business enterprise."

"That was all laid out in the note."

"Other than the note, what leads you to believe this is a suicide?"

With a snort Murphy leaned forward and put his elbows on his desk. "Let me give you a little lesson here in homicide investigation. The factors we have to look at. It's pretty simple, really."

Loveland, in no mood for a lecture, knew he was going to get one anyway. Murphy was going to dish out the information his way.

"You look at the wound first, of course," Murphy said, "to determine how close the weapon was to entry. Also the place of the wound. Most suicides are to the temple and the mouth. Some to the chest, not many to the stomach. Here we got it to the head. One shot. With suicide it's hard to do more. Then where is the weapon in relation to the body? Here, we got it on the floor near Burack's hand. We got residue on the hand. And there's one thing we don't have."

"What's that?"

"Evidence of a struggle. Burack was sitting calmly in a chair in his kitchen when he did this."

"Anything else?"

"Just the note, which is the final nail in the coffin. You'll pardon the expression."

"May I see it now?"

Murphy held up a white piece of paper. "Here's a copy."

"Where's the original?"

"Lab."

Loveland took the one-page note, a single-spaced, computer-generated document, and began to read.

My dream was to take us to the next level of human existence, to use computer technology to alter human consciousness in ways beyond our wildest dreams. I was opposed by everyone, so I had to do it myself. And I would have succeeded if given more time. But they found out about my lab. People started to disobey. I had to kill them. I had to cover it all up. When I did that, I realized something. What was I killing, really? Protoplasm. Chemicals in motion. A small part of the eternal recurrence Nietzsche spoke about. There is a bigger part! There is a higher experience than evolutionary progress trapped in time! That is what I go to experience, because I am too far ahead of everyone here.

I demand that the following be published upon my death:

Many die too late, and some die too early.

There is an old illusion: it is called good and evil.

There is no devil and no hell.

Hope is the worst of evils, for it prolongs the torments of man.

There are no eternal facts, as there are no absolute truths.

It was signed at the bottom, above a signature line that read "Dr. Lyle Burack, Ph.D., Harvard University."

"Crazy, huh?" Murphy said.

"Maybe."

"What's that supposed to mean?"

"Method in the madness perhaps."

Murphy tugged at his right eyebrow.

"Shakespeare," Loveland explained. "Doesn't this strike you as a bit too confessional?"

"I thought of that already," Murphy huffed. "But you line it up with everything else, all the other factors, and it makes a pretty strong presumption."

"You have a graphologist look at the signature?"

"A whosis?"

"Graphologist. Handwriting expert."

"I don't see any reason—"

"Look at the signature." He handed the paper back to Murphy, who scanned it.

"So?"

"Does the upsweep on the right side of the letters look any bolder to you?"

"Upsweep?"

"Oh, sorry. I guess you didn't take the same class in graphology I did at Quantico."

Murphy squinted. "Now, look—"

"It's not definitive, but it shouldn't be difficult to confirm. Lyle Burack may have been left-handed."

Cogs and wheels began churning behind Murphy's eyes.

"That's right," Loveland said. "Makes shooting himself in the right temple a bit of a trick, doesn't it?"

45

Waiting again. This time parked across the road from a Wendy's Old-Fashioned Hamburger place. It seemed to Janice, at first blush, like the proverbial needle in the haystack. But that's all they had at the moment.

Jed had been strangely quiet on the drive out. She chalked it up to his peculiar, tracker cogitations. Now, though, it seemed like something more. An indication of deeper waters below the surface.

She declined the informality of small talk, realizing that she had too much respect for him now to do that. She wondered, too, if there was more than respect going on here, and that made her nervous.

Almost as if he sensed her very feelings, Jed suddenly said, "Look, I want to say something to you, if you don't mind."

"No," she said, her voice squeaking involuntarily, as if it knew there was great import to what he was about to say.

"I work alone," he said. "This is new to me."

"Hey," said Janice, "it's new to *me* too."

"You put two people together, there's double the chance something can go wrong. There's also . . ."

Janice waited as his voice trailed off, giving him his own timing.

". . . the chance that personal stuff can happen."

"Personal?"

"Yeah. Like two people don't get along with each other. Or they get flat-out mad. Emotions get in there and make things more complicated."

"You feel that's happened with me here?"

"No. This is another complication. A man and a woman together."

Janice felt a sharp tingling run up her arms and down her back, a clear signal he was giving voice to what she felt too.

"I find myself," he said slowly, "attracted to you."

Unable to do a thing about it, Janice felt her pulse quicken and knew she could no longer deny feeling the same way.

"I had to tell you that," he said, "because it was going to fly out of me sooner or later. I had to clear the air."

"Jed—"

"No, let me finish. I don't know if the feeling is mutual or not, but before we go any further I feel like you deserve to know."

"Know what?"

"About me. About why I can't get involved with anybody again. You wanted to know about my daughter and all that?"

"I did, yes."

"All right, here it is. But as I talk, I want us both to look out the window. We're not here just to kill time."

"All right."

"It all started when I was eighteen years old and served at the tail end of Vietnam, just like Sterling."

When Jed got home, he was greeted with the derision of the public. That era was a time of deep divisions in the country, and for the first time in the history of American warfare, returning warriors were not welcomed back home with open arms. It was as if there was an embarrassed silence on the part of the government and a need for Jed's contemporaries—college-age kids—to express their animosity toward the war effort by despising the soldiers who fought it.

Jed's first reaction was to get high. In Nam he had gotten into drugs, mainly marijuana, and there was no good reason to stop now. Back in his old room at his parents' house in Oceanside, Jed spent his first full month doing nothing but going to the beach and clouding his mind with grass.

Sterling was, by this time, a full professor at Butler Theological Seminary in San Diego. Jed didn't find out until later, but Sterling took an early sabbatical in order to devote more time to helping his brother find his way back to normalcy.

He was persuasive and convinced Jed to use the GI Bill to reenroll in UC San Diego, where Jed had completed one year. Sterling knew a professor there in the religious studies department, the only staunch evangelical on the faculty, and he consented to take Jed under his wing. If all went well, Sterling would help Jed get into Butler.

Everything worked at first. Jed took to college as if it were a lifeline, and delving into religion was just what he needed after the life-disrupting experience of Vietnam. If there was meaning to this life, Jed wanted to find it.

And he thought he did the day he met Susie Howarth.

She was a poli sci major and a hippie, intelligent, with blue eyes and long blonde hair that fell to the middle of her back. She liked reading Whitman and Kerouac, as well as McLuhan and I. F. Stone. She could quote the *I Ching* and Frank Zappa. In short, she was beautiful and intelligent, with a verve for life Jed had long since lost.

For some reason she went for him.

Maybe he was something of a reclamation project for her. A Nam vet

who represented everything she despised but home with deep wounds—
mental, not physical. She laughed a lot at his jokes and feeble attempts to
act poetic. "You read poetry like Nixon," she once told him, a remark that
bothered him more than she knew.

But somewhere along the way she must have fallen in love because one
Friday at the end of his sophomore year they got married by a judge and
ran off for a three-day honeymoon in Tijuana.

For a while there everything was near perfect. They lived in a small,
one-bedroom apartment near the campus. Susie went to her organization
meetings and didn't insist Jed go. They had their share of arguments, of
course. He was, despite the war, still gung-ho about American military
imperatives. But maybe those controversies were what kept them
together, the way opposites attract and add spice.

Then in Jed's senior year Melody made her appearance.

It was an unplanned pregnancy, and at first Susie was pushing to have
an abortion. Susie had been a strong abortion advocate since high school,
three years before the Supreme Court had legalized the procedure in *Roe
v. Wade*.

Though he had never given the issue much thought—in fact, he
leaned toward letting women do pretty much what they wanted with
their bodies—Jed somehow felt this time it wasn't right. Maybe his
religious studies had given him a new valuation of life. Or maybe it was
simply the fact that Susie was carrying *his* baby, and there was something
primal about that. He *wanted* the baby and realized that was, for the first
time in years, giving him a reason to hope about the future—hope that
life had a purpose beyond mere existence.

The arguments about the abortion were fierce. Finally Susie, without
Jed's knowledge, scheduled the abortion for a morning in mid-December.
But at the last moment she didn't go through with it. Jed never knew why.
He only knew that Melody was born, and he was transformed. He never
knew he had that much love inside him.

Susie seemed happy about it, too, once she got used to Melody. But it wasn't the easiest thing to go to school with an infant daughter. Somehow Susie and Jed muddled through. The UC system hadn't caught on yet to the explosive need for good child care, so Jed and Susie had to juggle their schedules. But they managed, and for a time they were happy.

But with classes and flip-flopping care for Melody, they spent less and less time together. For Jed it wasn't the worst of trade-offs. He adored his baby daughter. But Susie seemed to grow more distant.

Jed graduated and was accepted as a divinity student at Butler. At last his life seemed to be operating on all cylinders. He was sure now that he could put to rest the demons of the past, the horrible Nam experience, and pretty much get things together.

Then it all blew up.

Jed had gone into the preaching program and was even doing some messages at a local church on Sundays. It wasn't so much a calling as it was a voyage of discovery. But Susie did not see it that way.

"You're too far out!" Susie shouted one Sunday when Jed came home. "You're taking this to the extreme!"

"What extreme?"

"Religion! I mean it's OK from a philosophical standpoint, but it's not practical."

"Oh really? Is that the latest word from the Marxist-Leninist Radical Campus Club?"

"At least we're *doing* something, not just talking about it!"

"Doing what? Blowing up government buildings? Kidnapping heiresses? Shooting cops? What?"

Melody, who had been sleeping, started crying. Susie snatched her out of the crib and started for the door.

"Where are you going?" Jed said.

"None of your business," Susie snapped, slamming the door behind her.

She didn't come back that night or the next day. Jed called the police, and two days later they found her at the house of a guy named Thomas Leeds.

●

"He was a local campus radical type," Jed told Janice. "One of the last of the revolutionary wannabes. Susie told me she was moving in with him."

"And Melody?"

"With Melody."

"What did you do?"

"Nothing, at first. I thought it would blow over. I thought she'd come back. I prayed to God that she would come back. I put on sackcloth and ashes. And guess what?"

"What?"

"She didn't come back."

Janice couldn't help turning toward him for a moment. Jed continued to stare ahead, lost in a former shadow.

●

Jed dropped out of Butler. Though Sterling tried to help, nothing anyone could say had any effect. It was as if the bottom had dropped out of his ship of faith, and the boat was sinking directly to the bottom of the sea.

There would be a custody fight. Jed was not going to give up seeing Melody, but Susie was determined to keep her from him. Once, when he showed up at Leeds's house unannounced, demanding to see Melody, he was roughed up by a couple of Leeds's radical lackeys and thrown out on the street, falling there like an unhinged tackling dummy.

That was the moment, lying in the street, when the course of his life took a turn that would change him forever.

Jed bought a gun—a Smith & Wesson .357 magnum, a six-shooter as powerful as a small rifle. Reportedly it could stop a moving vehicle, which is why the California Highway Patrol favored it. And if it had that much power, it could easily clean out a nest of pseudo-revolutionaries and one hateful ex-wife.

The plan was simple. Get wind of the next meeting at Leeds's house, then calmly walk in and commit mass murder. Take Melody and head for Mexico. Find a way to live.

Jed told no one about his intentions, but somehow, the way he always did, big brother Sterling sensed something bad was about to happen.

They had a tense confrontation on the very afternoon Jed was going to do it. Sterling pulled out all the emotional stops—anger, frustration, sadness, duty, honor—in an effort to get Jed to check himself into a psych hospital for help. The consuming fire of Jed's hatred wouldn't allow any of it to have an effect.

Finally, Sterling yelled, "What are you going to do?"

"Nothing," Jed lied.

"I can always tell when you lie, Jed. You're lying now. You're going to do something to mess up your life! What is it?"

"Nothing, I tell you. Get out of my face!"

"Kill her," Sterling said quietly. "That's what you're going to do."

"Get out of here, Sterling."

"You're crazy, Jed. You need help. Listen—"

"If you don't get out of here now, I may kill you!"

Jed would remember the look in Sterling's eyes forever after—the hurt, the pain. But it meant little then. There was just no caring left in Jed Brown.

"Before I go," Sterling said, "I want you to promise me you won't do anything or go anywhere until I talk to you again. Will you at least promise me that?"

Jed looked his brother in the face. "OK, I'll promise you that."

It was the best lie he ever told. Sterling left.

Jed spent the next two hours drinking liquid courage—a half-bottle of scotch. Just before packing his piece and heading out, he heard a car pull up on the street. He looked through the window. It was a black-and-white.

Sterling had tipped off the cops, he figured. Quickly, he slipped out the back, hopped on his motorcycle and rammed through the alley. He gunned the bike, as if being followed, zipping up and down side streets and in between traffic. If the cops had wanted to tail him, they didn't do much of a job. He was home free.

And heading for Leeds's place. The Smith & Wesson was hard against his back, stuck in his pants.

It was just before dark when he got there; his body was pumping adrenaline like it had the first time he'd seen action in Nam. And like that initial brush with death and danger, he felt the oddest sensation of removal from reality—as if he could stand outside his body and watch the carnage, like a teenager at a slasher flick. Somewhere inside him a voice tried to break the spell, but he suppressed it. Only later would he be able to reflect on how far he had fallen.

Parking his bike around the corner, Jed approached the house like a SWAT cop advancing on a sniper's lair. The place looked deserted, but he knew this guy Leeds liked secrecy. He wouldn't be advertising any meetings.

Determined to use the elements of shock and surprise, Jed gave a heavy boot to the door and burst into the house, his weapon ready to fire.

No one was home.

The place was partially cleaned out, as if someone had packed for a quick trip. Or been warned.

That was it, he was sure. His goody-goody brother! He must have come here to warn Susie, and she had taken off with Melody, along with that louse Leeds.

And gone where?

For a moment Jed considered turning the gun on himself. What was the point of going on? But then his desire for revenge saved him again. He would find them.

●

"Later," Jed explained to Janice, "I found one of Leeds's guys and . . . convinced him to tell me a few things. He didn't know where they'd gone, but he did say it was underground. The Feds were preparing an indictment against Leeds for interstate terrorism. It was a good time for them to take off and start a new life. That's when I became a tracker."

"Did you find them?"

"I have a natural talent."

●

It took two months, almost to the day, before Jed found them in Lincoln, Nebraska.

Starting with Leeds's transcripts, which Jed lifted from the college administration office, Jed managed to piece together a geography of Leeds's past. From there it was a simple matter of tracking down possible family members who might be providing aid and comfort. Leeds had been born in Lincoln. There were a lot of signposts from his past that were easy, though time-consuming, to follow.

But he found them.

And then he took his time. For several days he observed them, honing his surveillance skills, watching and waiting. Perversely, he wanted to let his obsession build, to allow it to become an unbearable force within him. That way, when the time finally came, he would release it in one raging torrent and in doing so, he hoped, purge himself of the driving hatred inside.

During his surveillance he saw just how much Leeds had taken away from him. Susie, but most of all Melody, seemed perfectly happy.

The more he saw, the more his hate burned, until he could stand it no more.

He waited until midnight, which seemed appropriate. Earlier he had observed Leeds working on a side window, and that was how he entered the house. Stealthily, into the dark two-story place, pulse pounding.

In his mind he had a map of the house, though he had never seen it. But from the outside view he figured that Melody had a room of her own on the second floor, at the northern corner. Susie and Leeds shared the bedroom on the opposite side.

Jed made his way up the stairs softly, careful with each step lest there be a creak or snap. His ascent was virtually soundless, and he felt empowered as never before. He could do this. He could probably do this for a living. Kill people for money. Hit man.

And why not? There was no point in anything else. In a way he was actually doing these people a favor. Removing them from this pointless existence. That's when he decided he'd include Melody.

Yes, Melody too. Better if she never had to face the rottenness of being alive.

At the end of the hall, he stopped outside the slightly opened door. Susie no doubt left it that way so she could hear Melody during the night. Her motherly instinct would be her downfall. Another of life's little ironies.

Jed removed the .357 magnum from his waistband.

This would be quick. He would dispatch the two lovers first, using a pillow to muffle the sound as best he could. Then Melody, quickly.

And then, he suddenly thought, himself. Why spare himself the relief he was giving to the others?

Yes, that would be best. Relieve the hatred, then go to rest forever.

Eternal nothingness.

Peace.

He reached for the door, pushed it open.

Took one step.

"Mommy!"

Melody's voice! From down the hall.

Unable to think, Jed stepped backward, finding a nook in the shadows.

"Mommy!"

A moment later Susie's form padded out of the room. "I'm coming, honey," she said sleepily as she moved toward her daughter's room.

Jed, frozen, listened. In the stillness of the house, he could hear the voices.

"I had a bad dream," Melody said in a half-crying voice.

"It's all right," Susie said. "It was just a dream. I'm right here."

"I'm scared."

"You don't have to be. There's nothing to be scared about."

Isn't there? Jed thought.

Then the little girl's voice said, "I miss Daddy."

Jed did not even hear Susie's response. It was as if a torrent of emotion swept into his head and blocked his hearing. When the tears started streaming down his face, he knew it was all over. His plans. Everything.

Instead of hate he became filled with revulsion for himself.

Then Susie came back toward her room. In the darkness Jed did everything he could not to make a sound. He breathed slowly through his mouth.

For a half hour he stood there, motionless, feeling only his chest expanding and retracting.

Then he quietly snuck down the stairs and out of the house. Out of Nebraska. Out of his past for good.

●

"I probably would have offed myself if I hadn't hit a ditch in New Mexico," Jed said. "Almost killed me anyway. I woke up in a hospital. I had only one eye."

"Did you ever see Melody again?" Janice asked.

"No." He said, still looking out the window toward Wendy's.

"Why not?"

"Because I looked at myself in the mirror. She didn't need a father like me hanging around. Live and let live."

"Don't you miss her?"

Jed kept his face straight ahead. "I used to. But I made myself stop."

The wall of ice was going up again. Janice waited in silence until she could stand it no longer. "Jed?" she said.

"Yeah?"

"Thank you for telling me."

Jed breathed in deeply. "Sure. Now we know we can keep things strictly business, right?"

There were too many conflicting thoughts for Janice to answer.

"Let's keep watching the place," Jed said.

46

Bently Davis paced his UniGen office like a prisoner in his cell. Along with Burack's suicide note had come publicity. Reporters. Curiosity seekers. Volunteers looking to take Burack's place. It was not quiet, and Davis could not work.

Though everything seemed neatly tied up, he could not shake the suspicion that there was still a loose end somewhere out there. At this stage he could not afford a slip.

The moment Karel Van Hoorn knocked on his office door, Davis made his decision. It was a difficult one, not because of any loyalty—that was an emotional reason and therefore not worthy of him—but because it would mean starting over. Time was what would be lost, but his mind told him it was for an offsetting gain. His mind won out, as it always did.

"Karel," Davis said to the big man. "Sit down."

Van Hoorn did as he was told, Davis noting a certain doglike obeisance to him. Good.

"You have hurt the enterprise, Karel," said Davis, who remained standing. "Above all things, that cannot be allowed to happen."

The big man only nodded, his head hanging down slightly.

"I have decided to give you another chance, however."

Van Hoorn looked up, as hopeful now as a child who expected a spanking but has a faint hope of reprieve.

"I have decided to make a clean slate of everything, Karel. With one exception, you, that will mean starting over at the beginning. Building this all up again. It will mean time and work, but the rewards will be there, for both of us. Are you willing?"

"Yes sir," Van Hoorn said immediately.

"Sam and the girl," Davis said, "must be eliminated. I want you to make it appear Sam has killed her and then taken his own life. We'll link him to Lyle's side, and that will be that. We will then have time to finish up Brown and the woman, and last of all Mr. Handleman. But you will start with Sam and the girl."

Without hesitation Van Hoorn said, "Yes sir. It will be done."

"I know it will," Davis said. "Go now."

Van Hoorn stood and nodded his assent, then quickly left the office. Davis smiled, feeling confident, then sat behind his desk. From a drawer he removed a syringe and vial and readied himself for another injection. He was feeling more like God all the time and couldn't wait to get the finishing touches.

●

Janice saw them first, getting out of a black sedan. A small, startled scream escaped her at the first sight of her daughter in five days. Her entire body tensed as if it were one giant ball of sinew reacting to some perceived danger. Without even thinking about it, her hand reached out and grabbed the door handle.

"Easy," Jed said.

Keeping her hand on the door, Janice said, "Do we just sit here?"

"Yes," said Jed.

"But we can take her; we can—"

"He might be armed. This isn't the place. We'll follow him."

A faint hysteria began to rise in her, born both of anxiety and fatigue. "But he might see us; he might call in help. What about calling Agent Loveland?"

"We still don't have anything to offer him," Jed said. "This is not the time. You want Lauren back, but I have a stake in this too. I want Davis. I want him for killing Sterling. Trust me just a little more."

Janice knew then she would trust him. After his opening up to her, she felt she could trust him with anything. It was a good feeling, too, one she hadn't felt for a man since Sam had ripped trust to shreds during their marriage.

"All right," she said finally. Then she looked back across the highway toward the hamburger place. Sam and Lauren had disappeared inside.

●

The smell of hamburgers and fries entered Lauren through her newly sensitive nasal passages. This was even richer and more satisfying than she'd remembered. What was happening to her was still confusing, though in a pleasurable way. Every experience seemed to take on a new texture, a deeper intensity.

Now as she stood contemplating her favorite foods, even her memories became more potent. She recalled in vivid detail one time when her mother took her out.

It was right after school one day, and Lauren had been sent to the principal's office for the first time in her young life. Discipline at school had never been a problem, but this day something had snapped inside her. It was a jigsaw puzzle that she couldn't quite figure out, and when the teacher told the class it was time to clean up, Lauren hadn't said or done anything. She just kept at it.

Finally the teacher, Miss Harold, had to come over and tell Lauren directly to put the puzzle away. At which point Lauren said, "Leave me alone."

That was as surprising to her as it was to Miss Harold, who decided to nip this thing in the bud. A trip to the principal's office also meant a call to her mother.

Waiting to be picked up, Lauren was sure that she had blown her entire future. She was convinced her mother was going to take her home and administer a severe discipline of her own. Two days before Lauren had also told her mother to "leave me alone."

To her surprise her mother took her to Wendy's. They sat to eat, her mother said a prayer (Lauren, remembering this now, felt a jolt of pain in her head), and then her mother had said, "The way you acted toward Miss Harold was wrong. You realize that, don't you?"

"Yes," said Lauren quietly

"And when you said the same thing to me, that was wrong too."

Lauren nodded.

"But I want to know if you know *why* it was wrong."

Lauren had thought about it and said, "Because I'll get in trouble?"

Her mother had smiled at that, though Lauren wasn't sure why. Then she reached out and stroked Lauren's hair and said, "That's not the reason, kiddo, but that's sure a consequence. No, the reason is that God says we are to honor our parents and those in authority over us. In the Bible, God . . ."

A white-hot spear of pain ripped through Lauren's head as she stood there with her father, remembering.

"Daddy, it hurts," she said, clutching the sides of her head. It was so intense she had to close her eyes.

Sam knelt beside her. "What are you thinking about?"

"Nothing."

"What *were* you thinking about?"

"Mommy."

"What else?"

"When we were at Wendy's. And I was in trouble and . . ."

"Yes, yes?"

"She told me why I wasn't supposed to talk in a bad way to my teacher."

"What did she tell you?"

Taking a deep breath, Lauren said, "That God—" The pain shot back. "It hurts, Daddy!"

"Don't think about God," Sam said.

Lauren tried not to, but it didn't work.

"I mean, think that God is dead," Sam instructed.

"Dead?"

"Yes. Dead like an animal. Don't ever think about God as good or alive, or it will hurt."

"I don't understand, Daddy."

"You will. Is that better?"

"No."

And then her father did something he had not done in years. He hugged her.

**47**

Bently Davis was god.

God I'll be.

As he looked over the faces of his lecture class, the bright, eager, shining ones, he felt now was the moment to bring a word from on high. He was feeling "high," in the sense they used to use back in the days when Leary had turned him on to LSD. This was so much better.

"Why is there such a need for our culture to look to supernatural or paranormal phenomena? Why, in this age of such superlative scientific achievements, are people still content to look to false gods and fairies?

"Let me suggest to you it is all about fear. Fear of death, fear of life without some sort of Tinker Bell to plink a magic wand over all the problems people face in the course of a life lived. What they fail to do is recognize the god of their own minds!"

Feeling the message take over his own mind, Davis allowed the full force of his evangelistic fervor to pour out of him. Waving his arms, lifting his voice, he began scaling rhetorical heights even he had never dreamed of.

"Each of you is more powerful than any god of religious superstition! You contain a trillion copies of a large, textual document written in a digital code, each copy as voluminous as a copious book. I'm talking, of course, of the DNA in your very cells! You don't have to be a scientist— you don't have to play with a Bunsen burner—in order to understand enough science to overtake your imagined need for gods and fairies and fill that gap with hard science, a science of hope!"

He paused to look out at the students, some of whom he knew would grow up in his world, be transformed by his genetic technologies, and rule. The new Nephilim were here in this room.

But so was someone else.

As Davis prepared to deliver his next broadside, he was momentarily stopped by someone standing in the back of the hall. He did not like the feeling of being, even momentarily, hushed by a circumstance.

But that's what happened when he saw that FBI agent, Loveland, watching him.

●

Following the black sedan Sam drove proved to be difficult, even for Jed. It took a turn out of traffic and into a commercial zone with few cars.

Janice prayed the whole time, and Jed used all his skill to hang back until the front car would disappear around a bend or corner. She admired his skills all the more.

But when they reached the final destination, an imposing warehouse surrounded by underdeveloped dirt and cement, Janice knew the next step would be the hardest—how to get Lauren out once and for all.

Jed parked the car a good one hundred yards away and said, "I have to try to get inside."

"I'm going with you," Janice said.

"No, not this time."

"Please."

Jed took her hand, a gesture both firm and full of concern, and said, "Believe me this time. It's too dangerous, for you and for Lauren. I'd like you to stay here and do one thing."

"Yes?"

"Pray."

●

Sam Ramsey felt as if his internal world, the one he had occupied for several years without qualm or regret, were now crumbling inside him like a condemned building under a wrecking ball. How could this have happened? This was not part of the plan or the promise.

Where was Davis? Why wasn't he here to answer questions? Questions such as, *Why am I so disturbed at what my daughter is going through?* This was all for her good, for the good of everyone in the world, and he had long ago made the rational decision to allow Davis to have his way with Lauren. Lauren was an experimental possibility, not a mere offspring. He had never felt any emotional uncertainty about it. So why now?

Lauren had obediently taken to the cot in the corner of a room that had once been an office. UniGen had acquired this site six months ago, keeping the transfer secret. That was easy since the name on the title was a front. Before UniGen, La Cosa Nostra had made good use of this place for trafficking in illegal computer parts.

Maybe, Sam thought, he was "running down," as it was sometimes put. The chips in his system were of uncertain duration. Regular injections were supposed to rejuvenate and recharge. Maybe he was building a resistance to the treatment. Maybe there was (planned?) obsolescence. Was that what was happening to him? Could that explain why he was feeling some sort of hot, unfamiliar, uncomfortable feeling toward his daughter?

Where was Davis?

Hearing a scuffing sound behind him, Sam whirled around.

**48**

"Nice of you to drop by," Davis said as Loveland approached him after the lecture. "Learn anything?"

"Fascinating stuff," Loveland said. "You really believe what you say?"

"Why shouldn't I?"

"Well, it sounds a little, I don't know, what my mother used to call 'the big head.'"

Davis laughed—forced, but sounding natural—and said, "I'm not known for being a shrinking violet. But I have a question for you."

"Yes?"

"Is that a federal crime?"

"Having a large ego? Not yet."

"Then that leads to another question. What are you doing here?"

The agent did something Davis found illogical and annoying. He smiled. It was a half smile but a smug one, the kind federal law enforcement agents used when they thought they knew something. It annoyed Davis because this man was not worthy to be taking any of his time at all.

"I have a simple request, Professor Davis. It's purely optional on your part."

"What is it?"

"Would you be willing to take a polygraph exam?"

Davis felt what he called "objective contempt" for Loveland. What an outrage that he would even think about keeping after him. "Still thinking about the big score, eh? Won't give up the thought of bagging a celebrity, is that it?"

"No," Loveland said, seeming calm. "No reason except to remove you once and for all as a subject of investigation."

"This is highly intrusive and inconvenient."

"You're free to say no."

"If I do take a lie detector exam, I expect you not only to leave me alone but to apologize."

"If you pass, of course."

Davis smiled. "Oh, I'll pass." And he knew he would. The Nephilim seed, strong within him, was his guarantee.

●

If that's the way they wanted to play, that's the way he'd play. If they wanted to clean him out, take his stuff, try to make him back down, he'd take them on. All of them. On their turf.

Data had already created not only a password for himself on the Harvard network but a completely new identity as well. He designated himself Q, after the omnipotent manifestation of the Q Continuum from episode one of *Next Generation.* These jokers didn't know who they were dealing with.

Nor had it been difficult to find a free computer at the Harvard Divinity School. Security wasn't much over there, no doubt due to a residual assumption about the protection of God, but Data wasn't worried about that. The divinity school, as everyone knew, had long since abandoned any pretense of believing in the supernatural intervention of God. Why should God do anything for the divinity school?

Managing to lock himself into a faculty office at lunch hour, Data quickly hacked his way into Davis's mailbox. Having a photographic memory helped. Access codes from the hard drive that was now missing still stood out in Data's head like neon signs. Once he found the incriminating messages again, Data would install a backdoor so he could easily have Loveland access the same material instantly.

In seconds he found the mailbox and entered it. And found nothing. Gone. Everything. Completely cleaned out.

For a long moment Data sat there, staring at the screen, the cursor blinking mockingly at him, challenging him. "I am Q," he said out loud, as if the incantation would give him powers of thought above and beyond the norm.

Apparently, it worked. His next step presented itself to him instantly. It would be bold, but that's what made it so good.

●

Karel Van Hoorn stood in the doorway, gun in hand. Sam knew instantly that he was there to kill him and Lauren.

In that moment of realization, Sam sensed many things simultaneously. That the grand experiment had failed, that it would always fail. That human biology would rebel against the attempt to reshape it. That some things that were not measurable were still tangible—like the feelings he had for his daughter. She was not just a thing, as he thought he believed, but part of him in some way that was beyond science to put a value on.

He knew, too, that he had lived a life of denial of the reality of something beyond nature. Davis called it the God part of the brain and an accident of nature, but somehow, in this moment before his death, Sam knew without knowing how he knew, that God was real and that he had turned his back on him.

All of this flashed through Sam's mind in that split second between seeing Van Hoorn in the doorway and hearing the blast of the gun.

●

In the car Janice heard the muffled but unmistakable report of a gun. Jed? Lauren? Sam? There was no way she would wait here to find out. She threw open the door, jumped out, and ran toward the warehouse.

●

Jed jumped Van Hoorn just after the second shot.

Surprise was with him. Van Hoorn's muscles were loose as Jed pulled him into a chokehold from behind. In what have must been an instinctive maneuver, Van Hoorn dropped his gun and put both hands on the arm Jed had wrapped around his neck.

Jed felt the callused hands dig into his flesh like iron teeth. But he held.

Van Hoorn's legs, though, were unencumbered. He backed quickly through the open doorway, out into the hall, and slammed Jed into the facing wall.

Jed felt hot knives of pain up his spine but held on, pulling hard against the carotid artery of the bigger man. Then Van Hoorn jerked forward and down, and Jed felt himself lifted up and over massive shoulders.

49

The foyer was empty, and, Janice sensed, so was the entire first floor. She tried one door that opened up into an enormous, empty space of discarded cubicles and broken lights. Indeed, the only light shining into this area was coming through the open door behind her. She saw a second-floor corridor and knew that's where they were.

She ran back into the foyer and looked for the stairwell. In seconds she was there and up the stairs.

Pure instinct took her down one corridor. No sign of anyone. She reached a divide and stopped, listened, and heard a groaning.

Stepping carefully now so as not to be heard, she crept along one wall toward the sound. It was a man's voice, in obvious pain.

Quickening her step, she came to a corner and peered around it. Her breath left her.

Sam was lying almost at her feet. Behind him was a trail of blood on the floor, as if he had crawled to this spot gravely wounded.

"Sam!" Janice said in a loud whisper. She hadn't forgotten what he had become, but now, as he lay there perhaps mortally wounded, she couldn't help feeling some sorrow for him.

Kneeling beside him, she said, "Where is Lauren?"

Sam rolled onto his back, and Janice saw the awful wound in the middle of his chest. Sam's eyes, which had once held both an animalistic rage and an eerie glow, were now dull and, somehow, more human.

"Janice," he said, his voice raspy.

"Yes, Sam."

"Forgive me."

The shock of the words was even more powerful than the realization that he was about to die.

"Sam, hold on," she said.

"Forgive me," he said once more, and then his eyes closed, and his head slumped to one side.

"Sam!"

He was gone.

●

Jed felt the sensation of total weightlessness as he and Van Hoorn tumbled over a railing and fell.

This is bad was the thought that shot through his brain at that moment. But the fall was cushioned by Van Hoorn beneath him. It could have been the other way around. Fortunately Jed was on top as the hard floor stopped the two falling men.

Jed's head went light for a moment, but he quickly recovered and scrambled to his feet.

Karel Van Hoorn lay motionless on the floor.

●

Lauren! Where is Lauren?

Sam was dead now. Lauren was alone in this building somewhere. Janice had followed the blood trail Sam had left. It led to an old office. There was even a bed there. But no Lauren.

"Jed!" she called. Her voice echoed through the abandoned corridors. "Lauren!"

She waited, listened. Then from somewhere on the first floor, Jed called to her. "Janice, are you all right?"

"I'm up on the second floor! Is Lauren with you?"

"No. I'm coming up."

Where is Lauren?

Janice heard a clicking sound and turned around. Lauren stood against a wall.

"Baby!" Janice cried and took two steps toward her, then stopped, horrified.

Lauren held up a revolver—pointed directly at her mother.

"Lauren!" Janice said, hearing the horrible incredulity in her voice, followed by the terrible realization—Lauren, her daughter, was transformed. They had done it to her. She was one of them!

There was a faint glow in Lauren's eyes.

Janice looked deeply into those eyes, not recognizing them. She wanted to run to Lauren, throw her arms around her, squeeze out all of the bad. But something stopped her. An internal danger signal.

Instead of moving forward, Janice raised her arms outward, an invitation to Lauren to run to her.

"Baby," Janice said softly, tears coming to her eyes even as she tried to fight them back. "It's me. It's Mommy."

Lauren did not move, did not even blink. She held the gun steady.

"It's over now," Janice whispered. In her mind she saw Lauren a week ago, the smiling, happy girl who would never hurt anyone. She put that image over the Lauren standing in front of her, willing the old Lauren to break through.

Janice risked one, small step forward.

"You don't have to be afraid," she said.

Her daughter did not move. She held the gun as if she were an accomplished target shooter, at home with the weapon.

"I'm here now," Janice pleaded. "God is here. He'll protect us."

At the mention of God, Lauren's eyes came alive with emotion. Janice felt a surge of relief. Was she getting through at last?

She opened her arms wider. "Come here, Lauren. Please."

Her daughter seemed to have a shot of pain. She blinked her eyes hard and shook her head but still kept the gun aloft.

"It's OK, baby," Janice said.

She took another full step toward her daughter, then stopped. Something wasn't right.

Lauren said, "All truths are soaked in blood."

And then she fired.

50

There was a pleasant warmth in the air that actually felt intensely personal to Bently Davis. It was as if nature itself were bowing to him, acknowledging him as the one who, if not its creator, was its master. Indeed, as he strolled across the Harvard campus, sucking on a grape Tootsie Roll Pop (his favorite indulgence), he almost verbalized an acknowledgment to the sun. *I approve of you,* he thought. *Well done.*

I approve also of myself. Now to begin again.

The events of last week had played themselves out in an even more resonant tone than he had intended. It was like the last note of a master symphony which, upon completion, one tags with the label genius.

If he had believed in fate, he would have chalked it up to that. Or if he had been completely nuts, he might have said it was the alignment of the planets or some other New Age nonsense. But he believed in none of those things, only himself, and he had done it. *God I'll be.*

As he turned toward the north end of campus, he gave his sucker that final crunch which always marked the beginning of the pleasurable end. From hard candy to chewy chocolate center. And he thought, in the same way, I have transformed my own destiny.

The woman was dead, shot by her own daughter, in what he thought was a wonderful irony. Shakespeare couldn't have scripted it any better. The bounty hunter was arrested for several violations, and Karel would say nothing from his cell. He had told Karel he would be well taken care of. The authorities would try to put together some puzzlelike image, something to make sense of it all, but would fail miserably.

And he, Bently Davis, was completely in the clear. Not only had he cleaned out every electronic vestige of the Nephilim project, but he had passed the lie detector test with flying colors. It was easy enough to fool the machine as a mere human, but programmed as a new master of the earth, it was child's play.

Keeping himself occupied with visions of his new project—the selection of subjects, the laying of a fresh foundation, and the delicious thought of enemies destroyed—Davis was on what he used to call a natural high when he got to his office.

What brought him out of his reverie was the sight of the one man he had no desire to talk to—Loveland.

What was this all about? Davis had put to rest any suspicions about himself with the polygraph test. And hadn't Loveland promised to leave him alone after that? So much for the word of the federal government.

Davis's new assistant, a pretty young graduate student he was grooming for the new project, looked at her boss with consternation and said, "I couldn't do anything."

"It's all right," Davis said to calm her. "Call Berkowitz. Have him come right over."

"Yes sir," she said. Professor Howard Berkowitz of the Harvard Law School was not only one of the most respected legal minds in the country but also a personal friend and sometimes representative of Bently Davis. He'd put an end to this infringement in short order.

To Loveland, Davis said, "I will not talk to you personally. You can talk to my attorney."

"That's fine," Loveland said. "I think he ought to hear this too."

"Hear what?"

"Can I talk to you personally then?"

"Don't play games."

"Let's wait for your lawyer."

Reluctantly Davis entered his office with the agent. As he sat at his desk, he had a thought. *What would it take to set up the death of an FBI agent in such a way as not to be caught?* Scenarios zipped through his brain like computer code. Which, he mused, it was.

Berkowitz was in his office in ten minutes. With his curly, thinning, sand-colored hair and rumpled suit, Howard Berkowitz looked more the absent-minded professor than the attorney who had won four times in the U.S. Supreme Court. But looks were deceiving.

"What's up, Bent?" Berkowitz said, looking at Loveland. Loveland showed him his credential and explained that he would like to ask a few questions.

"Does this relate to an ongoing investigation?" Berkowitz asked.

"It does."

"Then you can address me."

"Does your client refuse to answer?"

"I'll decide what he answers."

Good, Howard, good, thought Davis. *Hardball.*

"Fine," Loveland said. "Excuse me one moment." He took out a wireless phone, punched in a number, then said, "Come up."

"What's this all about?" Berkowitz demanded.

"Colleagues," said Loveland.

"Look," Berkowitz said, "you were let in here voluntarily, and you can be asked to leave. You haven't got a search warrant."

"You want me to get one?"

"On what cause?"

"The usual, Mr. Berkowitz. That incriminating evidence may be found here."

Davis watched as Berkowitz's neck reddened. The pit bull. Loveland didn't know what he was in for.

"Don't play games with me," Berkowitz said. "Or with the law. You will either give me a good reason to continue listening to you, or you'll leave. Now."

There was a knock at the door, and the assistant stuck her head in, looking frantic. "Three more people!" she sputtered.

For the first time in a long time, Davis felt his skin start to prickle, the way it did when he had been nervous as a kid. He felt an anger creeping up in him next, at the idea that this agent, whatever he had cooked up, was feeling smug enough to corner him in his office. Well, Berkowitz was here, and this thing could be wrapped up right now.

"Let them in," Davis said, and his skin moved again on his arms as he saw Loveland smile and Berkowitz rub his hair.

But it was nothing compared to the shock that hit him when Janice walked into his office, her right arm in a sling—*She's supposed to be dead!*—followed by Jed Brown and some skinny, crazy looking guy who was holding some papers in his hands. For an instant he thought he recognized the crazy one, but there was no way. A face like that he would have remembered.

Standing, Davis said, "What is all this?"

"Let me," said Berkowitz. Then to Loveland: "What is all this?"

Loveland said, "I believe you know Janice Taylor and Jed Brown," said Loveland.

Davis did not acknowledge them.

Ignoring him, Loveland said, "And this is Data," Loveland said, motioning to the skinny guy.

"Data?" said Berkowitz. "What kind of a name is that?"

"One that inspires fear throughout the galaxy!" Data snapped. Berkowitz looked at Davis as if seeking an explanation for the circus that had suddenly pitched its tent.

"All right," Berkowitz said, "I'm taking over this whole thing. I will give you two minutes to explain"—he held up two stubby fingers to Loveland—"and then it's over."

"All right," said Loveland. "I can see from the professor's face that he is surprised to see Miss Taylor, the former Mrs. Sam Ramsey, standing here. We let it out that she had died. It was in our interest to give the professor a feeling that all was well."

"What's the connection?" Berkowitz demanded.

"Your client will tell you the truth, I'm sure, since you seem to have such a close bond."

Berkowitz flashed a quick look at Davis, a nascent questioning in his eyes. Davis shook his head at the lawyer, telling him to dismiss the statement.

"Keep going," said Berkowitz.

Loveland made a gesture to Janice, who stepped forward. "We just wanted the professor to relax. After he passed the lie detector test, and with the news that witnesses were dying off, we thought he might let his guard down, allow something to turn up."

"Witnesses to what?" Berkowitz said. "You haven't asserted any criminality yet."

Janice said, "How about murder, conspiracy, and a twisted plan to remake humanity?"

Berkowitz's forehead began to redden under his thinning hair. "You'd better have something to back this up, or we'll begin looking at slander."

Davis, his neck starting to itch, glared at Janice. He wanted to throw her out of the office. Physically. How dare she come into his private sanctuary with all this!

Then she looked directly at him and said, "We know what you did. Everything. I know what you did to my daughter, to make her do this—"

she held up her slinged arm—"and I wanted to look into the face of the man who thinks he can play God. And tell him personally, it's all over."

Berkowitz started to say something, but Davis stopped him with a raised hand. Then he said to Janice, "You're not worthy to clean my fingernails. None of you. Your limited minds, your superstitions—"

"Now then," Berkowitz interrupted, "before we have any more words, let me make a simple point here. I have not seen any evidence of anything. And I won't allow people to stand here and make outrageous statements about God or conspiracies or anything else. So unless you're prepared to show me some hard evidence, I'm going to have to ask you to get out of here."

Janice put her hand out to Data, who handed her a sheaf of papers.

"What are those?" Berkowitz asked.

"What we have here is a partial manuscript," said Janice, "of what looks to be a novel that's heavy on philosophy."

Davis felt a sharp popping in his brain, as if a circuit had overloaded. *How did they get this?* he thought.

Janice said, "Agent Loveland asked Professor Davis at the polygraph exam if he had ever heard the term *Nephilim* before. He said no. The machine backed him up. But now let me read a passage from this document."

Head starting to throb, Davis kept his face passive.

"What has God ever brought us but pain and suffering?" Janice read. "Guilt and imprisonment? Despair and agony? God is dead. Science has proved it. The brave ones have lived it. Those who deny this fundamental truth are the lost ones. They who seek to be saved are lost. Irony is the watchword of history! But their time is past. The forces of time and nature and the free mind of man shall take their course. They who cling to superstition will die out. I will help them in that process. I will live on the side of nature. And if I shall be resisted, what then? The fittest shall survive. I shall be the fittest. Survive. And thrive. And they shall call me Nephilim."

There was a short silence, and then Davis said, "So?"

"Professor Davis," said Loveland. "This document came from this office."

How could this be? Davis thought, his brain in an odd state of arrest, as if it could not itself process the fact that something had gone so wrong.

"What do you mean by that?" said Berkowitz.

"It was stolen," said Loveland.

"By me!" Data said proudly. "My name is Victor Padilla, security guard." He pulled out an ID card, complete with picture, from his pocket. "Fake," he said.

That's it! Davis thought. He'd seen that face in passing two nights ago, leaving the building. A security guard! He'd thought nothing of it. In fact, he'd felt safe.

"This is outrageous!" Davis shouted.

"Outrageous enough," said Loveland, "to make out a case. We couple this document with your denials and with the statements of the witnesses we have so far, and we might just be able to convince a jury."

Berkowitz shouted, "You listen to me now! This farce is over! I don't know what your theory is, or anything about this ridiculous story, but you will never get to use that document. I'll bring a motion to suppress the evidence. It was illegally obtained!"

"That's right!" Davis shouted. "I want them all arrested!"

"I'll look into that," said Berkowitz, and then he snatched the document from Janice's hands.

"That's a copy," Janice said calmly.

"I don't care what it is," said Berkowitz. "You'll never show that document in any court anywhere. I'll move to suppress!"

"The motion will be denied," Janice said.

"Do you know who I am?" Berkowitz demanded. "You think you can tell me what the law is? Who do you think you are?"

"Just a member of the Illinois Bar," Janice said, "who's admired some of your legal writings, Professor Berkowitz."

"I don't give a rip," said Berkowitz. "You're not going to use that document. Ever."

"Professor Berkowitz," Janice said, "I'm sure you're aware of the *Burdeau* rule."

To Davis it seemed that Berkowitz flinched slightly. The pounding in his head reached new levels.

Berkowitz said, "What about it?"

As Janice spoke, it looked to Davis as if she thought she was standing in front of the Supreme Court or something! "In *Burdeau v. McDowell,* the United States Supreme Court, in 1921, held that the Fourth Amendment protection against unlawful searches and seizures applies only to governmental action, not the action of private citizens. That case had facts quite similar to this. Private detectives stole books and papers from the office of Mr. McDowell, to present to the grand jury as evidence of mail fraud. His lawyers tried to get the evidence back, citing the Fourth Amendment. The trial court granted the motion, but the Supreme Court reversed, saying there was no involvement by federal officials."

Davis's head was pounding, pounding. He looked at Berkowitz. "What is she saying?"

"She's saying," said Berkowitz, "that because this guy who stole the manuscript is a private citizen, not an FBI agent, that the evidence can still be used."

"Can it?" Davis said.

Berkowitz paused and ruffled his sparse but curly hair. "Maybe, unless I can show that Agent Loveland here was encouraging this in some way."

Loveland looked at Data, "Did I encourage you, son?"

Data curled back his lip. "I don't like FBI agents."

"All that doesn't change the fact that he broke the law," said Berkowitz. "We'll be sure he's prosecuted for that."

"And he'll get a lawyer," Janice said. "Me. *Pro bono.*"

Davis felt several snaps in his brain, as if someone had started a fire-works display in his head. He could take no more of this.

"You all," he said, letting the venom spill out. "You all think you have the right to challenge me, even to talk to me? You poor excuses for humanity? I'll see to it—"

"Hold on, Bent," Berkowitz said.

"I won't stand for this! Not from this *scum!*"

The one calling himself Data, the *ersatz* security guard, said, "Uh-oh, meltdown."

"Get out!" Davis screamed. "Get them all out!"

"Calm down, Bent," Berkowitz said, looking anything but calm.

"You'll hear from us," said Janice. "We'll let you know when the indictment is handed down and we can arrange for the surrender of your client."

With that the intruders left. Davis wanted to shout something more, but a white-hot ball of gas in his head blinded him, burned the inside of his skull, rendering him speechless.

51

The doctor, a diminutive Chinese-American named Yeh, nodded at Janice outside the OR. "Very strange," he said, wiping his hands on a towel.

"What is?" Janice said. She reached for Jed's arm to steady herself.

"Her blood. Color of her blood I have never seen. Transfusion will help, I hope."

"Will she be all right? I mean . . ." What did she mean? She meant would she ever see her daughter again, normal, a loving child, not the monster who had shot her so coldly.

"Time," Dr. Yeh said. "Only time will tell."

Time was sluggish, ticking by interminably. In the waiting room she and Jed said hardly a word. She leaned on him, at one point falling asleep, then waking up feeling his arm around her. It was a safe feeling.

At another point he said to her, "You were great back there in Davis's office. When you made that argument about the Fourth Amendment, I thought Berkowitz was going to fall on his keester."

She smiled and thought to herself, *Yeah, it was a pretty good argument, all from a case I remembered from first year Con Law.*

370

When the nurse said she could come in now and see Lauren, Janice's heart flew up into her throat. She was almost breathless when she entered the room and saw Lauren, hooked up to an IV unit, looking so small and frail on the adult-sized bed. It was cold in the room, but when Lauren turned her head toward Janice and smiled, Janice felt like the summer sun had come out and warmed her all over.

"Hi, Mommy," Lauren said. "I missed you."

●

Standing on top of the building, the cold wind whipping around his body, Bently Davis laughed.

It was just like in *The Fountainhead* by Ayn Rand, he mused. That opening where the perfect man, Howard Roark, laughs standing on top of a cliff. Laughter at the knowledge he is perfect. Like him.

Below him and to the east, he could see the glittering lights of Boston Harbor and Waterfront Park. He thought of all the happy tourists there, happy in their mediocrity, never able to transcend the prison of their own skins. That was the way all people were now.

It was just like that note he prepared for Burack, the "suicide" note. He had written, *There is a bigger part! There is a higher experience than evolutionary progress trapped in time! That is what I go to experience, because I am too far ahead of everyone here.*

He believed that.

Berkowitz had told him there would at least be a trial, though they had a good chance to win it. Sure. And he, Bently Davis, would never be able to work in peace again. This world did not deserve him anymore. He would deprive it of his genius and let them suffer.

But he would go on into the eternal recurrence Nietzsche taught and come back again, stronger. *God I'll be.* He laughed again, looked downward, and stepped off the edge.

52

"Been thinking about Job," Jed said.

"How so?" said Janice.

They were in the kitchen of her apartment, chopping vegetables. Outside her kitchen window the stars shone brightly over the city. It was a perfect view, Janice thought, dreamlike. Since settling back into her Chicago world a week ago, Janice had to keep reminding herself that it was real. She had to remind herself that Lauren was all right now, miraculously so. It was such a stunning reversal that Johns Hopkins had called twice already to inquire about allowing them to do research on Lauren.

Janice had turned them down. She wanted to give her child back her innocence. She glanced over to the sofa where Lauren sat watching an old Tex Avery cartoon on TV. That was innocence enough for now.

"The bet God made with Satan," said Jed, handing Janice a chopping board full of chopped celery. "About putting Job to the test. When I was in seminary, that was the book I spent the most time in. The idea that God allows suffering always threw me."

Janice nodded, waiting for him to finish the thought.

"I never really got around that to the other part, though. The part where God restores him. Thought that was just sort of tacked on there to make everybody feel good. I never thought it could actually be the truth until now."

Janice stopped cutting the carrot in front of her and looked at him. She felt a warmth inside. "Why now?"

"You remember my little man?" Jed said, pointing to his middle.

"Sure."

"Remember how he was talking so loud about finding Lauren at Wendy's?"

"Yes."

"Well, I wonder if that wasn't the voice of God. Ever since I met you, things have had sort of a supernatural feel to them. Like somebody up there is watching."

"Somebody is," she said.

"And Sterling. Weird, but I keep feeling like he's watching too."

"Yes."

"It's like what Dewey said."

Janice flashed on an image of Dewey and made a mental note to call him. She was still his lawyer, even after working out a deal to have him treated in a mental hospital on a plea of guilty by reason of insanity. Loveland had helped enormously with that, explaining to the local authorities about Dewey's cooperation in the ever-unfolding UniGen story. When the full story emerged and the physiological effects became fully explained, Janice was sure Dewey would be exonerated and given a clean bill of health.

"Dewey talked about that God part," said Jed. "He thought maybe it was real, put there by God, the place where he actually gets through to us. Maybe it's true."

Janice smiled and felt a communion then with both Jed and God, as if for that one moment they were a triangle, connected and strong. From the look on his face, Janice sensed that Jed was going to make it all the way back to the God from whom he had once run away. Her own "little man" was telling her just that, and she knew then it was the still, small voice of God.

Dinner was a success, especially for Lauren. She couldn't get enough of "this big guy," as she kept calling Jed. Janice told her all about the brave things he had done to help find her, and Lauren kept asking him for more stories about hunting bad guys all across the country.

Lauren also insisted that Jed be the one to tell her a bedtime story. When he asked her which one she wanted to hear, she gave him a choice—David and Goliath or Daniel in the lion's den. When Jed said it had been a long time since he'd read those stories, Lauren had him sit in a chair while *she* told the stories. Jed listened with a slight smile but seemed to drink in every word.

After tucking Lauren into bed, Janice joined Jed in the living room. He was looking out the window, through the blinds.

"Where are you?" she asked.

"I was in Boston for a minute," he said. "I spoke to Loveland today, and he told me Van Hoorn was talking. And you want to hear the kicker? He's going to hire Data to do some cyber sleuthing for him. Can you see Data helping the FBI?"

"It's a stretch," said Janice. But it made a certain, circular sense. It was like a perfect ending to a *Next Generation* episode with Data as the reluctant hero.

There was a long silence in which Jed seemed to struggle to find words. "What is it?" Janice said finally.

He took her hand then and faced her. "I've been alone for so long," he said. He didn't have to go on. Janice knew this was his way of asking her if she could find a place in her life for him. In his voice and look were the vulnerabilities of a man who had been fleeing from life for years and didn't quite know what stopping would mean for him.

"It's been so long I guess I just don't know what to do next," he said.

Janice smiled. She reached her hand behind his neck and pulled him gently toward her, kissing him softly on the cheek. Then she whispered something in his ear.

"Improvise," she said.